A PERFECT FAILURE

FANTE BUKOWSKI THREE

NOAH VAN SCIVER

FANTAGRAPHICS BOOKS

Seattle, New York, London

FANTAGRAPHICS BOOKS INC.
7563 Lake City Way NE
Seattle, Washington, 98115

Editor and Associate Publisher: Eric Reynolds
Book Design: Keeli McCarthy
Production: Paul Baresh
Publisher: Gary Groth

ISBN 978-1-68396-131-4
Library of Congress Control Number: 2015935147

First printing: September 2018
Printed in China

A PERFECT FAILURE

FANTE BUKOWSKI THREE

NOAH VAN

FANTAG

Seat

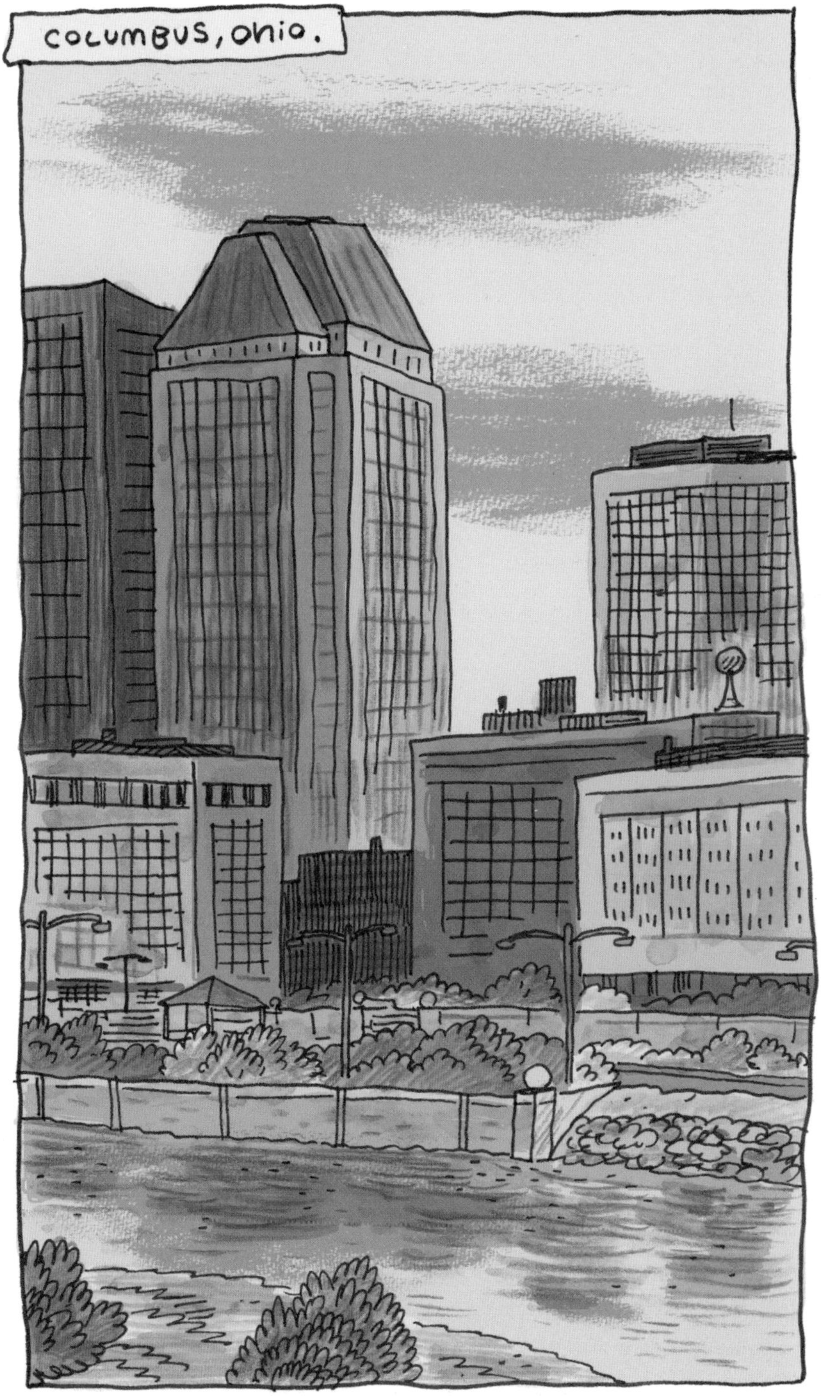
COLUMBUS, OHIO.

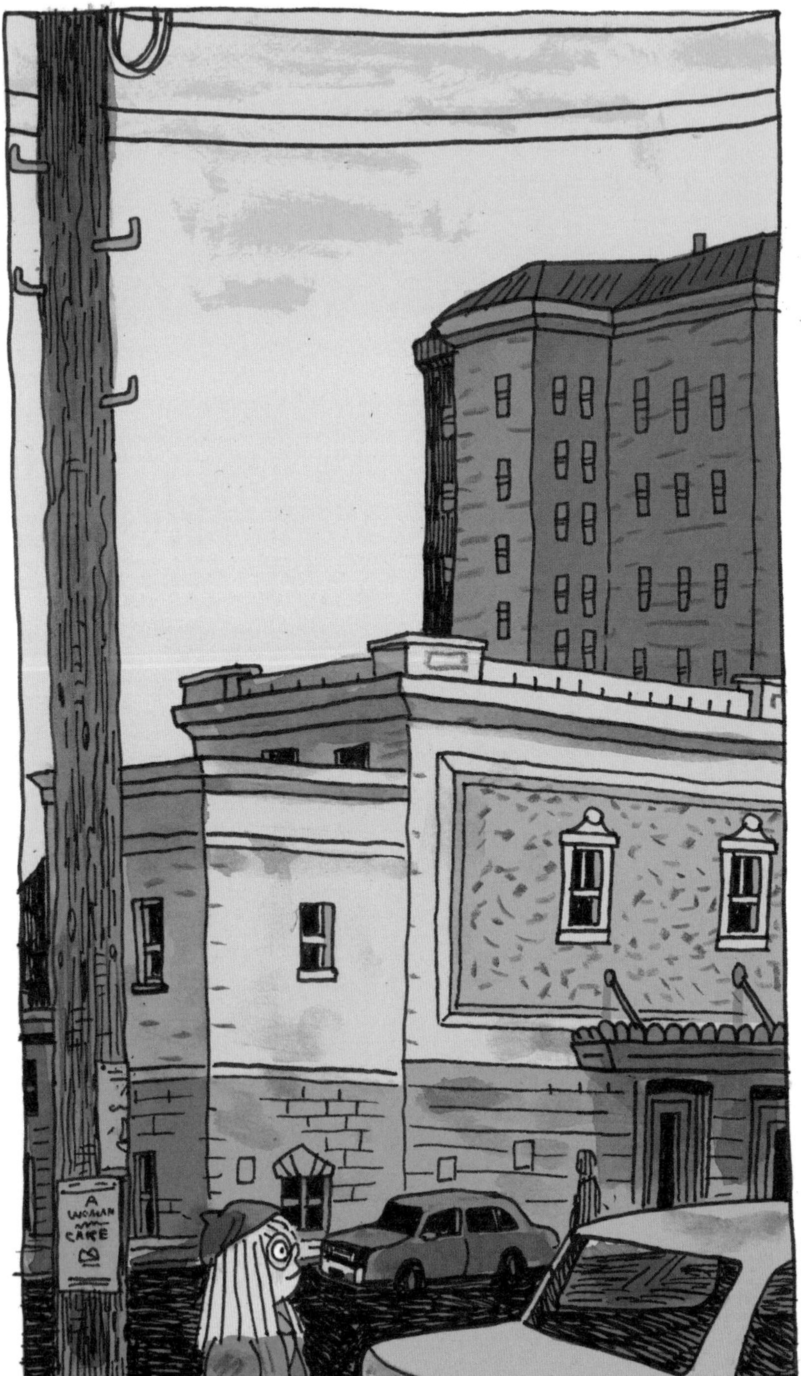
A
WOMAN
CAKE

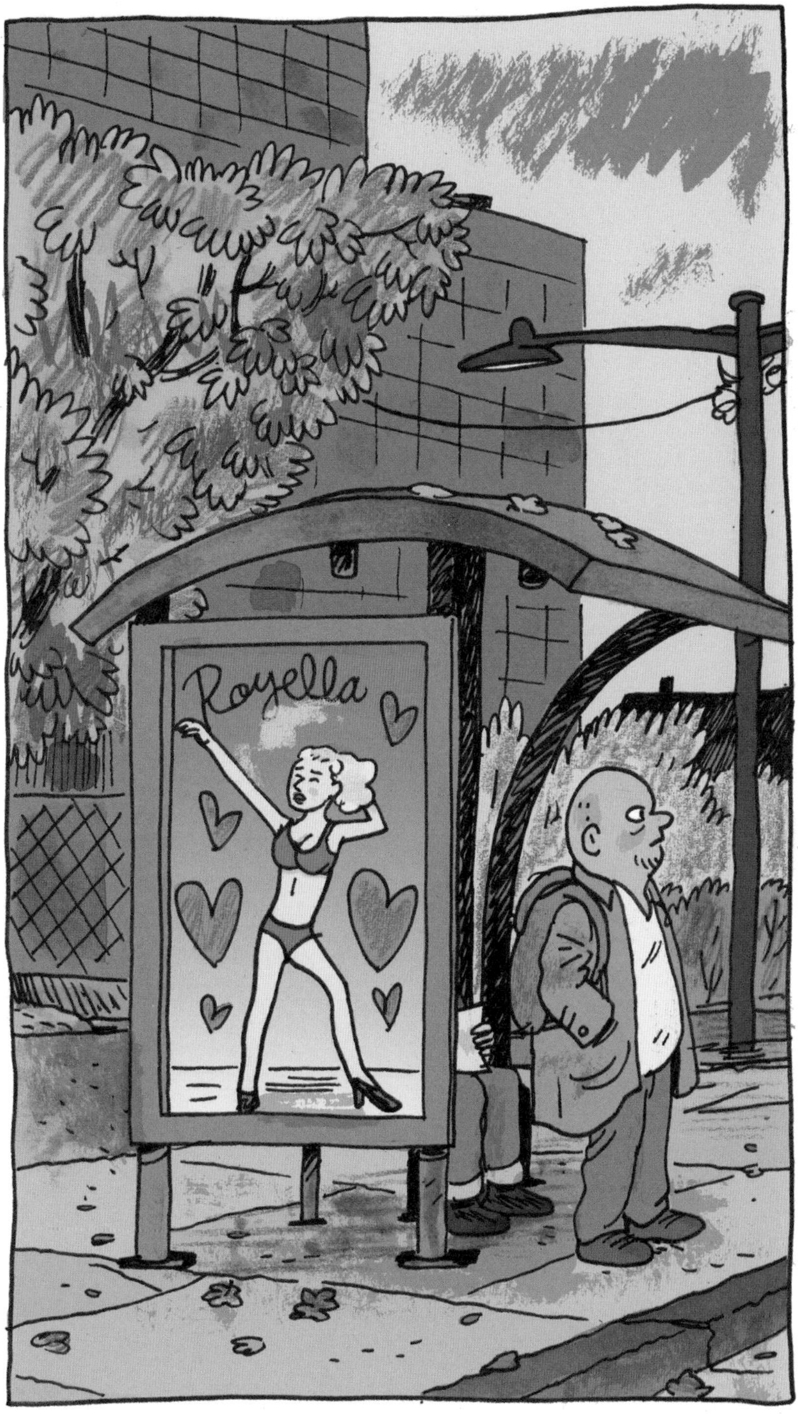
Royella

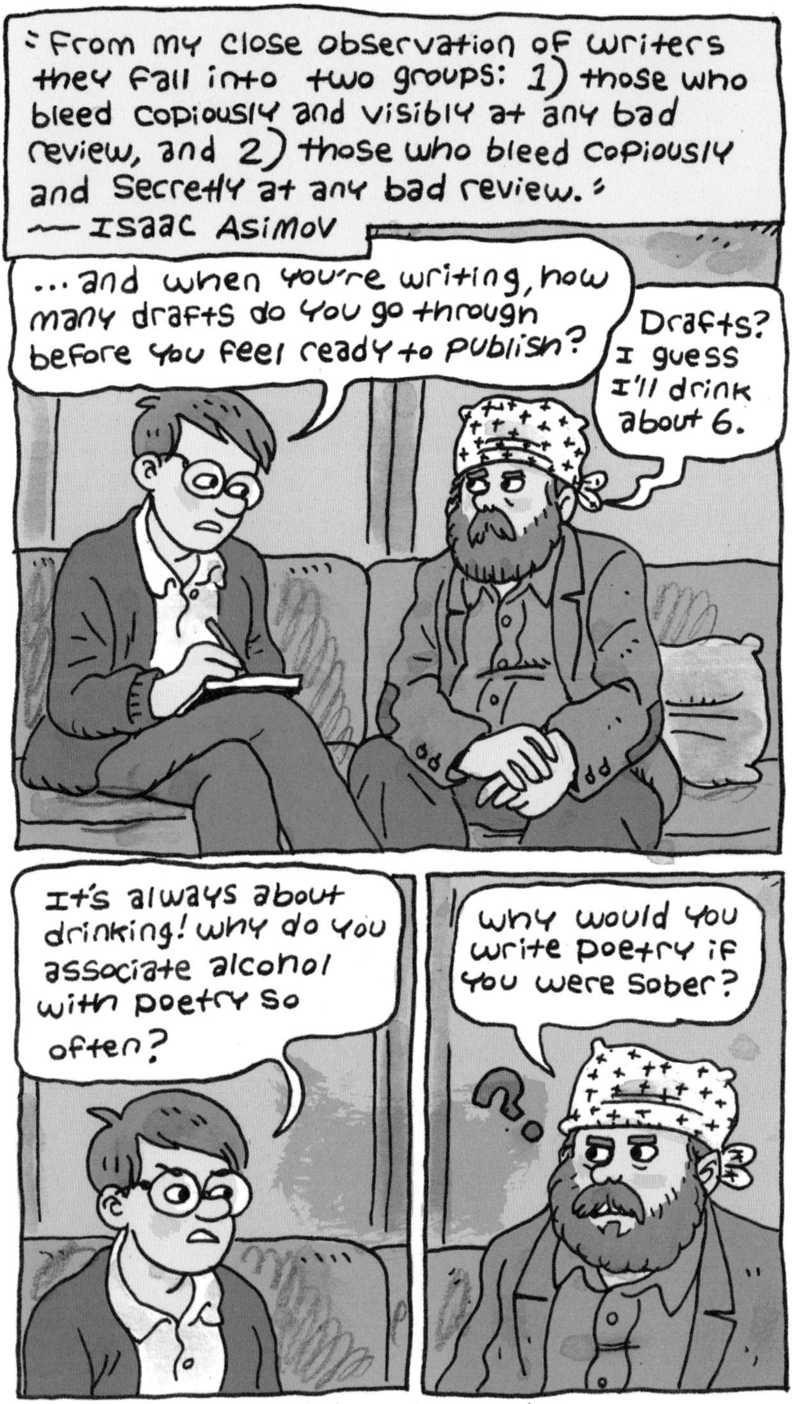
"From my close observation of writers they fall into two groups: 1) those who bleed copiously and visibly at any bad review, and 2) those who bleed copiously and secretly at any bad review."
— Isaac Asimov
...and when you're writing, how many drafts do you go through before you feel ready to publish?
Drafts? I guess I'll drink about 6.
It's always about drinking! Why do you associate alcohol with poetry so often?
Why would you write poetry if you were sober?
?

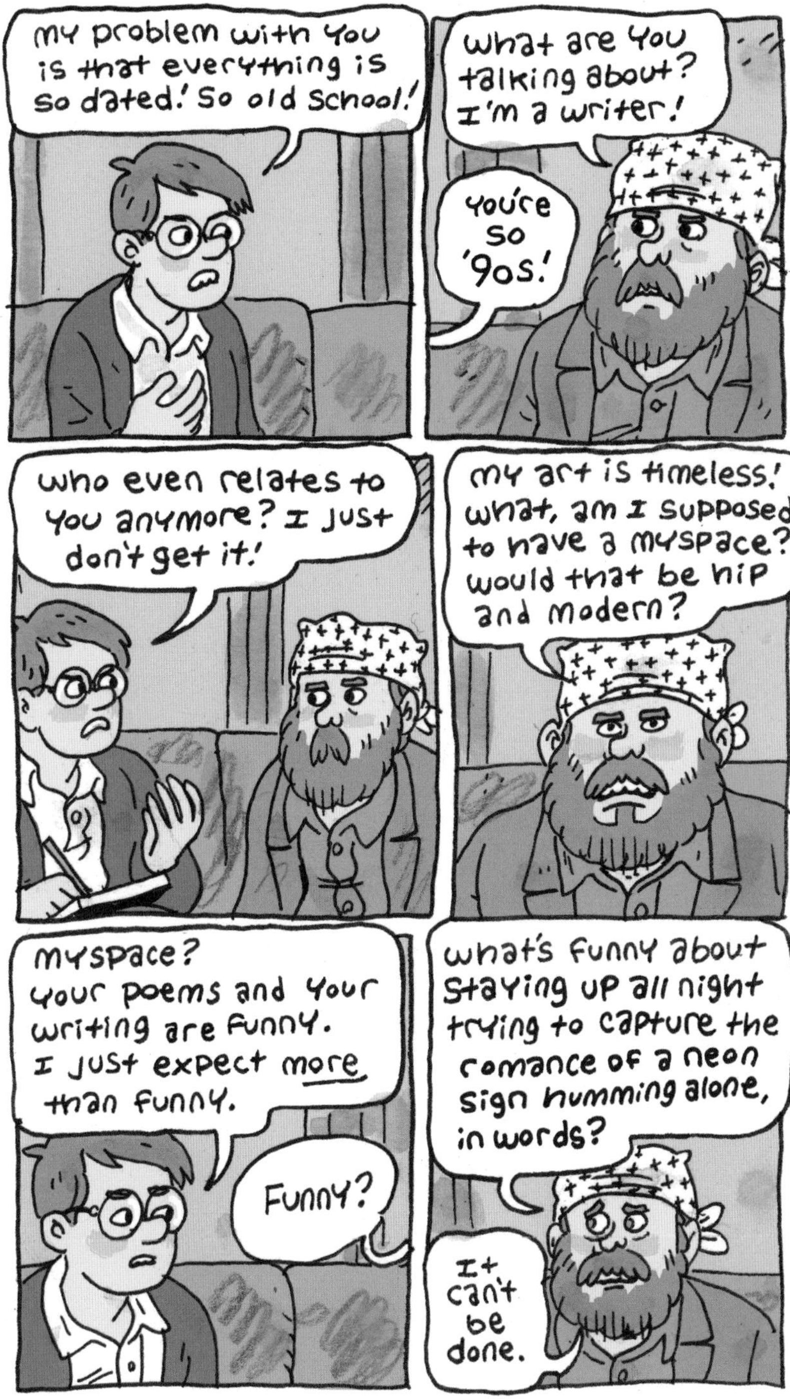
my problem with you is that everything is so dated! So old school!
what are you talking about? I'm a writer!
you're so '90s!
who even relates to you anymore? I just don't get it!
my art is timeless! what, am I supposed to have a myspace? would that be hip and modern?
myspace? your poems and your writing are funny. I just expect more than funny.
Funny?
what's funny about staying up all night trying to capture the romance of a neon sign humming alone, in words?
It can't be done.

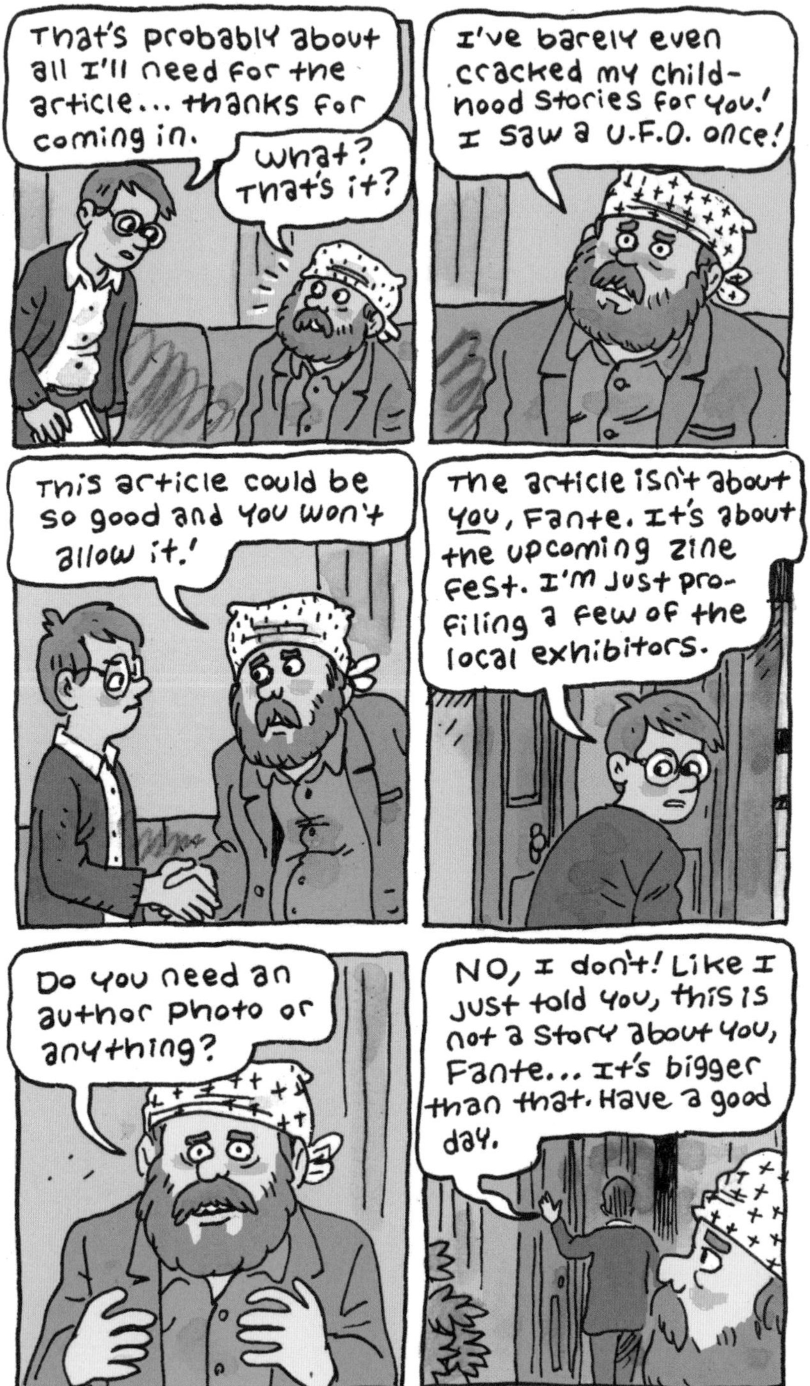
That's probably about all I'll need for the article... thanks for coming in.
What? That's it?
I've barely even cracked my childhood stories for you! I saw a U.F.O. once!
This article could be so good and you won't allow it!
The article isn't about you, Fante. It's about the upcoming zine fest. I'm just profiling a few of the local exhibitors.
Do you need an author photo or anything?
NO, I don't! Like I just told you, this is not a story about you, Fante... It's bigger than that. Have a good day.

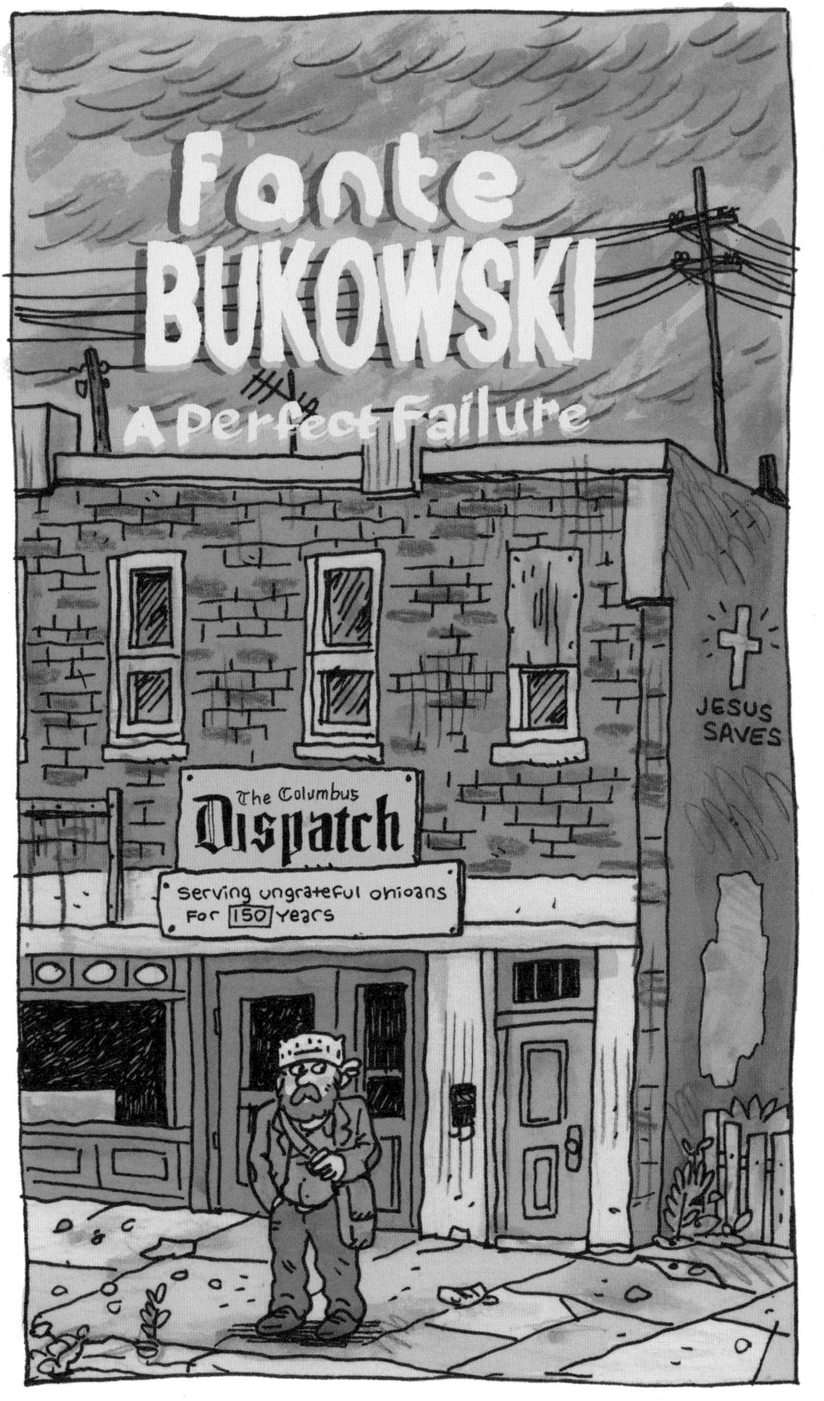
Fante
BUKOWSKI
A Perfect Failure
JESUS
SAVES
The Columbus
Dispatch
Serving ungrateful ohioans
For 150 Years

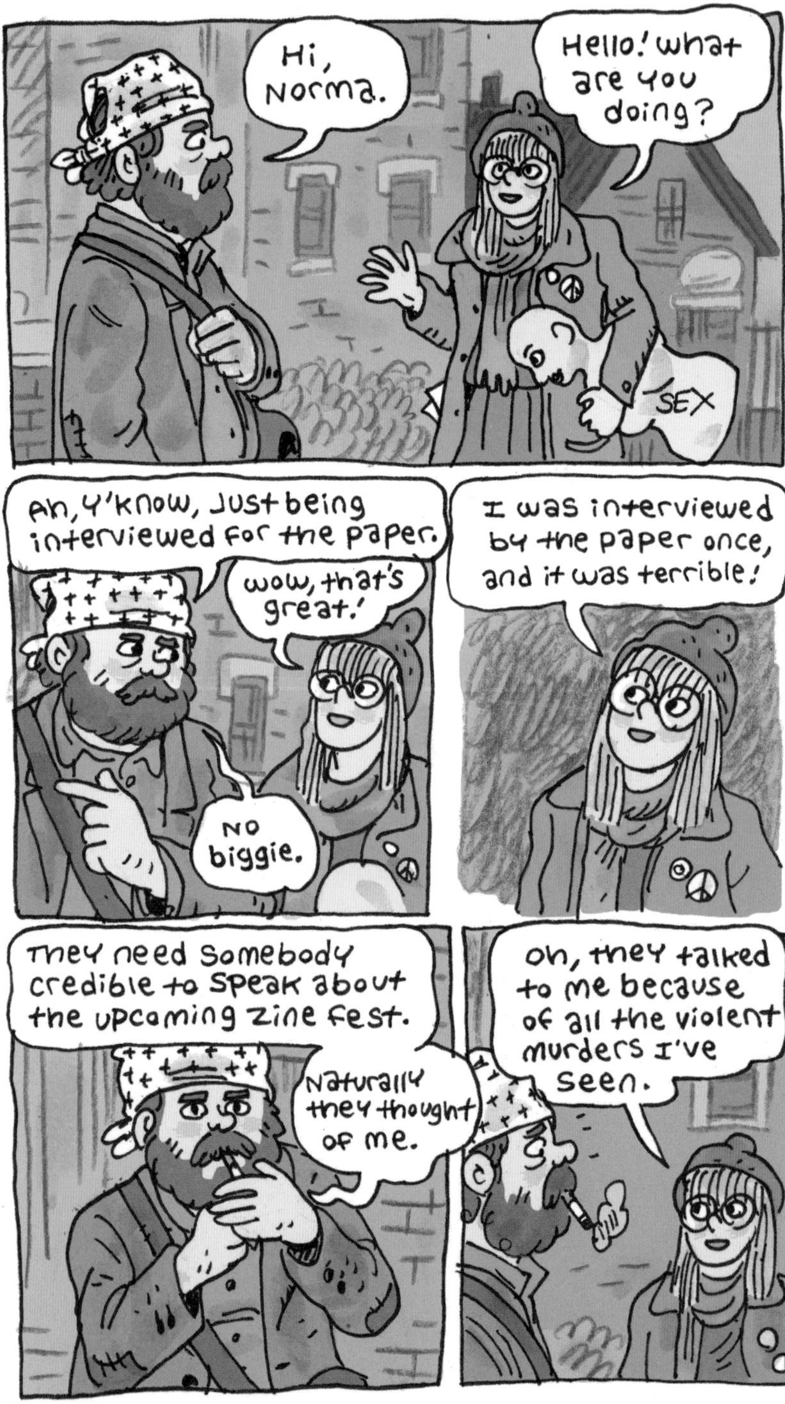
Hi, Norma.
Hello! what are you doing?
SEX
Ah, y'know, just being interviewed for the paper.
wow, that's great!
No biggie.
I was interviewed by the paper once, and it was terrible!
They need somebody credible to speak about the upcoming zine fest.
Naturally they thought of me.
Oh, they talked to me because of all the violent murders I've seen.

I'm promoting my new performance piece at Blockfort gallery!

DECEMBER 10th
A WOMAN MADE OF CAKE

A NEW PERFORMANCE BY NORMA LEE

This is 2 months from now, Norma! Why are you handing these out today?

This will be my final piece! I wanna build a lot of hype! It's gonna be big!

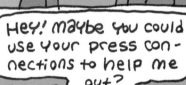

Hey! Maybe you could use your press connections to help me out?

I think my connections are exclusive to me, unfortunately. Sorry, Norma.

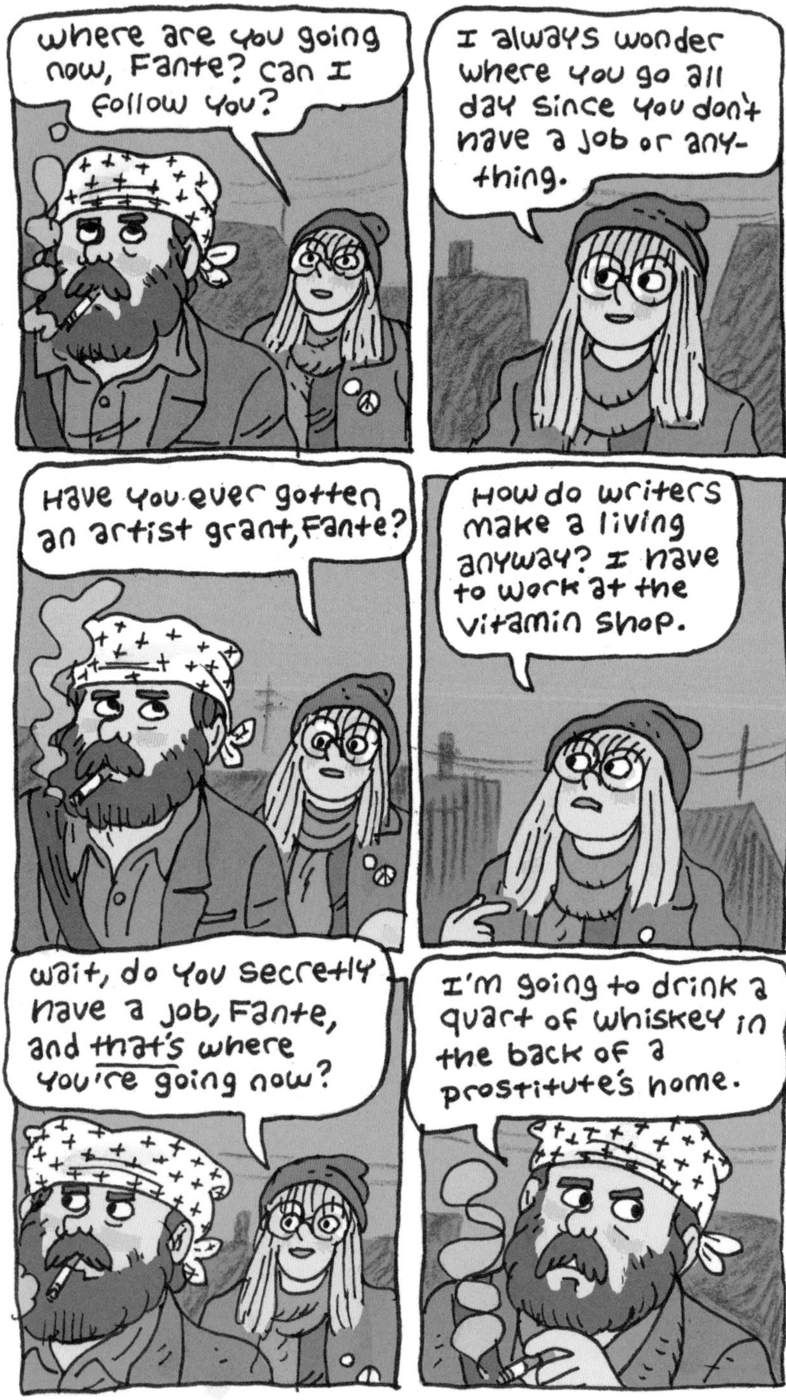
where are you going now, Fante? Can I follow you?
I always wonder where you go all day since you don't have a job or any-thing.
Have you ever gotten an artist grant, Fante?
How do writers make a living anyway? I have to work at the vitamin shop.
wait, do you secretly have a job, Fante, and that's where you're going now?
I'm going to drink a quart of whiskey in the back of a prostitute's home.

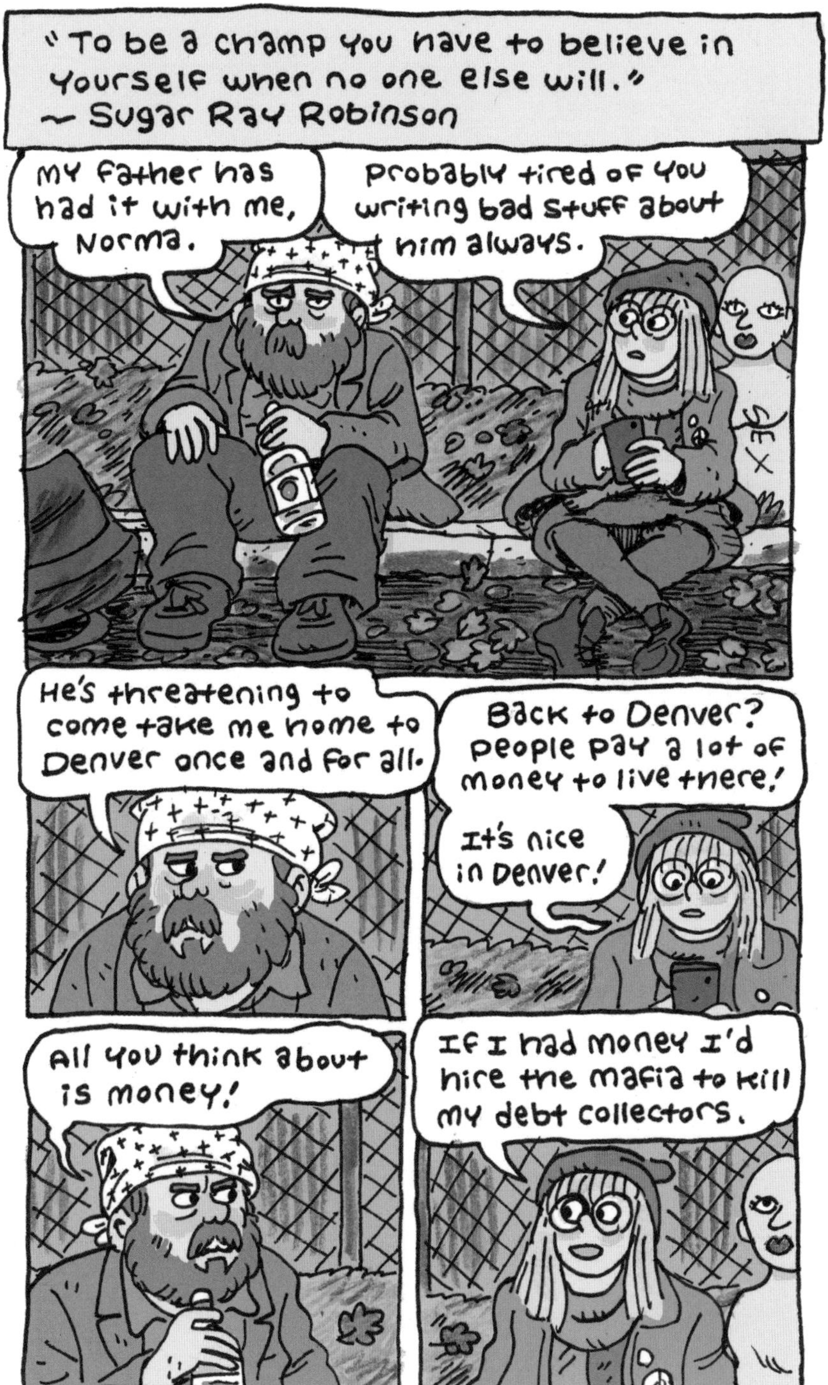
"To be a champ you have to believe in yourself when no one else will."
~ Sugar Ray Robinson
My father has had it with me, Norma.
Probably tired of you writing bad stuff about him always.
SEX
He's threatening to come take me home to Denver once and for all.
Back to Denver? People pay a lot of money to live there!
It's nice in Denver!
All you think about is money!
If I had money I'd hire the mafia to kill my debt collectors.

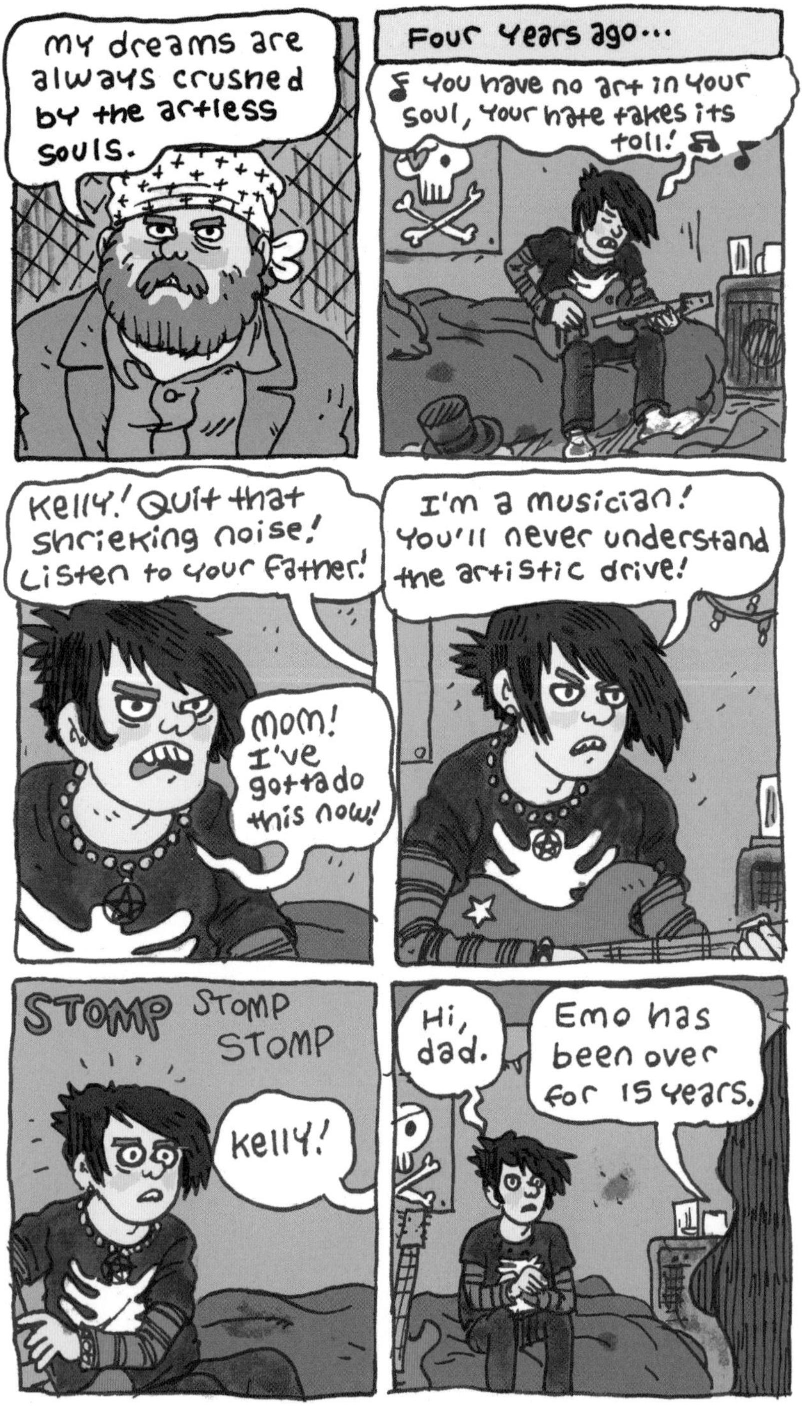
my dreams are always crushed by the artless souls.
Four years ago...
You have no art in your soul, your hate takes its toll!
Kelly! Quit that shrieking noise! Listen to your father!
mom! I've gotta do this now!
I'm a musician! You'll never understand the artistic drive!
STOMP STOMP STOMP
Kelly!
Hi, dad.
Emo has been over for 15 years.

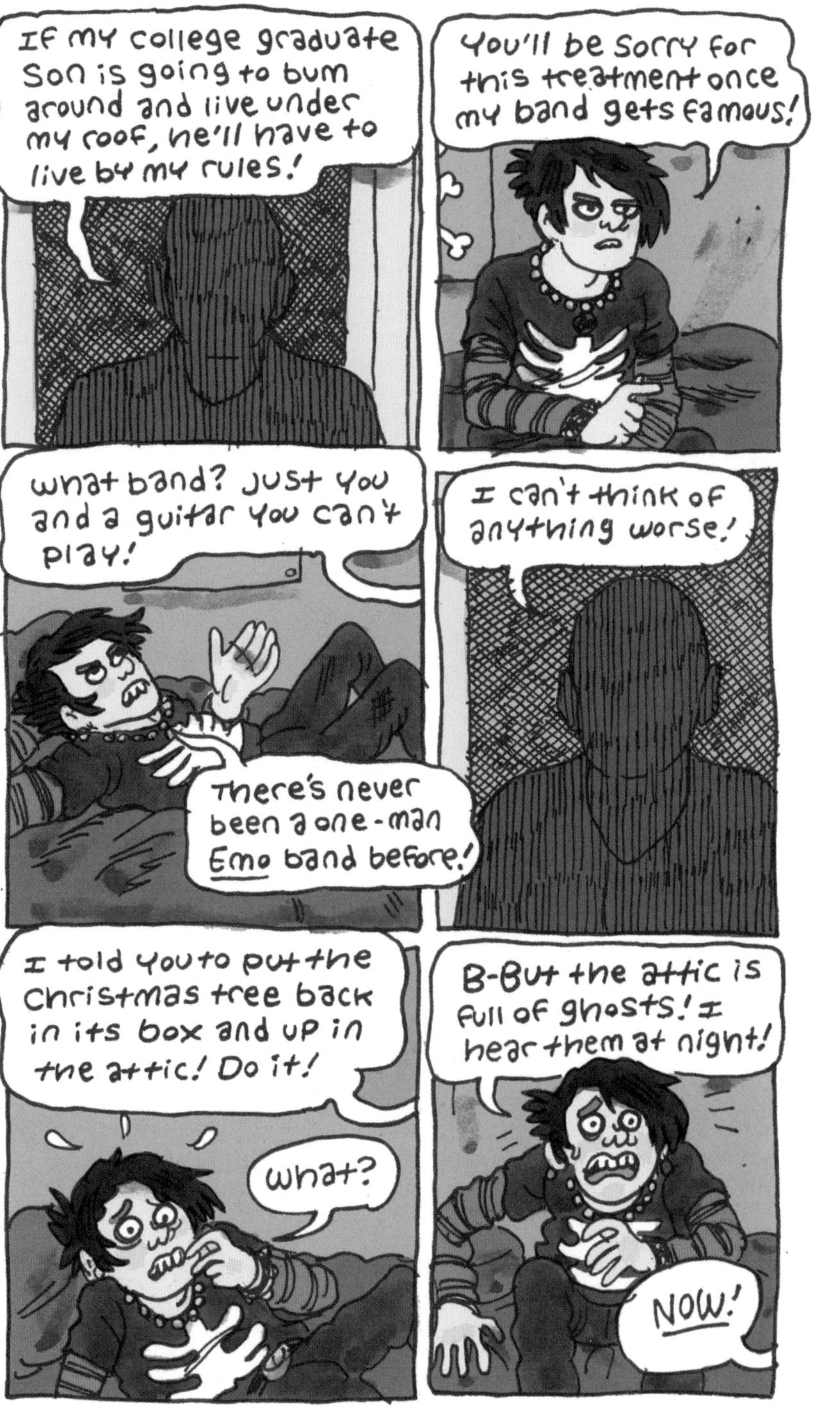
If my college graduate son is going to bum around and live under my roof, he'll have to live by my rules!
You'll be sorry for this treatment once my band gets famous!
What band? Just you and a guitar you can't play!
There's never been a one-man Emo band before!
I can't think of anything worse!
I told you to put the Christmas tree back in its box and up in the attic! Do it!
What?
B-But the attic is full of ghosts! I hear them at night!
NOW!

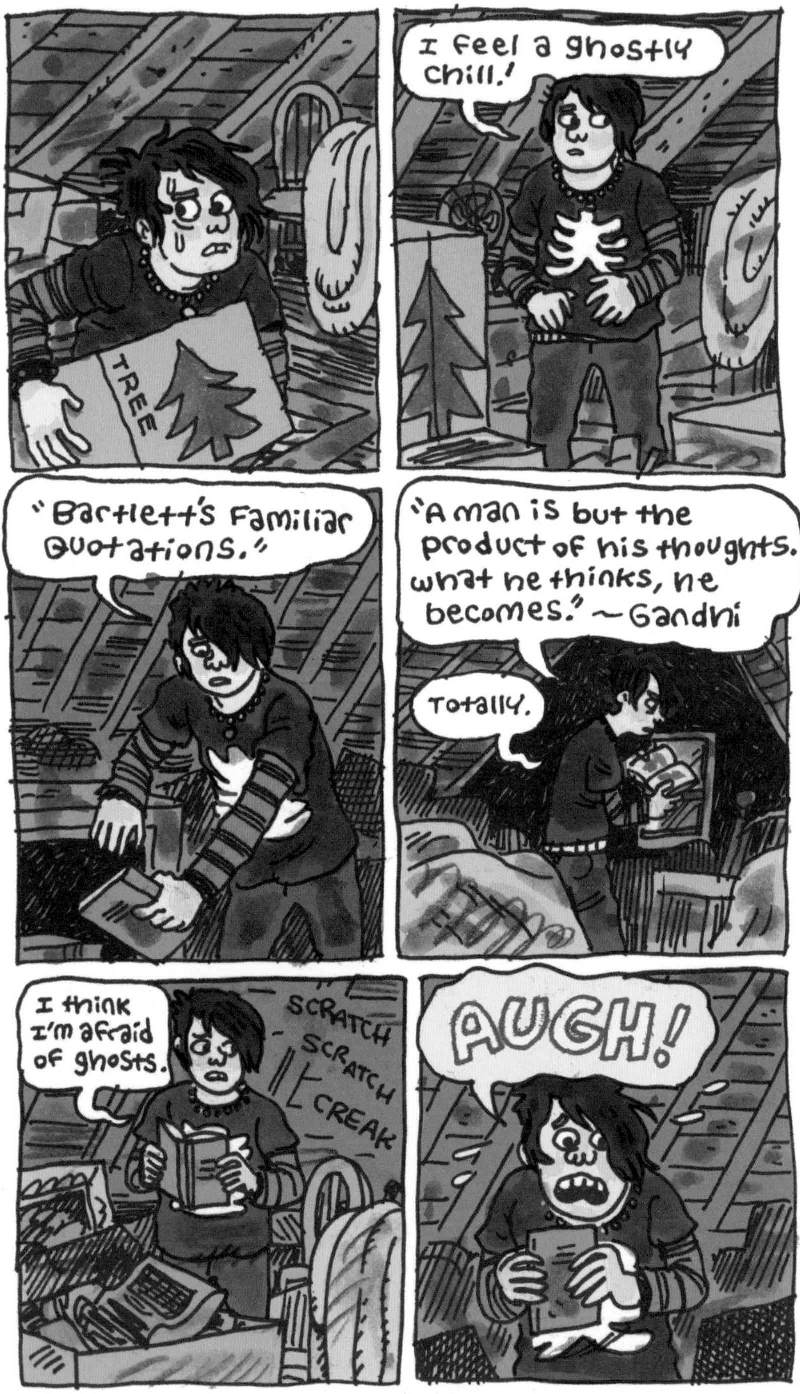

TREE
I feel a ghostly chill!
"Bartlett's Familiar Quotations."
"A man is but the product of his thoughts. What he thinks, he becomes." ~Gandhi
Totally.
I think I'm afraid of ghosts.
SCRATCH
SCRATCH
CREAK
AUGH!

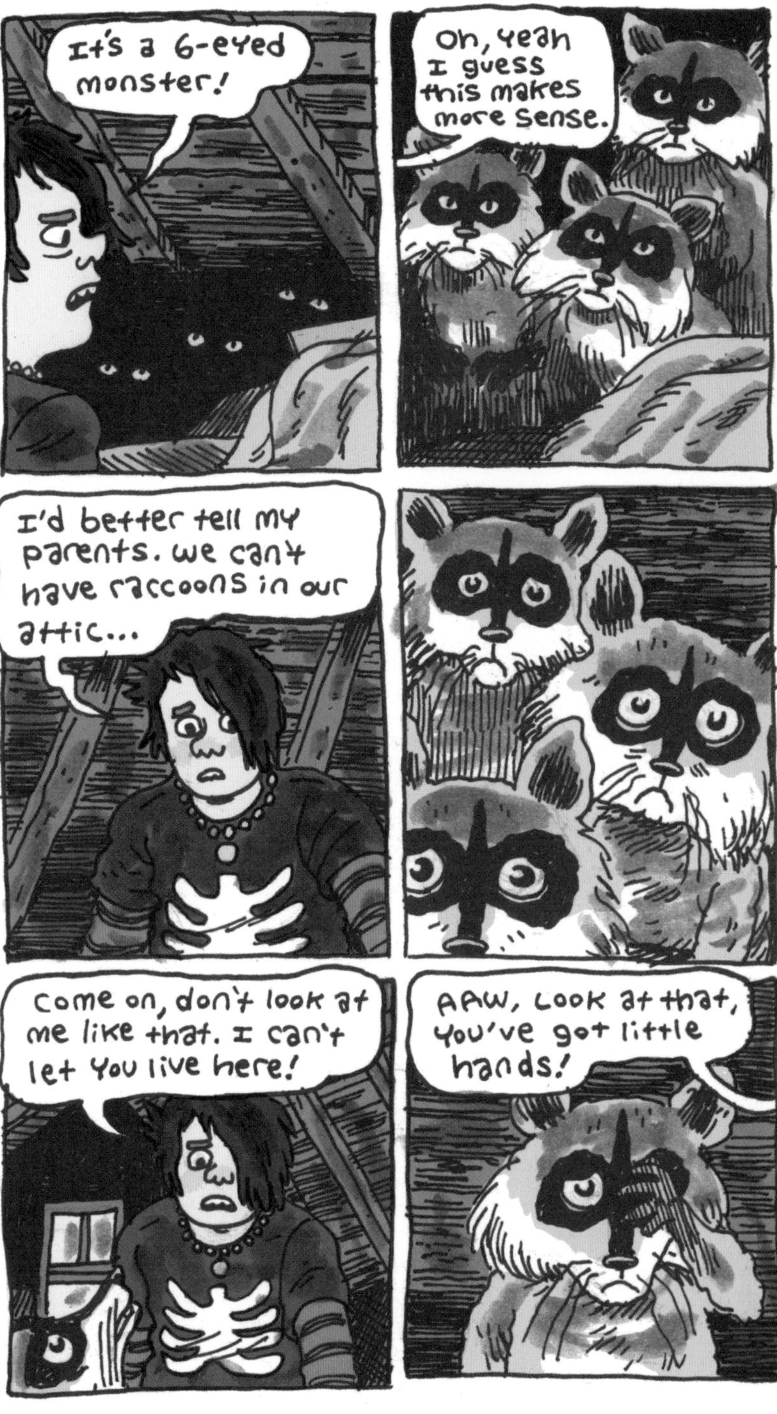
It's a 6-eyed monster!
Oh, yeah I guess this makes more sense.
I'd better tell my parents. we can't have raccoons in our attic...
Come on, don't look at me like that. I can't let you live here!
AAW, look at that, you've got little hands!

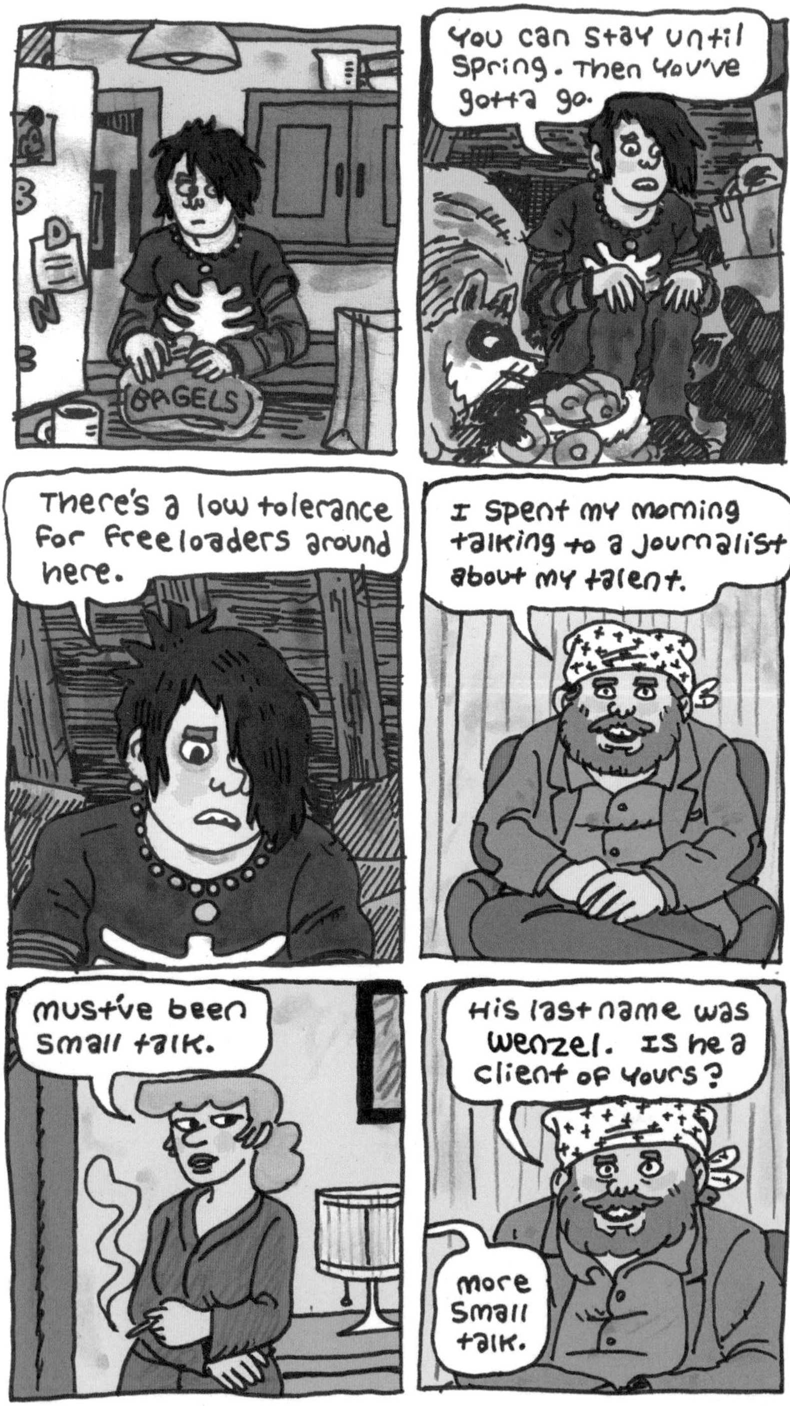
BAGELS
You can stay until Spring. Then you've gotta go.
There's a low tolerance for freeloaders around here.
I spent my morning talking to a journalist about my talent.
Must've been small talk.
His last name was Wenzel. Is he a client of yours?
More small talk.

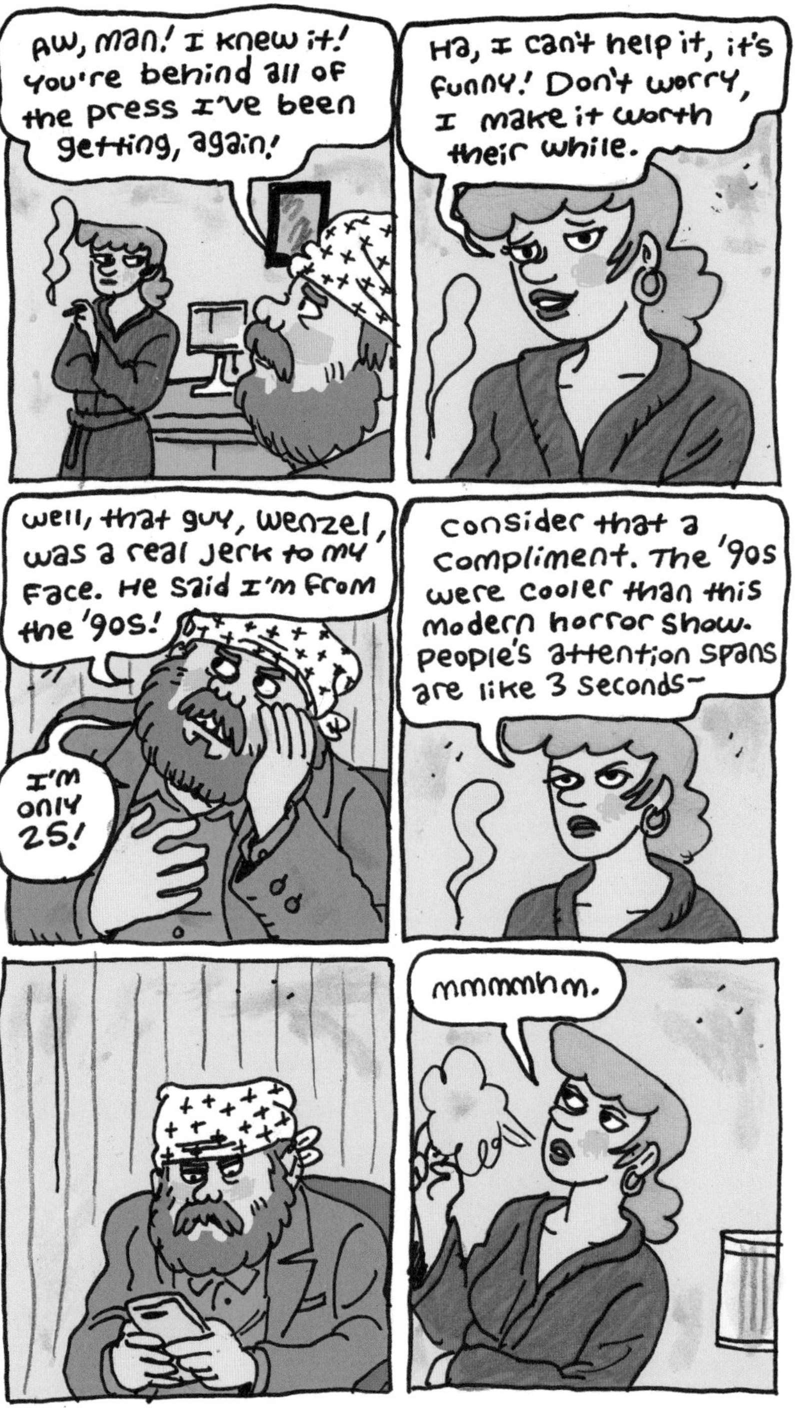
AW, MAN! I KNEW IT! YOU'RE BEHIND ALL OF THE PRESS I'VE BEEN GETTING, AGAIN!
HA, I CAN'T HELP IT, IT'S FUNNY! DON'T WORRY, I MAKE IT WORTH THEIR WHILE.
WELL, THAT GUY, WENZEL, WAS A REAL JERK TO MY FACE. HE SAID I'M FROM THE '90S!
I'M ONLY 25!
CONSIDER THAT A COMPLIMENT. THE '90S WERE COOLER THAN THIS MODERN HORROR SHOW. PEOPLE'S ATTENTION SPANS ARE LIKE 3 SECONDS–
MMMMHM.

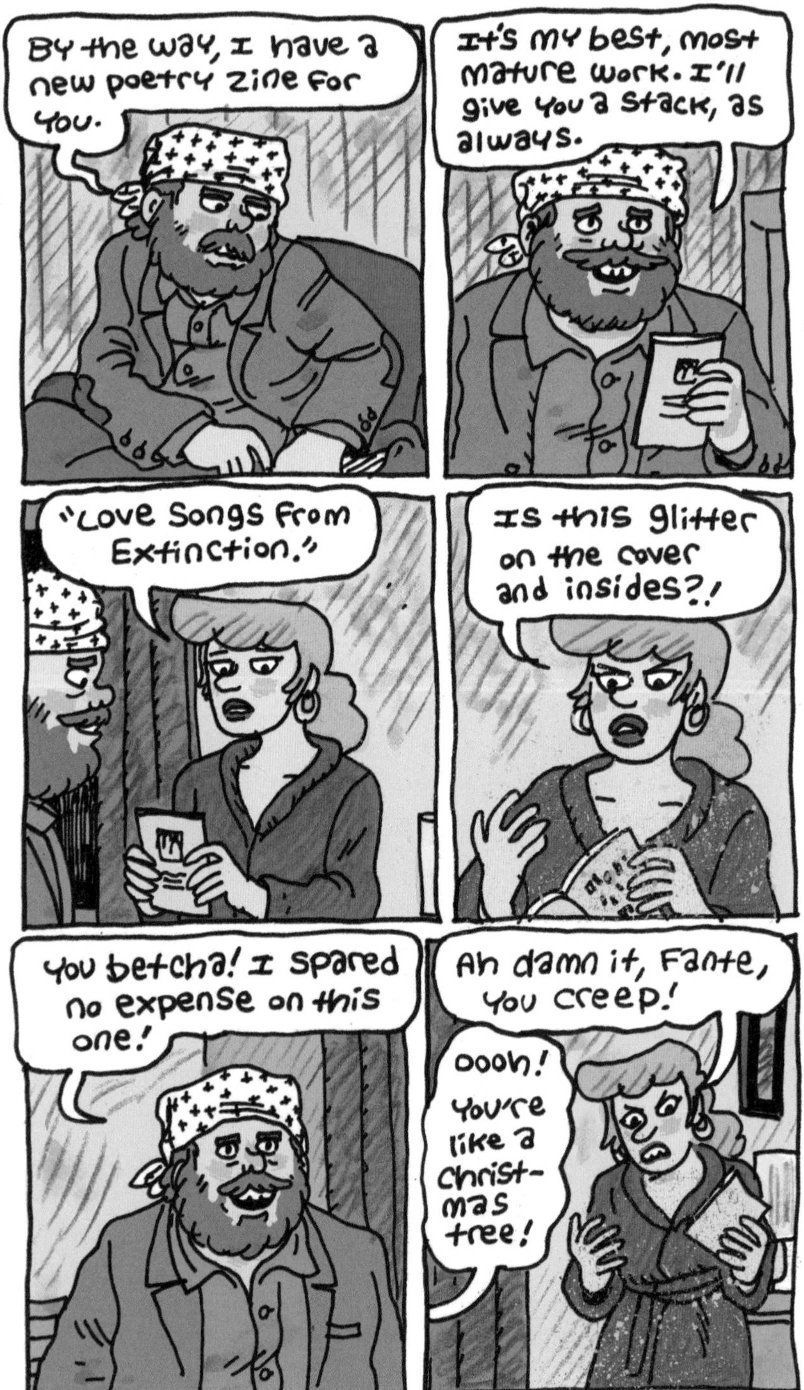
By the way, I have a new poetry zine for you.
It's my best, most mature work. I'll give you a stack, as always.
"Love Songs from Extinction."
Is this glitter on the cover and insides?!
You betcha! I spared no expense on this one!
Ah damn it, Fante, you creep!
Oooh! You're like a Christ-mas tree!

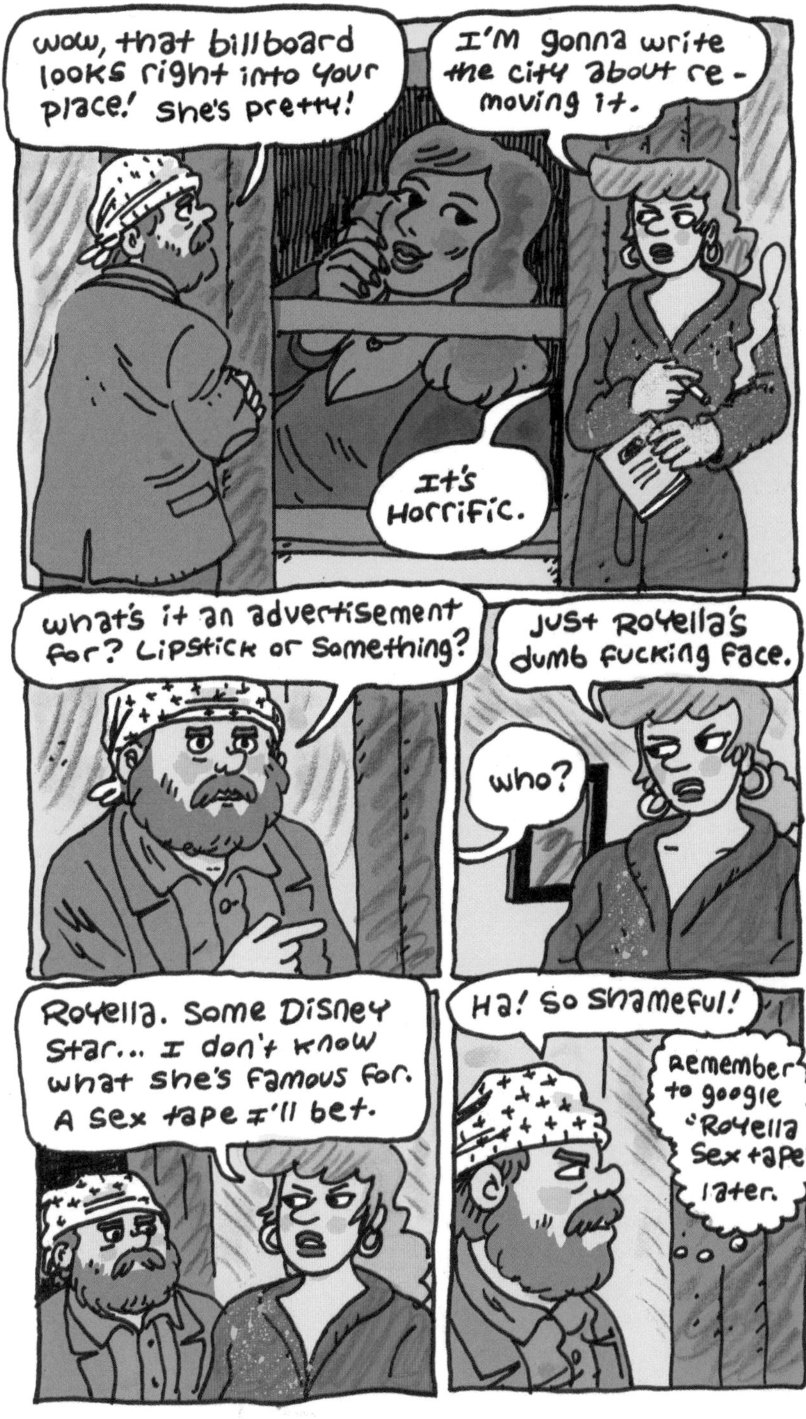
wow, that billboard looks right into your place! she's pretty!
I'M gonna write the city about re-moving it.
It's Horrific.
what's it an advertisement for? Lipstick or Something?
Just Royella's dumb fucking face.
who?
Royella. Some Disney Star... I don't know what she's famous for. A sex tape I'll bet.
Ha! So shameful!
Remember to google "Royella Sex tape" later.

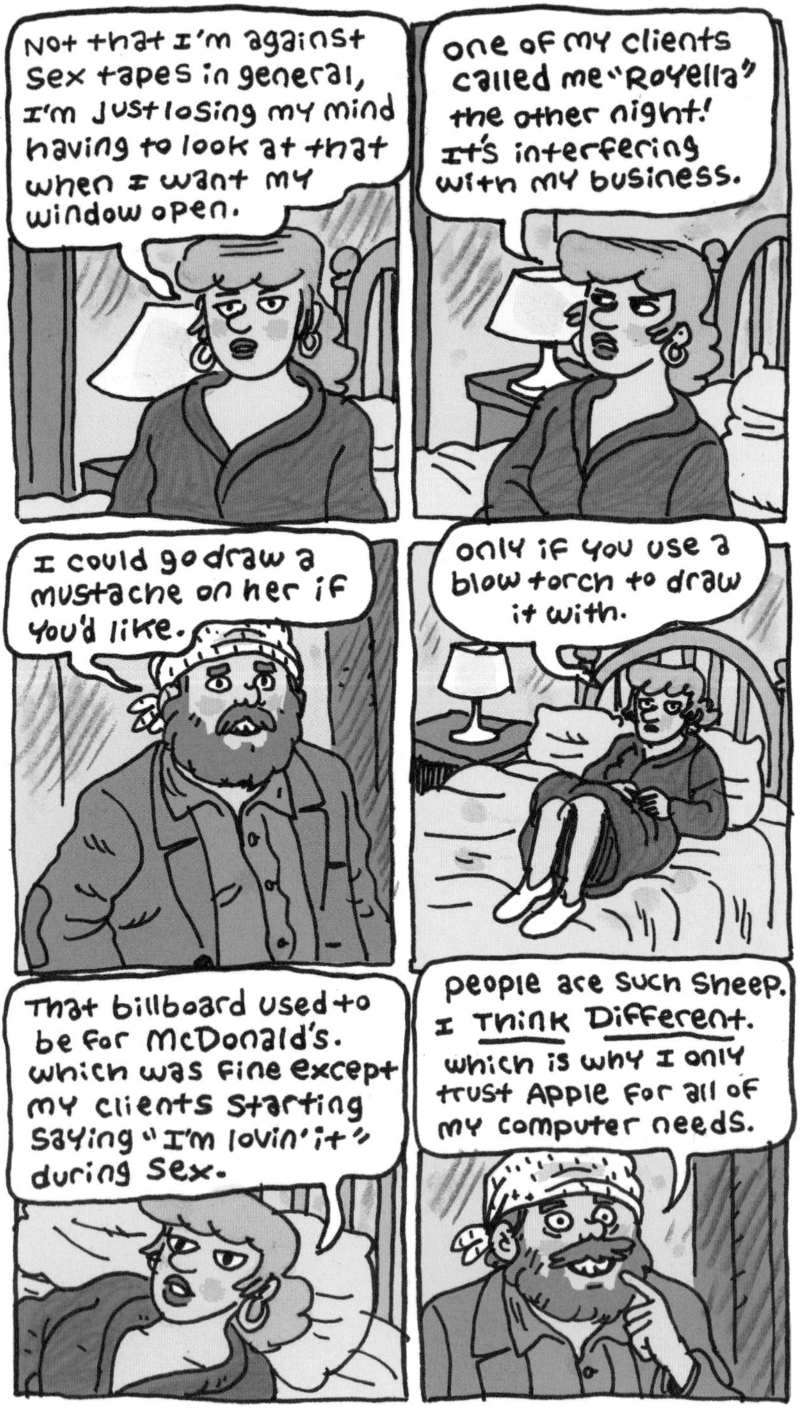
Not that I'm against sex tapes in general, I'm just losing my mind having to look at that when I want my window open.
One of my clients called me "Royella" the other night! It's interfering with my business.
I could go draw a mustache on her if you'd like.
Only if you use a blow torch to draw it with.
That billboard used to be for McDonald's. which was fine except my clients starting saying "I'm lovin' it" during sex.
People are such sheep. I Think Different. which is why I only trust Apple for all of my computer needs.

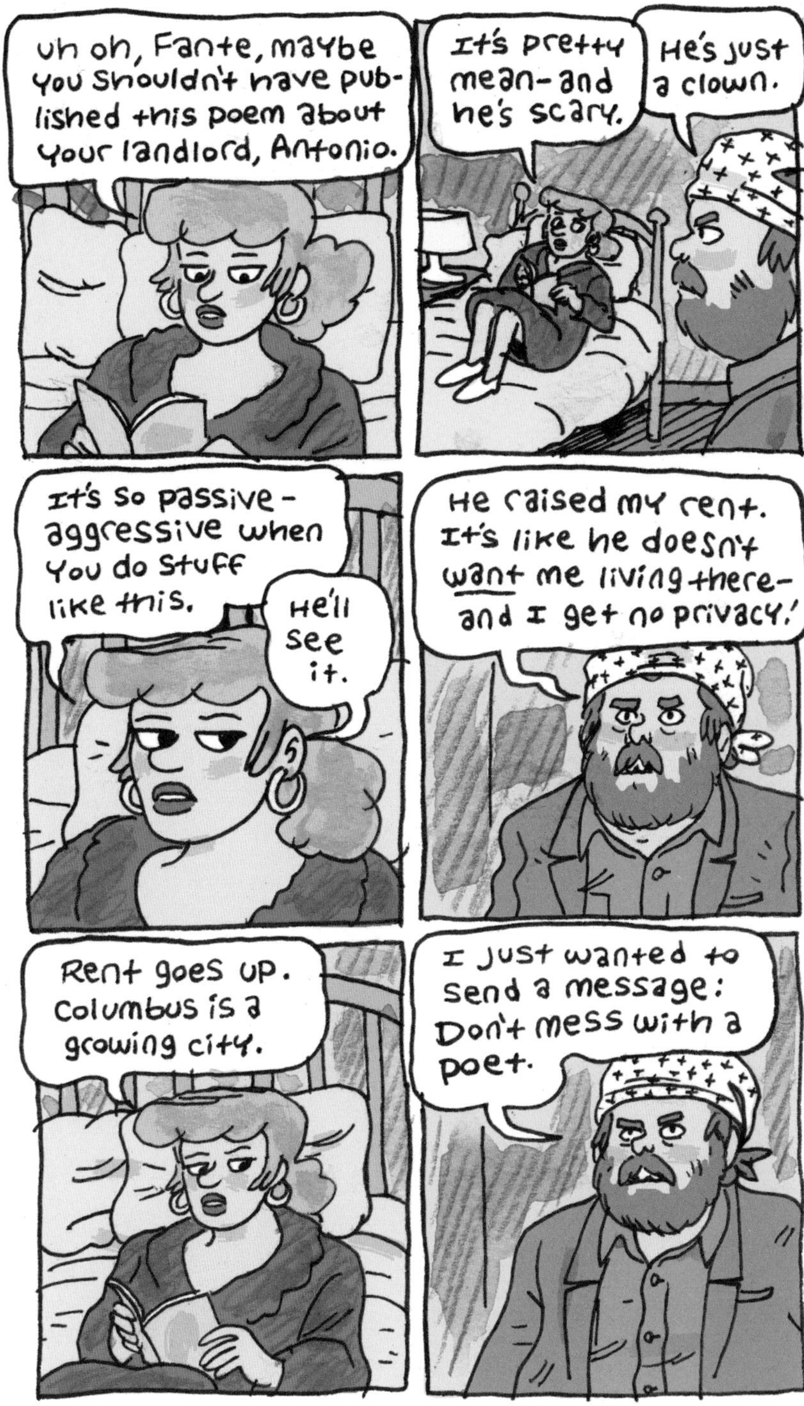
Uh oh, Fante, maybe you shouldn't have published this poem about your landlord, Antonio.
It's pretty mean–and he's scary.
He's just a clown.
It's so passive-aggressive when you do stuff like this.
He'll see it.
He raised my rent. It's like he doesn't want me living there–and I get no privacy!
Rent goes up. Columbus is a growing city.
I just wanted to send a message: Don't mess with a poet.

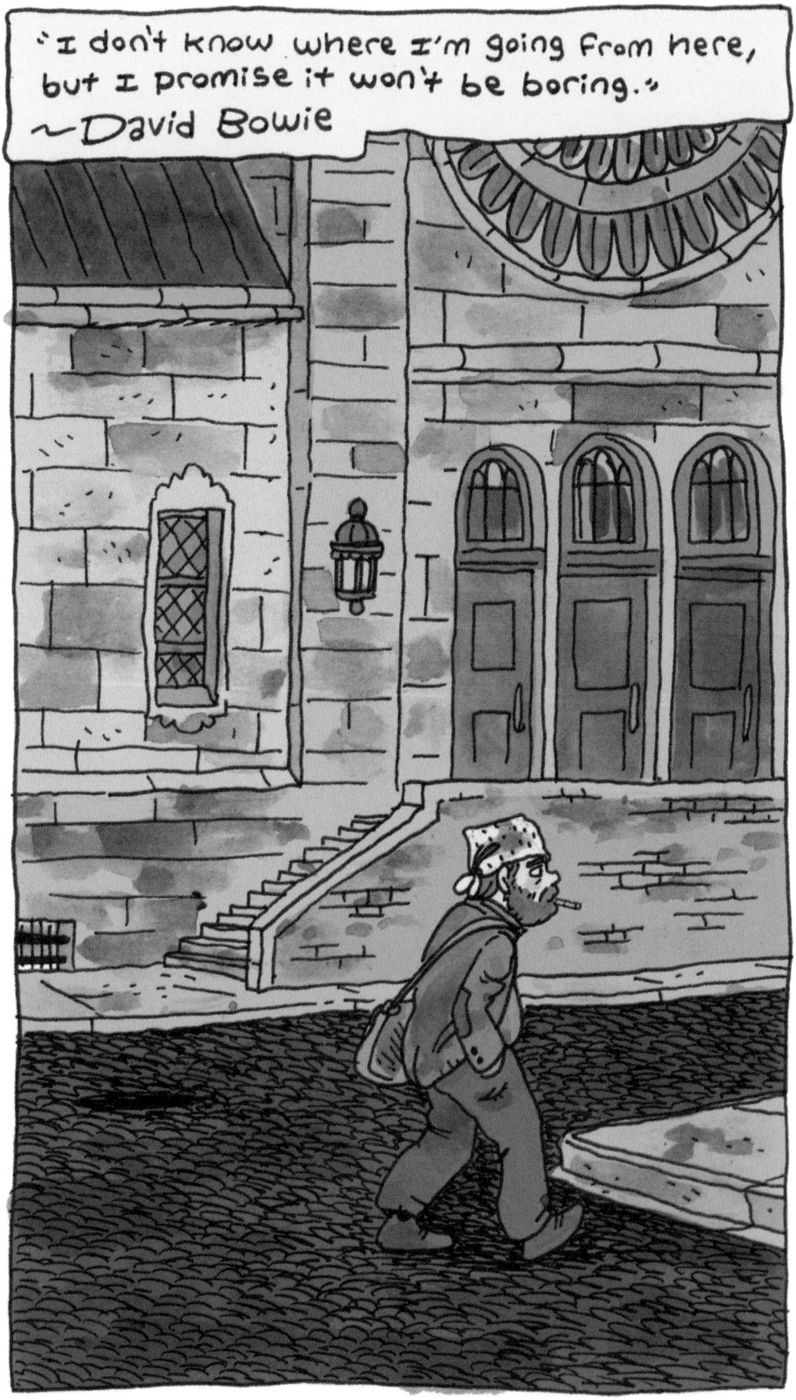
"I don't know where I'm going from here, but I promise it won't be boring."
~David Bowie

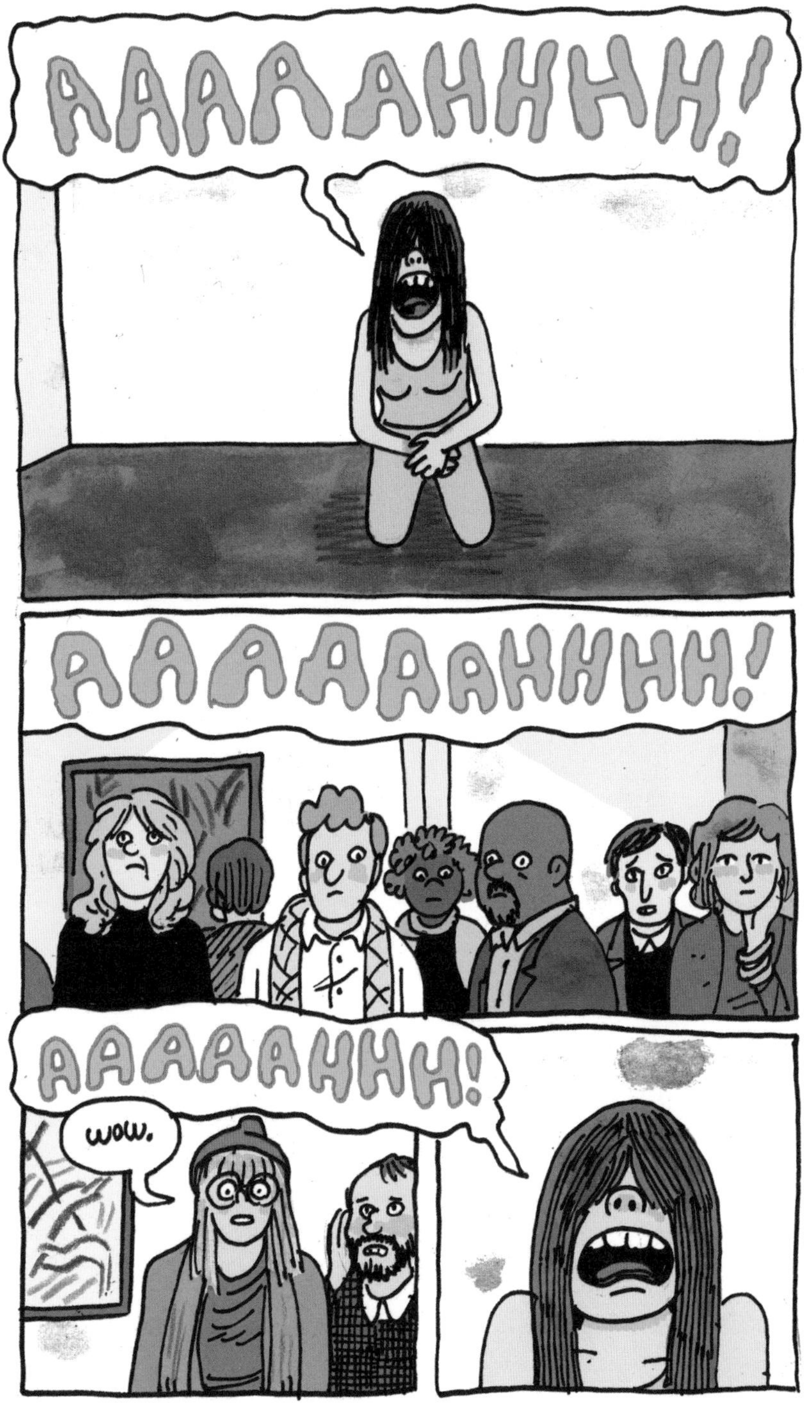

AAAAAHHHH!
AAAAAAHHHH!
AAAAAHHH!
wow.

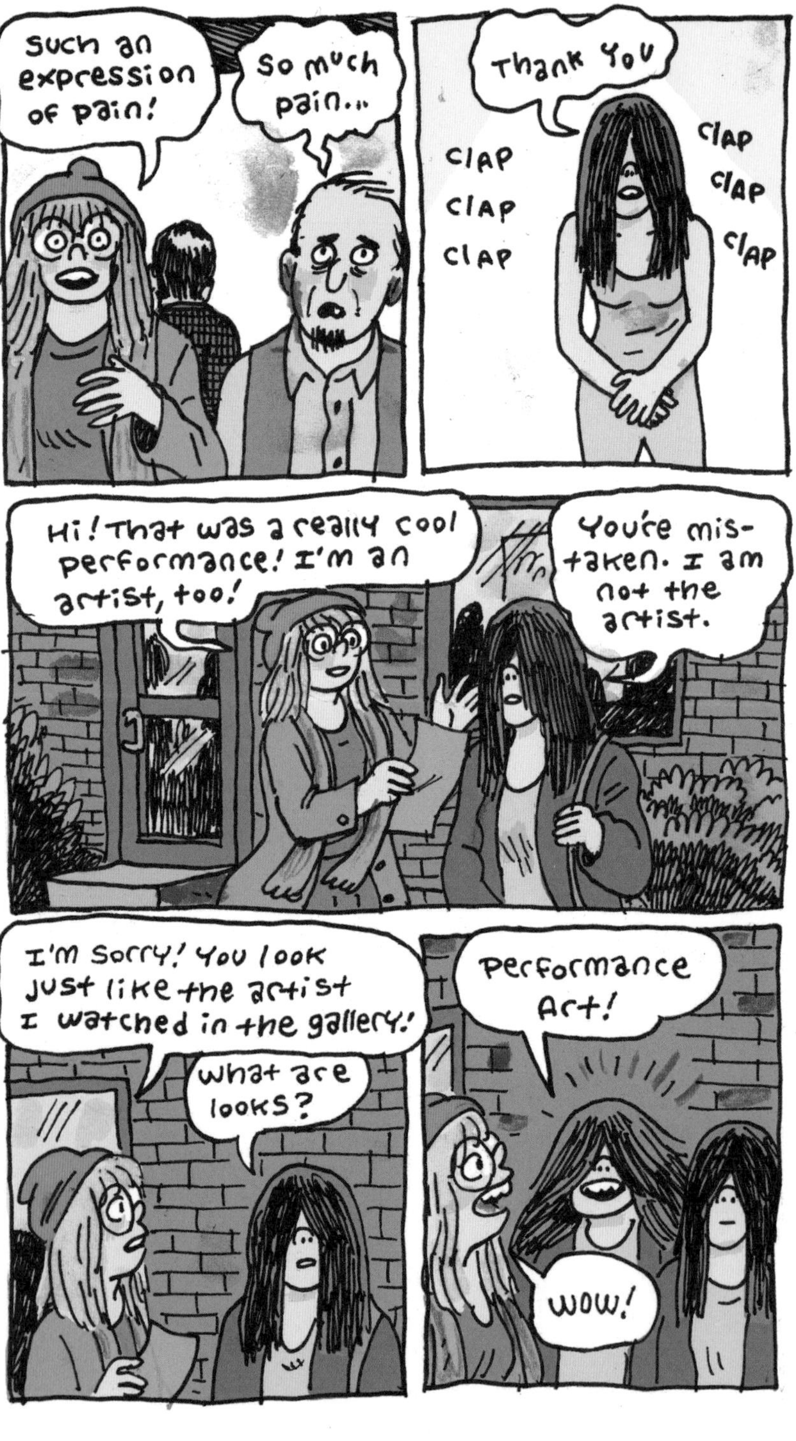
Such an expression of pain!
So much pain...
Thank you
CLAP
CLAP
CLAP
CLAP
CLAP
CLAP
Hi! That was a really cool performance! I'm an artist, too!
You're mistaken. I am not the artist.
I'm sorry! You look just like the artist I watched in the gallery!
What are looks?
Performance Art!
WOW!

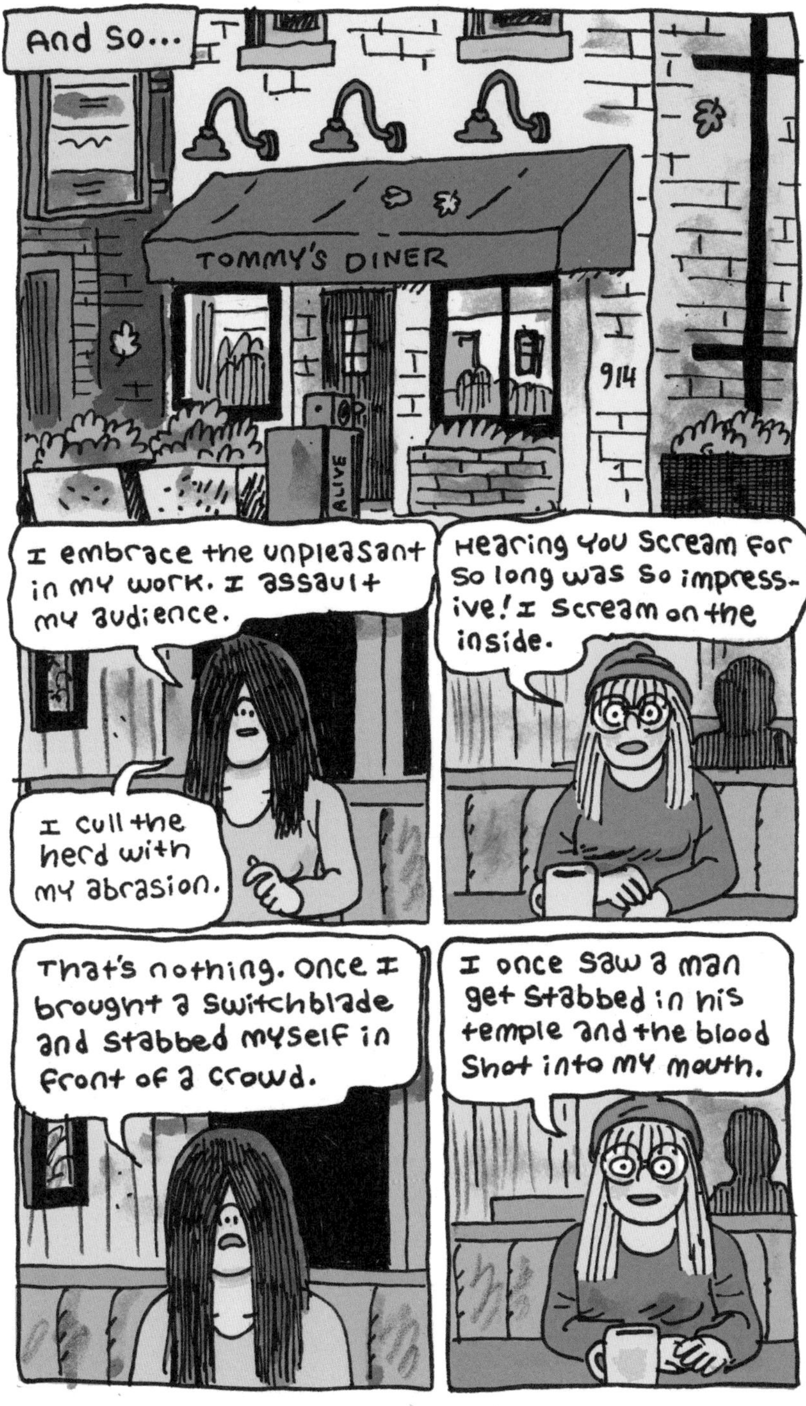
And so...
TOMMY'S DINER
914
ALIVE
I embrace the unpleasant in my work. I assault my audience.
I cull the herd with my abrasion.
Hearing you scream for so long was so impress-ive! I scream on the inside.
That's nothing. Once I brought a switchblade and stabbed myself in front of a crowd.
I once saw a man get stabbed in his temple and the blood shot into my mouth.

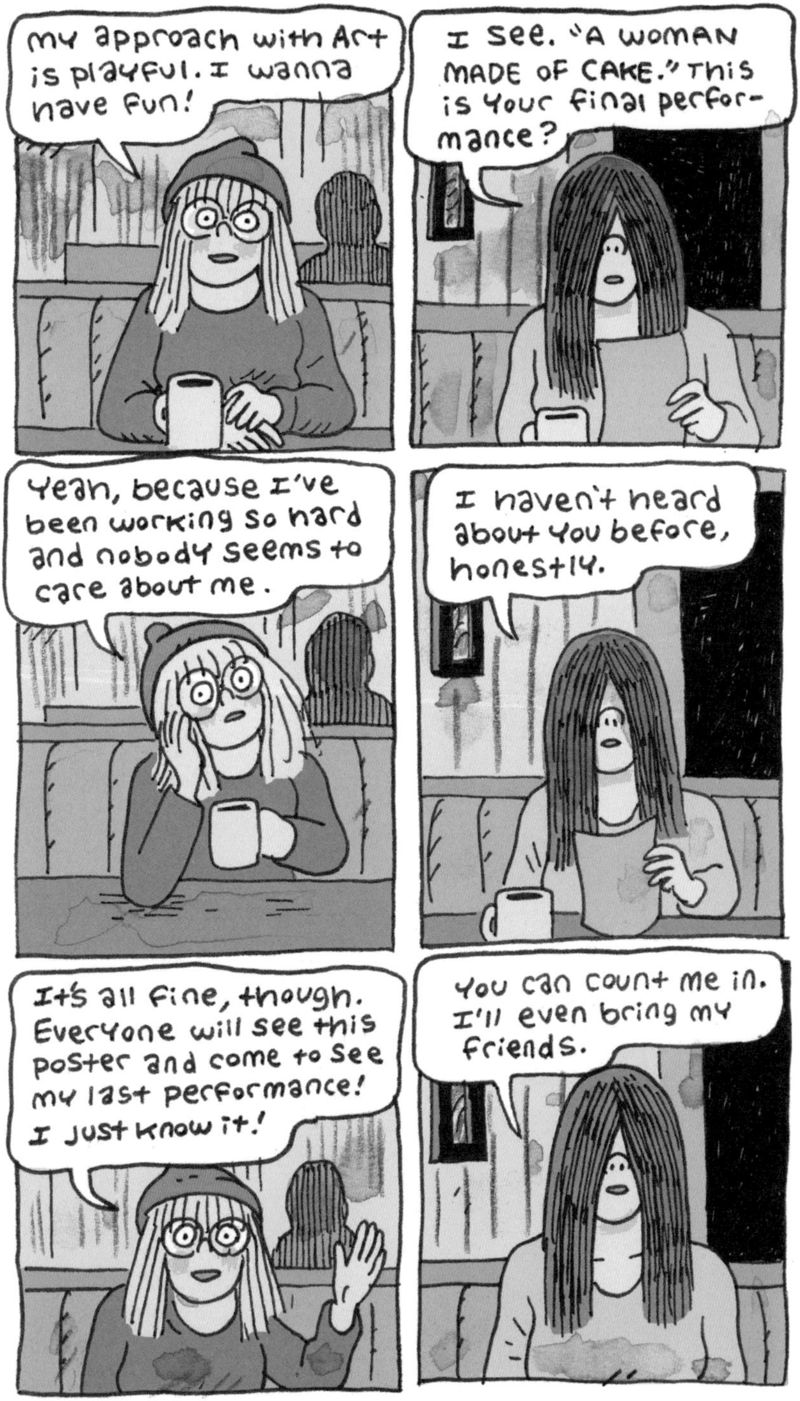
my approach with Art is playful. I wanna have fun!
I see. "A WOMAN MADE OF CAKE." This is your final performance?
Yeah, because I've been working so hard and nobody seems to care about me.
I haven't heard about you before, honestly.
It's all fine, though. Everyone will see this poster and come to see my last performance! I just know it!
You can count me in. I'll even bring my friends.

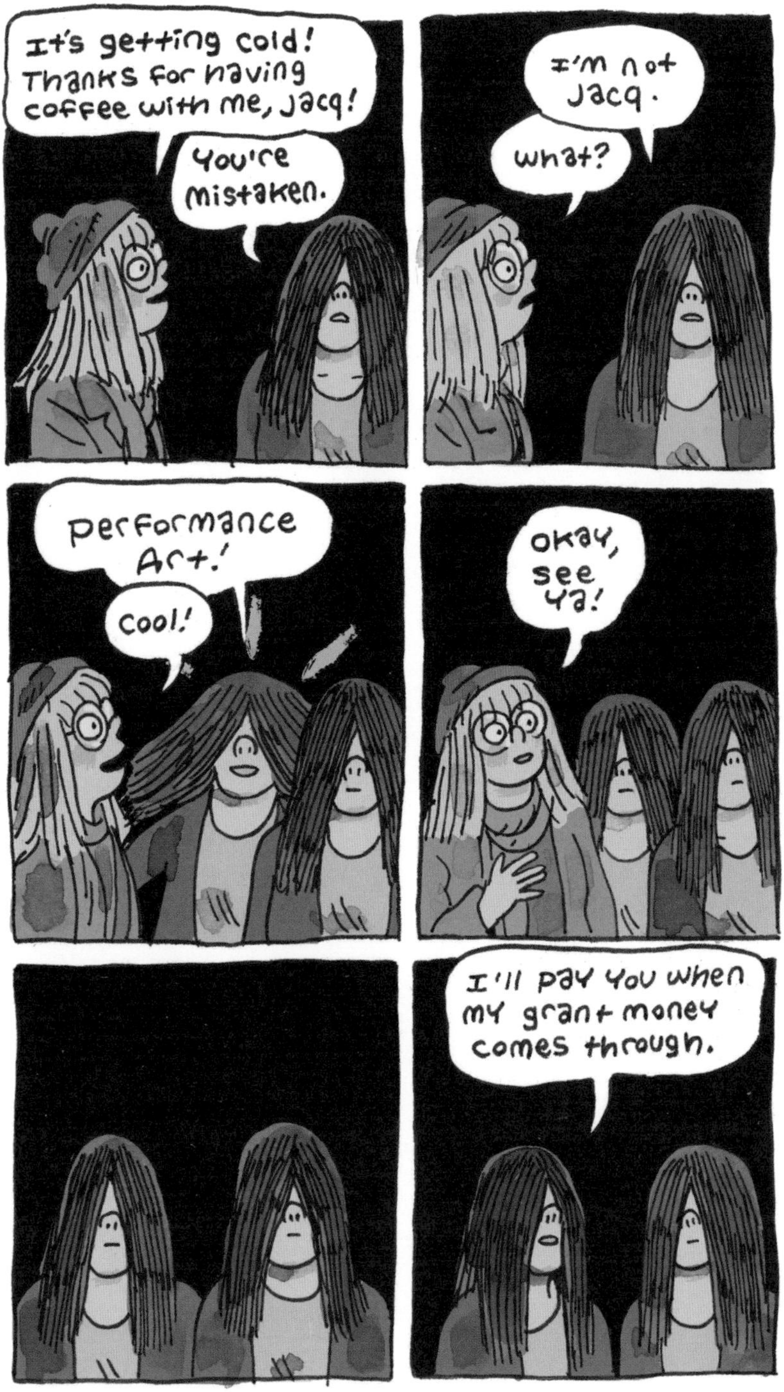
It's getting cold! Thanks for having coffee with me, Jacq!
You're mistaken.
I'm not Jacq.
What?
Performance Art!
Cool!
Okay, see ya!
I'll pay you when my grant money comes through.

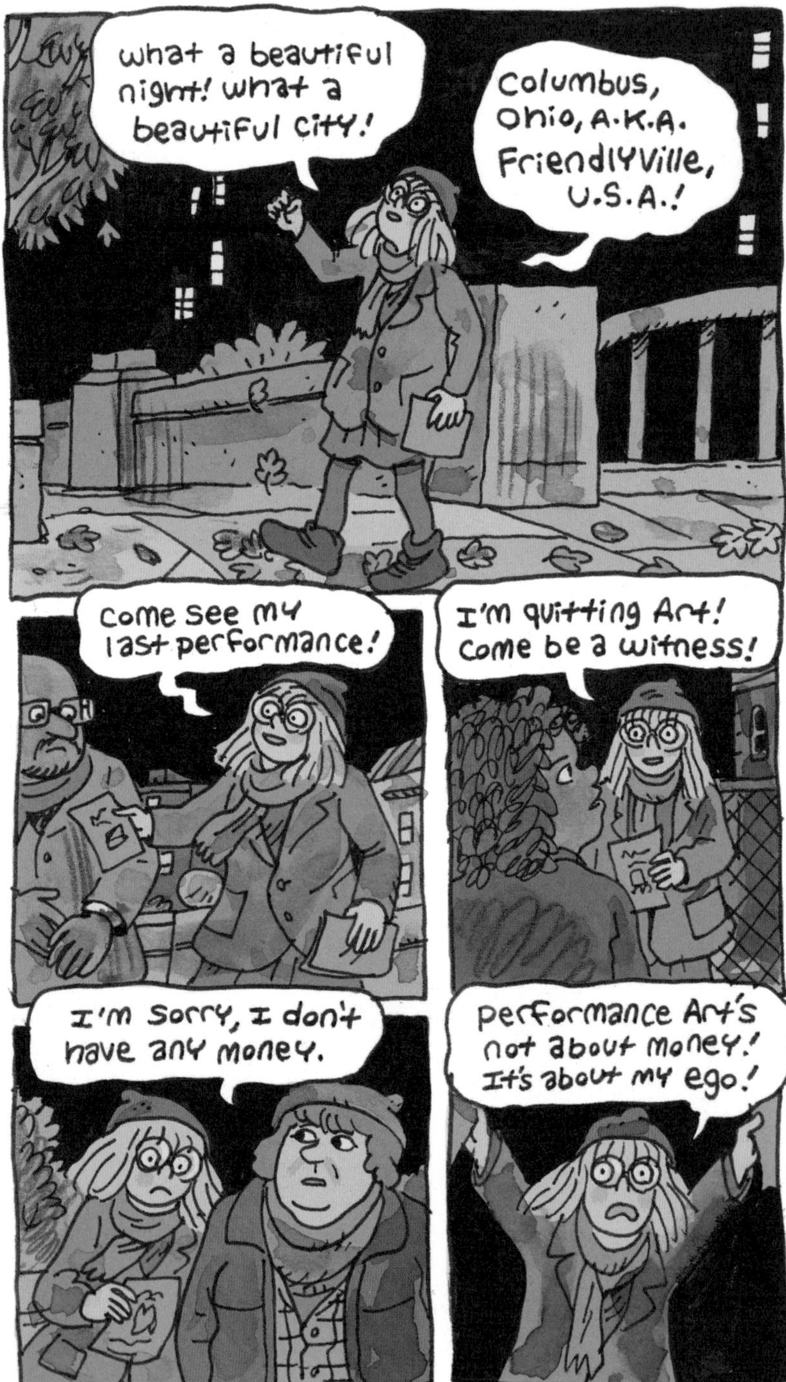
what a beautiful night! what a beautiful city!
Columbus, Ohio, A.K.A. FriendlyVille, U.S.A.!
Come see my last performance!
I'm quitting Art! Come be a witness!
I'm sorry, I don't have any money.
Performance Art's not about money! It's about my ego!

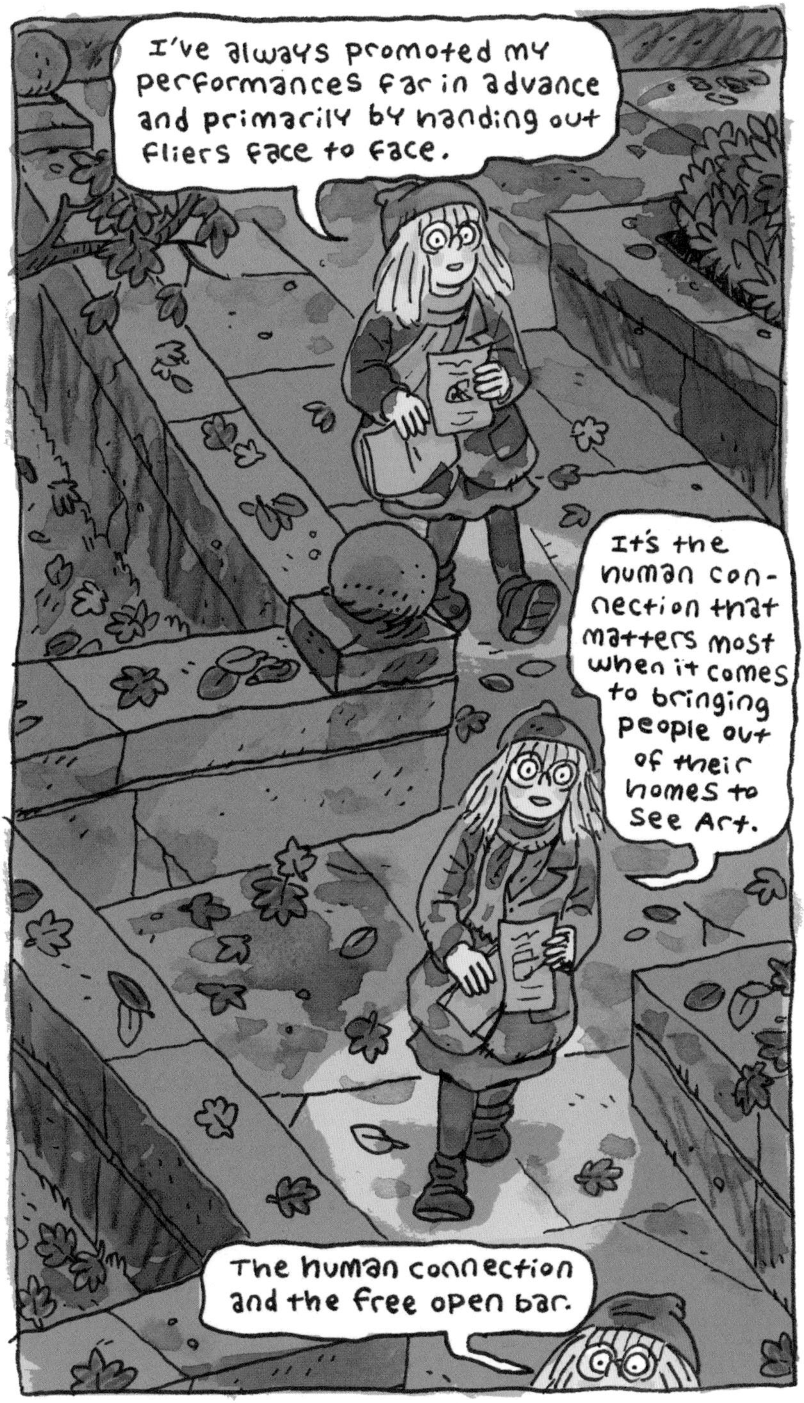
I've always promoted my performances far in advance and primarily by handing out fliers face to face.
It's the human connection that matters most when it comes to bringing people out of their homes to see Art.
The human connection and the free open bar.

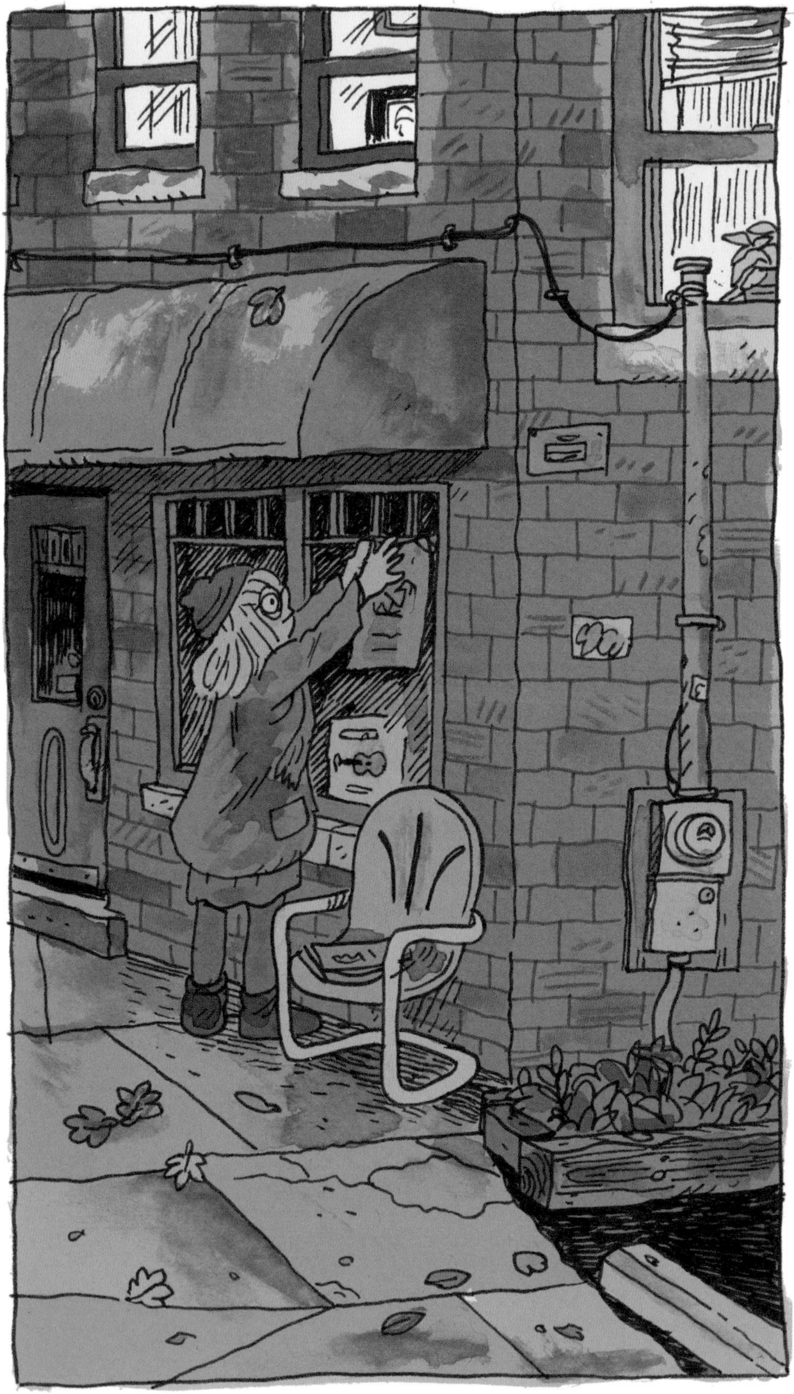

Fante e-mails his father

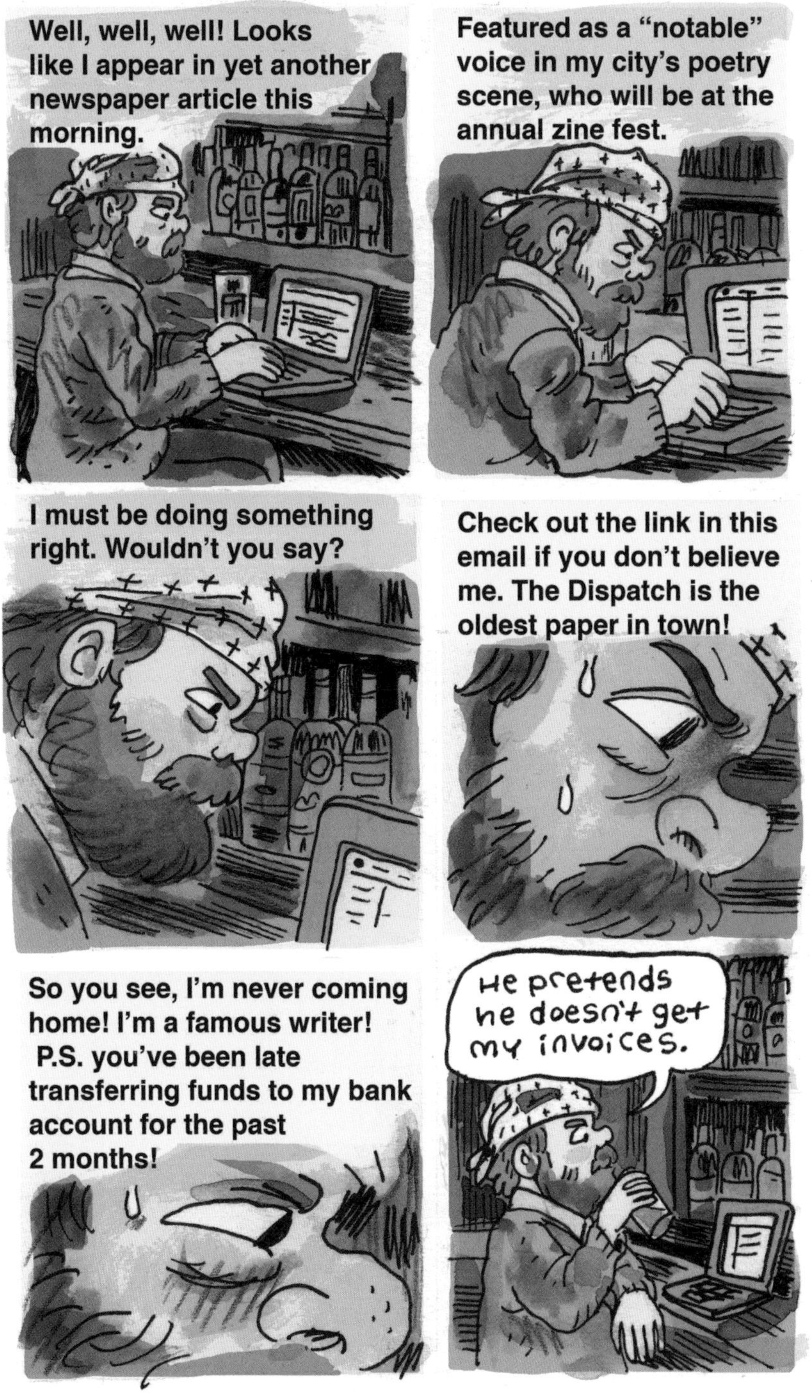
Well, well, well! Looks like I appear in yet another newspaper article this morning.
Featured as a "notable" voice in my city's poetry scene, who will be at the annual zine fest.
I must be doing something right. Wouldn't you say?
Check out the link in this email if you don't believe me. The Dispatch is the oldest paper in town!
So you see, I'm never coming home! I'm a famous writer! P.S. you've been late transferring funds to my bank account for the past 2 months!
He pretends he doesn't get my invoices.

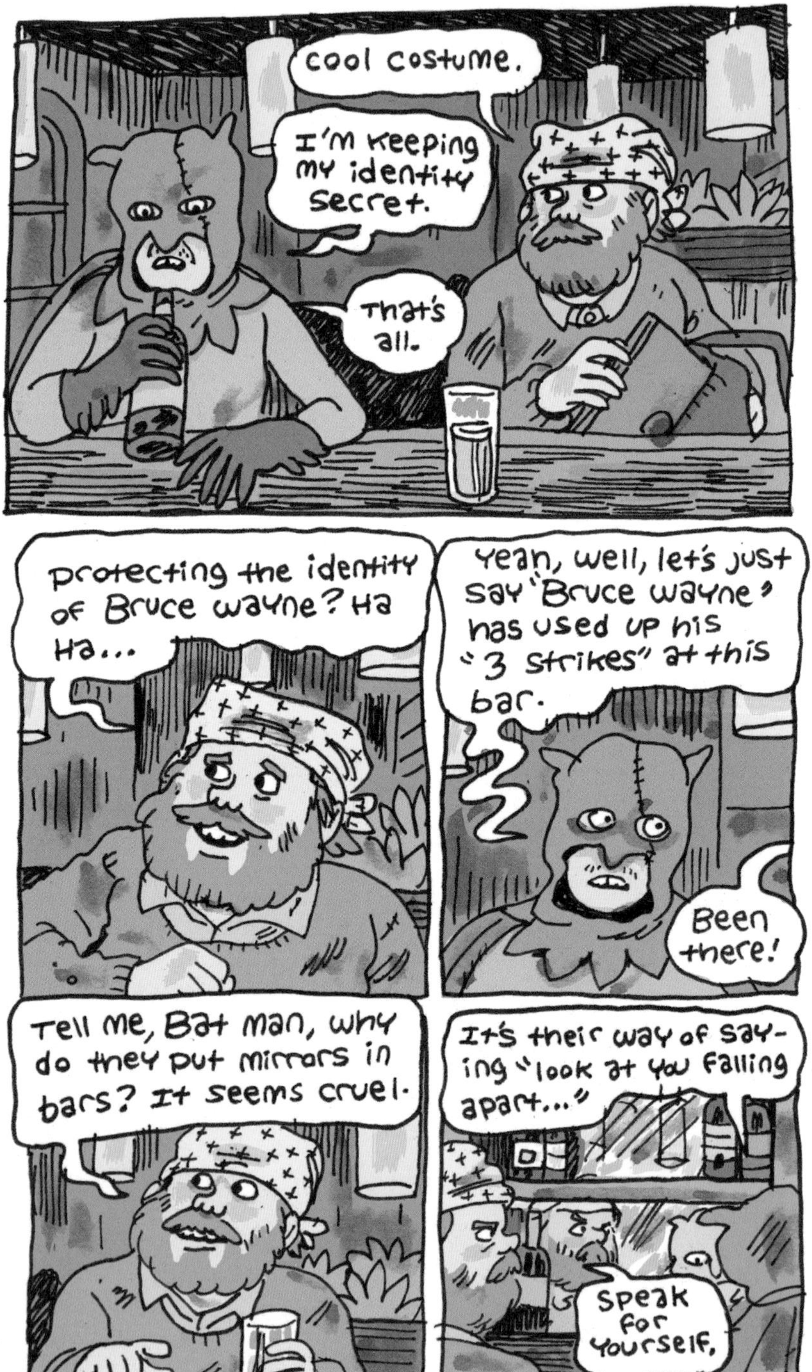
cool costume.
I'm keeping my identity secret.
That's all.
protecting the identity of Bruce wayne? Ha Ha...
yeah, well, let's just say "Bruce wayne" has used up his "3 strikes" at this bar.
Been there!
Tell me, Bat man, why do they put mirrors in bars? It seems cruel.
It's their way of say-ing "look at you falling apart..."
Speak for yourself.

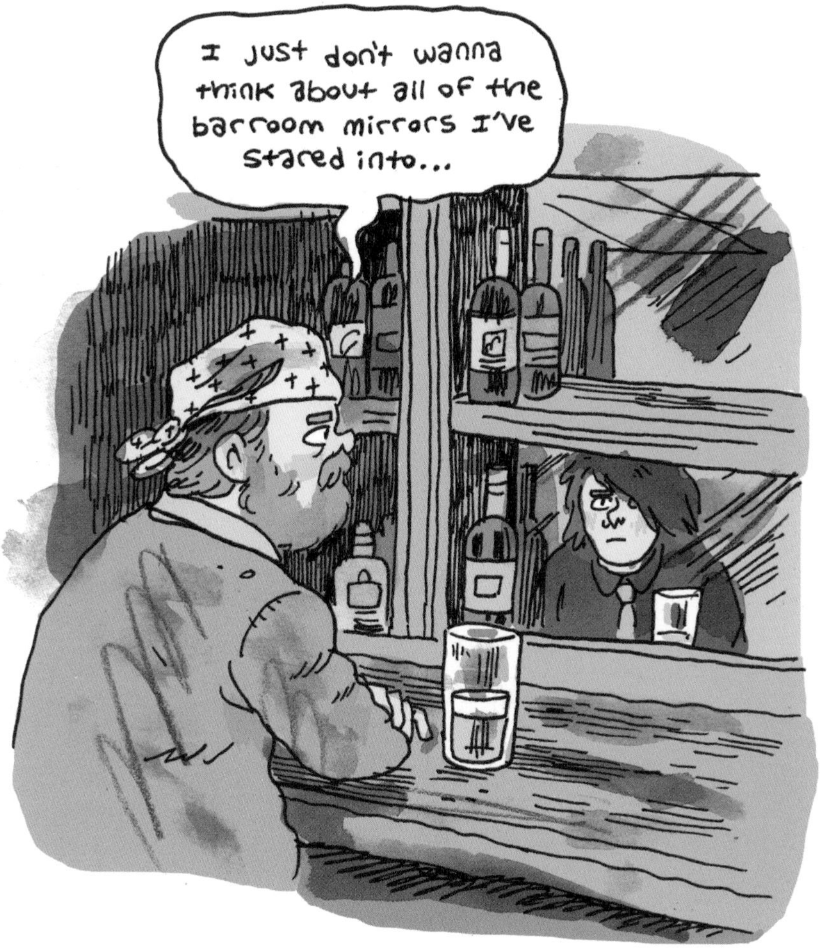
I just don't wanna think about all of the barroom mirrors I've stared into...

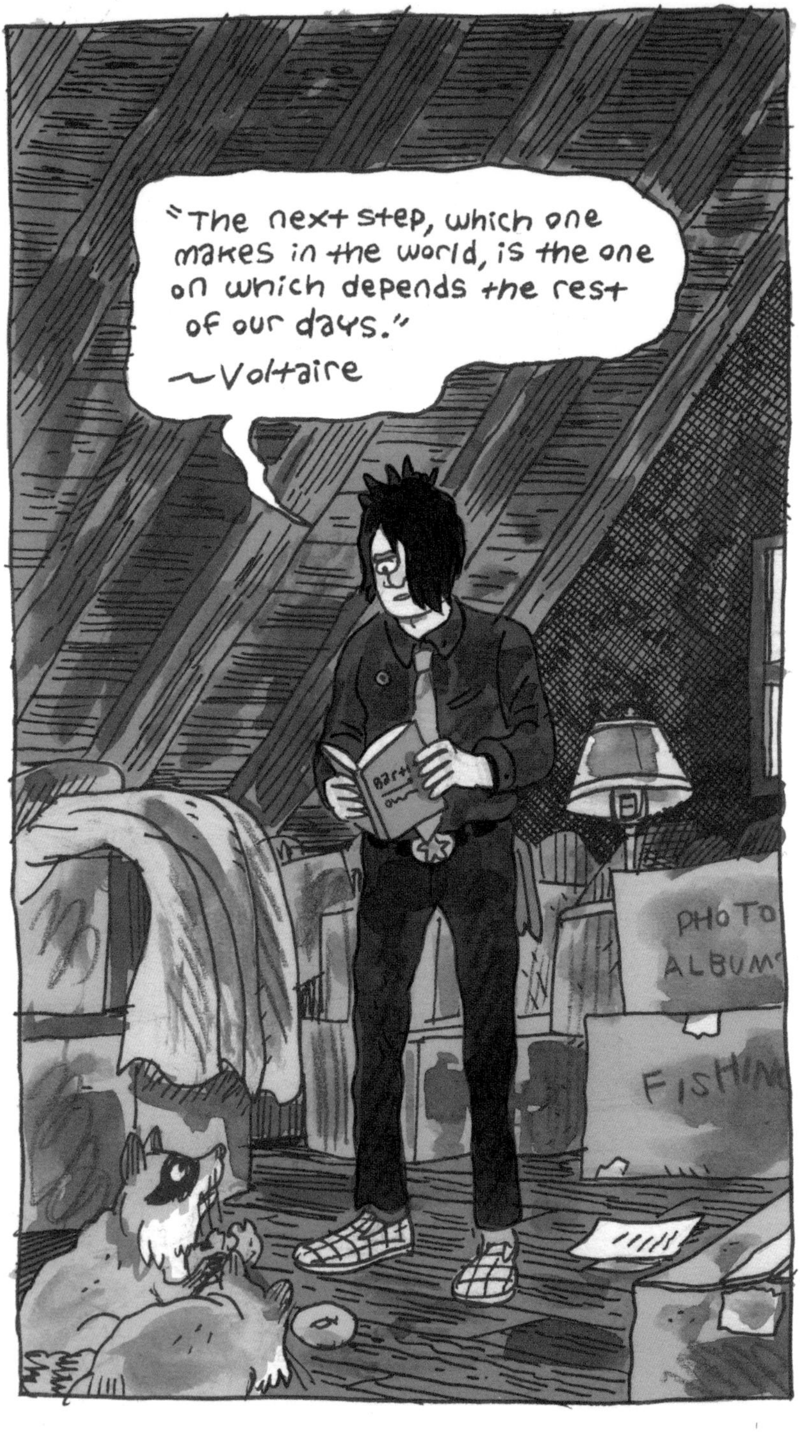
"The next step, which one makes in the world, is the one on which depends the rest of our days."
~Voltaire
PHOTO ALBUM

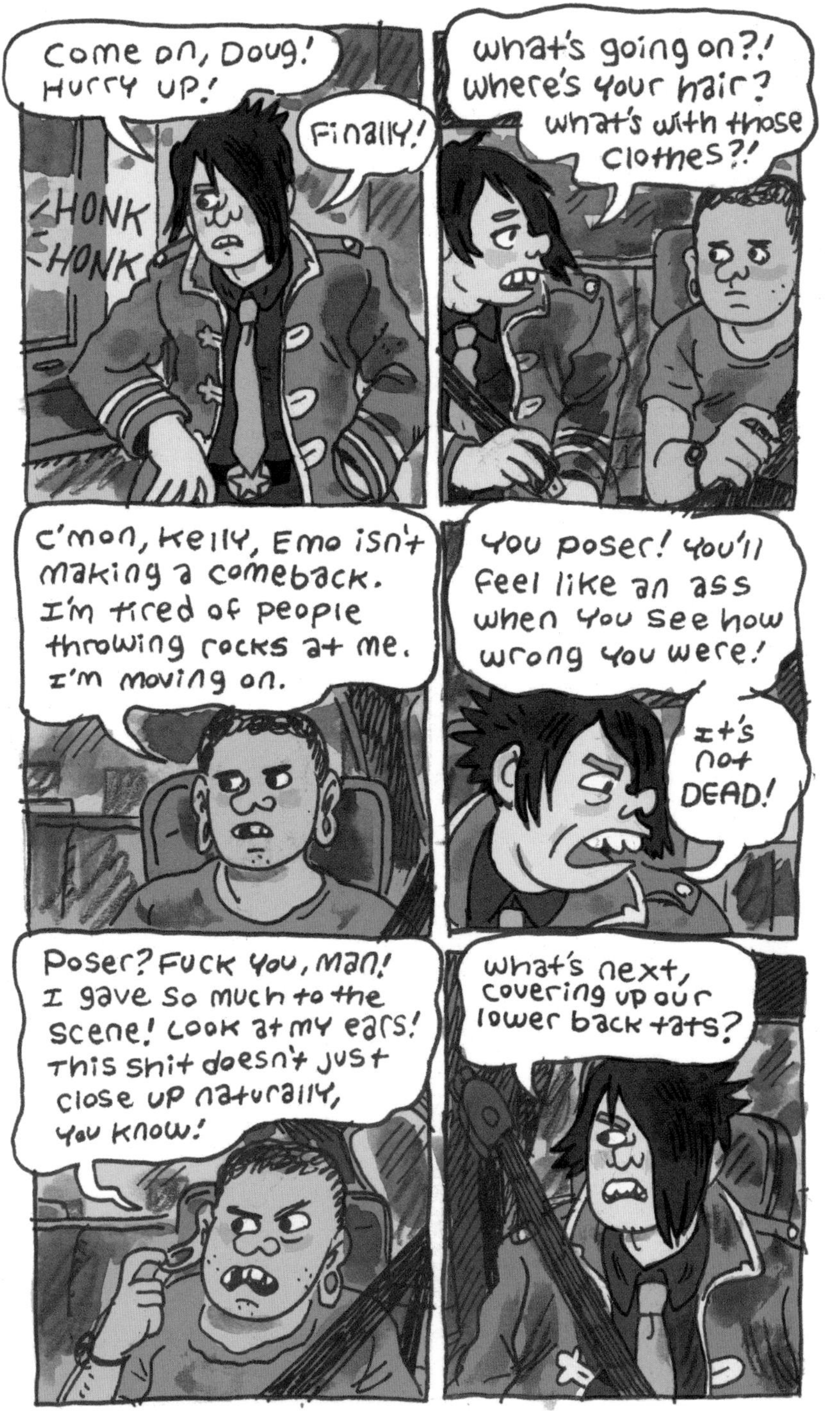
Come on, Doug! Hurry up!
HONK
HONK
Finally!
What's going on?! Where's your hair? What's with those clothes?!
C'mon, Kelly, Emo isn't making a comeback. I'm tired of people throwing rocks at me. I'm moving on.
You poser! You'll feel like an ass when you see how wrong you were!
It's not DEAD!
Poser? Fuck you, man! I gave so much to the scene! Look at my ears! This shit doesn't just close up naturally, you know!
What's next, covering up our lower back tats?

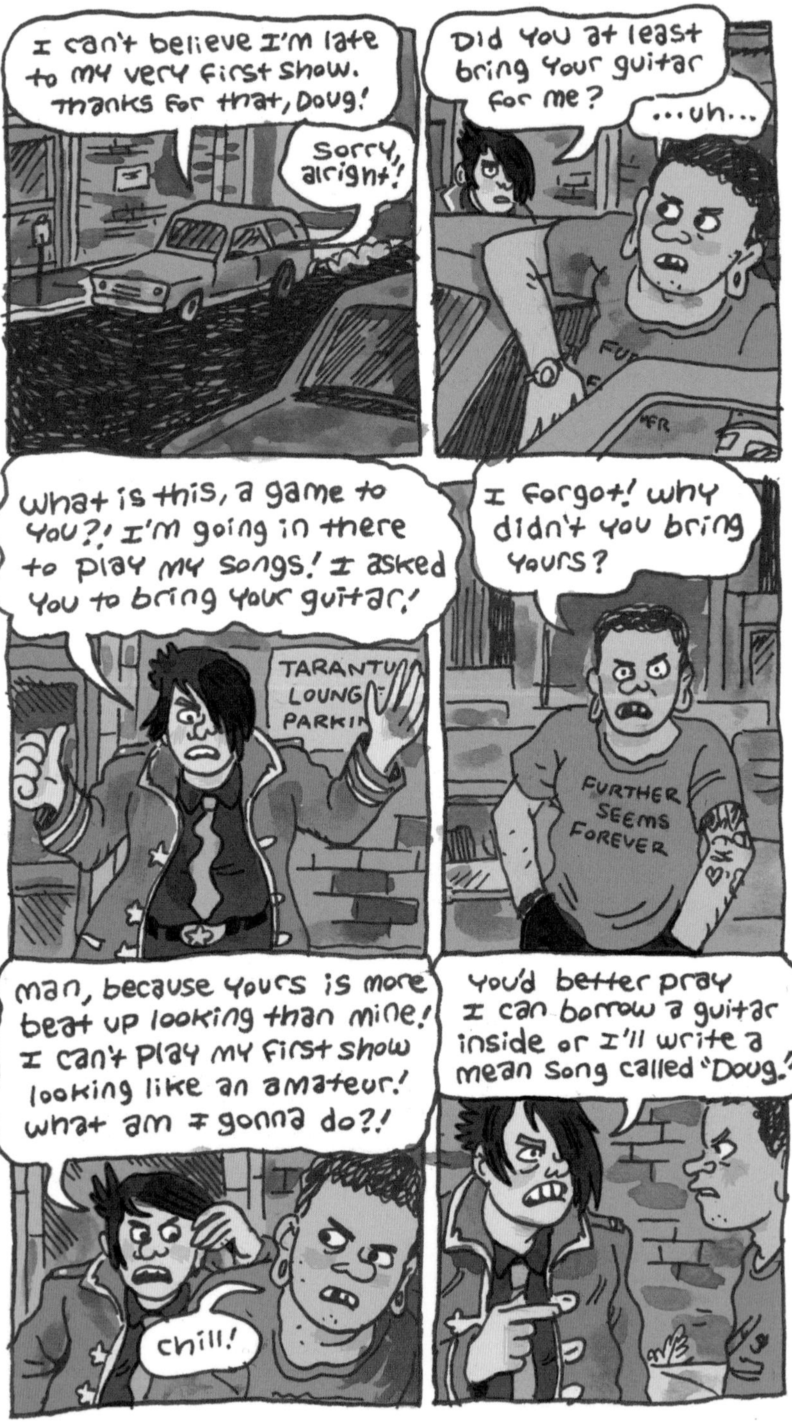
I can't believe I'm late to my very first show. Thanks for that, Doug!
Sorry, alright!
Did you at least bring your guitar for me?
...uh...
What is this, a game to you?! I'm going in there to play my songs! I asked you to bring your guitar!
TARANTU
LOUNG
PARKI
I forgot! Why didn't you bring yours?
FURTHER SEEMS FOREVER
Man, because yours is more beat up looking than mine! I can't play my first show looking like an amateur! What am I gonna do?!
Chill!
You'd better pray I can borrow a guitar inside or I'll write a mean song called "Doug."

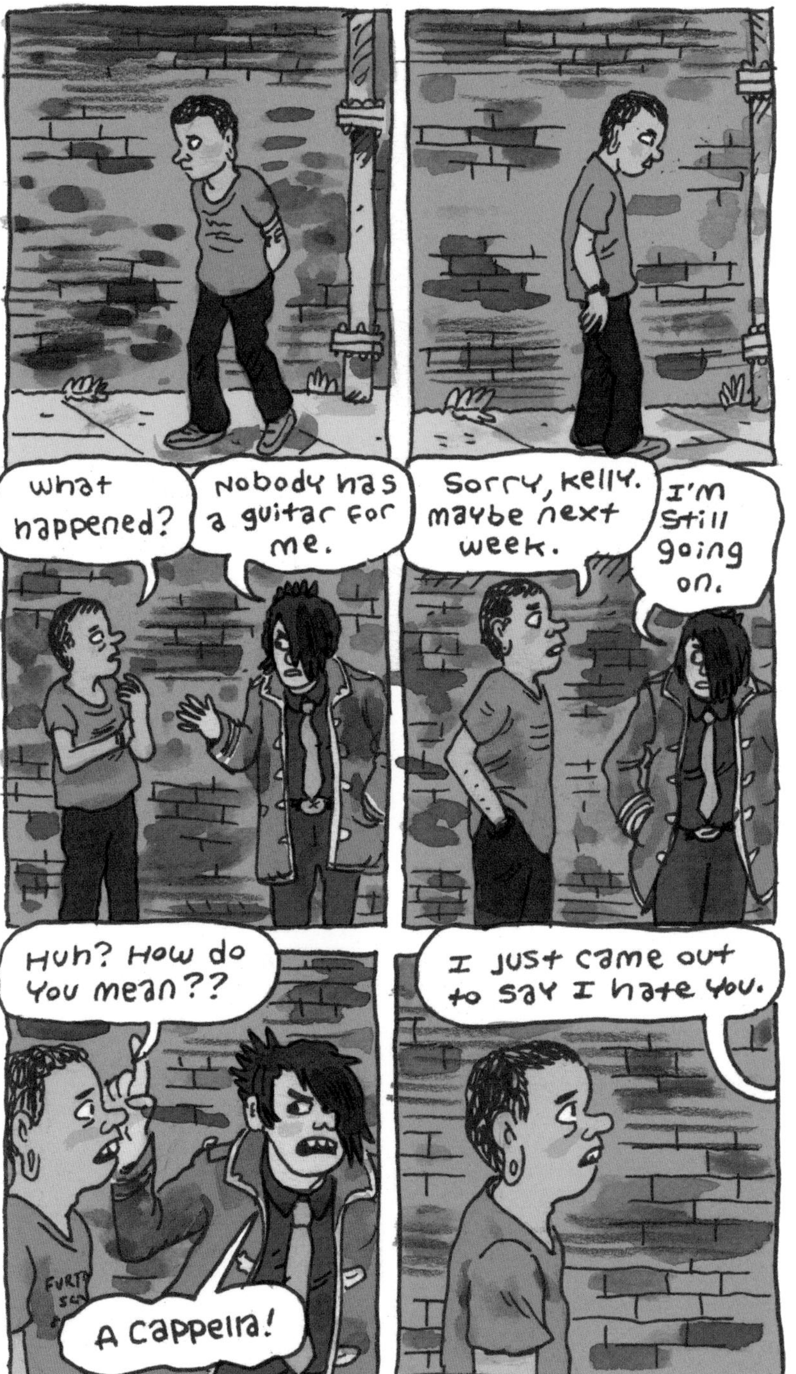
What happened?
Nobody has a guitar for me.
Sorry, Kelly. Maybe next week.
I'm still going on.
Huh? How do you mean??
A cappella!
I just came out to say I hate you.

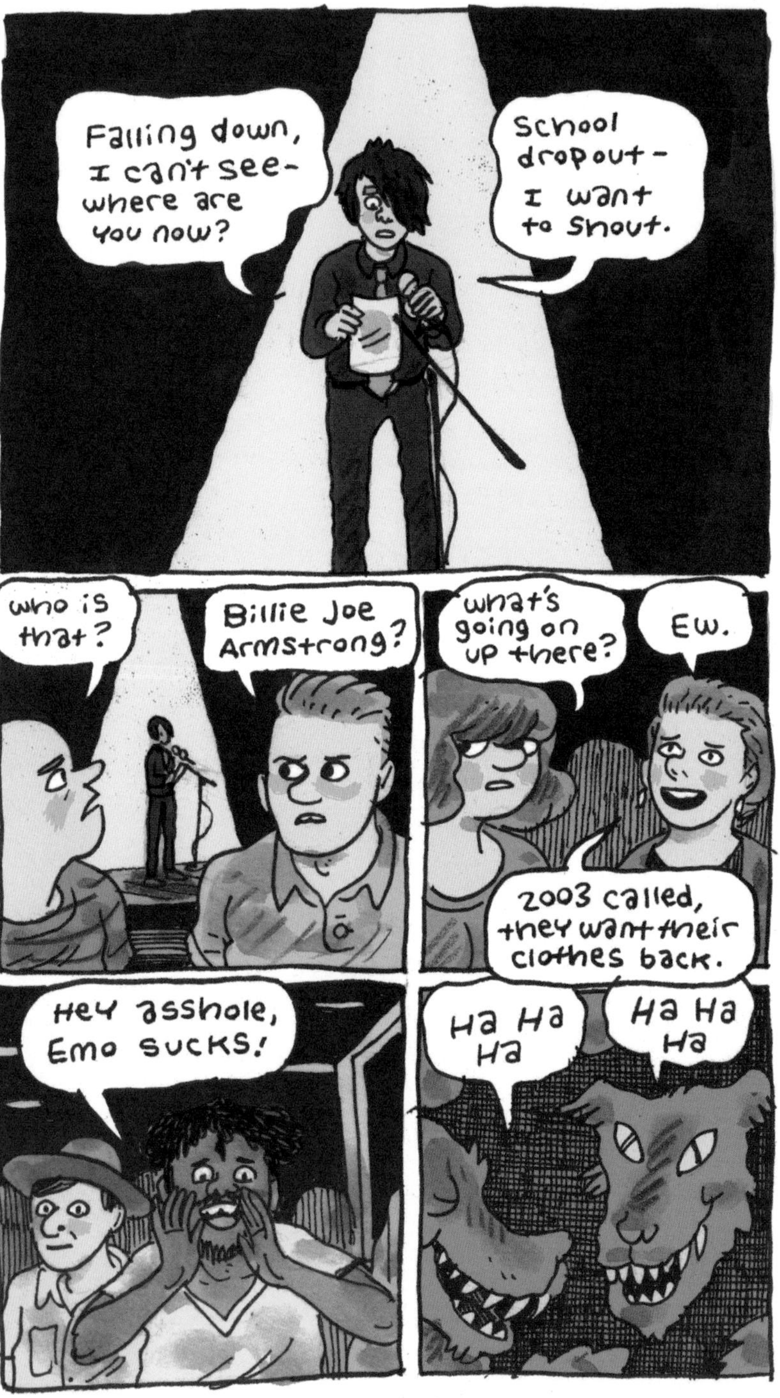
Falling down, I can't see- where are you now?
School dropout - I want to shout.
who is that?
Billie Joe Armstrong?
what's going on up there?
Ew.
2003 called, they want their clothes back.
Hey asshole, Emo sucks!
Ha Ha Ha
Ha Ha Ha

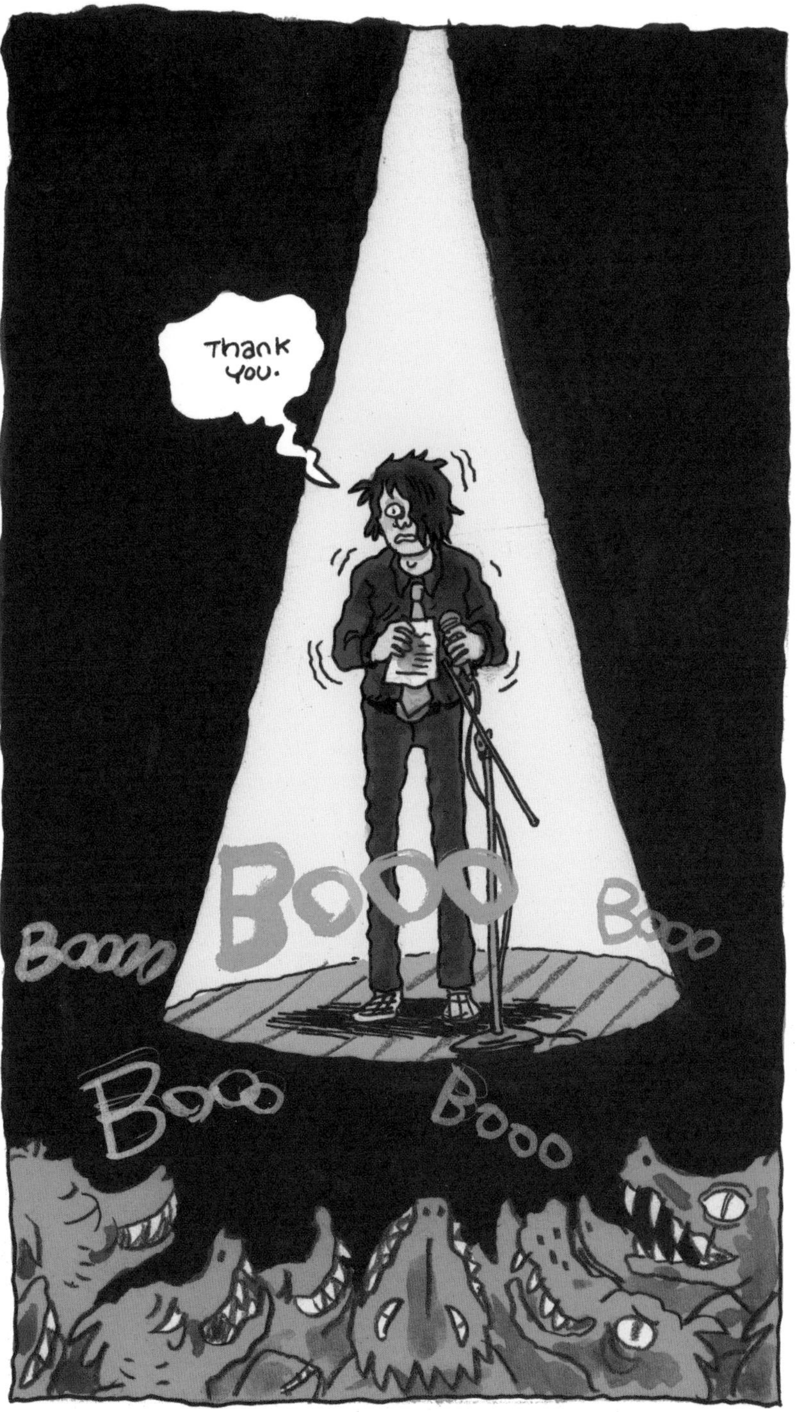
Thank you.
BOOO
Boooo
Booo
Booo
Booo

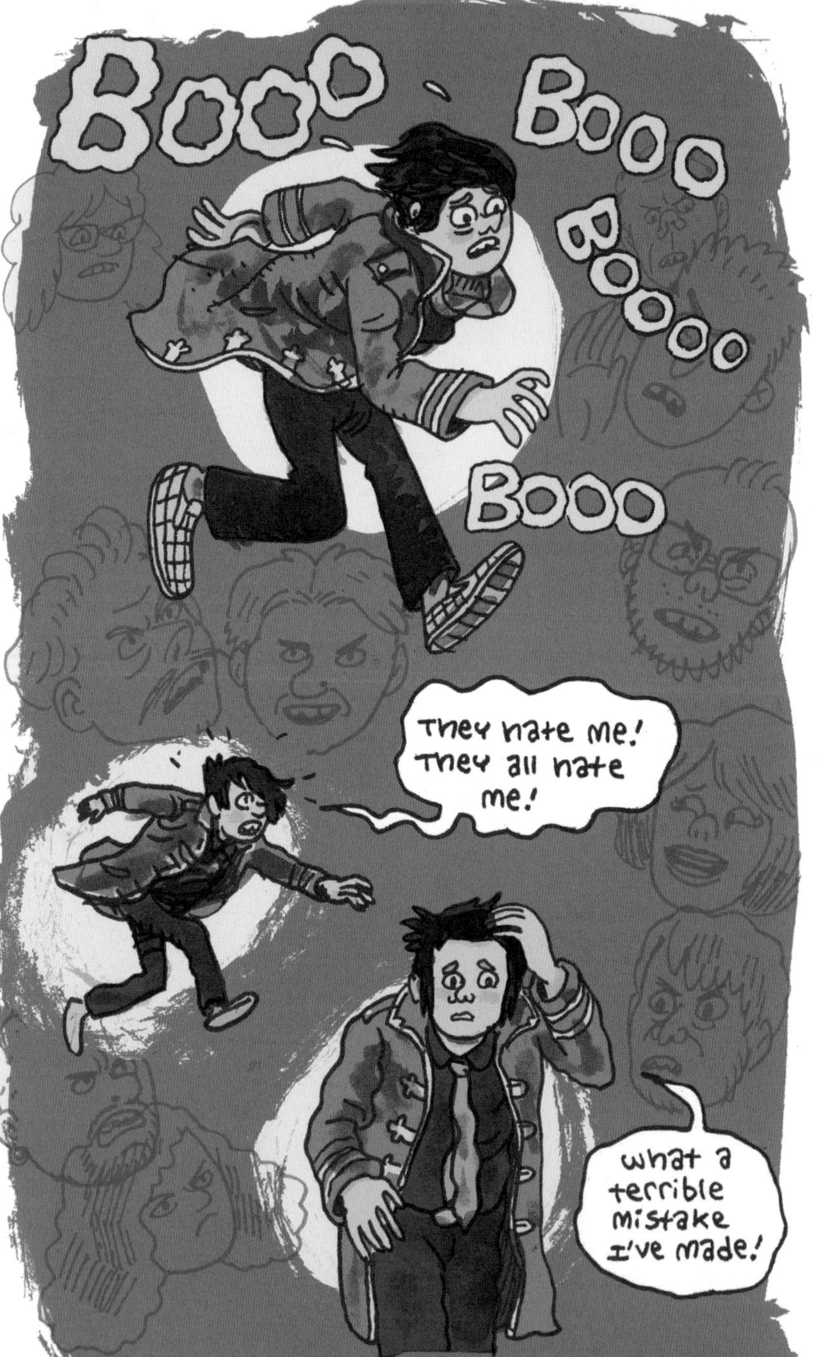
BOOO BOOO BOOOO BOOO
They hate me! They all hate me!
what a terrible mistake I've made!

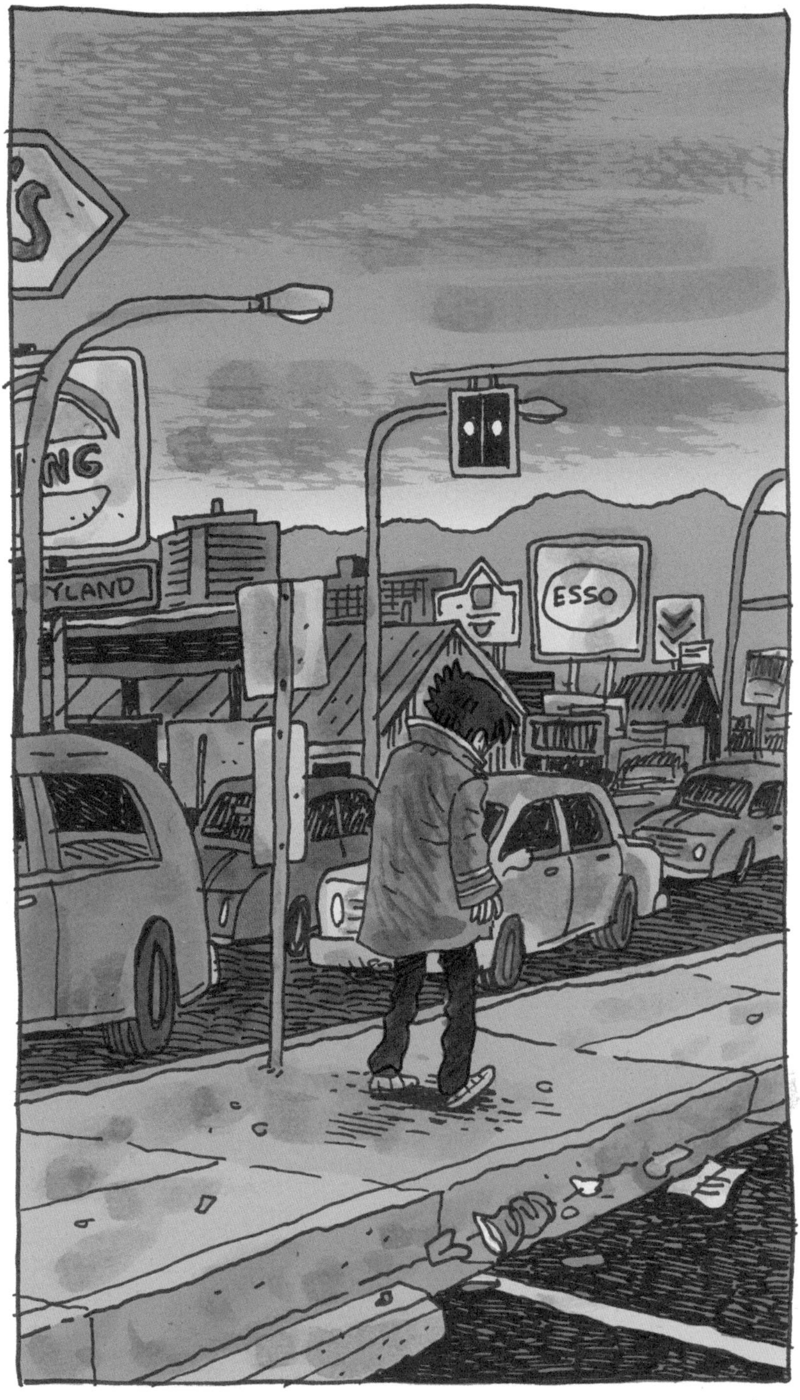

ESSO
YLAND

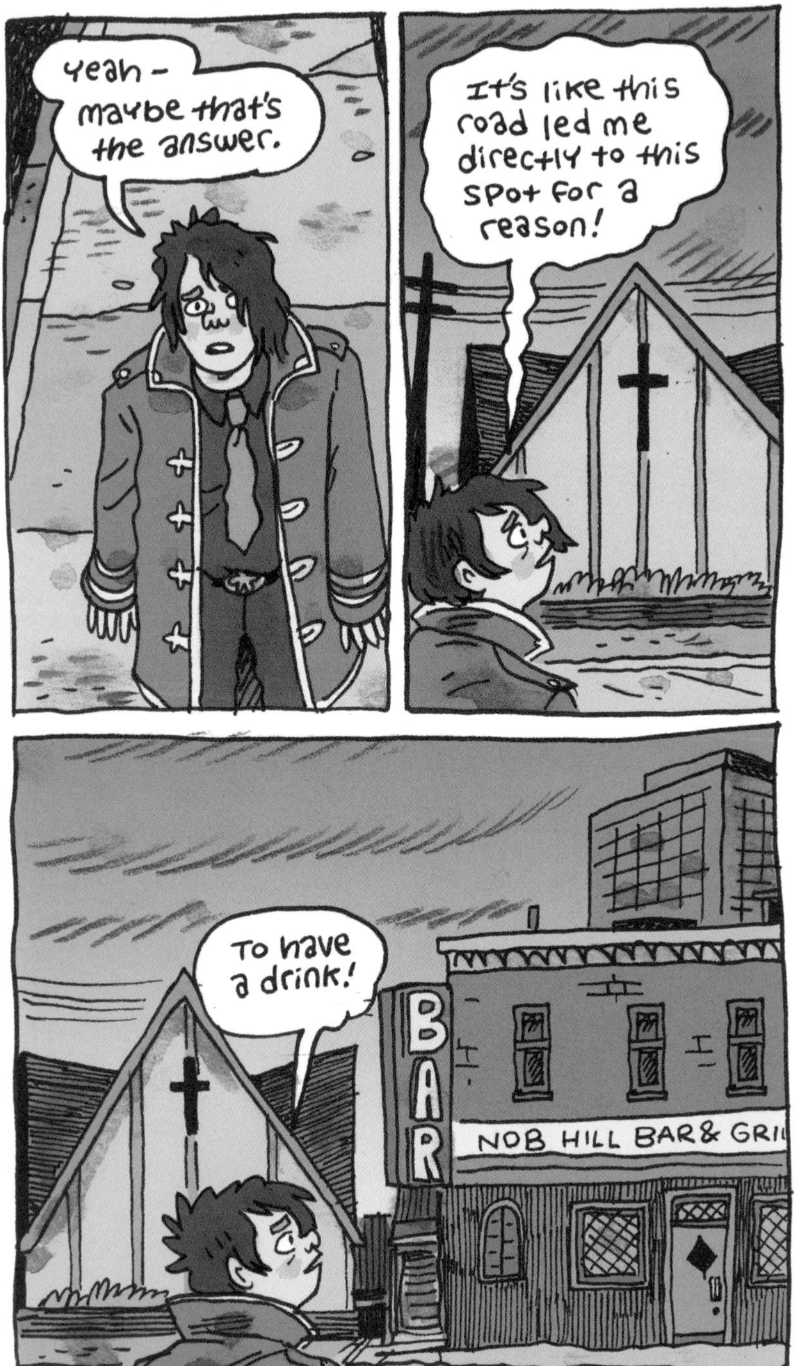
yeah - maybe that's the answer.
It's like this road led me directly to this spot for a reason!
To have a drink!
BAR
NOB HILL BAR & GRI

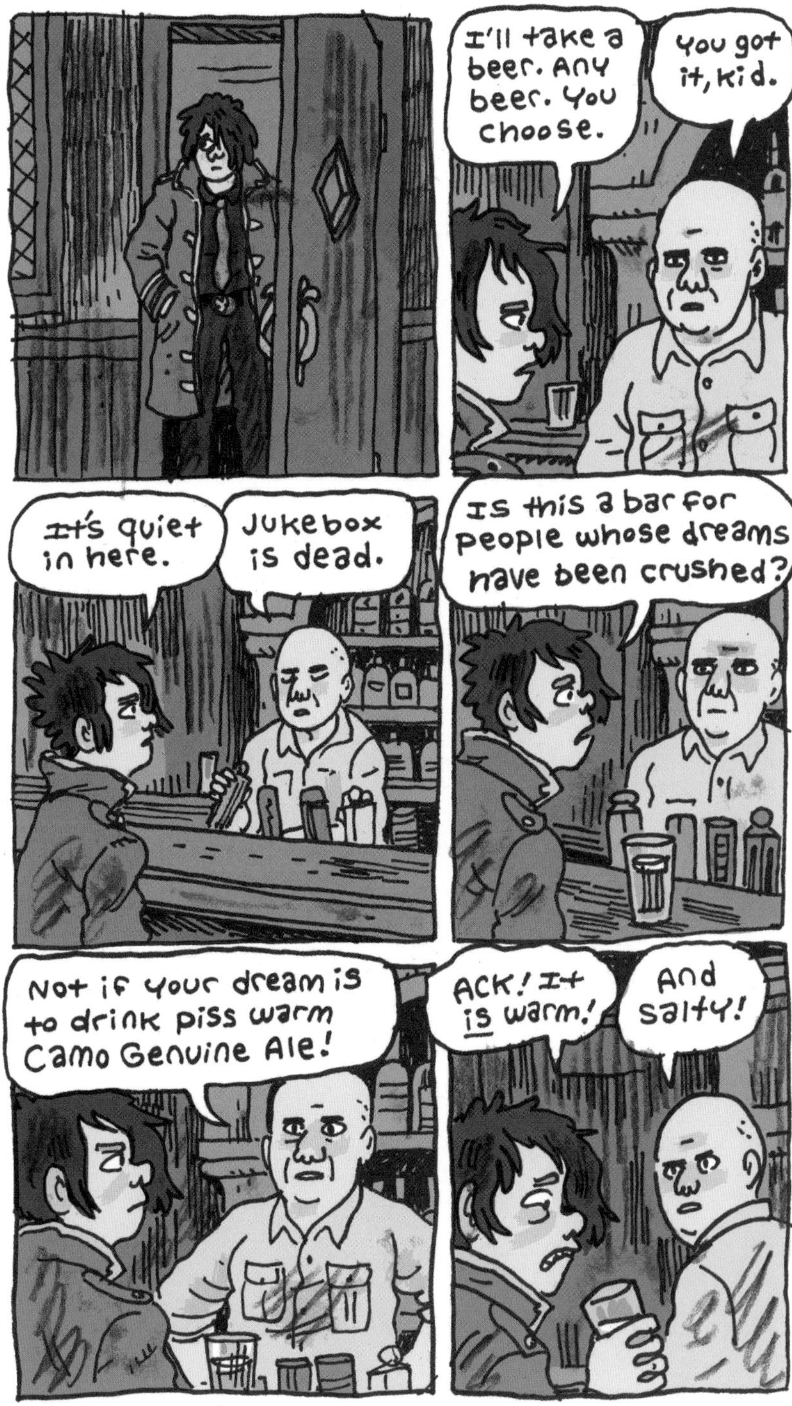

I'll take a beer. Any beer. You choose.
You got it, kid.
It's quiet in here.
Jukebox is dead.
Is this a bar for people whose dreams have been crushed?
Not if your dream is to drink piss warm Camo Genuine Ale!
ACK! It is warm!
And salty!

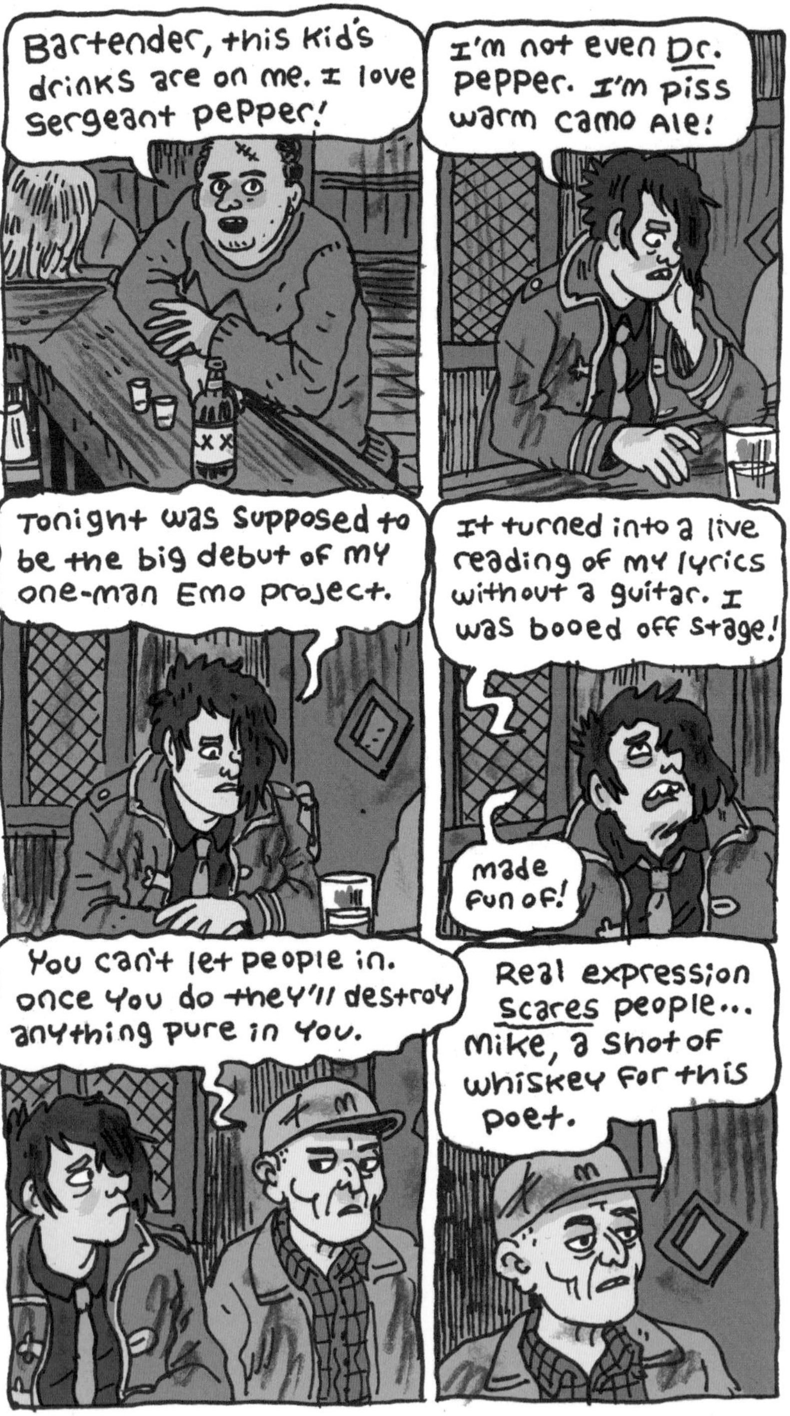
Bartender, this kid's drinks are on me. I love sergeant pepper!
I'm not even Dr. pepper. I'm piss warm camo Ale!
Tonight was supposed to be the big debut of my one-man Emo project.
It turned into a live reading of my lyrics without a guitar. I was booed off stage!
made fun of!
You can't let people in. once you do they'll destroy anything pure in you.
Real expression scares people... Mike, a shot of whiskey for this poet.

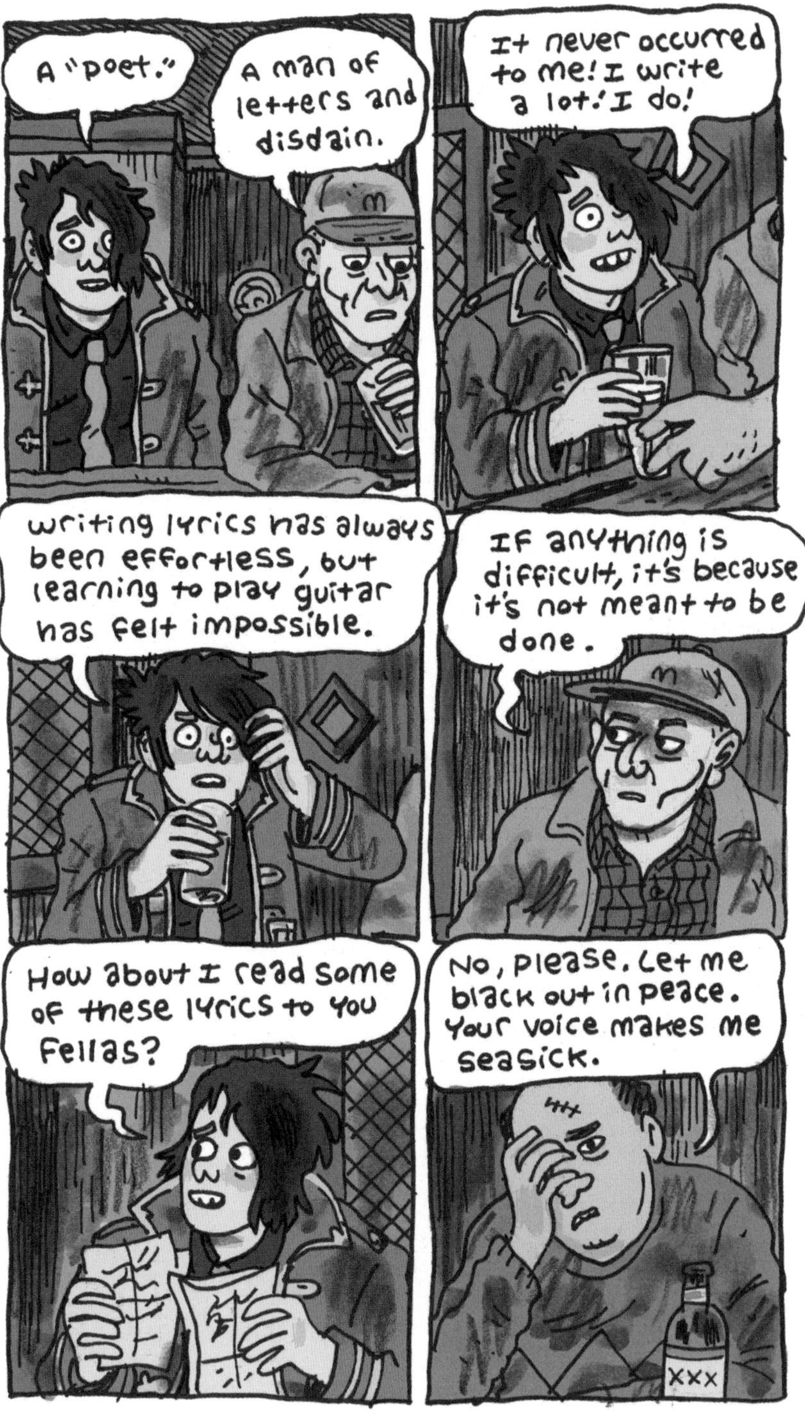
A "poet."
A man of letters and disdain.
It never occurred to me! I write a lot! I do!
Writing lyrics has always been effortless, but learning to play guitar has felt impossible.
If anything is difficult, it's because it's not meant to be done.
How about I read some of these lyrics to you fellas?
No, please. Let me black out in peace. Your voice makes me seasick.
XXX

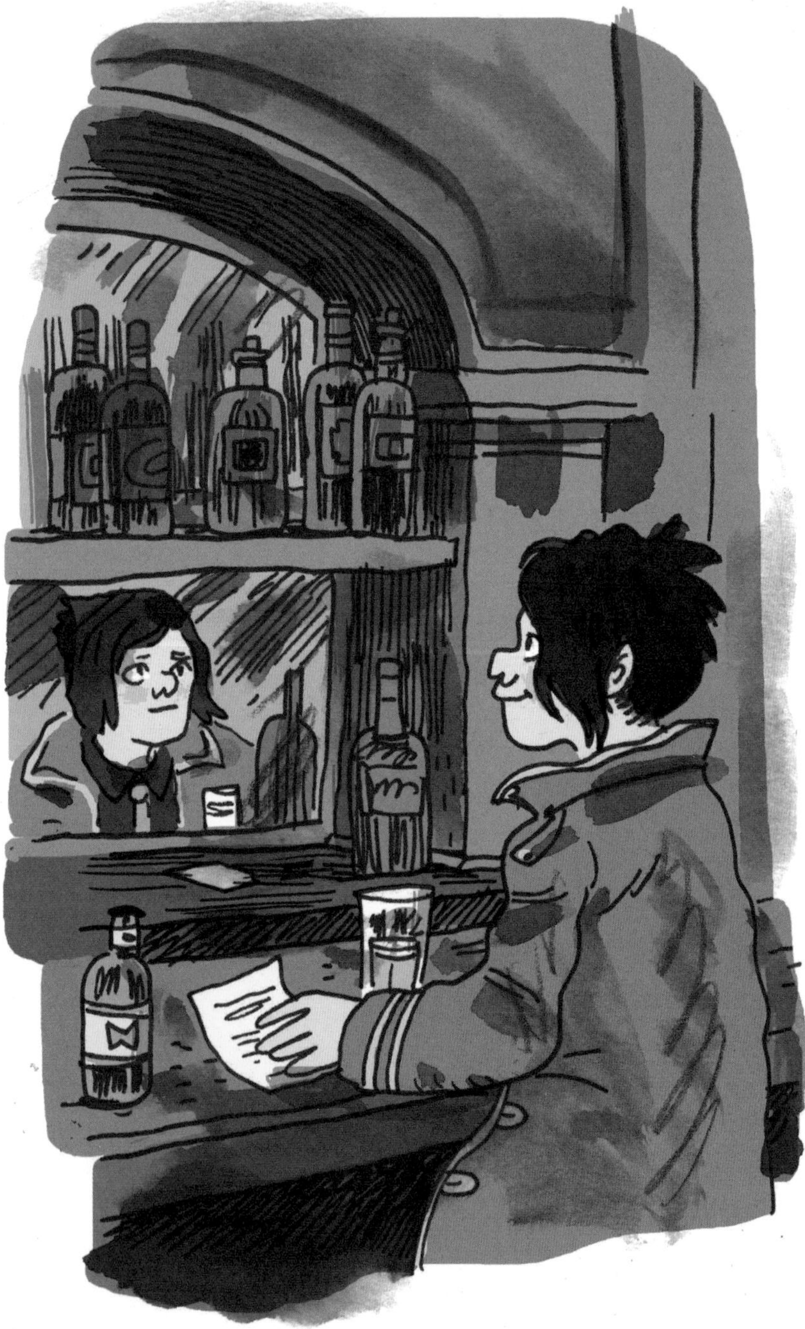

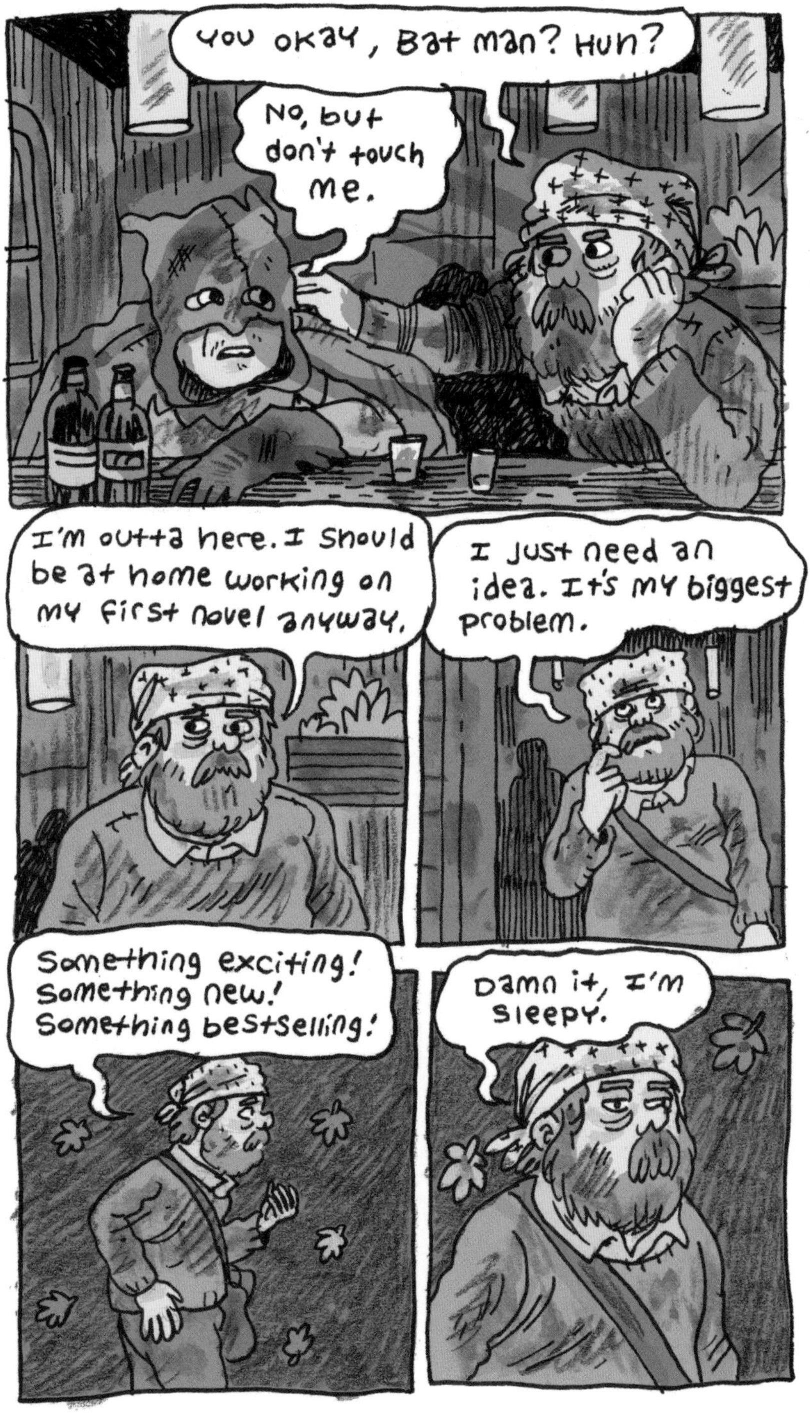
You okay, Bat man? Huh?
No, but don't touch me.
I'm outta here. I should be at home working on my first novel anyway.
I just need an idea. It's my biggest problem.
Something exciting! Something new! Something bestselling!
Damn it, I'm sleepy.

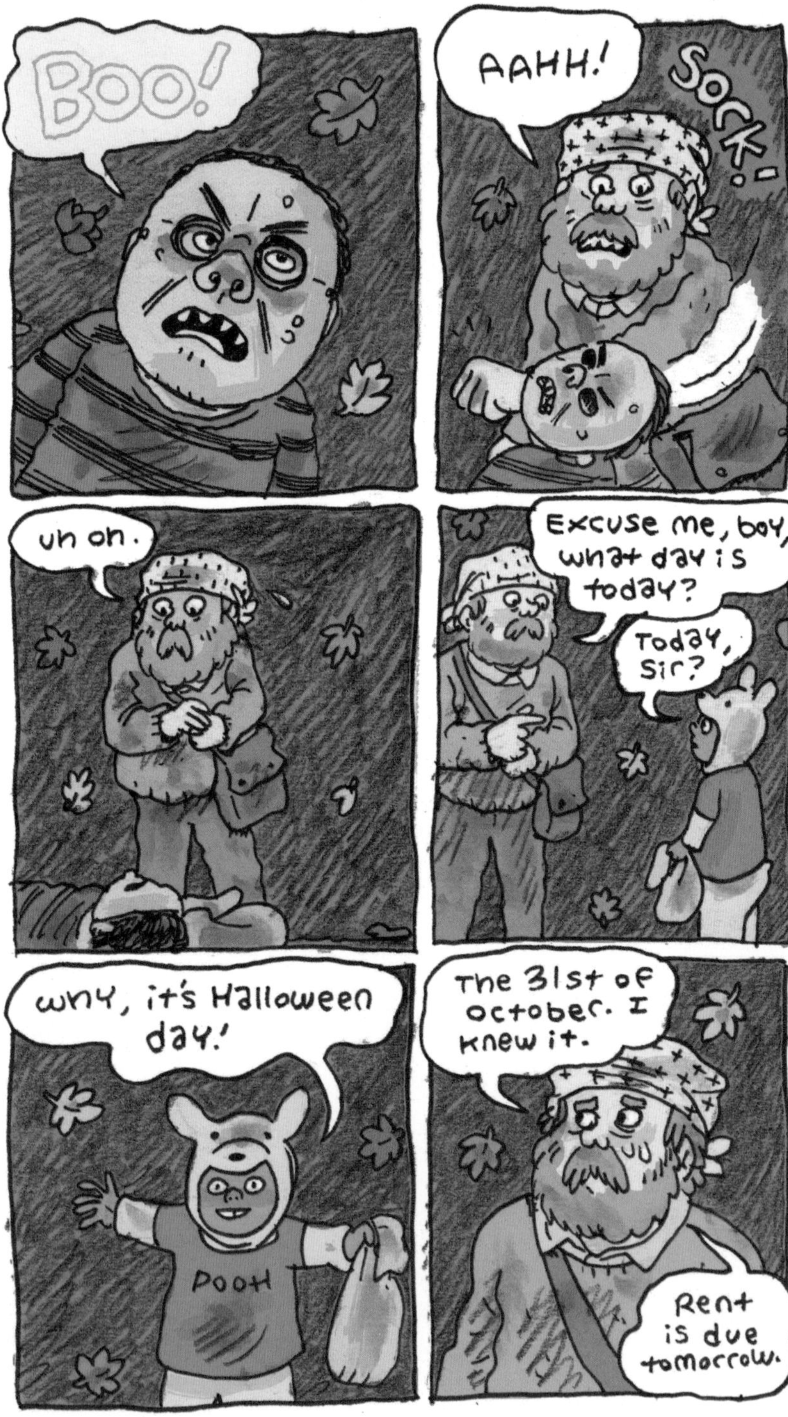
BOO!
AAHH!
SOCK!
uh oh.
Excuse me, boy, what day is today?
Today, sir?
why, it's Halloween day!
POOH
The 31st of october. I knew it.
Rent is due tomorrow.

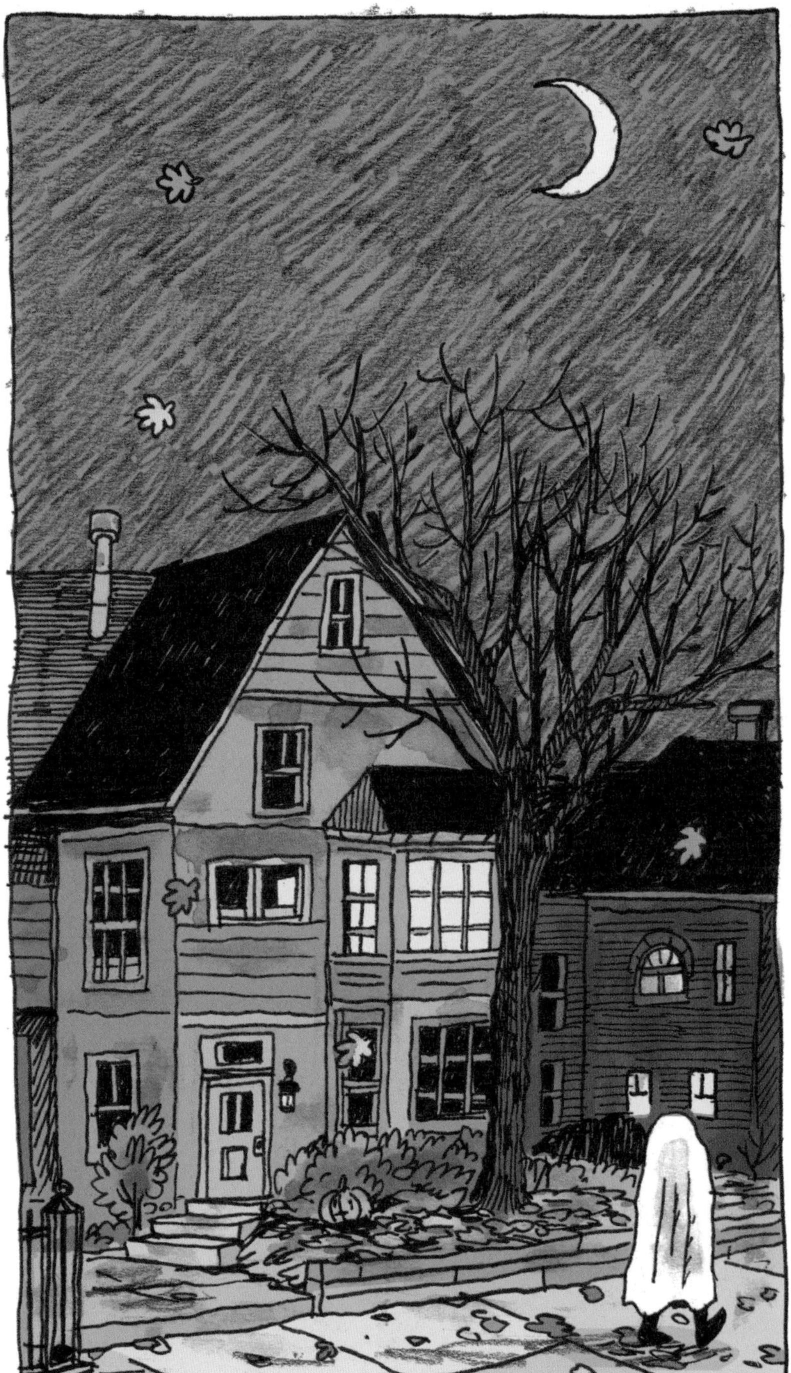

Fante gets no peace.

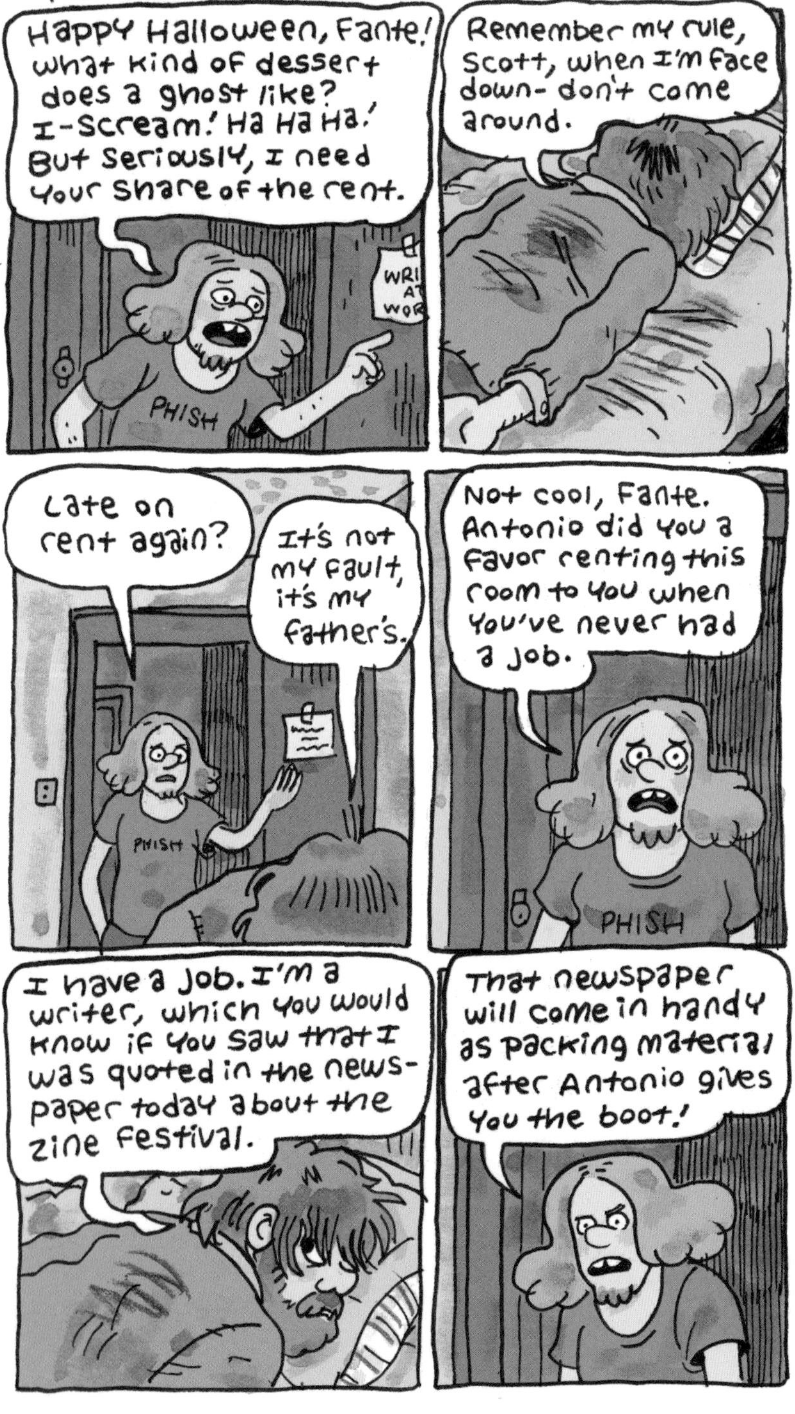
Happy Halloween, Fante! what kind of dessert does a ghost like? I-Scream! Ha Ha Ha! But seriously, I need your share of the rent.
PHISH
Remember my rule, Scott, when I'm face down- don't come around.
Late on rent again?
It's not my fault, it's my father's.
PHISH
Not cool, Fante. Antonio did you a favor renting this room to you when you've never had a job.
PHISH
I have a job. I'm a writer, which you would know if you saw that I was quoted in the newspaper today about the zine festival.
That newspaper will come in handy as packing material after Antonio gives you the boot!

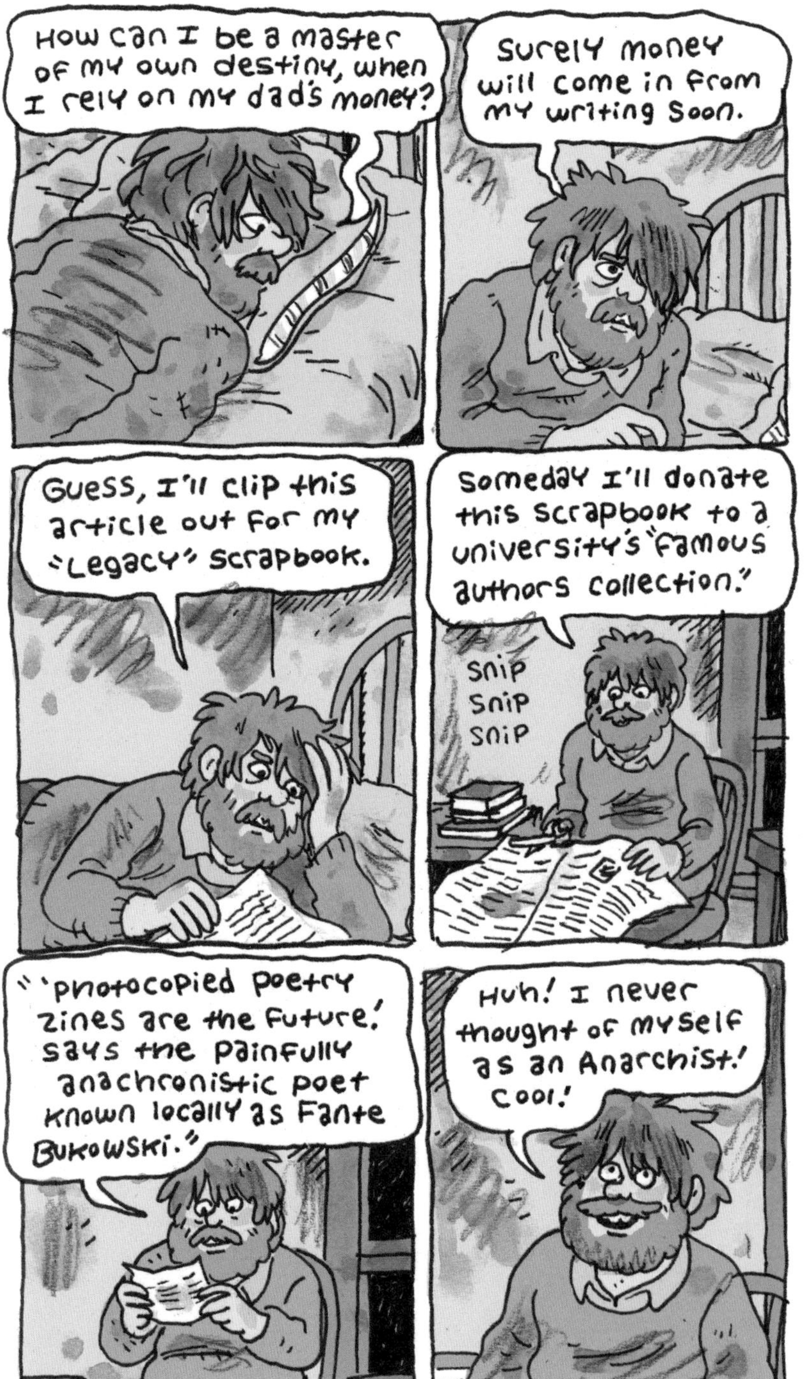
How can I be a master of my own destiny, when I rely on my dad's money?
Surely money will come in from my writing soon.
Guess, I'll clip this article out for my "Legacy" scrapbook.
Someday I'll donate this scrapbook to a university's "Famous authors collection."
snip snip snip
"'Photocopied poetry zines are the future,' says the painfully anachronistic poet known locally as Fante Bukowski."
Huh! I never thought of myself as an Anarchist! Cool!

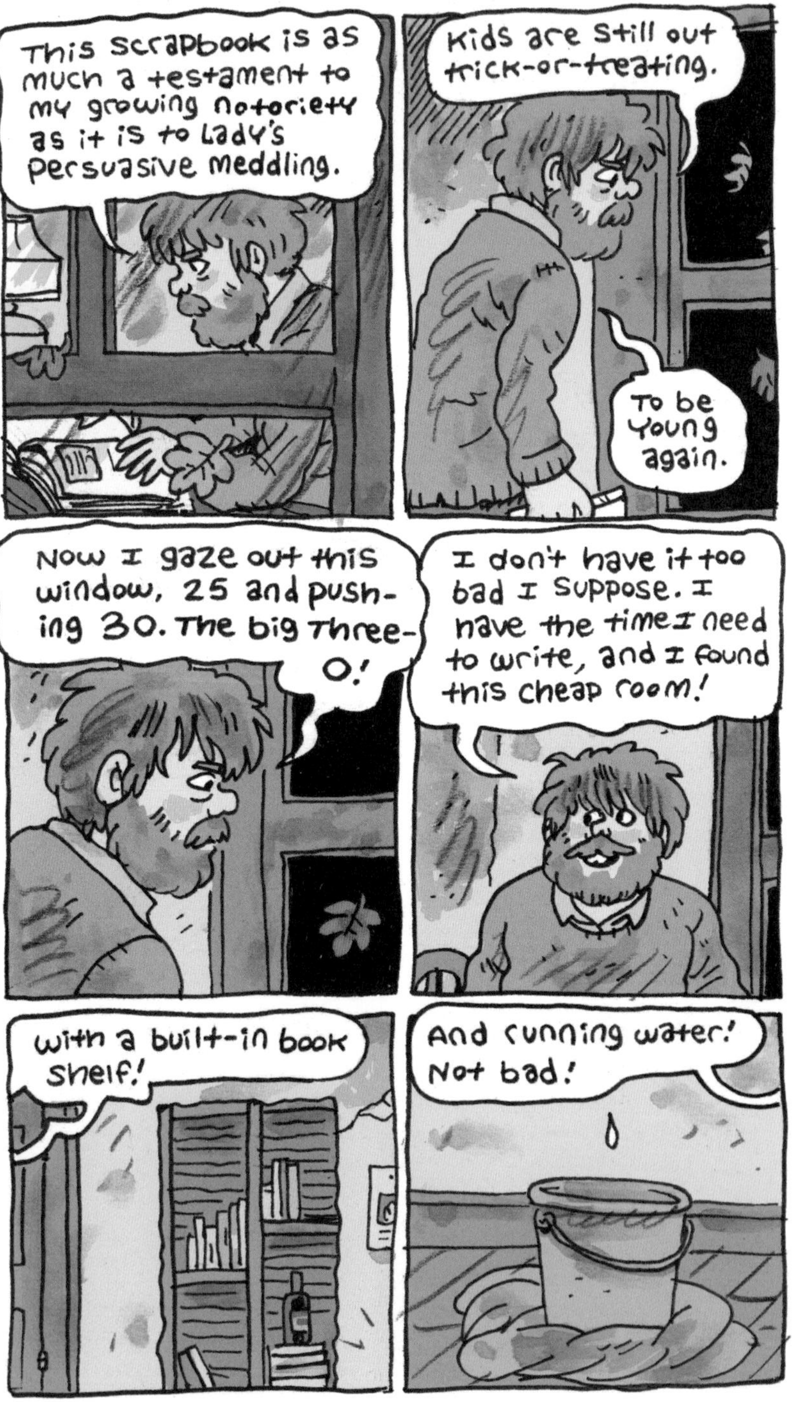
This scrapbook is as much a testament to my growing notoriety as it is to Lady's persuasive meddling.
Kids are still out trick-or-treating.
To be young again.
Now I gaze out this window, 25 and pushing 30. The big three-O!
I don't have it too bad I suppose. I have the time I need to write, and I found this cheap room!
with a built-in book shelf!
And running water! Not bad!

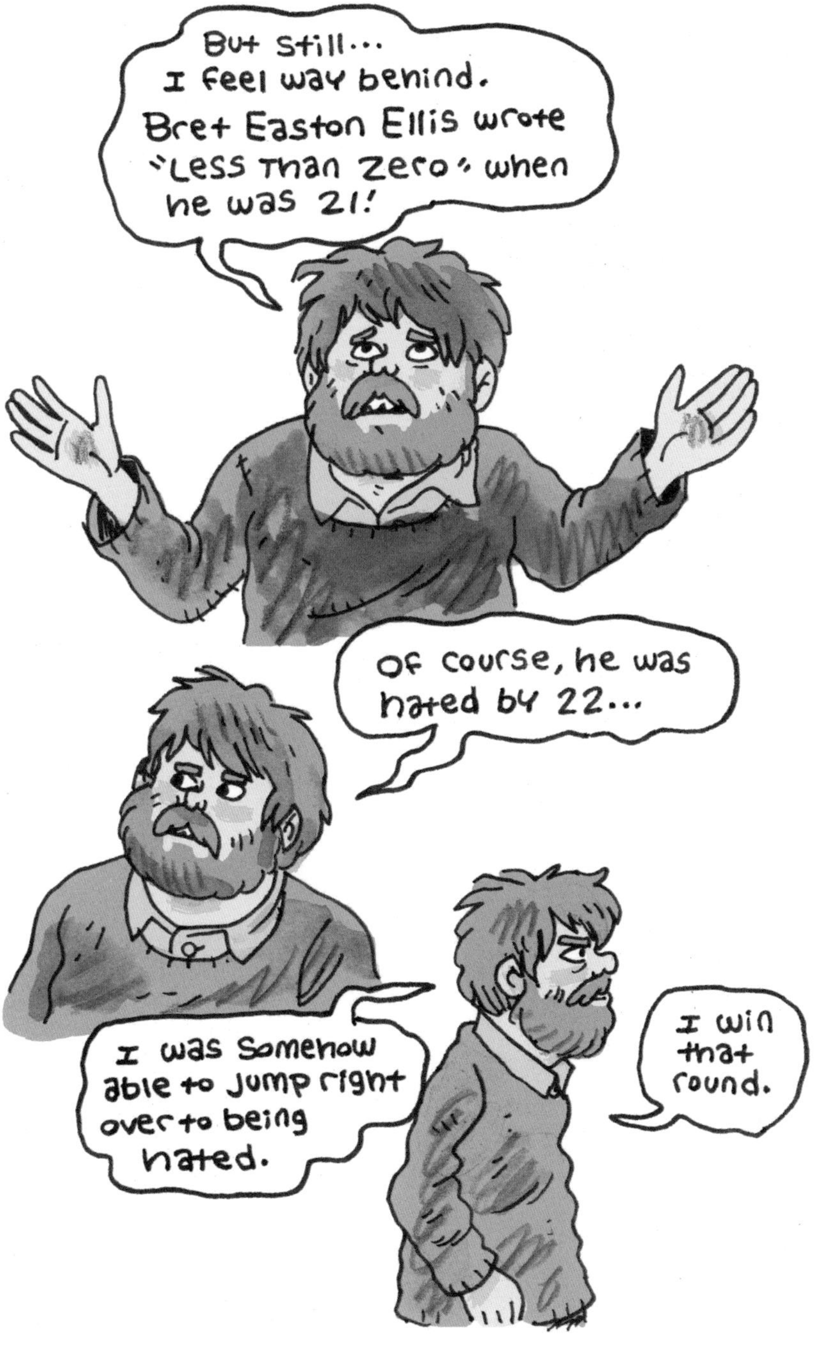
But still...
I feel way behind.
Bret Easton Ellis wrote "Less Than Zero" when he was 21!
Of course, he was hated by 22...
I was somehow able to jump right over to being hated.
I win that round.

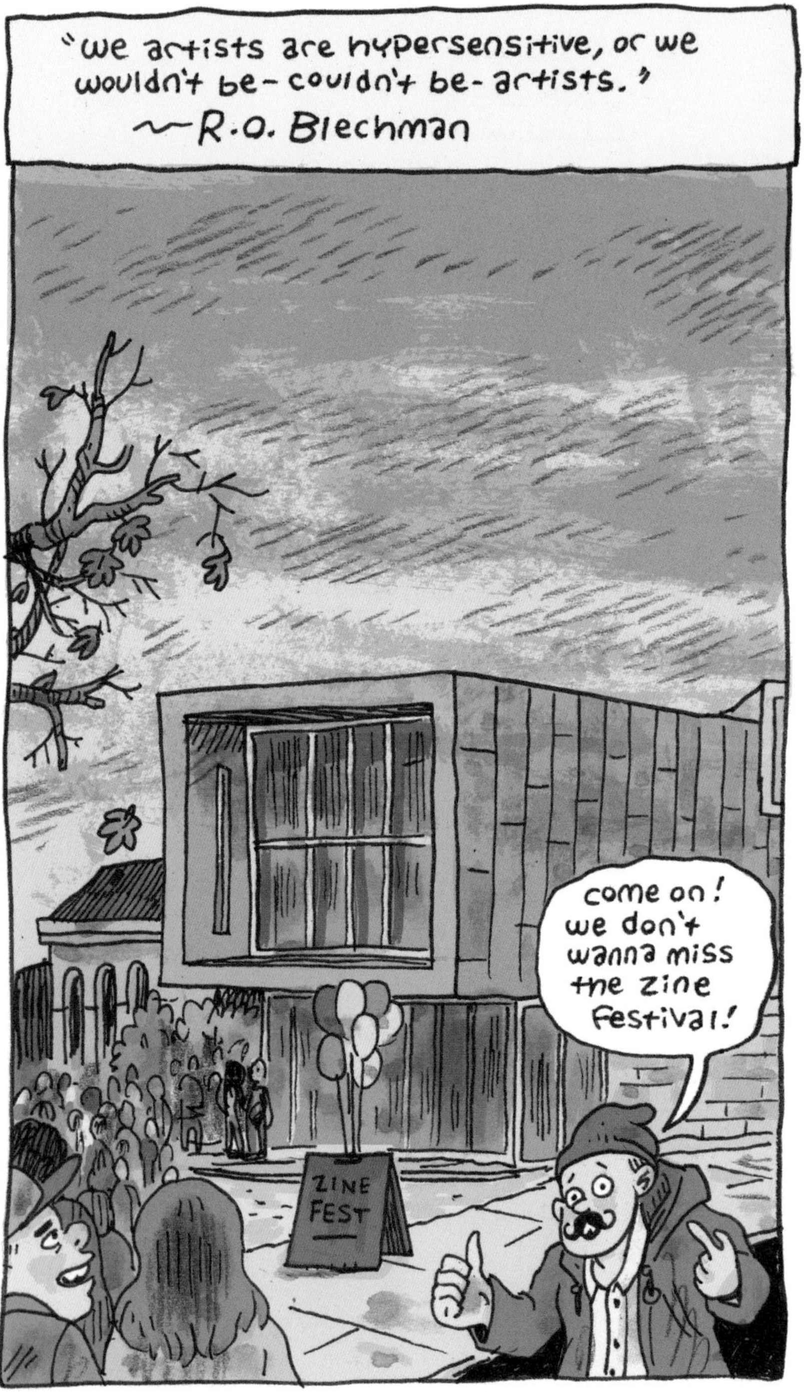
"we artists are hypersensitive, or we wouldn't be-couldn't be-artists."
~R.O. Blechman
come on! we don't wanna miss the zine festival!
ZINE FEST

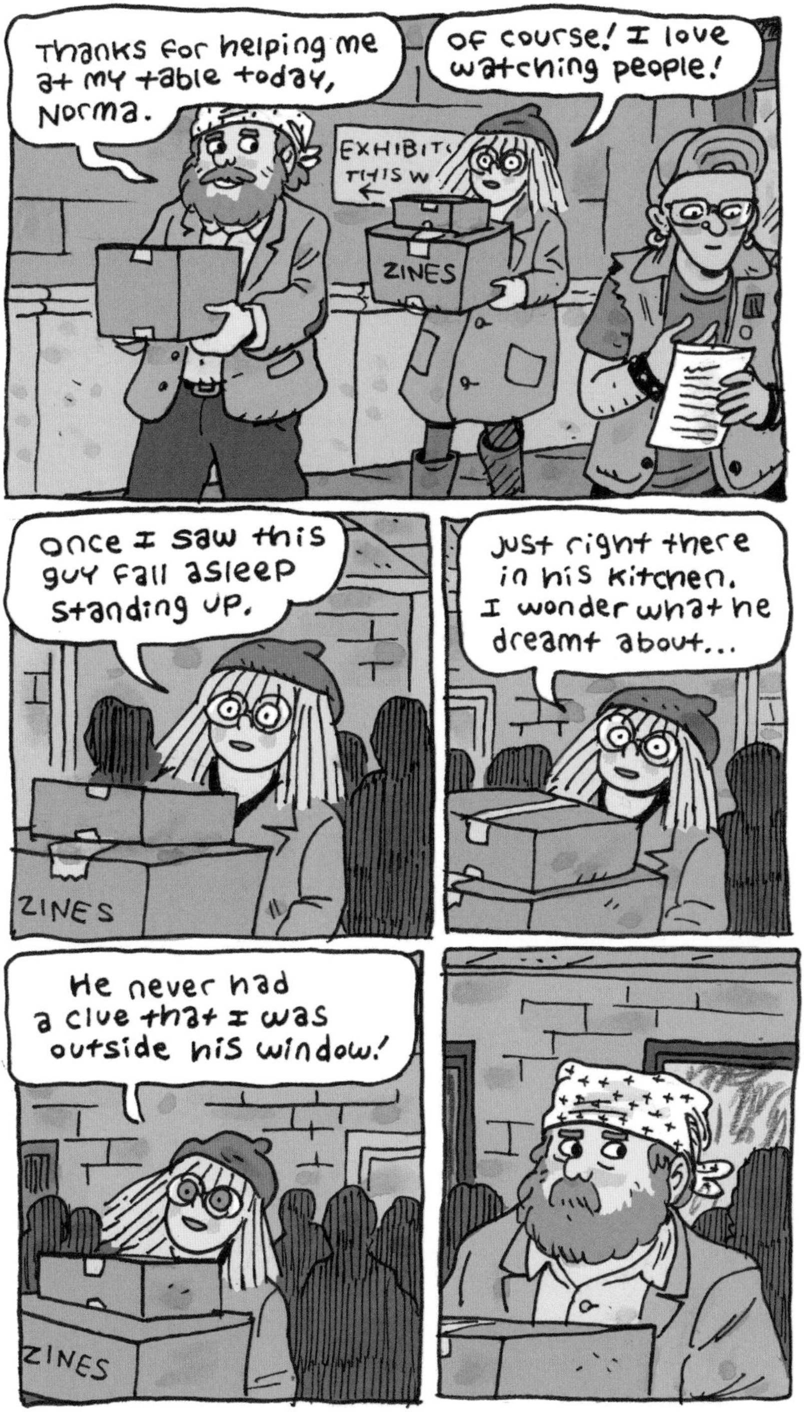
Thanks for helping me at my table today, Norma.
Of course! I love watching people!
EXHIBIT
THIS W
ZINES
Once I saw this guy fall asleep standing up.
ZINES
Just right there in his kitchen. I wonder what he dreamt about...
He never had a clue that I was outside his window!
ZINES

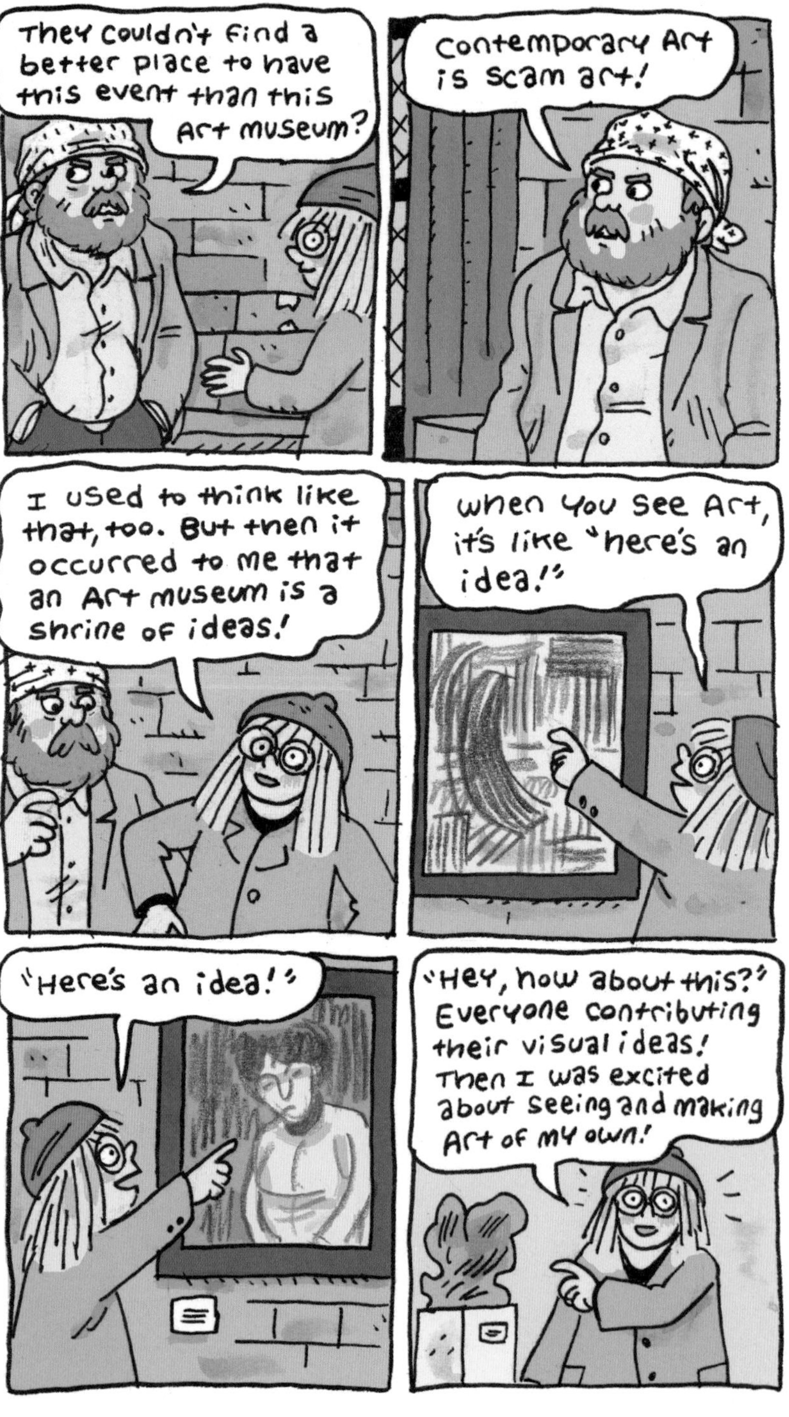
They couldn't find a better place to have this event than this Art museum?
Contemporary Art is scam art!
I used to think like that, too. But then it occurred to me that an Art museum is a shrine of ideas!
When you see Art, it's like "here's an idea!"
"Here's an idea!"
"Hey, how about this?" Everyone contributing their visual ideas! Then I was excited about seeing and making Art of my own!

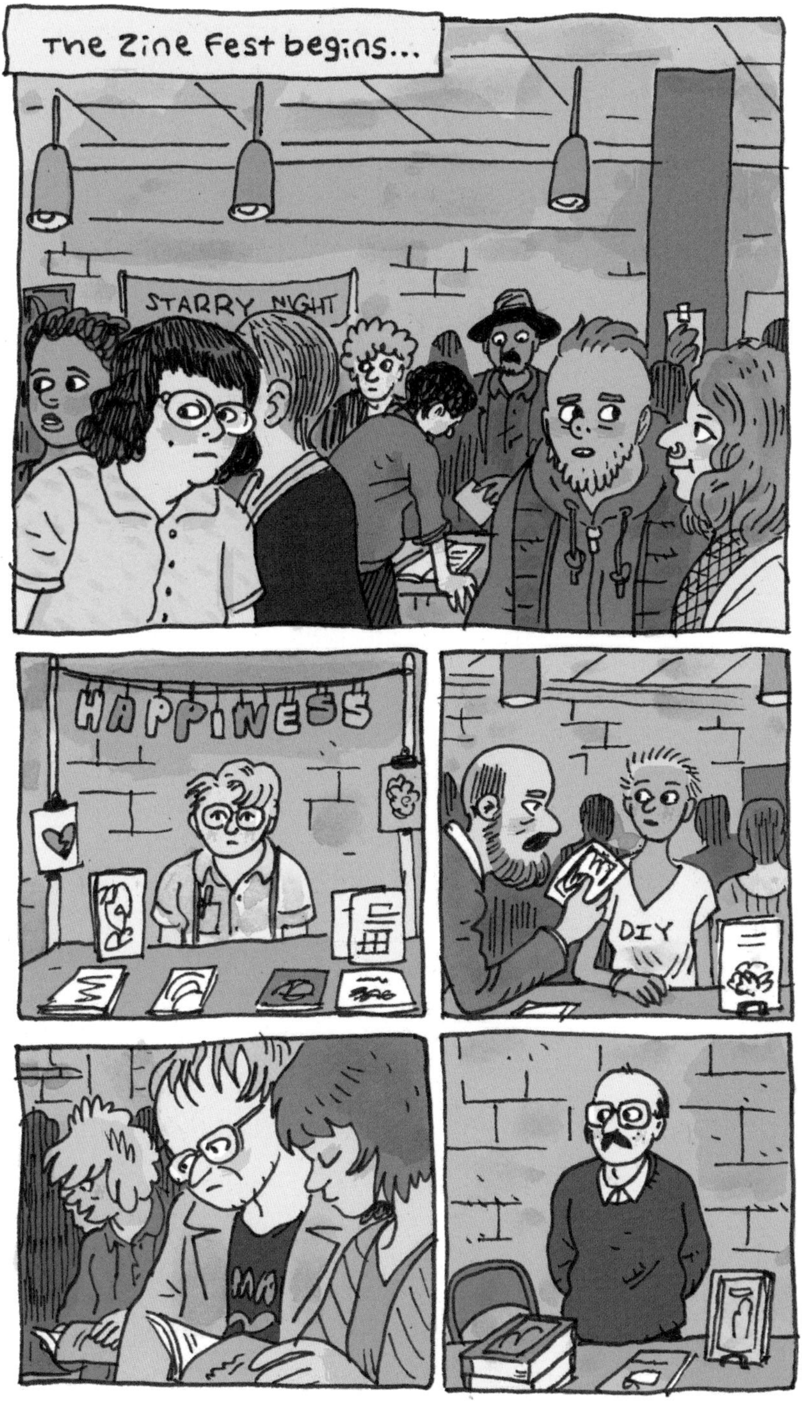
The Zine Fest begins...
STARRY NIGHT
HAPPINESS
DIY

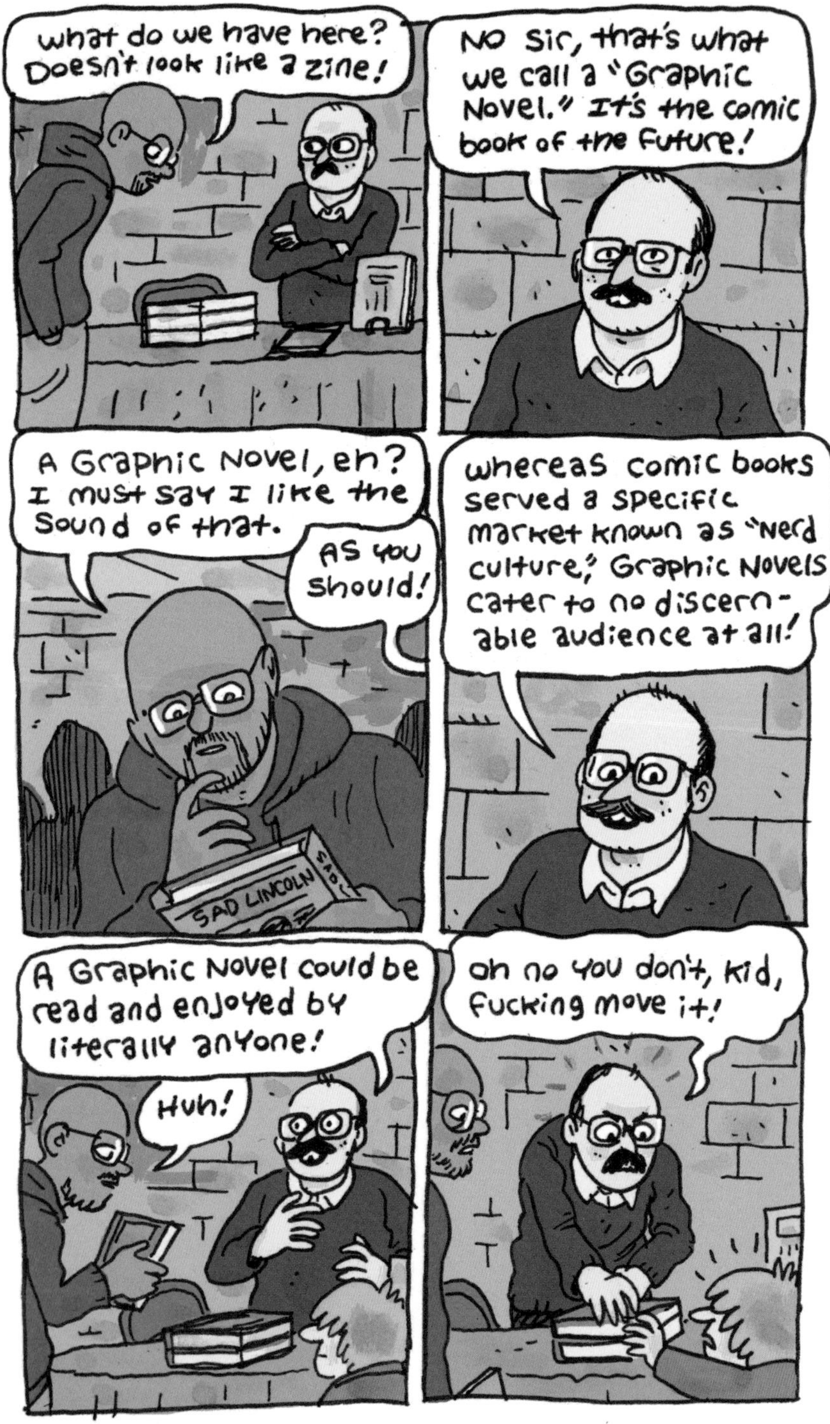
what do we have here? Doesn't look like a zine!
No sir, that's what we call a "Graphic Novel." It's the comic book of the future!
A Graphic Novel, eh? I must say I like the sound of that.
As you should!
whereas comic books served a specific market known as "nerd culture," Graphic Novels cater to no discern-able audience at all!
SAD LINCOLN
A Graphic Novel could be read and enjoyed by literally anyone!
Huh!
oh no you don't, kid, fucking move it!

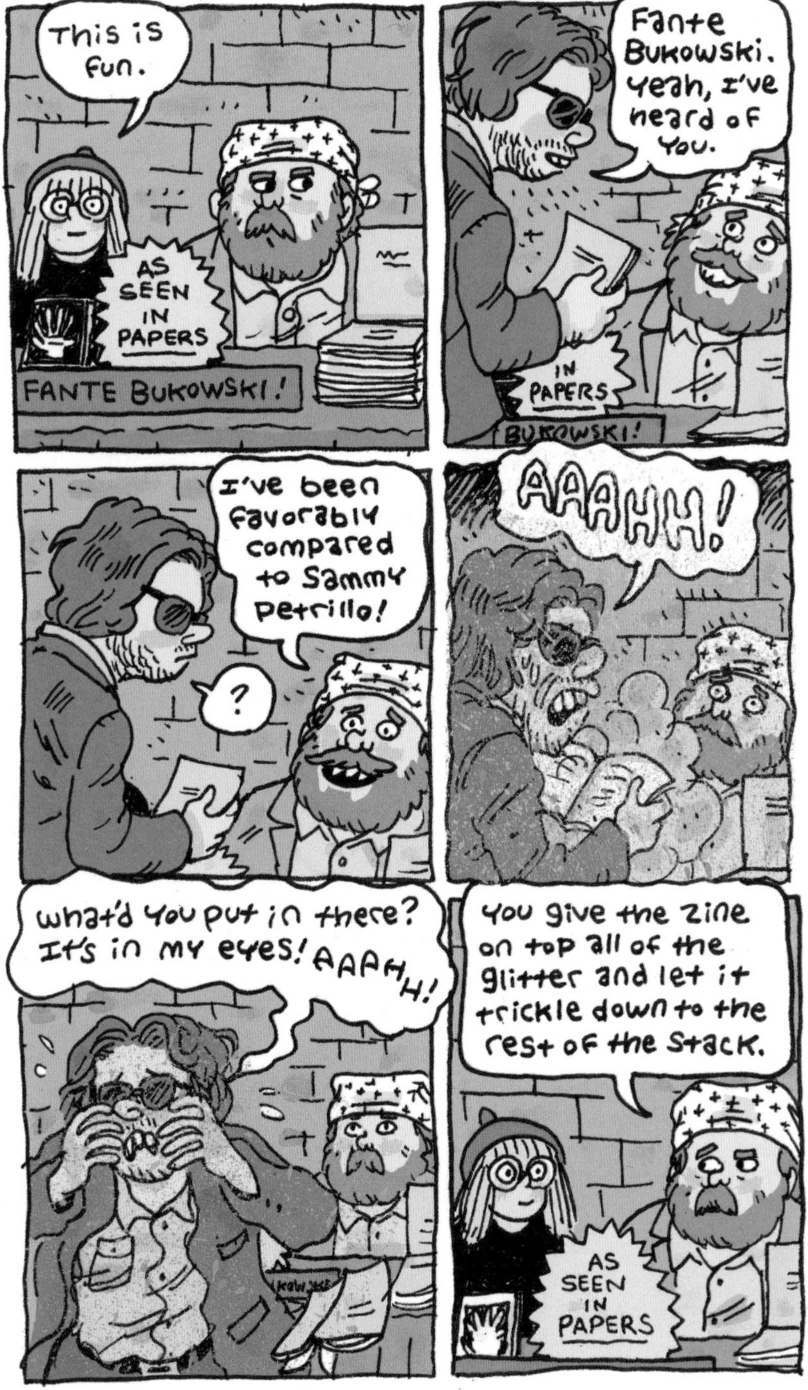
This is fun.
AS SEEN IN PAPERS
FANTE BUKOWSKI!
Fante Bukowski. yeah, I've heard of you.
IN PAPERS
BUKOWSKI!
I've been favorably compared to Sammy Petrillo!
?
AAAHH!
what'd you put in there? It's in my eyes! AAAHH!
you give the zine on top all of the glitter and let it trickle down to the rest of the stack.
AS SEEN IN PAPERS

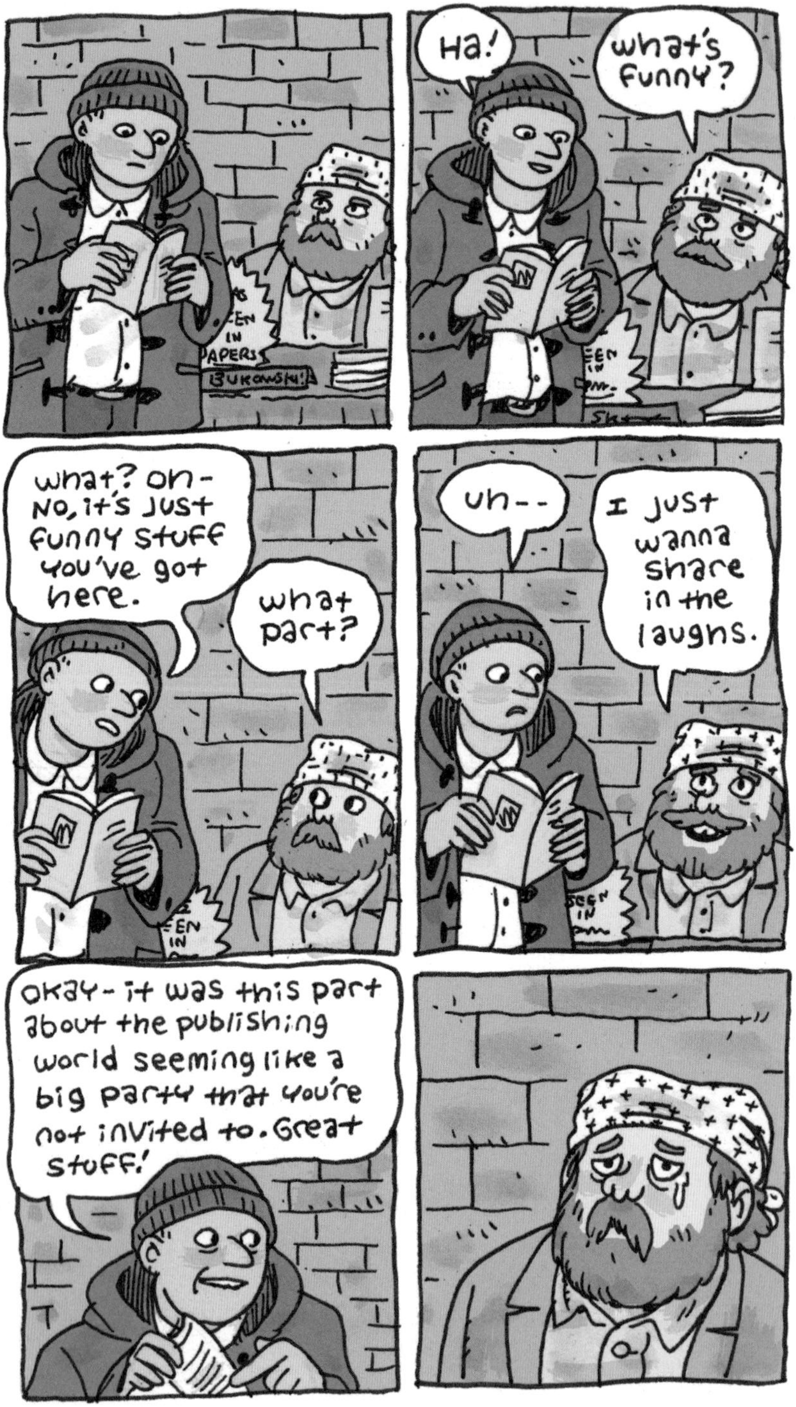
BUKOWSKI!
Ha!
what's funny?
what? oh-
No, it's just funny stuff you've got here.
what part?
uh--
I just wanna share in the laughs.
okay- it was this part about the publishing world seeming like a big party that you're not invited to. Great stuff!

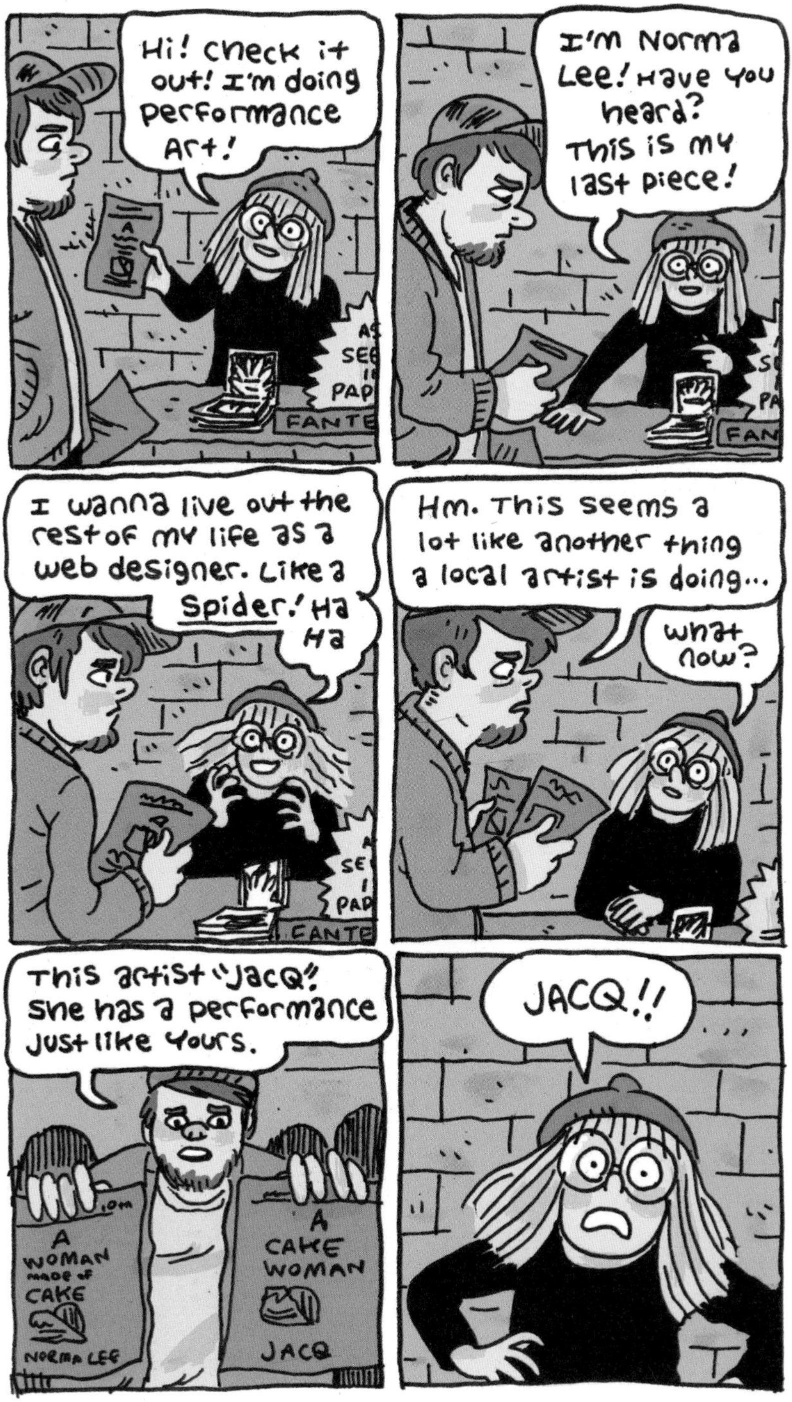
Hi! check it out! I'm doing performance Art!
AS SEEN IN PAP
FANTE
I'm Norma Lee! Have you heard? This is my last piece!
I wanna live out the rest of my life as a web designer. Like a Spider! Ha Ha
Hm. This seems a lot like another thing a local artist is doing...
what now?
This artist "Jacq!" She has a performance just like yours.
A WOMAN MADE OF CAKE
NORMA LEE
A CAKE WOMAN
JACQ
JACQ!!

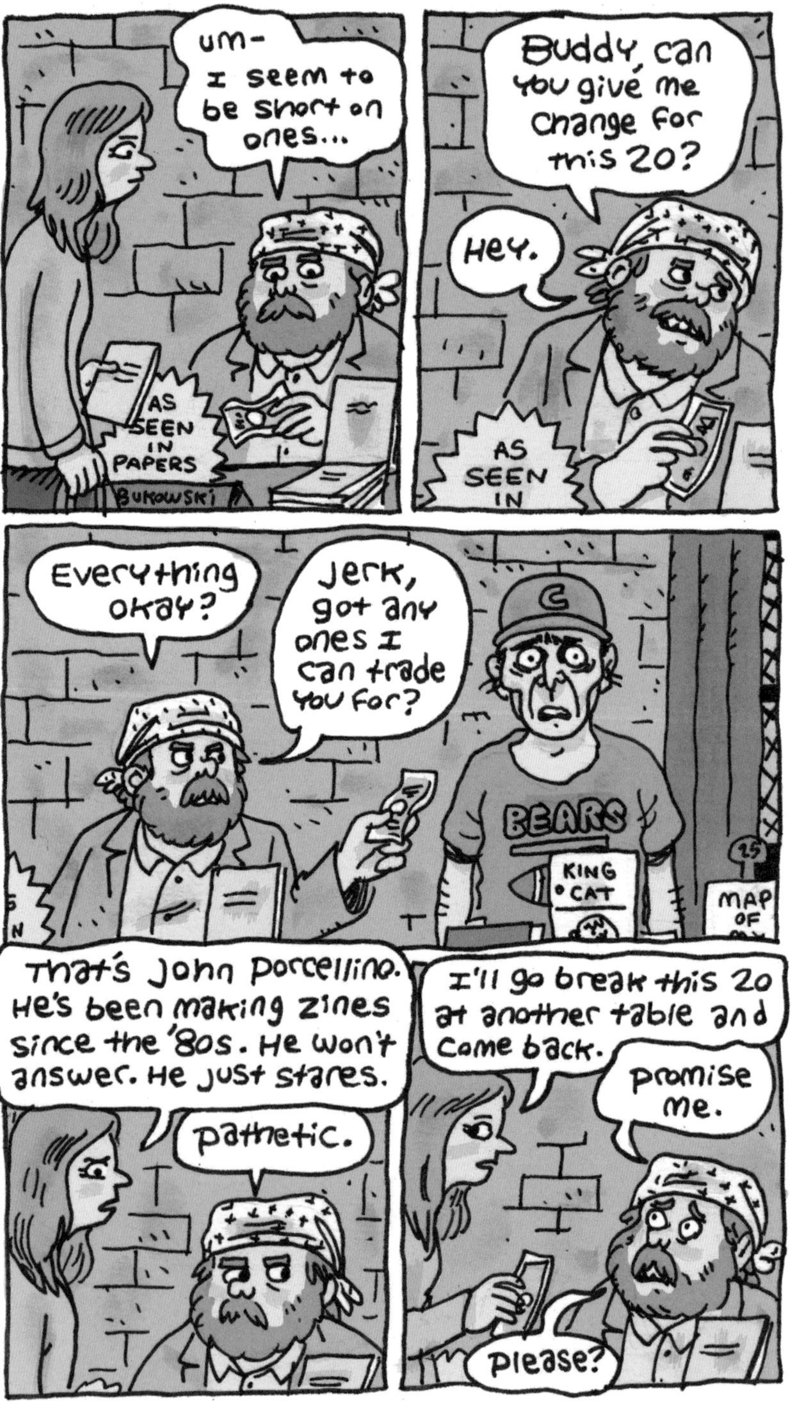
um-
I seem to be short on ones...
AS SEEN IN PAPERS
BUKOWSKI
Buddy, can you give me change for this 20?
Hey.
AS SEEN IN
Everything okay?
Jerk, got any ones I can trade you for?
BEARS
KING CAT
MAP OF
That's John Porcellino. He's been making zines since the '80s. He won't answer. He just stares.
pathetic.
I'll go break this 20 at another table and come back.
promise me.
please?

Hours snuffle by...

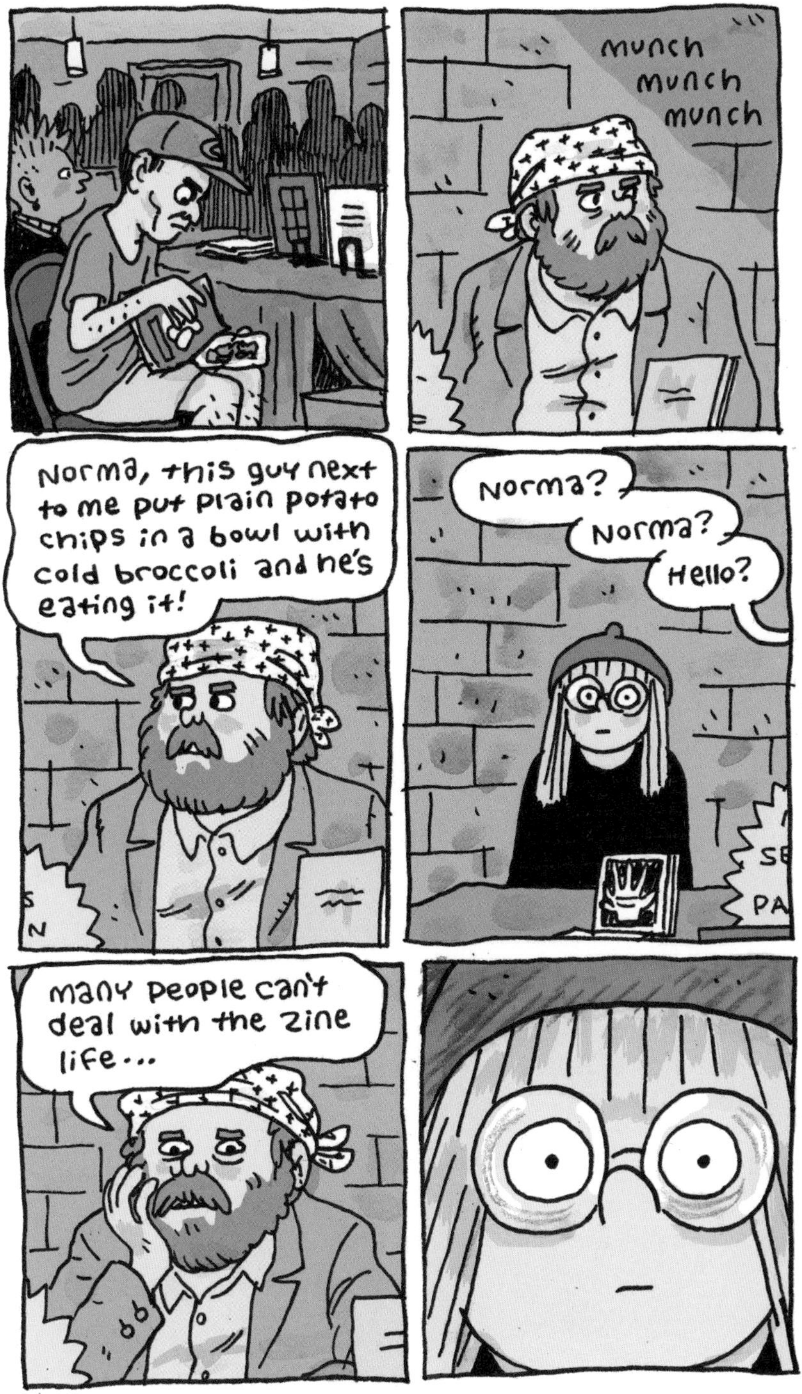
munch
munch
munch
Norma, this guy next to me put plain potato chips in a bowl with cold broccoli and he's eating it!
Norma?
Norma?
Hello?
many people can't deal with the zine life...

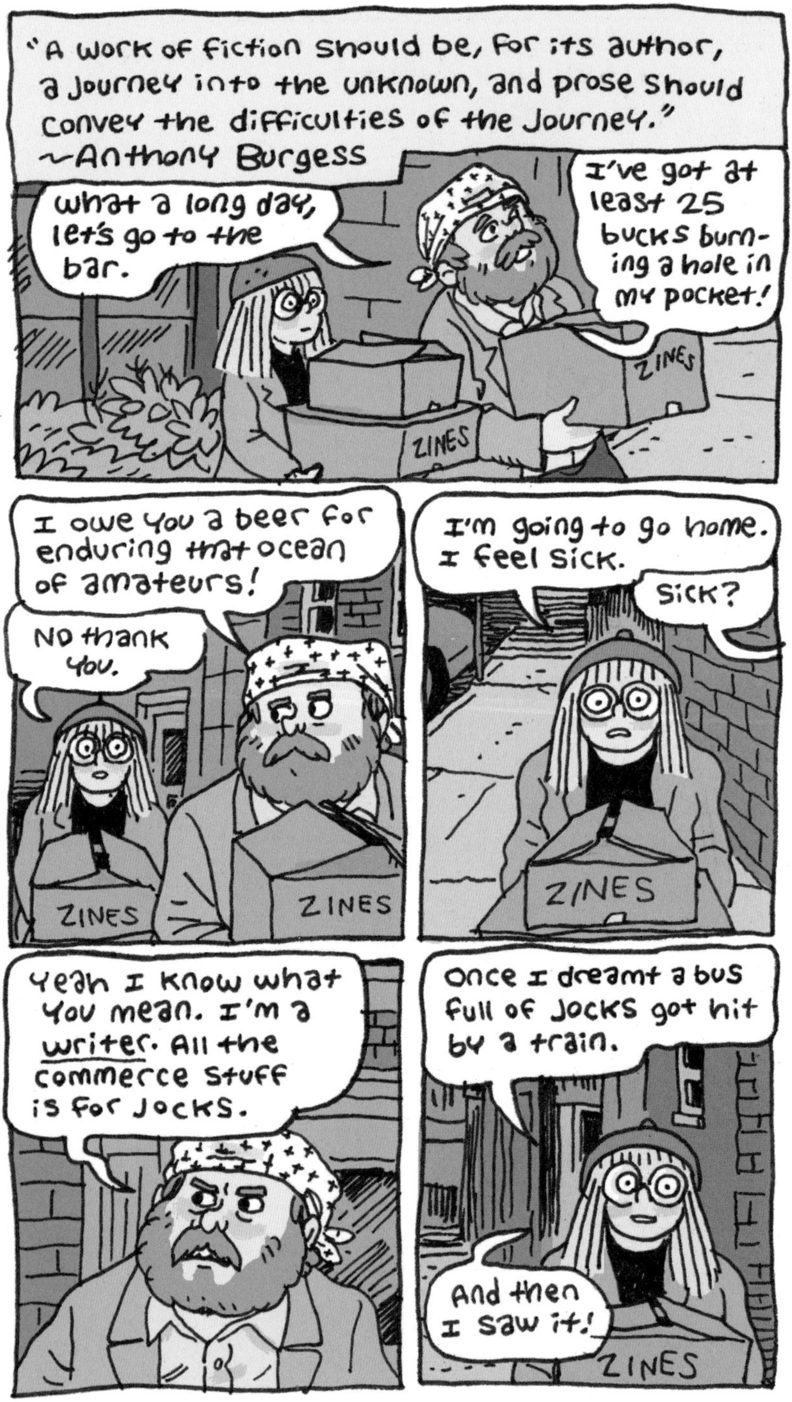
"A work of fiction should be, for its author, a journey into the unknown, and prose should convey the difficulties of the journey." ~Anthony Burgess
what a long day, let's go to the bar.
I've got at least 25 bucks burning a hole in my pocket!
ZINES
ZINES
I owe you a beer for enduring that ocean of amateurs!
No thank you.
ZINES
ZINES
I'm going to go home. I feel sick.
Sick?
ZINES
Yeah I know what you mean. I'm a writer. All the commerce stuff is for jocks.
Once I dreamt a bus full of jocks got hit by a train.
And then I saw it!
ZINES

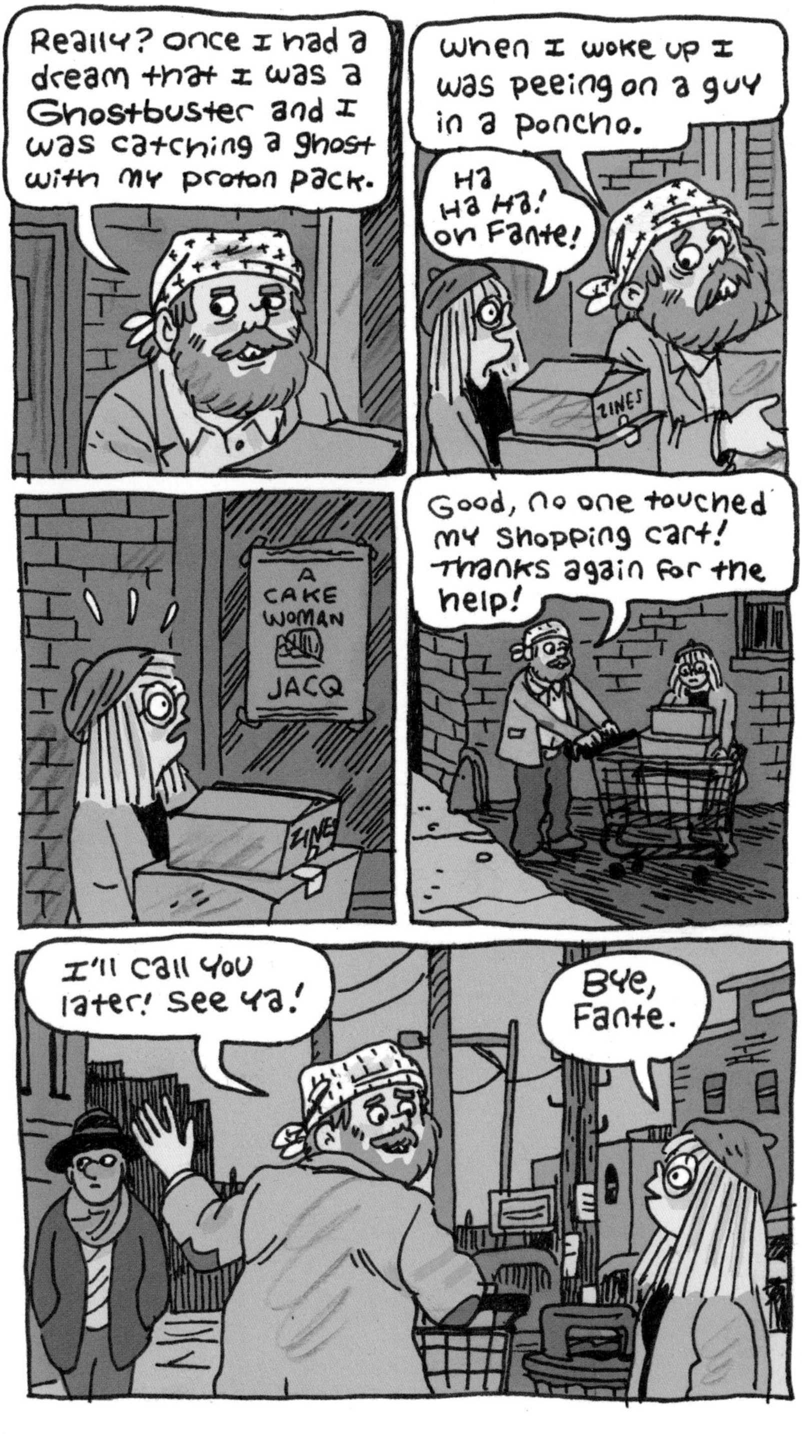
Really? Once I had a dream that I was a Ghostbuster and I was catching a ghost with my proton pack.
When I woke up I was peeing on a guy in a poncho.
Ha Ha Ha! Oh Fante!
ZINES
A CAKE WOMAN JACQ
ZINES
Good, no one touched my shopping cart! Thanks again for the help!
I'll call you later! See ya!
Bye, Fante.

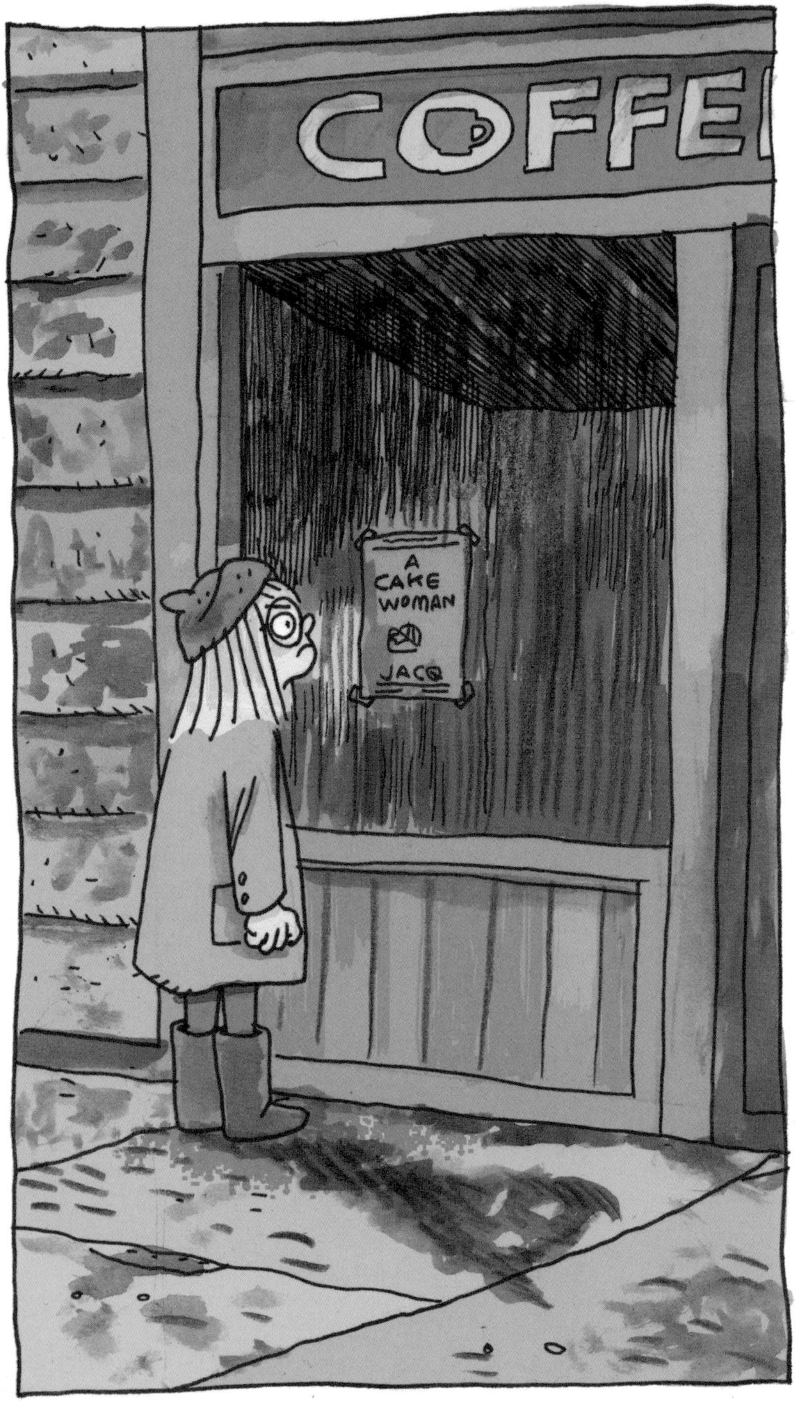
COFFE
A CAKE WOMAN
JACQ

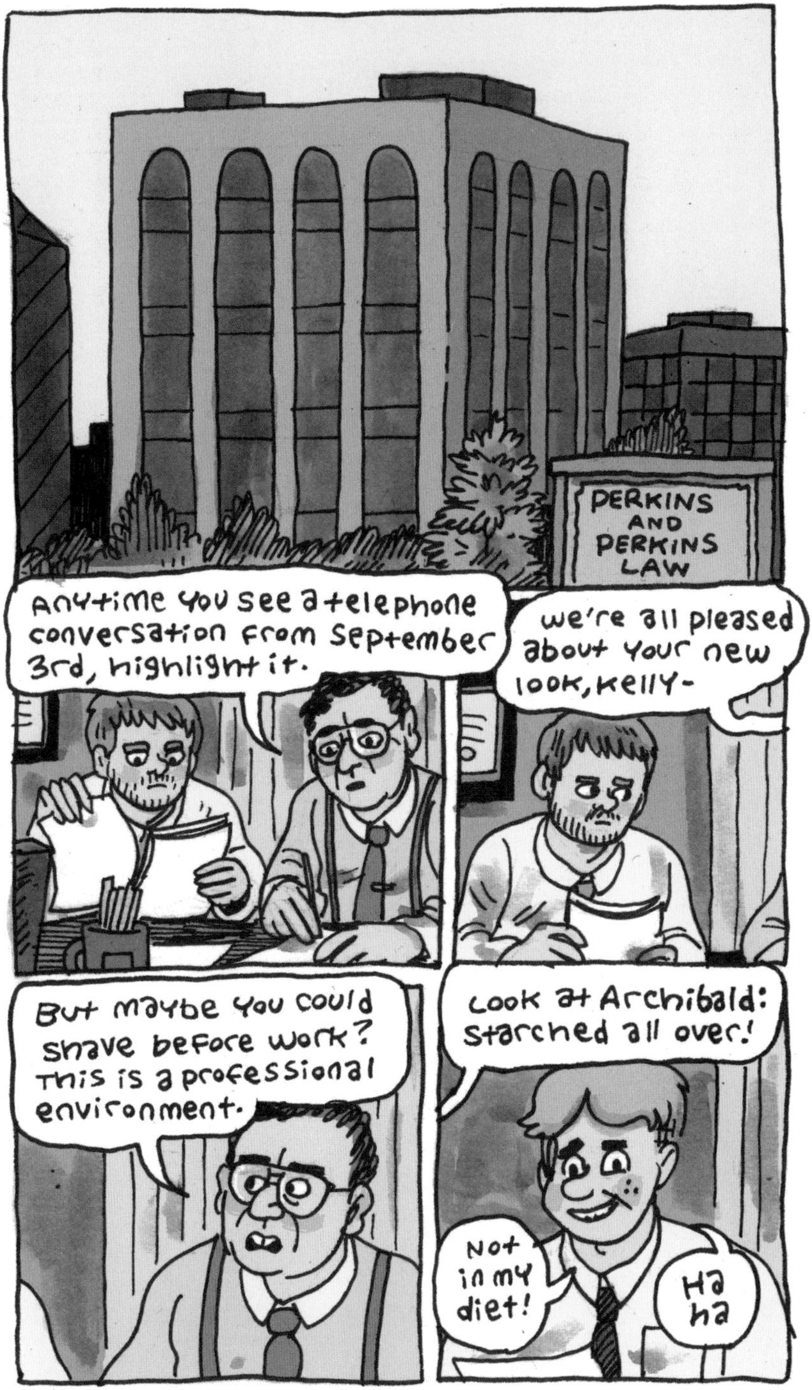
PERKINS AND PERKINS LAW
Anytime you see a telephone conversation from September 3rd, highlight it.
we're all pleased about your new look, Kelly-
But maybe you could shave before work? This is a professional environment.
Look at Archibald: starched all over!
Not in my diet!
Ha ha

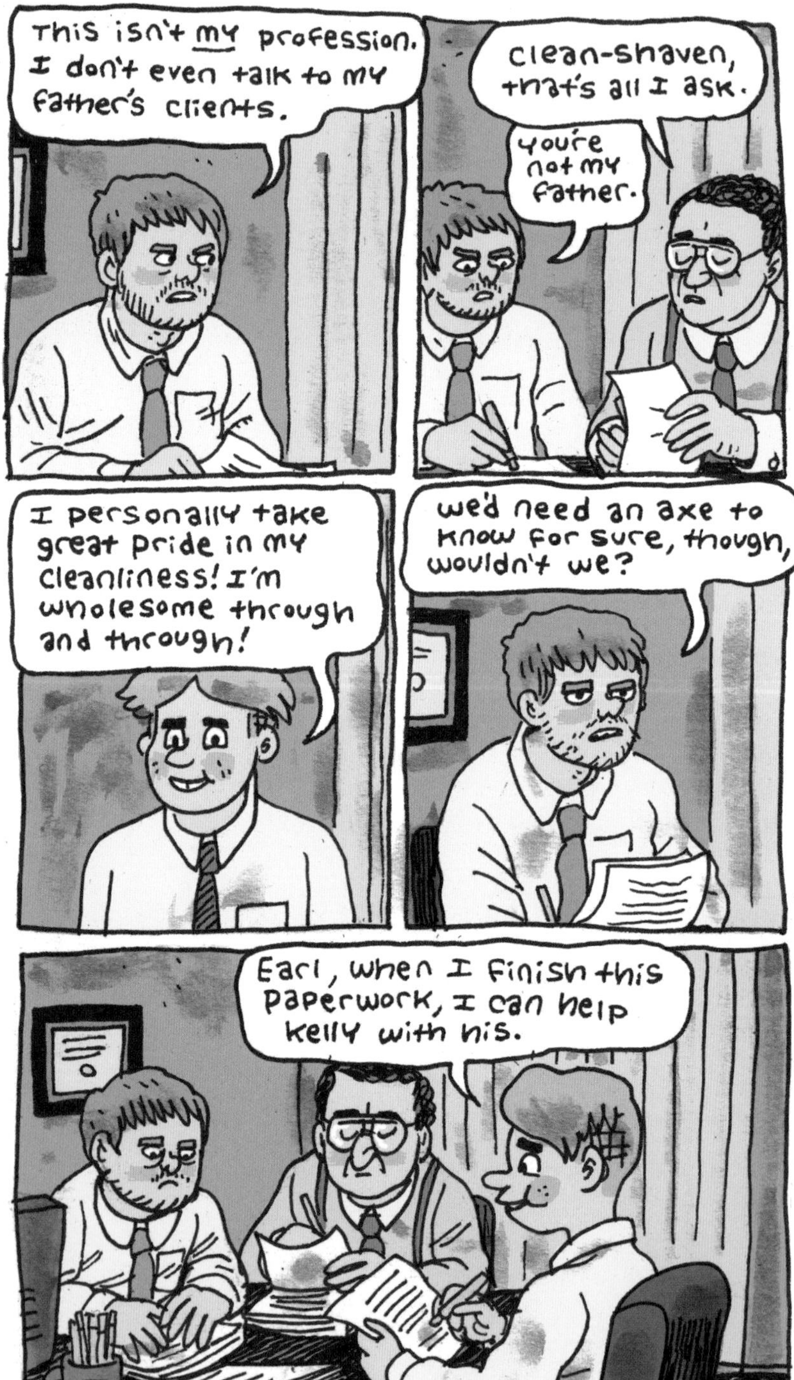
This isn't my profession. I don't even talk to my father's clients.
Clean-shaven, that's all I ask.
You're not my father.
I personally take great pride in my cleanliness! I'm wholesome through and through!
We'd need an axe to know for sure, though, wouldn't we?
Earl, when I finish this paperwork, I can help Kelly with his.

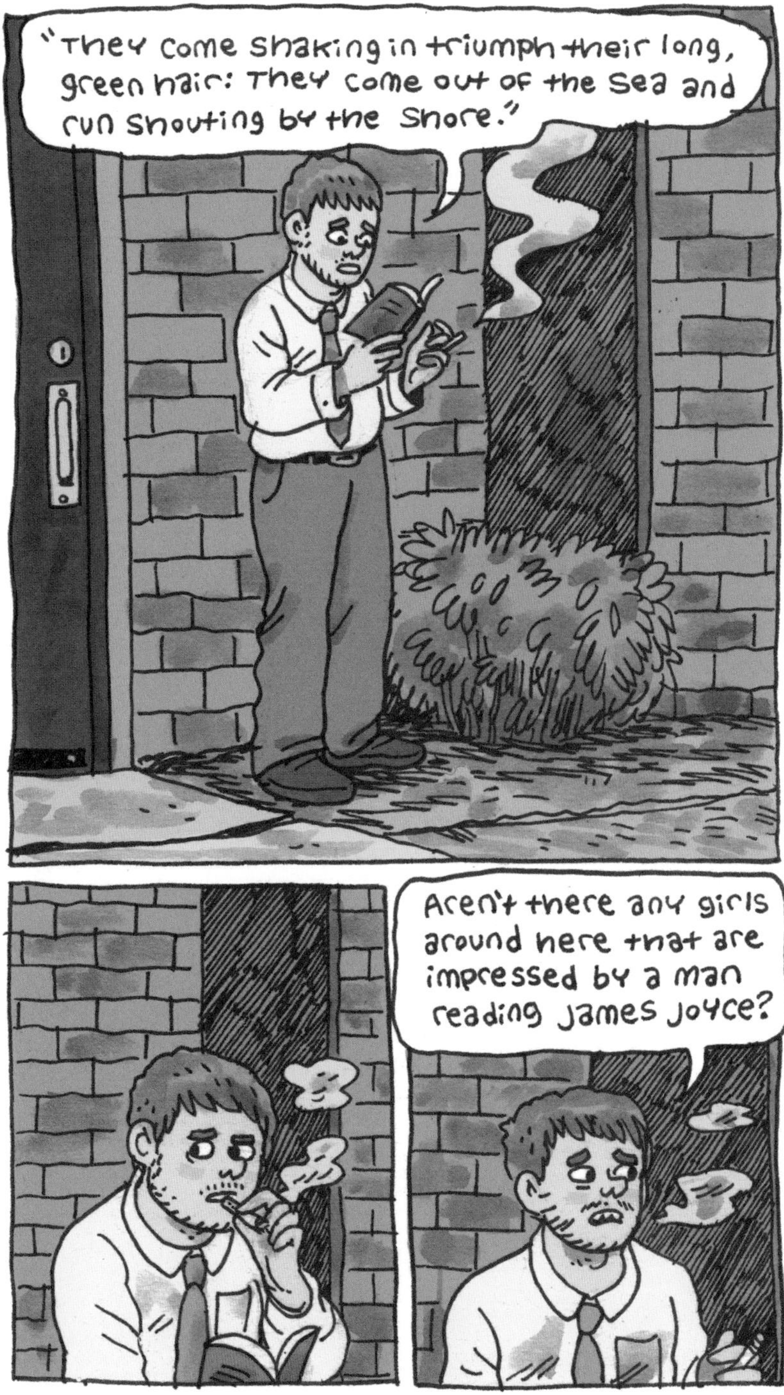
"They come shaking in triumph their long, green hair: They come out of the sea and run shouting by the shore."
Aren't there any girls around here that are impressed by a man reading James Joyce?

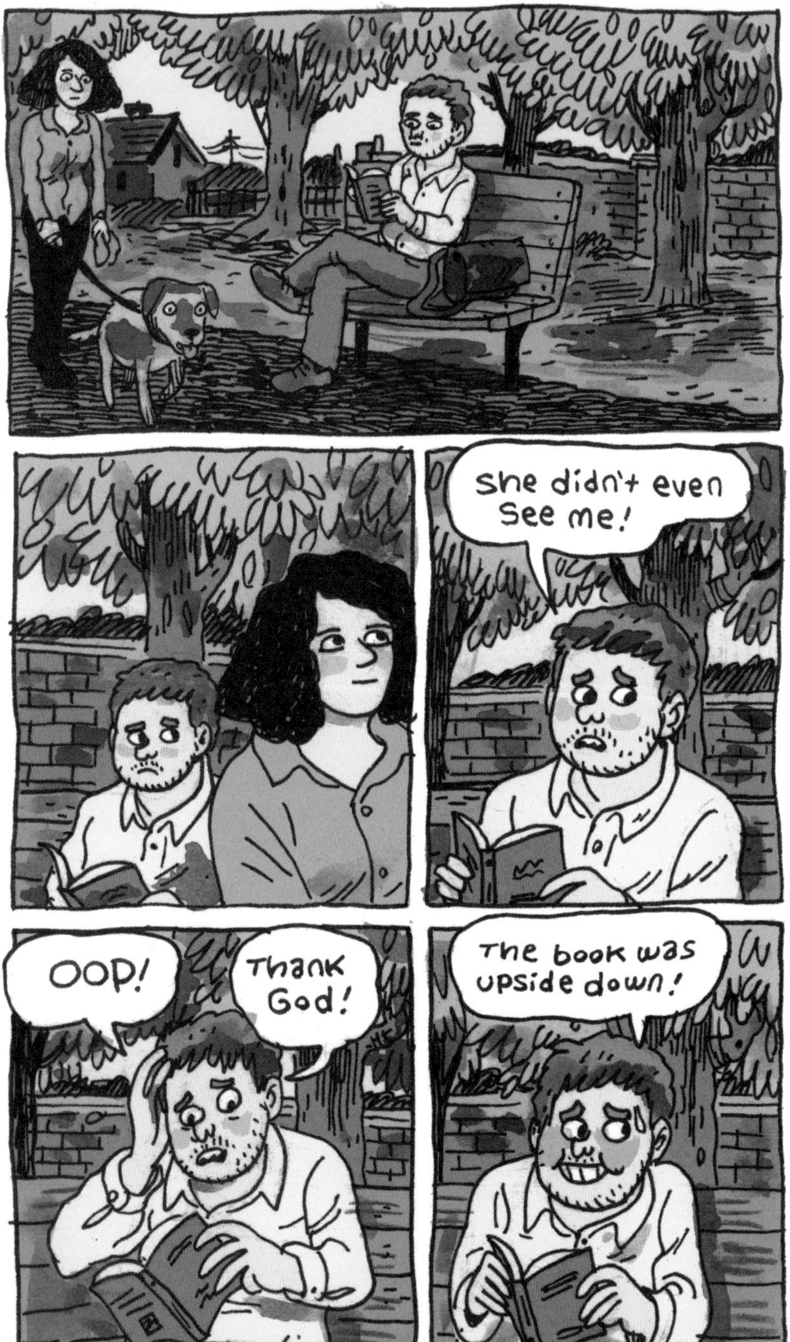
She didn't even See me!
OOP!
Thank God!
The book was upside down!

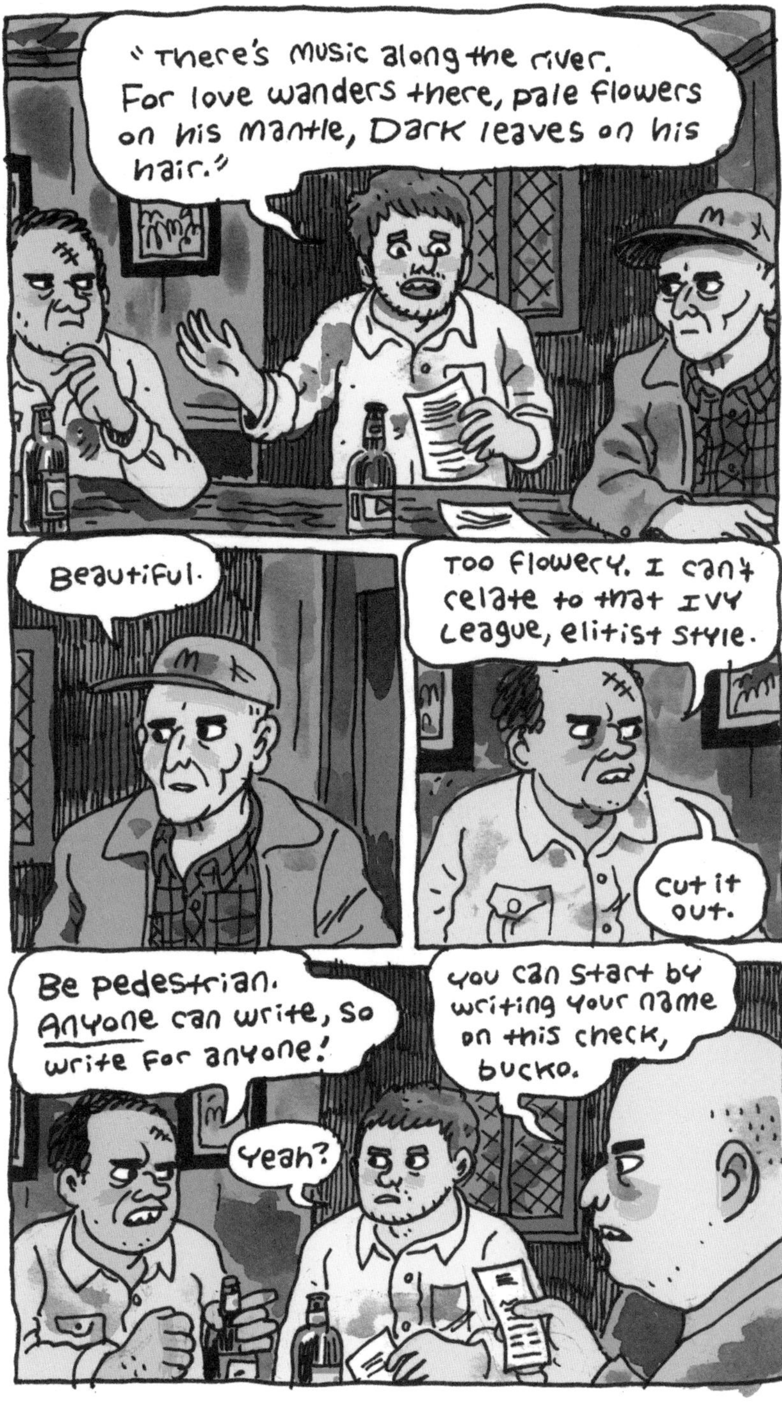
"There's music along the river. For love wanders there, pale flowers on his mantle, Dark leaves on his hair."
Beautiful.
Too flowery. I can't relate to that Ivy League, elitist style.
Cut it out.
Be pedestrian. Anyone can write, so write for anyone!
Yeah?
You can start by writing your name on this check, bucko.

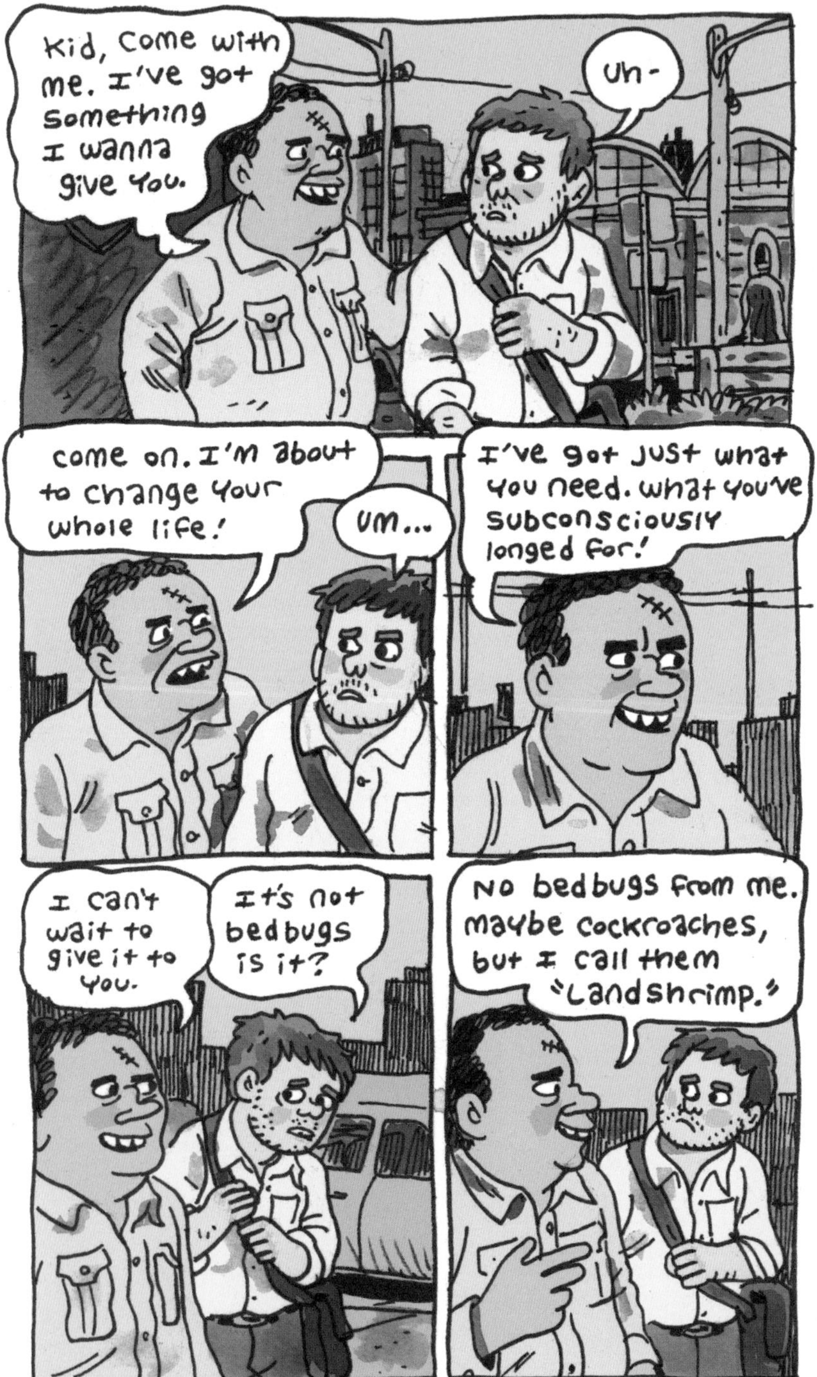
Kid, come with me. I've got something I wanna give you.
Uh-
come on. I'm about to change your whole life!
UM...
I've got just what you need. what you've subconsciously longed for!
I can't wait to give it to you.
It's not bedbugs is it?
No bedbugs from me. maybe cockroaches, but I call them "Landshrimp."

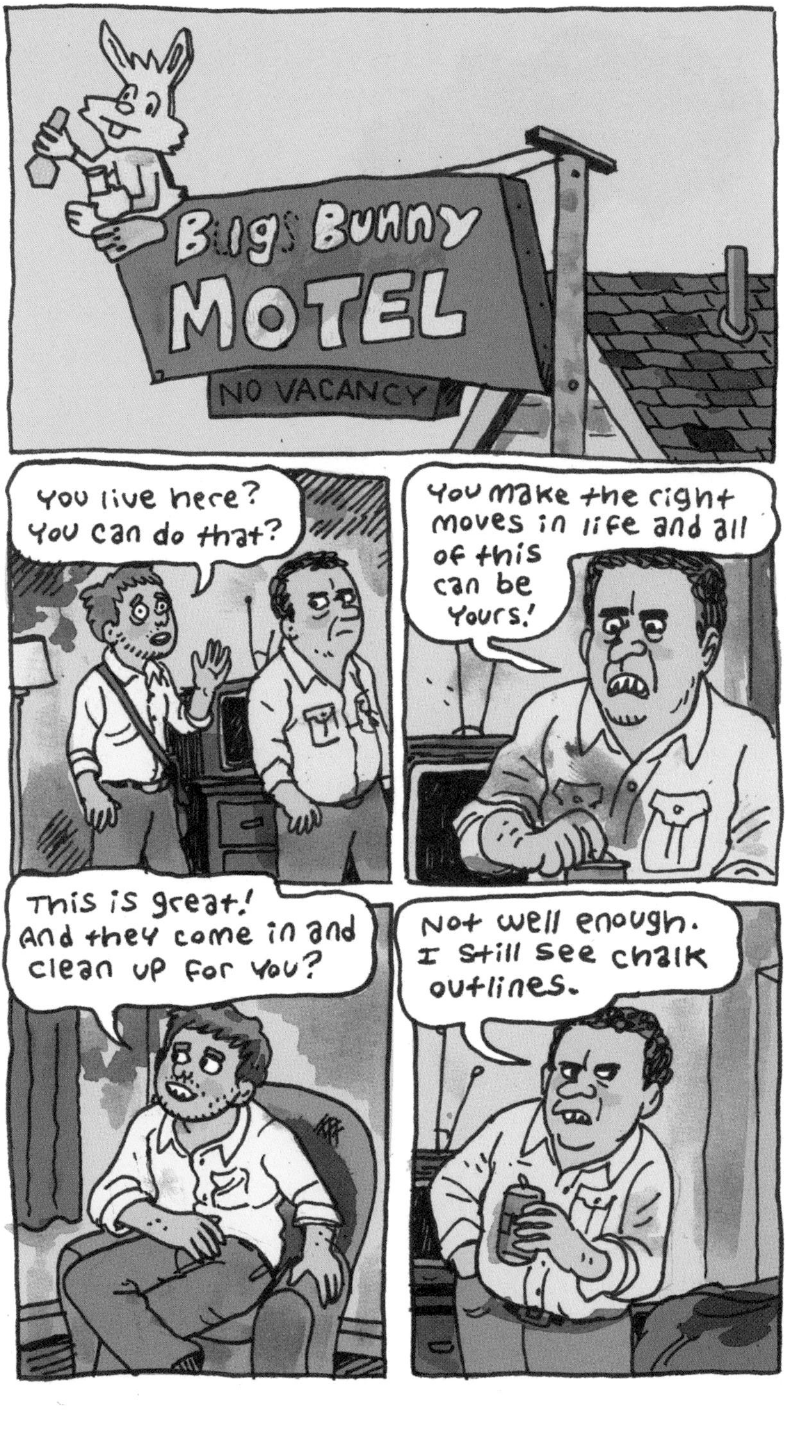

Big Bunny
MOTEL
NO VACANCY
You live here? You can do that?
You make the right moves in life and all of this can be Yours!
This is great! And they come in and clean up for you?
Not well enough. I still see chalk outlines.

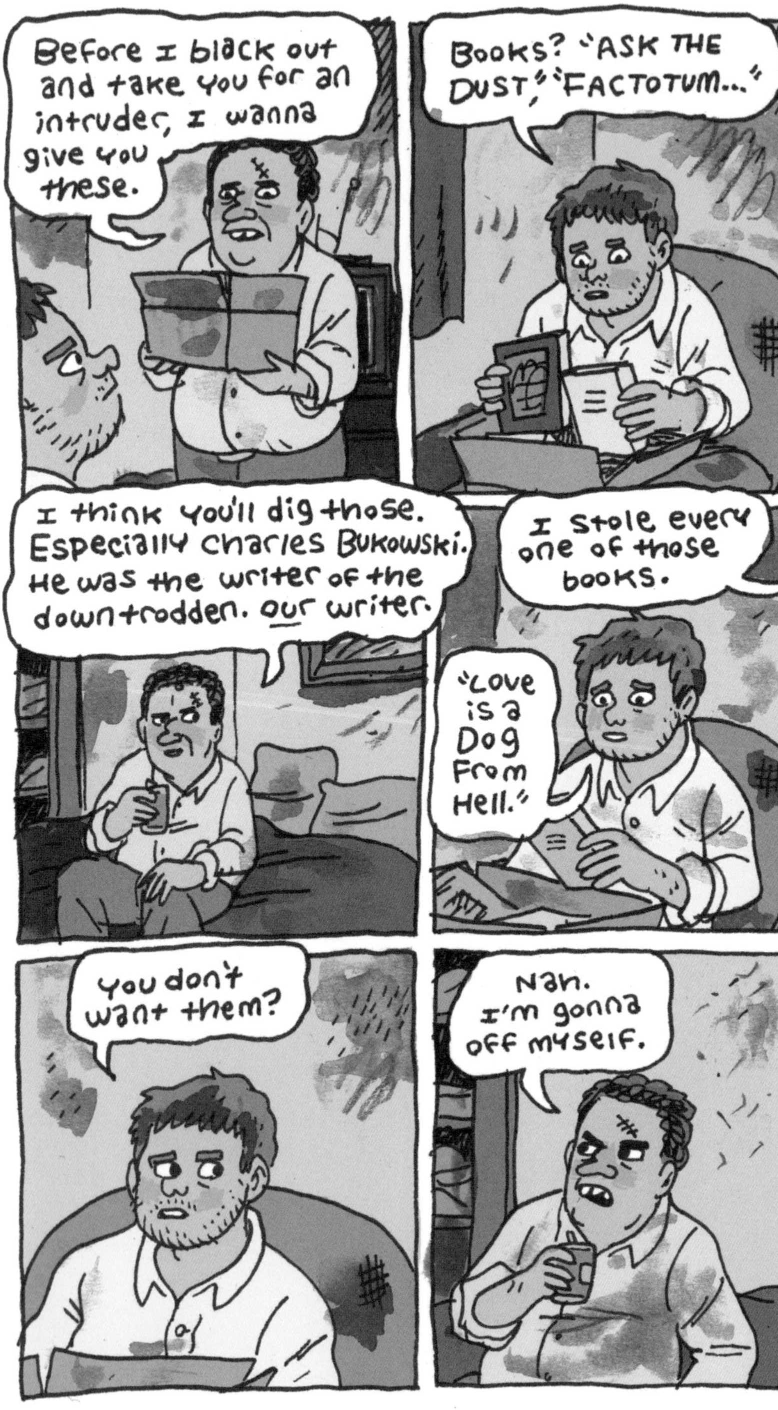

Before I black out and take you for an intruder, I wanna give you these.
Books? "ASK THE DUST," "FACTOTUM..."
I think you'll dig those. Especially Charles Bukowski. He was the writer of the downtrodden. our writer.
I stole every one of those books.
"Love is a Dog From Hell."
You don't want them?
Nah. I'm gonna off myself.

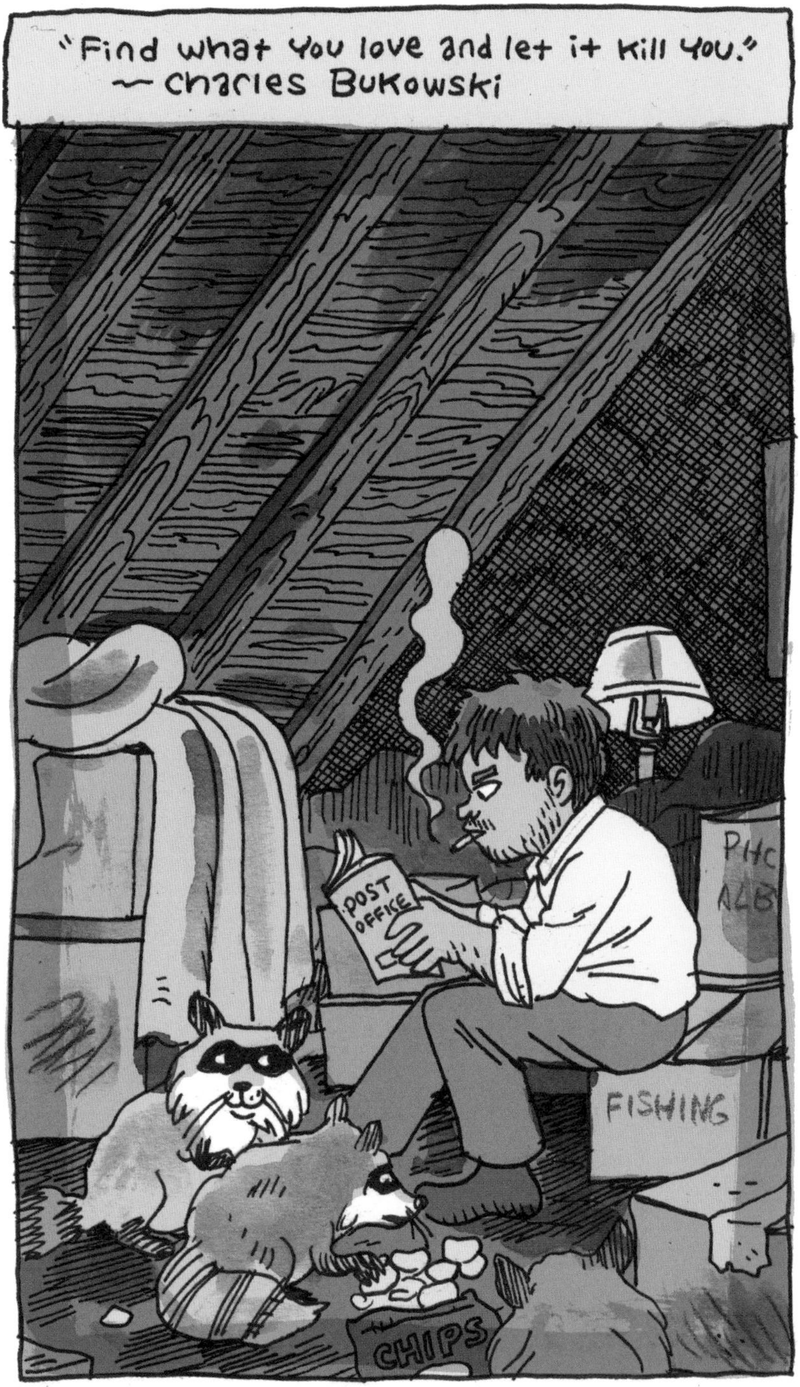
"Find what you love and let it kill you."
~Charles Bukowski
POST OFFICE
FISHING
CHIPS

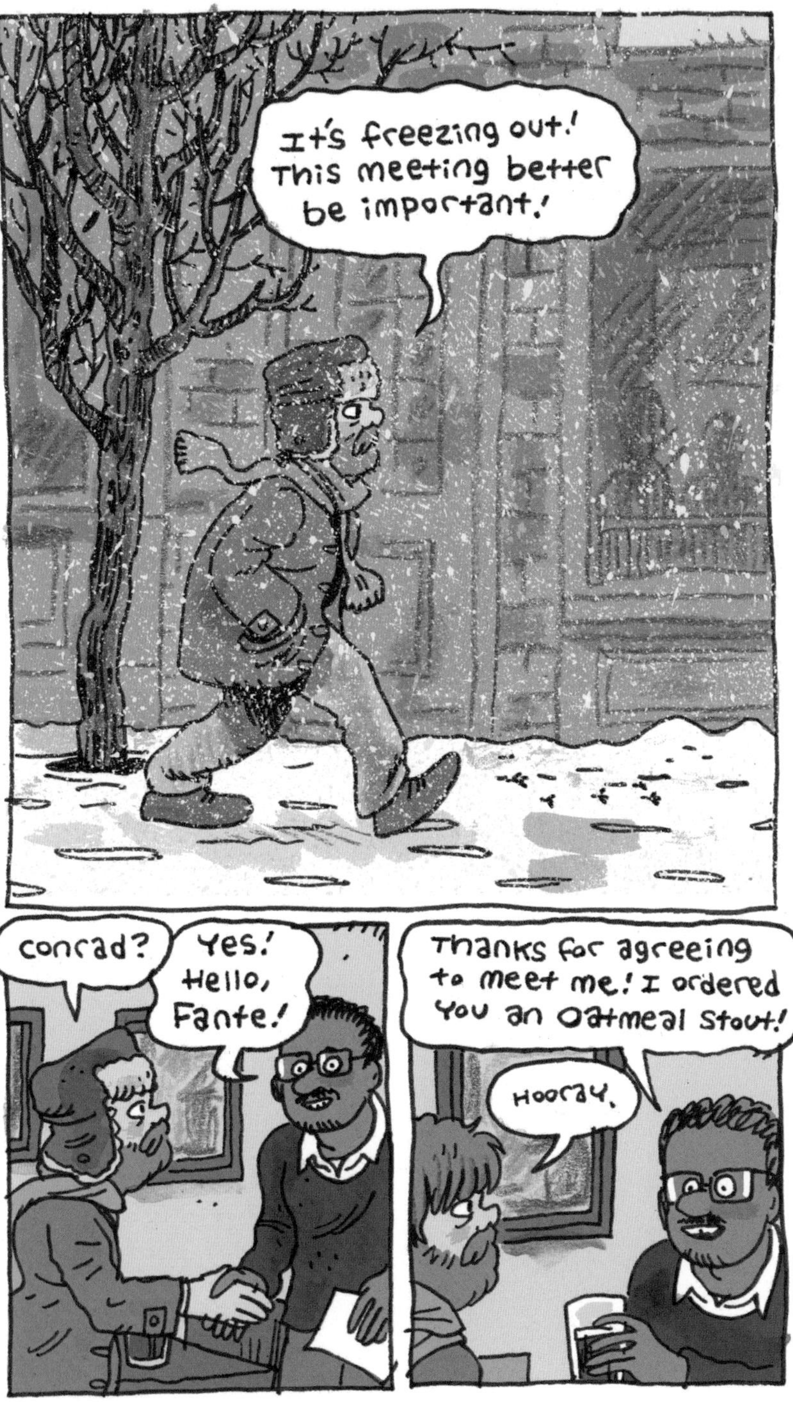
It's freezing out! This meeting better be important!
Conrad?
Yes! Hello, Fante!
Thanks for agreeing to meet me! I ordered you an oatmeal stout!
Hooray.

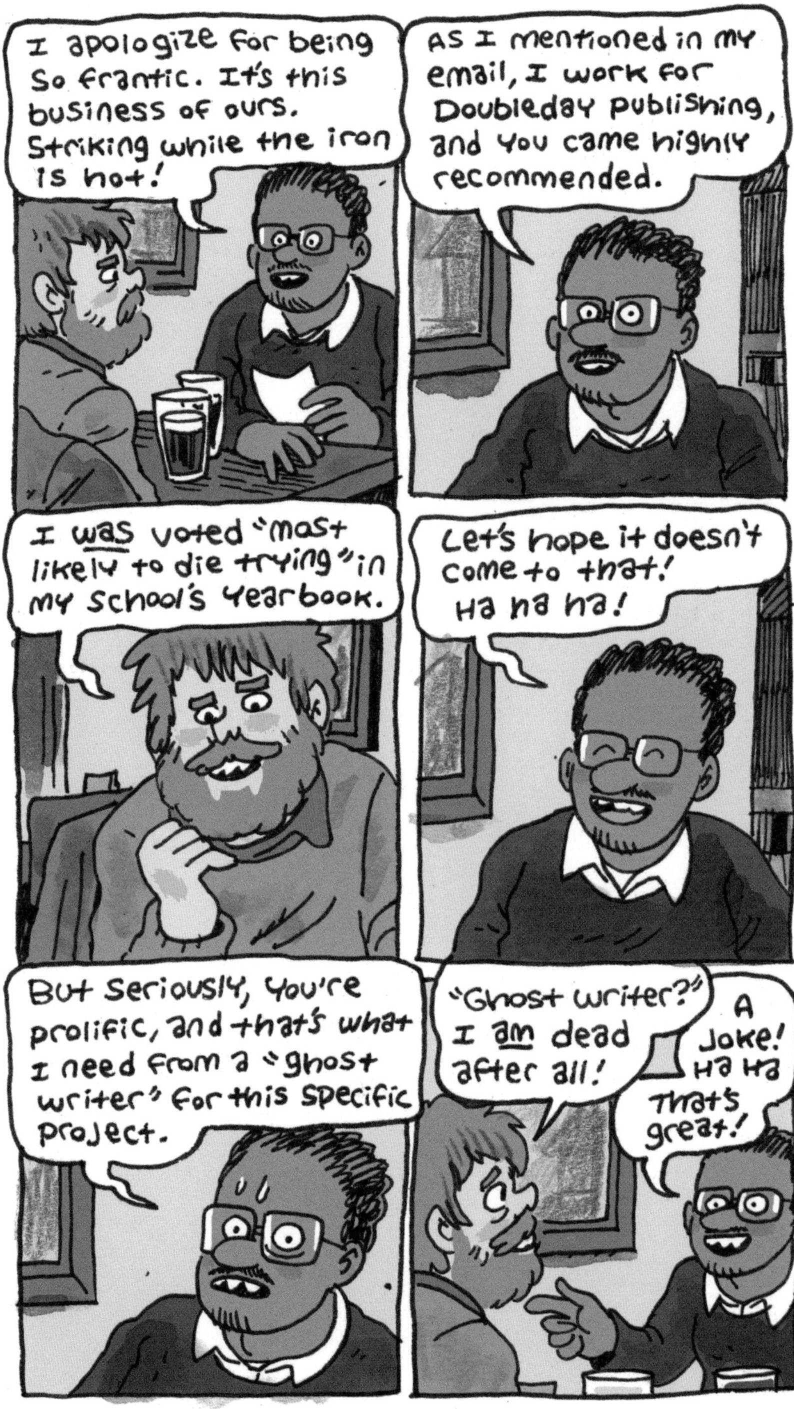

I apologize for being so frantic. It's this business of ours. Striking while the iron is hot!
As I mentioned in my email, I work for Doubleday publishing, and you came highly recommended.
I was voted "most likely to die trying" in my school's yearbook.
Let's hope it doesn't come to that! Ha ha ha!
But seriously, you're prolific, and that's what I need from a "ghost writer" for this specific project.
"Ghost writer?" I am dead after all!
A joke! Ha ha That's great!

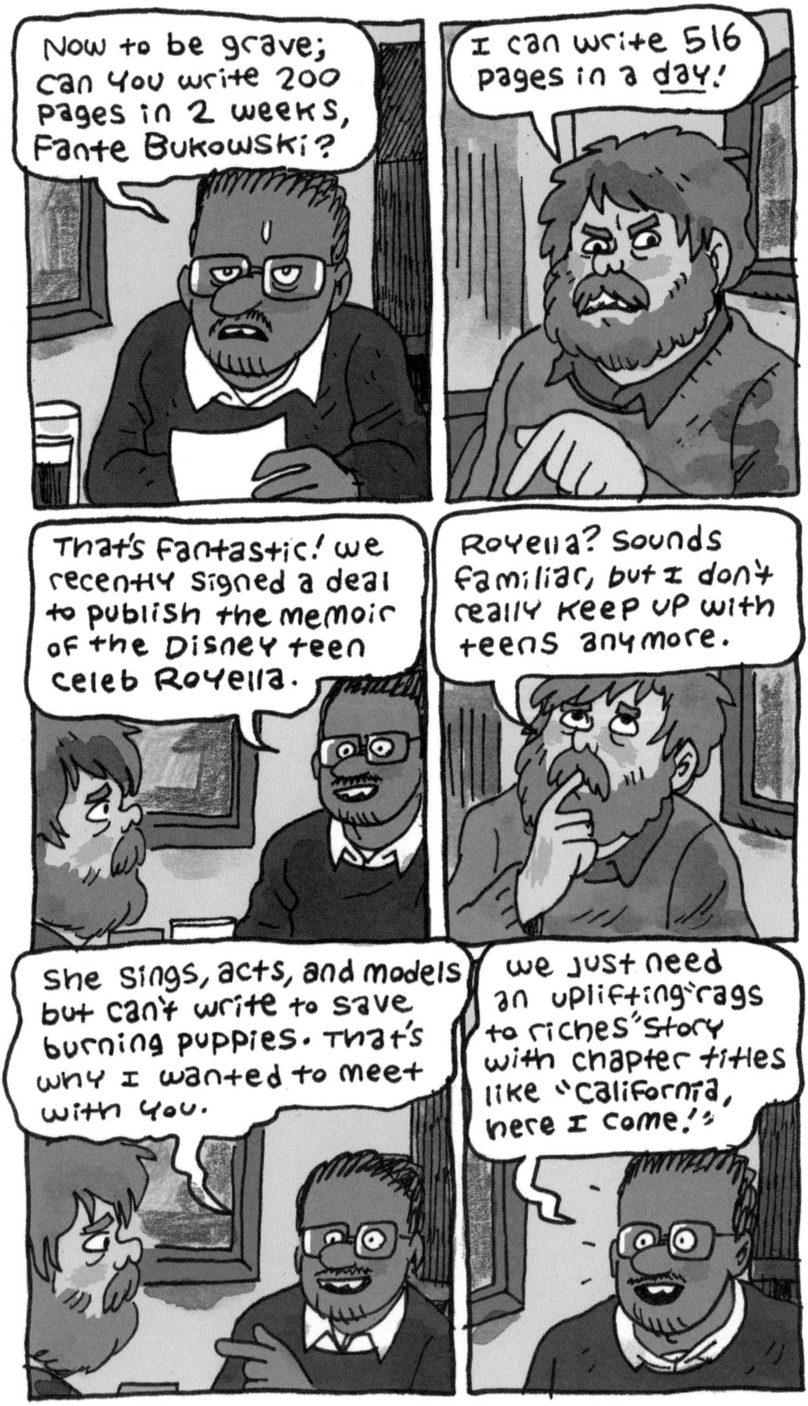

Now to be grave; can you write 200 pages in 2 weeks, Fante Bukowski?
I can write 516 pages in a day!
That's fantastic! we recently signed a deal to publish the memoir of the Disney teen celeb Royella.
Royella? Sounds familiar, but I don't really keep up with teens anymore.
She sings, acts, and models but can't write to save burning puppies. That's why I wanted to meet with you.
we just need an "uplifting" rags to riches "story" with chapter titles like "California, here I come!"

But I don't know anything about her life!

I have a packet of biographical info. Just connect the dots.

You couldn't screw up that bad. Disney stars are mostly fictional creations anyway.

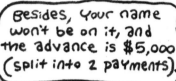

Besides, your name won't be on it, and the advance is $5,000 (split into 2 payments).

5 grand?

uh- plus I'm paying for these oatmeal stouts...

Can I have a check today?

If you'll sign the contract.

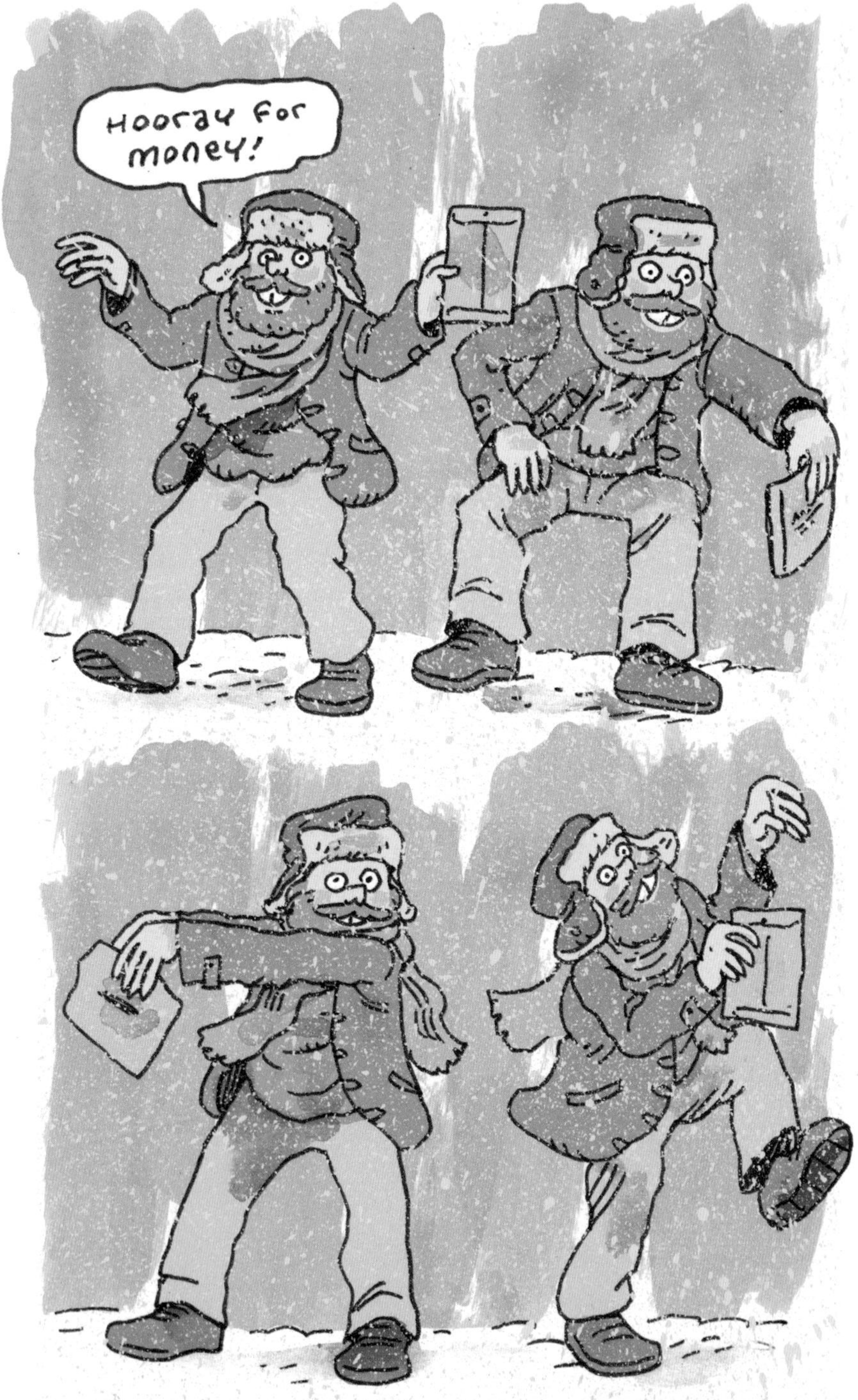
Hooray for money!

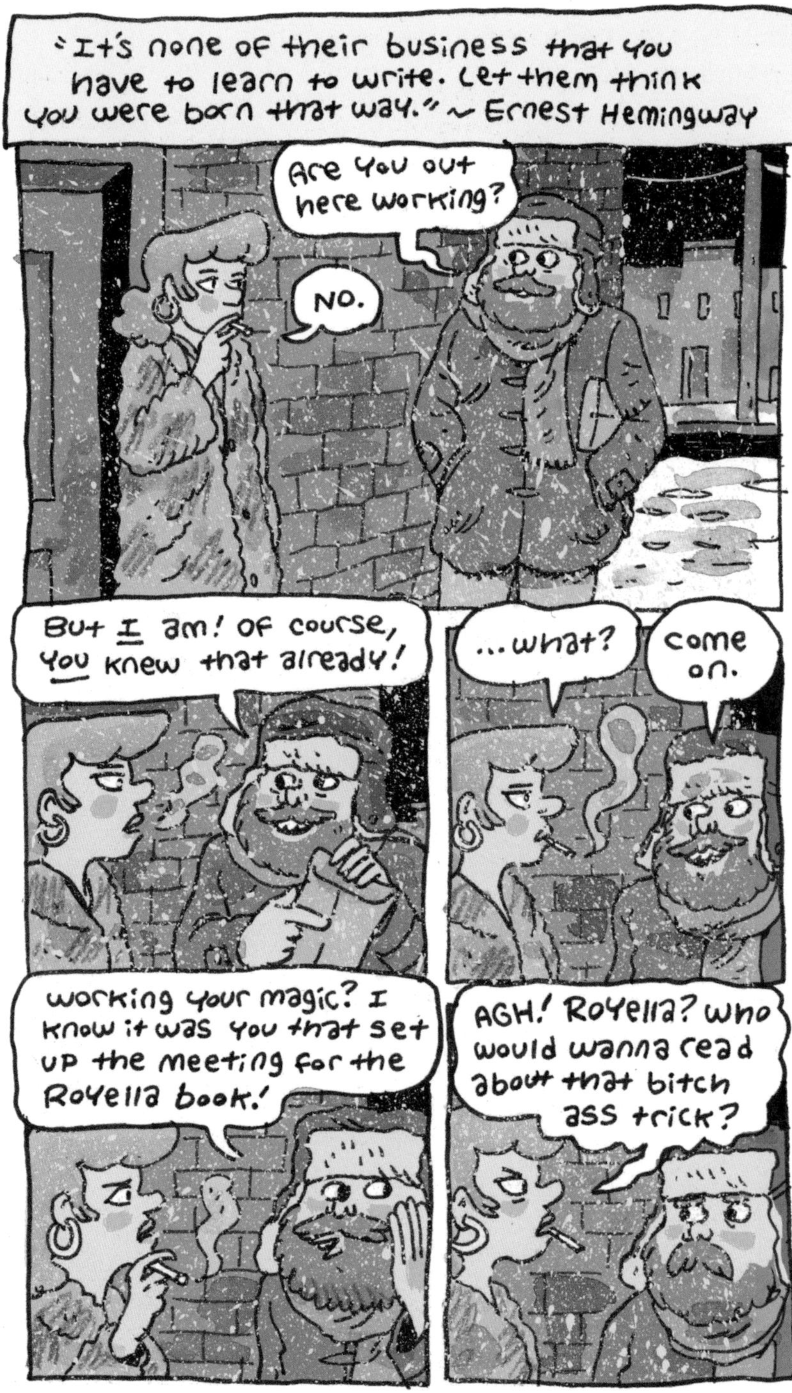
"It's none of their business that you have to learn to write. Let them think you were born that way." ~ Ernest Hemingway
Are you out here working?
No.
But I am! Of course, you knew that already!
...what?
come on.
working your magic? I know it was you that set up the meeting for the Royella book!
AGH! Royella? who would wanna read about that bitch ass trick?

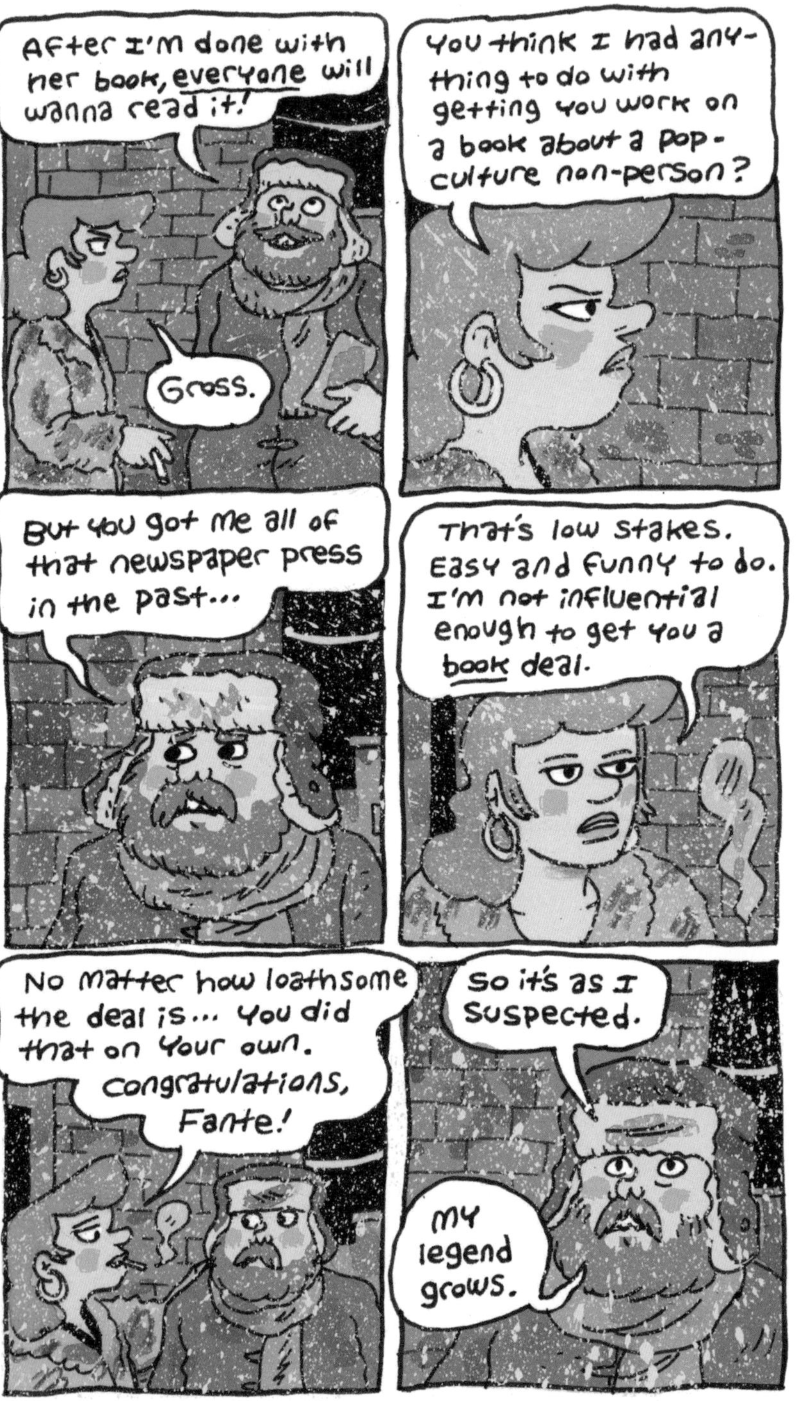
After I'm done with her book, everyone will wanna read it!
Gross.
You think I had anything to do with getting you work on a book about a pop-culture non-person?
But you got me all of that newspaper press in the past...
That's low stakes. Easy and funny to do. I'm not influential enough to get you a book deal.
No matter how loathsome the deal is... You did that on your own.
Congratulations, Fante!
So it's as I suspected.
My legend grows.

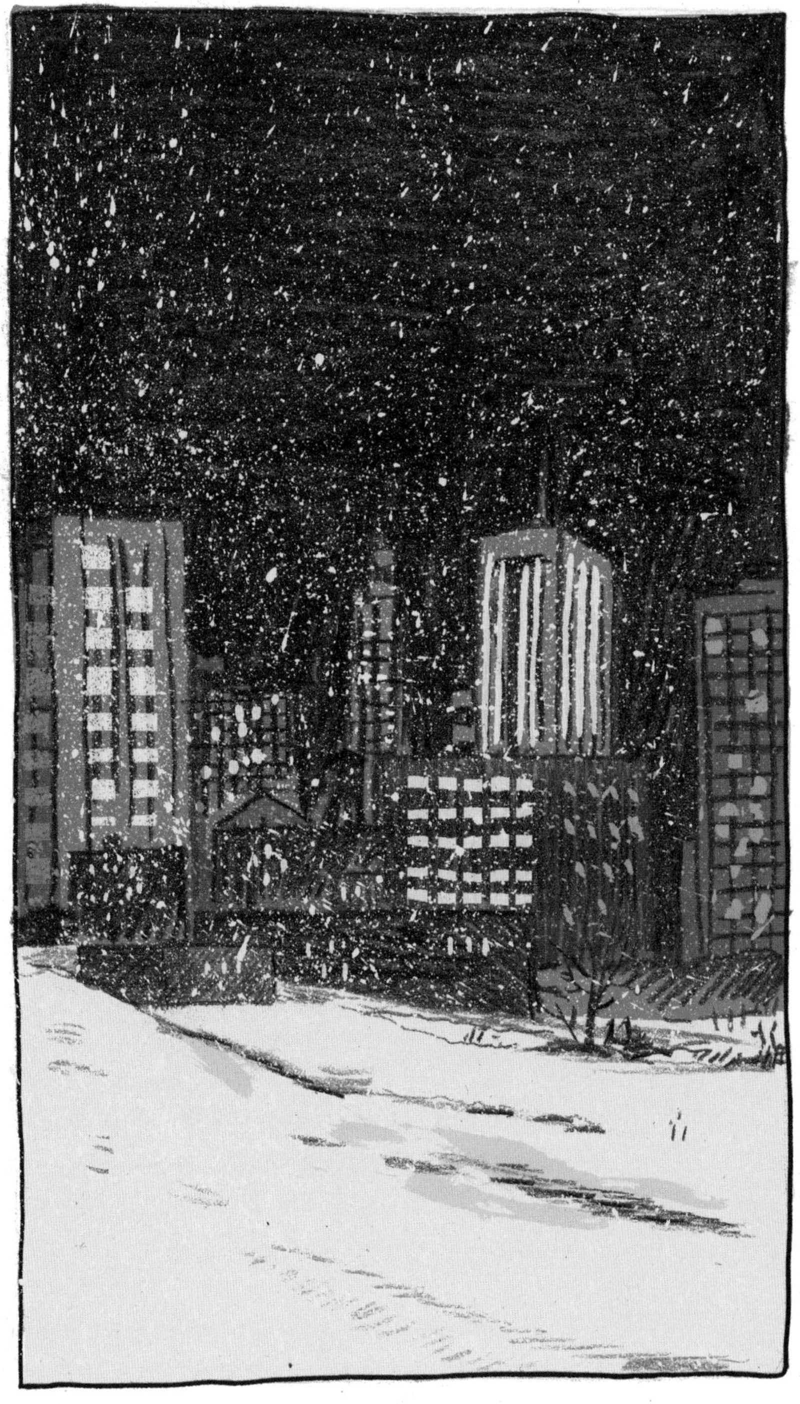

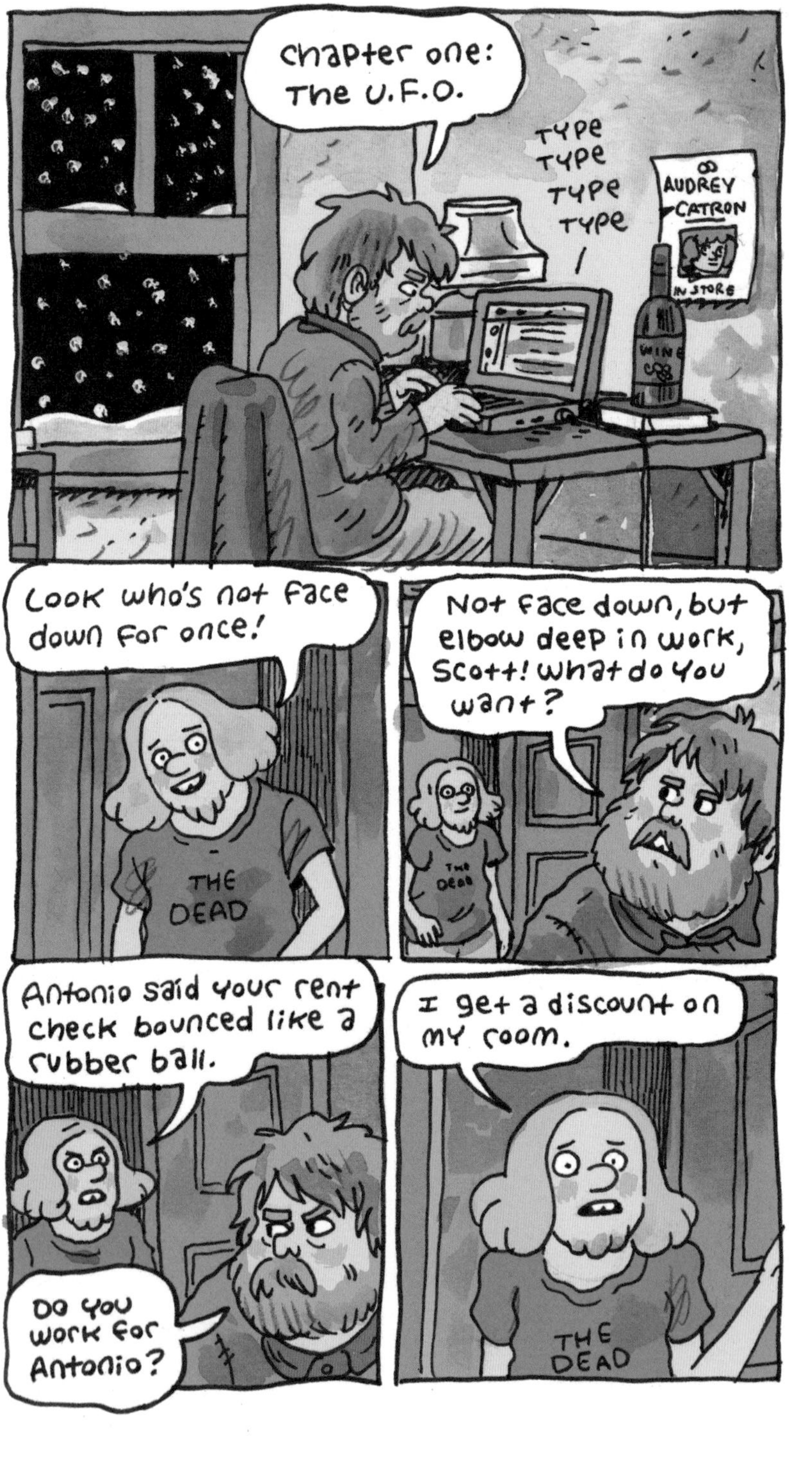
Chapter one: The U.F.O.
TYPE TYPE TYPE TYPE
AUDREY CATRON
IN STORE
WINE
Look who's not face down for once!
THE DEAD
Not face down, but elbow deep in work, Scott! What do you want?
THE DEAD
Antonio said your rent check bounced like a rubber ball.
Do you work for Antonio?
I get a discount on my room.
THE DEAD

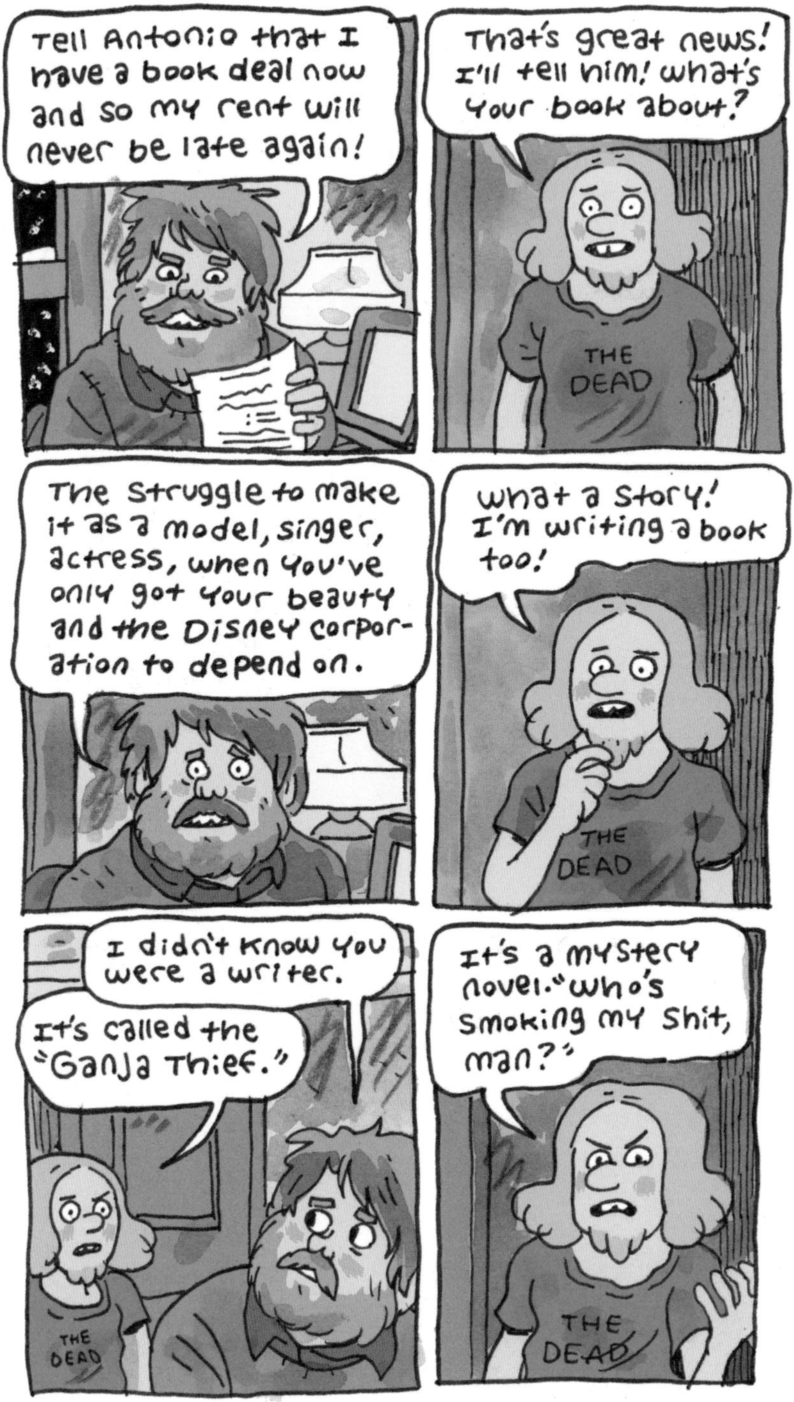
Tell Antonio that I have a book deal now and so my rent will never be late again!
That's great news! I'll tell him! what's your book about?
THE DEAD
The struggle to make it as a model, singer, actress, when you've only got your beauty and the Disney corporation to depend on.
what a story! I'm writing a book too!
THE DEAD
I didn't know you were a writer.
It's called the "Ganja Thief."
THE DEAD
It's a mystery novel. "who's smoking my shit, man?"
THE DEAD

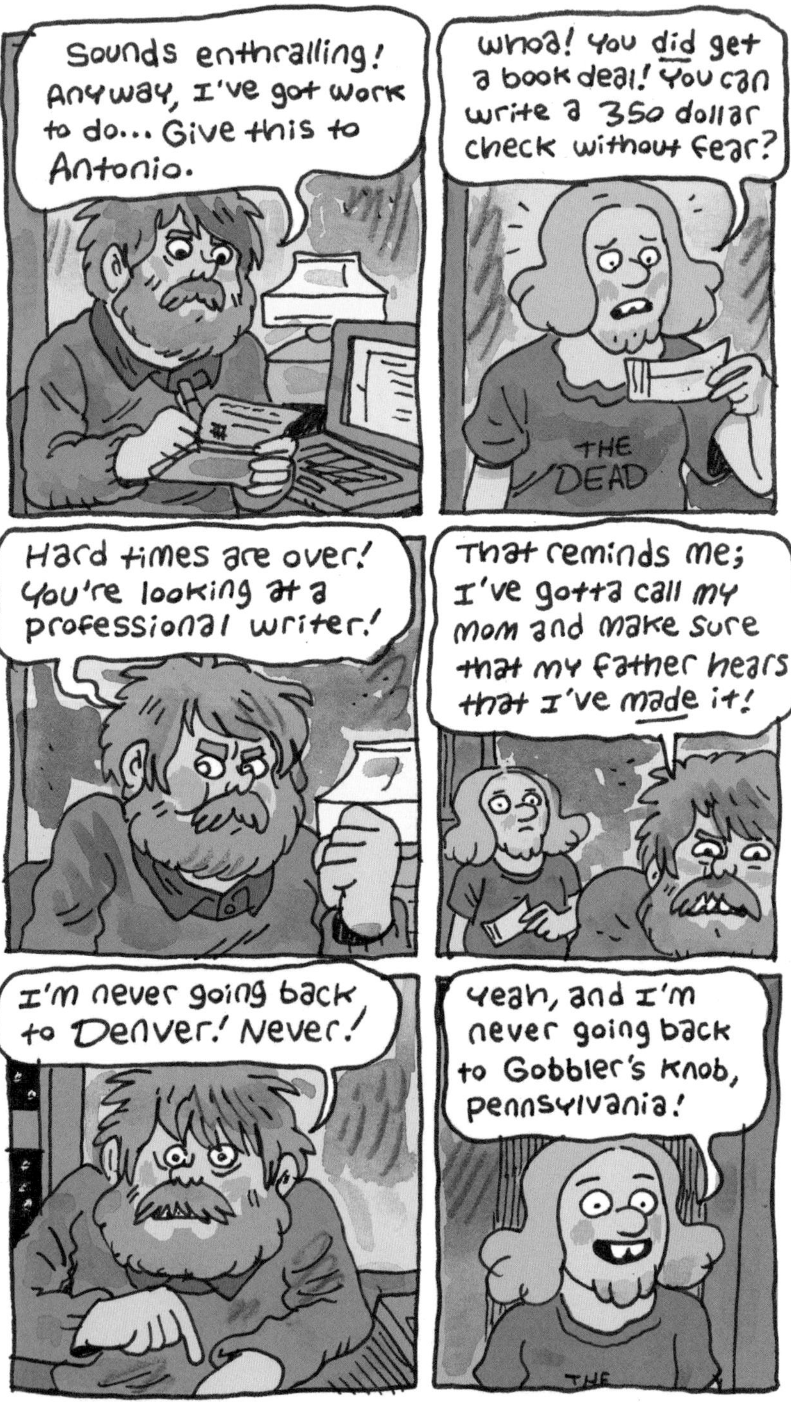
Sounds enthralling! Anyway, I've got work to do... Give this to Antonio.
Whoa! You did get a book deal! You can write a 350 dollar check without fear?
THE DEAD
Hard times are over! You're looking at a professional writer!
That reminds me; I've gotta call my mom and make sure that my father hears that I've made it!
I'm never going back to Denver! Never!
Yeah, and I'm never going back to Gobbler's Knob, Pennsylvania!
THE

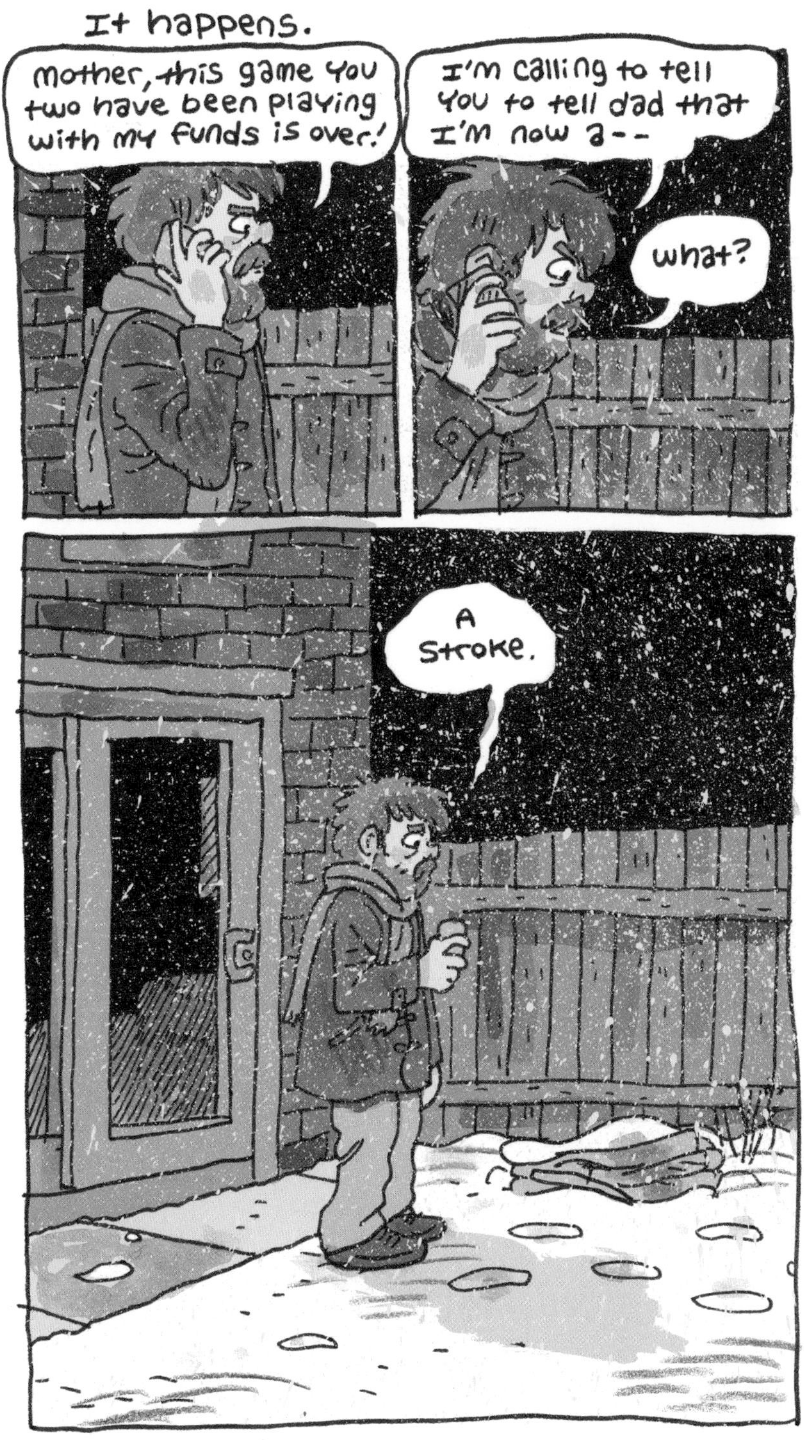
It happens.
Mother, this game you two have been playing with my funds is over!
I'm calling to tell you to tell dad that I'm now a--
what?
A stroke.

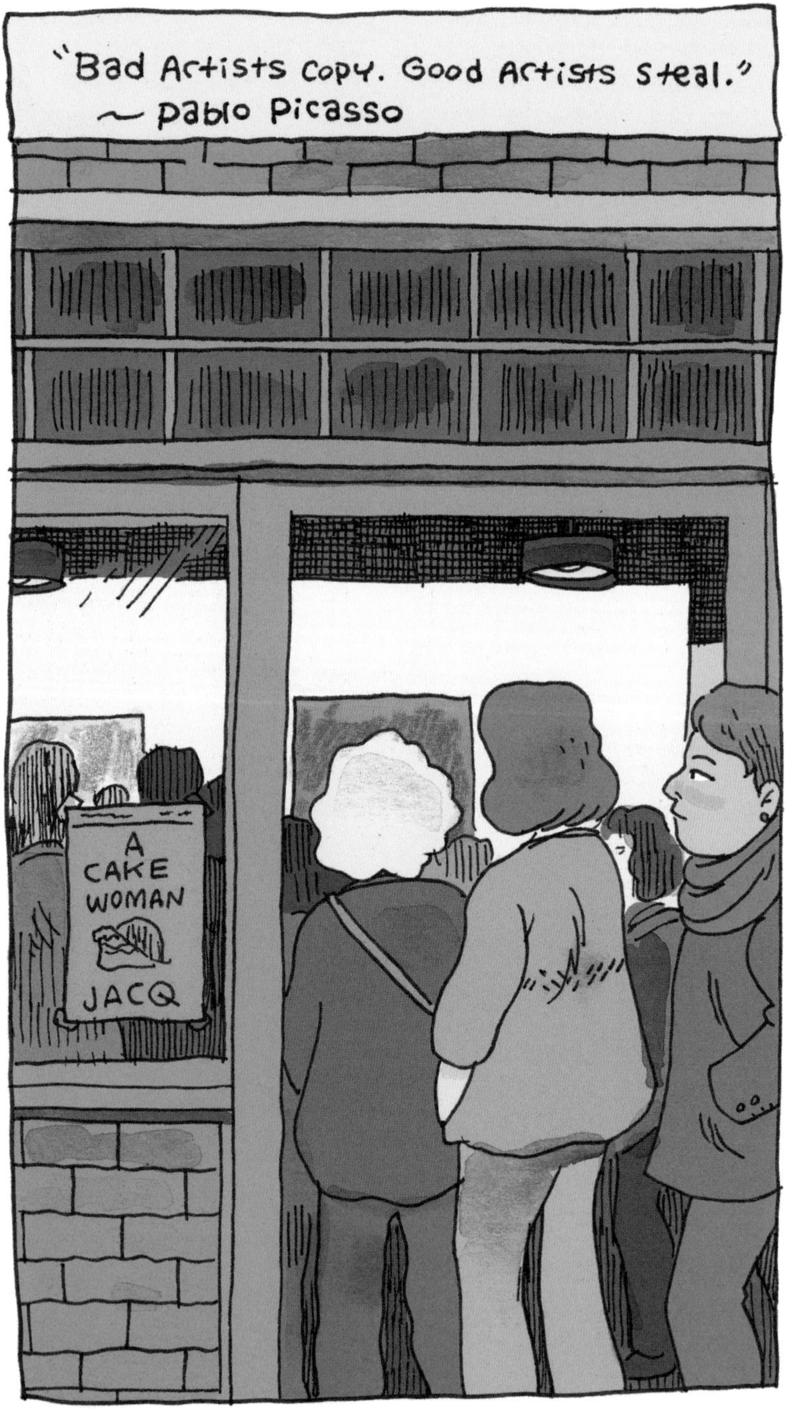
"Bad Artists copy. Good Artists steal."
~ Pablo Picasso
A CAKE WOMAN
JACQ

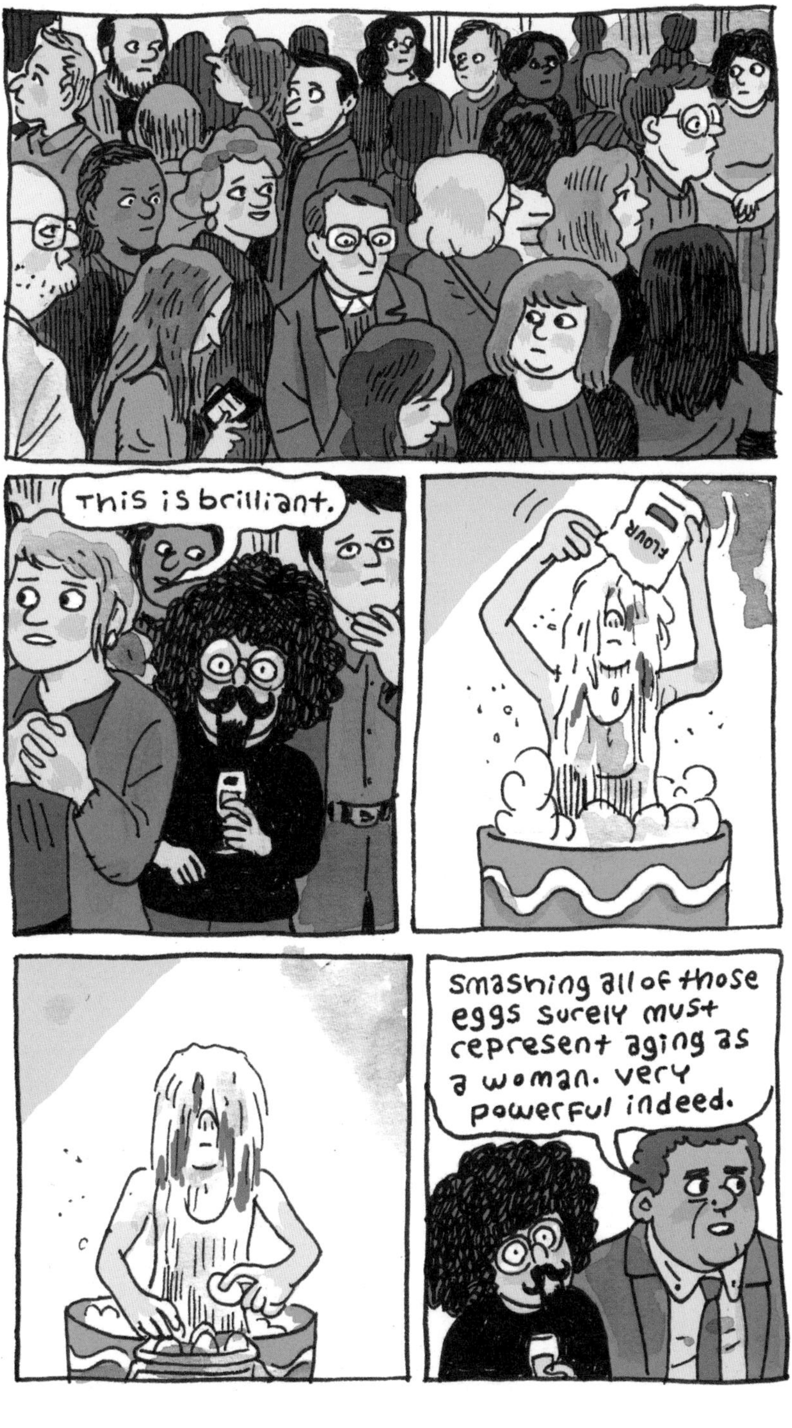
This is brilliant.
FLOUR
Smashing all of those eggs surely must represent aging as a woman. Very powerful indeed.

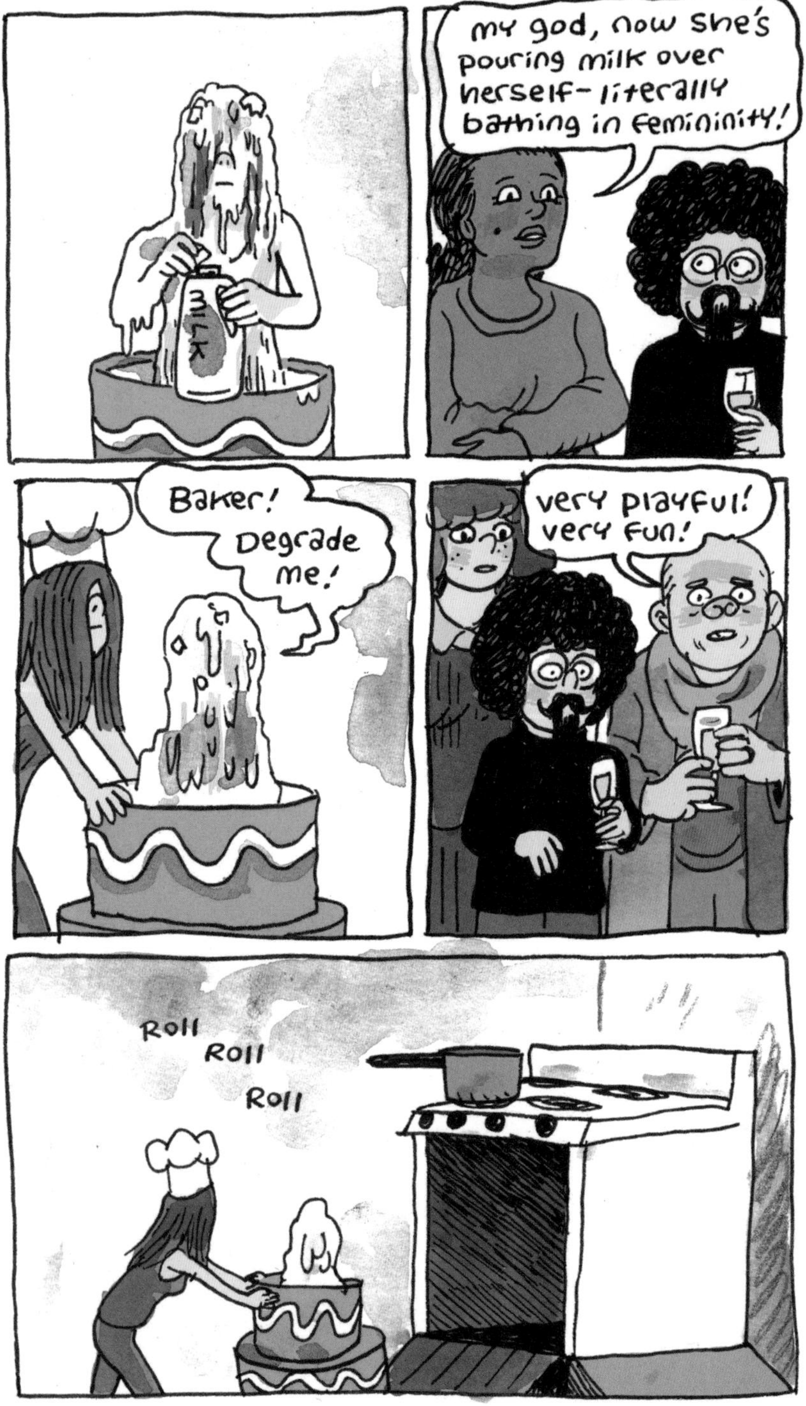

MILK
my god, now she's pouring milk over herself- literally bathing in femininity!
Baker! Degrade me!
very playful! very fun!
Roll
Roll
Roll

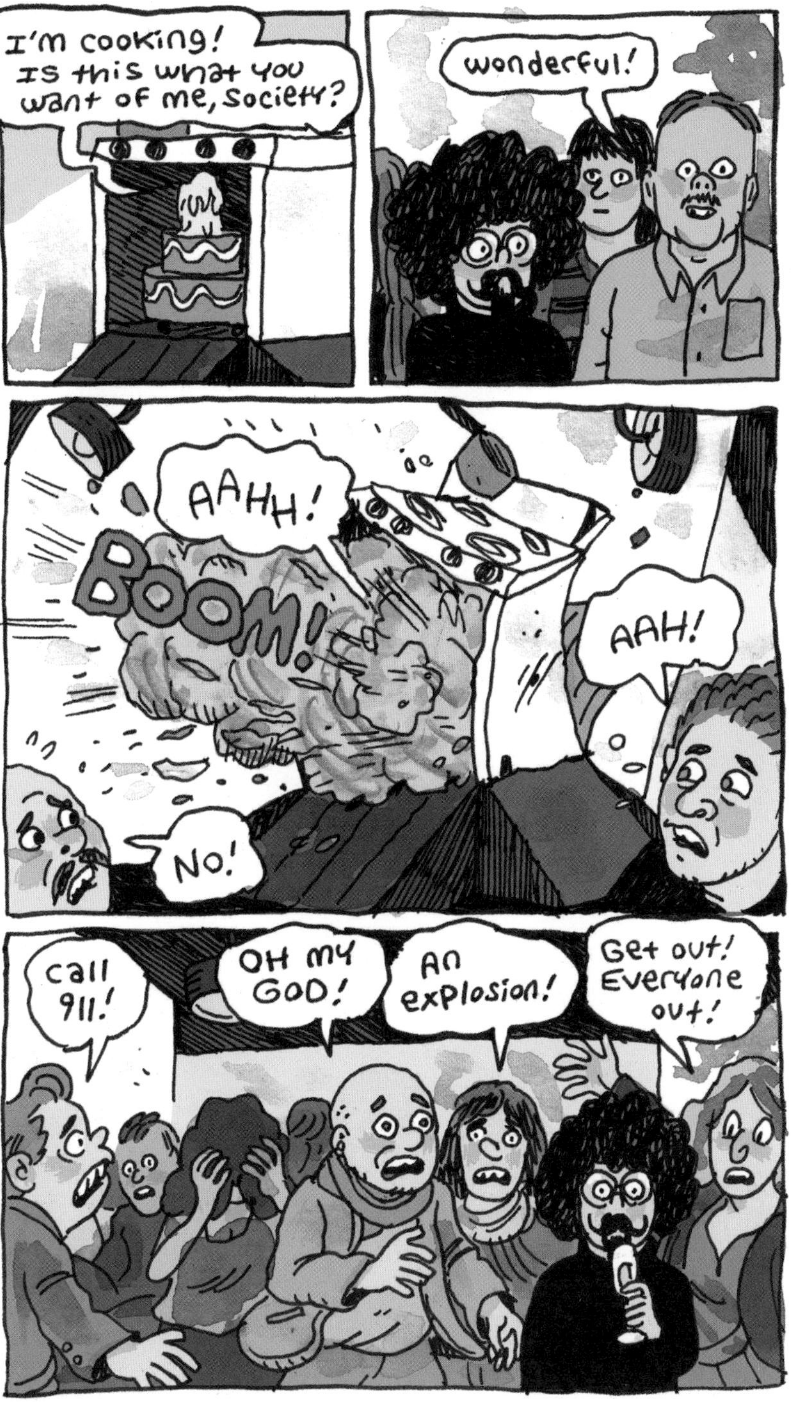
I'm cooking! Is this what you want of me, society?
wonderful!
AAHH!
BOOM!
AAH!
No!
call 911!
OH my GOD!
An explosion!
Get out! Everyone out!

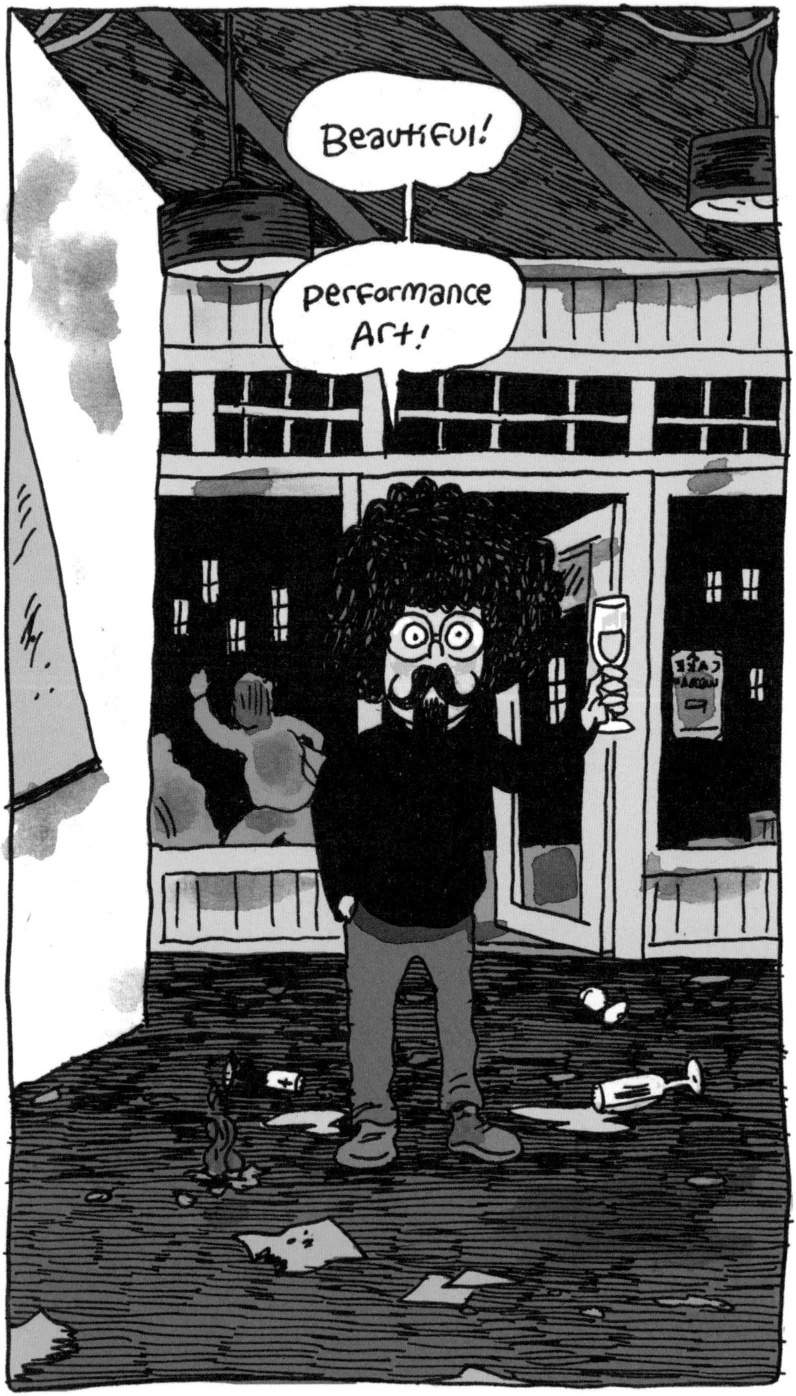
Beautiful!
Performance Art!

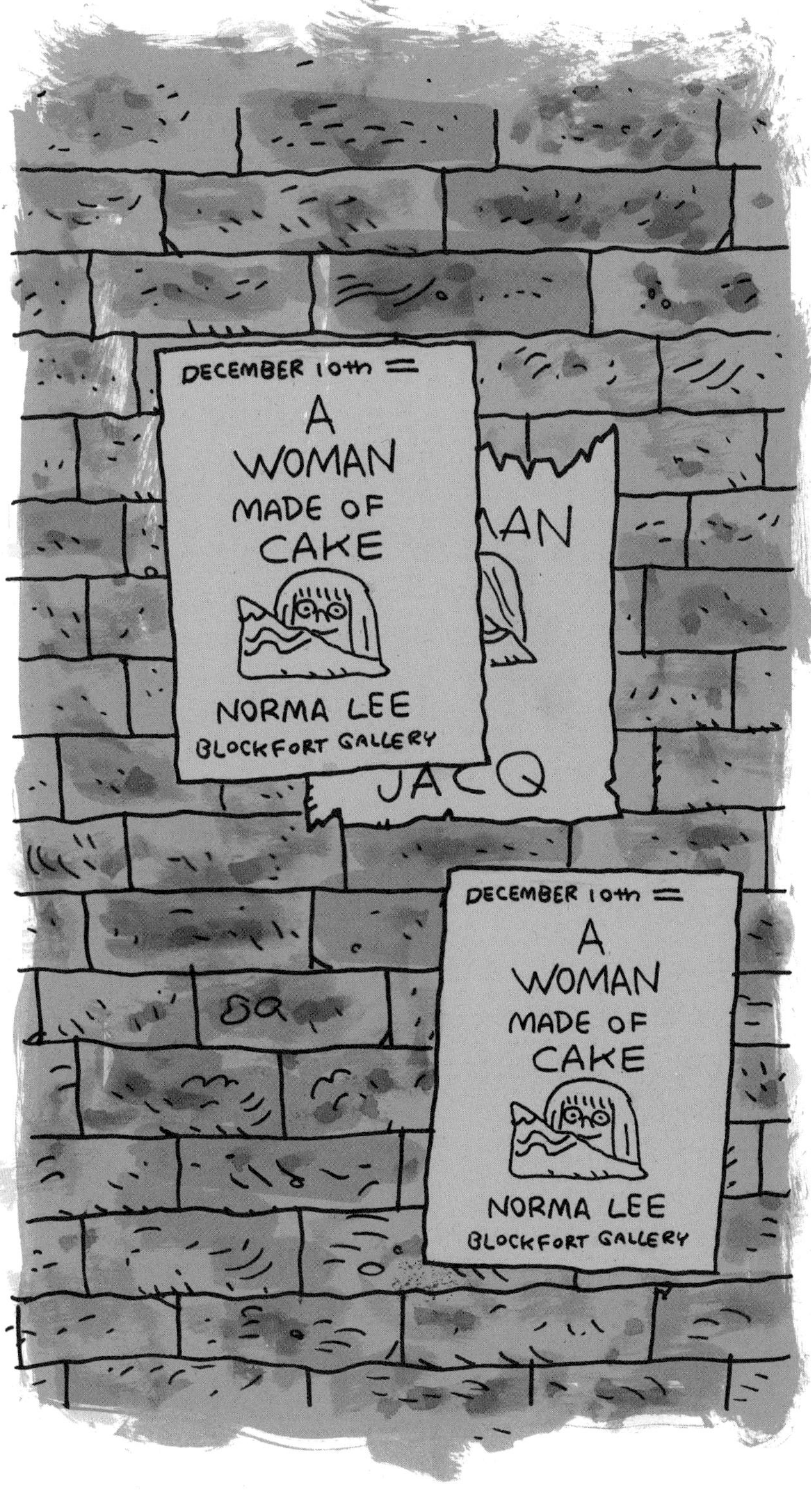
DECEMBER 10th =
A WOMAN MADE OF CAKE
NORMA LEE
BLOCKFORT GALLERY
MAN
JACQ
DECEMBER 10th =
A WOMAN MADE OF CAKE
NORMA LEE
BLOCKFORT GALLERY

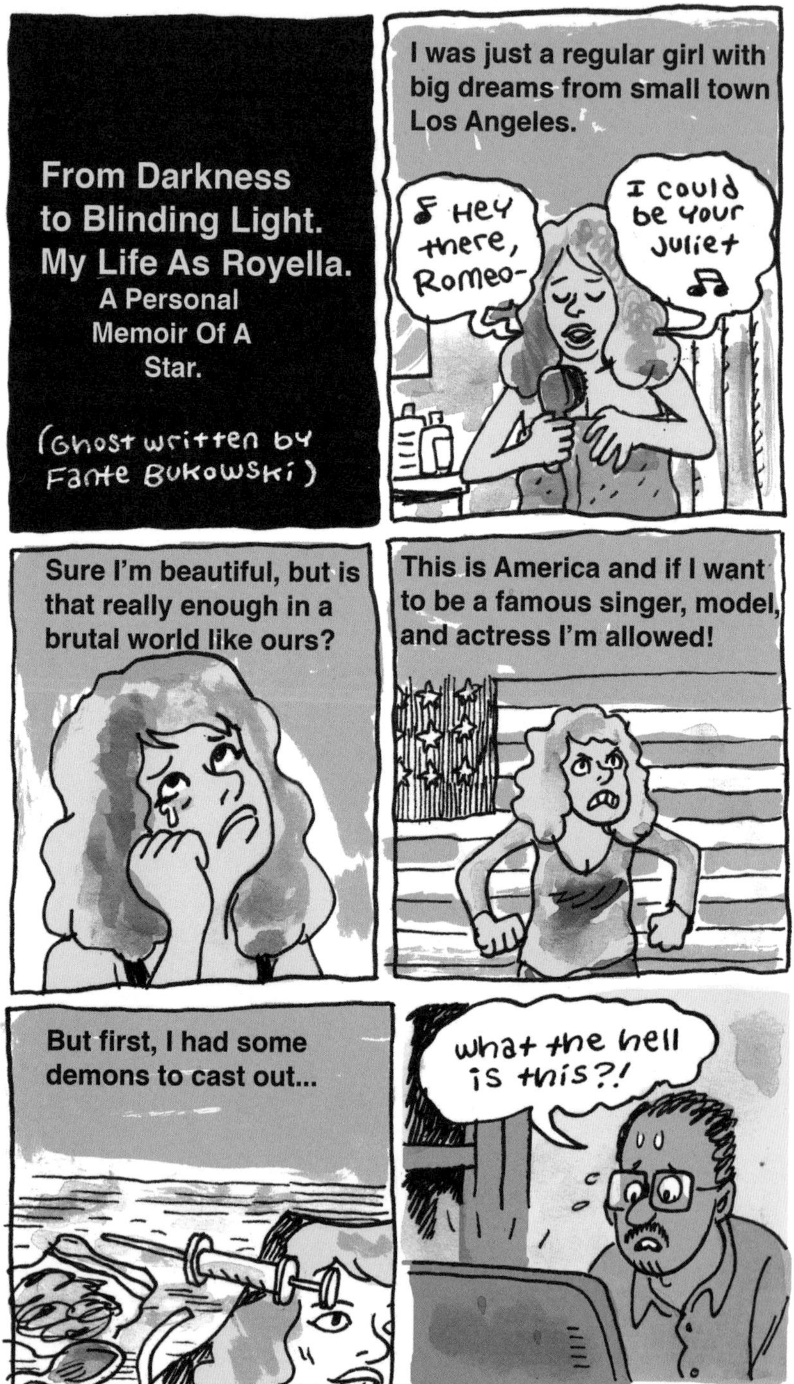

From Darkness to Blinding Light. My Life As Royella.
A Personal Memoir Of A Star.
(Ghost written by Fante Bukowski)
I was just a regular girl with big dreams from small town Los Angeles.
Hey there, Romeo-
I could be your Juliet
Sure I'm beautiful, but is that really enough in a brutal world like ours?
This is America and if I want to be a famous singer, model, and actress I'm allowed!
But first, I had some demons to cast out...
what the hell is this?!

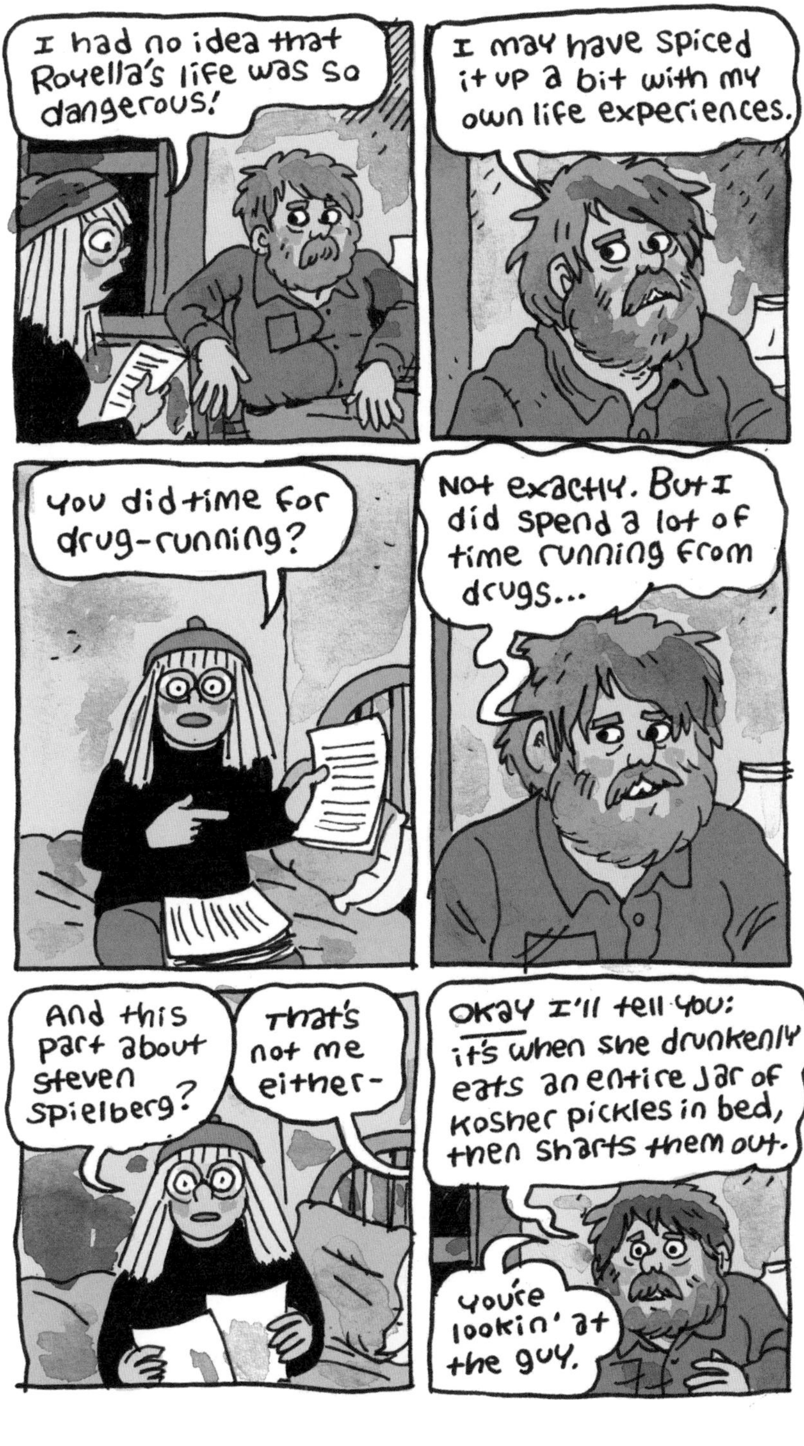
I had no idea that Royella's life was so dangerous!
I may have spiced it up a bit with my own life experiences.
You did time for drug-running?
Not exactly. But I did spend a lot of time running from drugs...
And this part about Steven Spielberg?
That's not me either-
Okay I'll tell you: it's when she drunkenly eats an entire jar of kosher pickles in bed, then sharts them out.
You're lookin' at the guy.

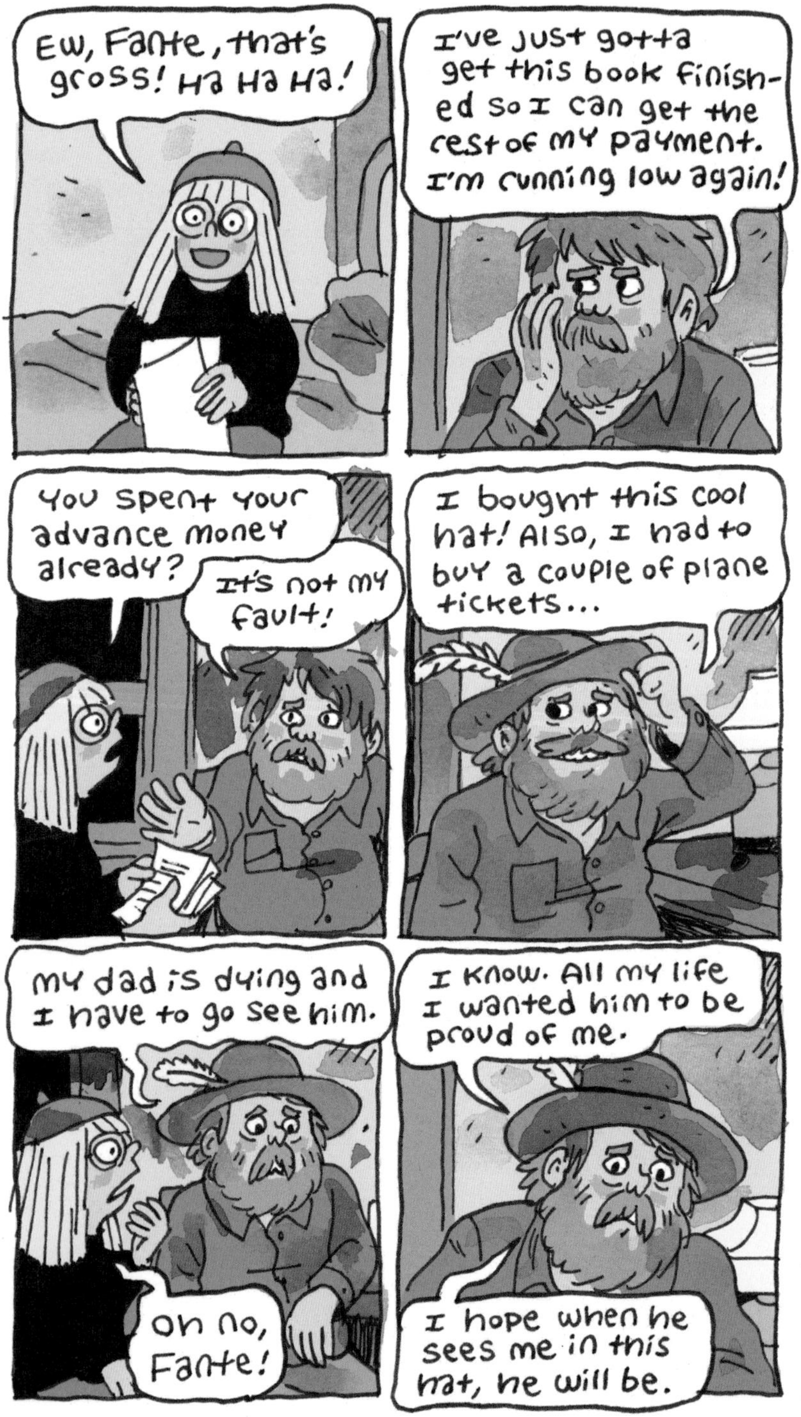
Ew, Fante, that's gross! Ha Ha Ha!
I've just gotta get this book finished so I can get the rest of my payment. I'm running low again!
You spent your advance money already?
It's not my fault!
I bought this cool hat! Also, I had to buy a couple of plane tickets...
My dad is dying and I have to go see him.
Oh no, Fante!
I know. All my life I wanted him to be proud of me.
I hope when he sees me in this hat, he will be.

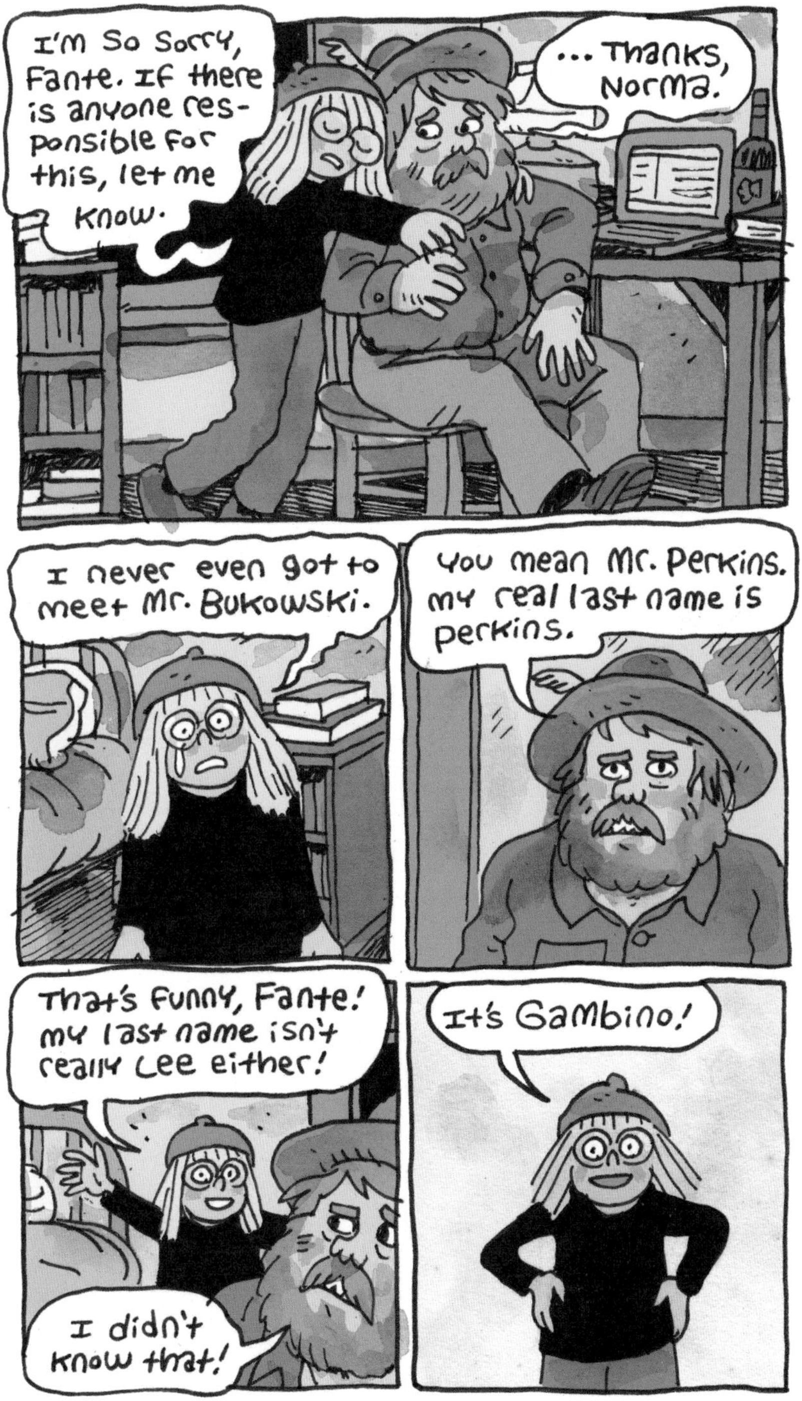
I'm So Sorry, Fante. If there is anyone res-ponsible for this, let me know.
...Thanks, Norma.
I never even got to meet Mr. Bukowski.
You mean Mr. Perkins. My real last name is Perkins.
That's funny, Fante! My last name isn't really Lee either!
I didn't know that!
It's Gambino!

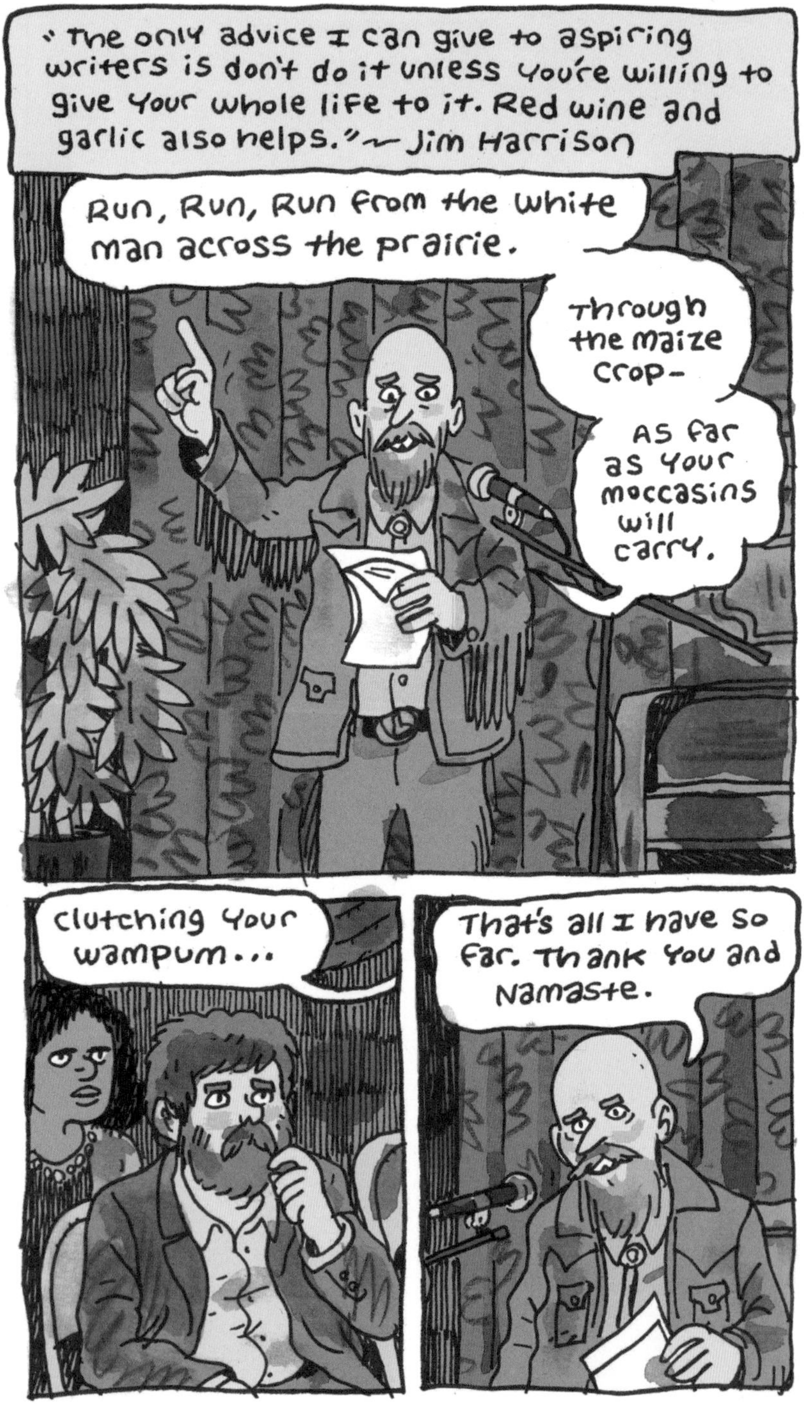
"The only advice I can give to aspiring writers is don't do it unless you're willing to give your whole life to it. Red wine and garlic also helps." ~ Jim Harrison
Run, Run, Run from the white man across the prairie.
Through the maize crop–
As far as your moccasins will carry.
Clutching your wampum...
That's all I have so far. Thank you and Namaste.

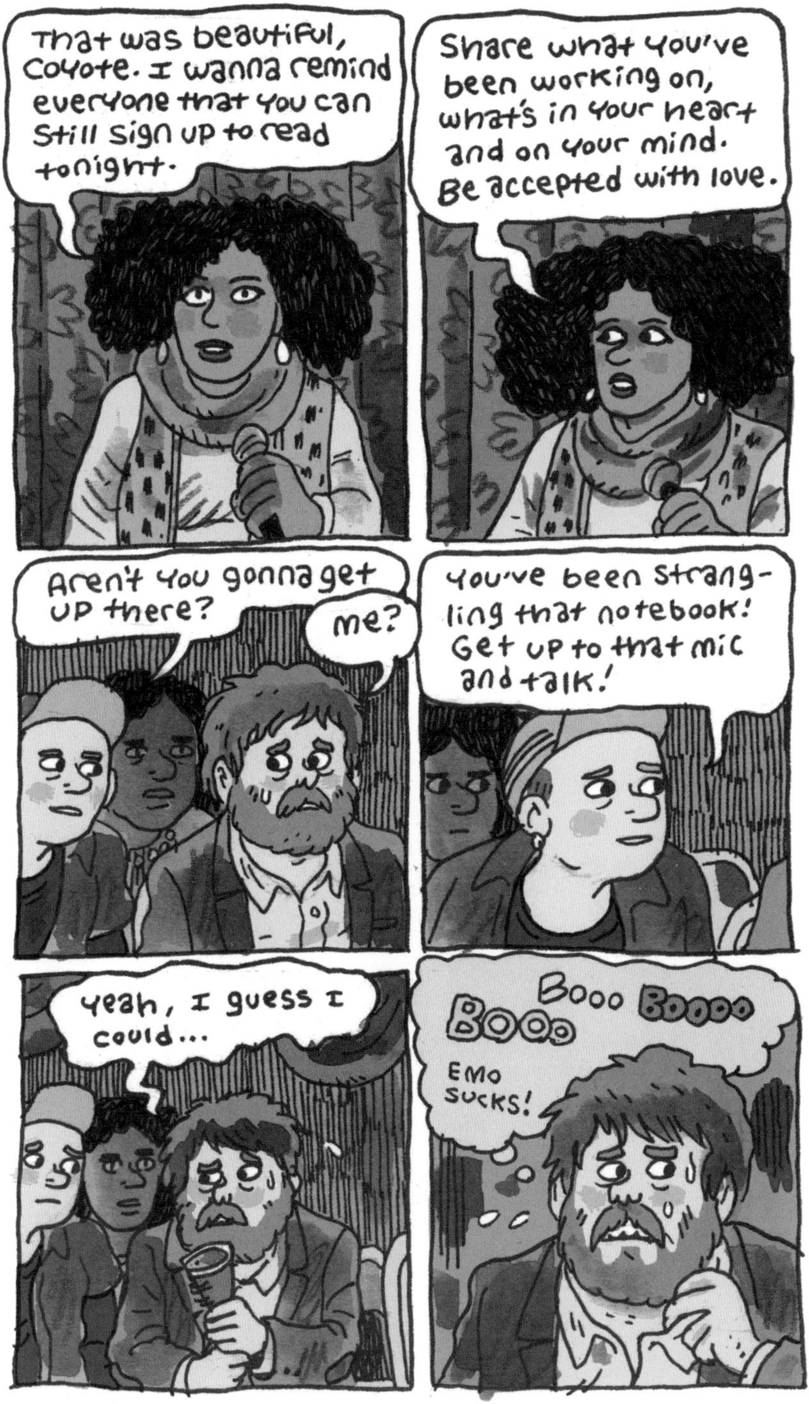
That was beautiful, Coyote. I wanna remind everyone that you can still sign up to read tonight.
Share what you've been working on, what's in your heart and on your mind. Be accepted with love.
Aren't you gonna get up there?
me?
You've been strangling that notebook! Get up to that mic and talk!
yeah, I guess I could...
Booo Boooo BOOo
EMO SUCKS!

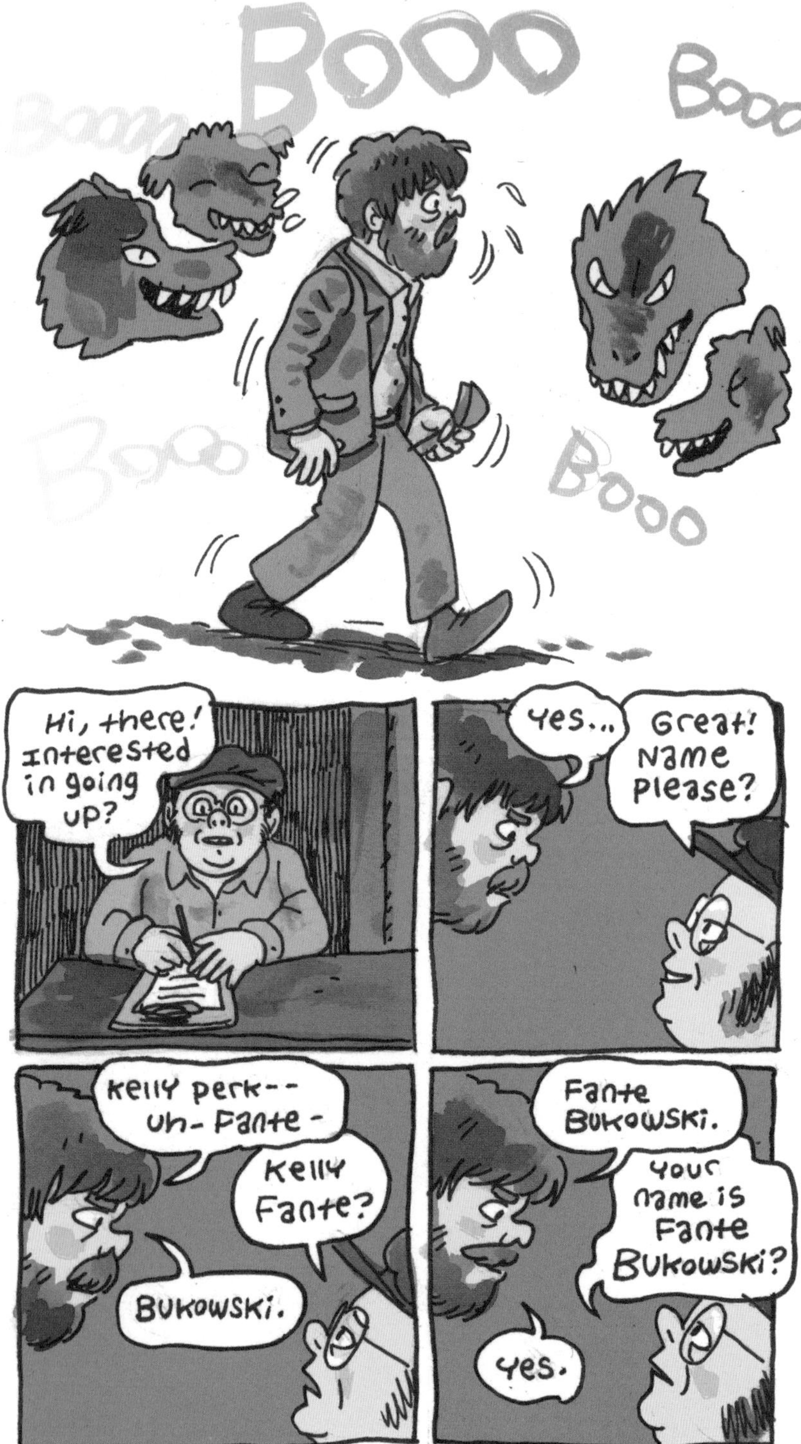
BOOO
Booo
Booo
Booo
Booo
Hi, there! Interested in going up?
Yes...
Great! Name please?
Kelly Perk-- uh- Fante-
Kelly Fante?
Bukowski.
Fante Bukowski.
Your name is Fante Bukowski?
Yes.

Next up to the mic is the "Struggling writer," Mr. Fante Bukowski. Give him a warm acceptance.

clap clap clap clap

Hello. This is my premiere...

Here's a short story I've been working on titled "Date Night with Bourbon."

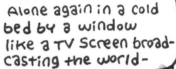

Alone again in a cold bed by a window like a TV screen broadcasting the world—

Shuffling and hustling about like an ant colony.

Only this bottle of bourbon to soften the room like the padded walls of a cell.

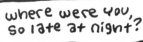
where were you, so late at night?

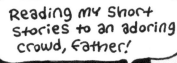
Reading my short stories to an adoring crowd, father!

I'm a writer now!

And I call myself, "Fante Bukowski!"

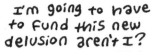
I'm going to have to fund this new delusion aren't I?

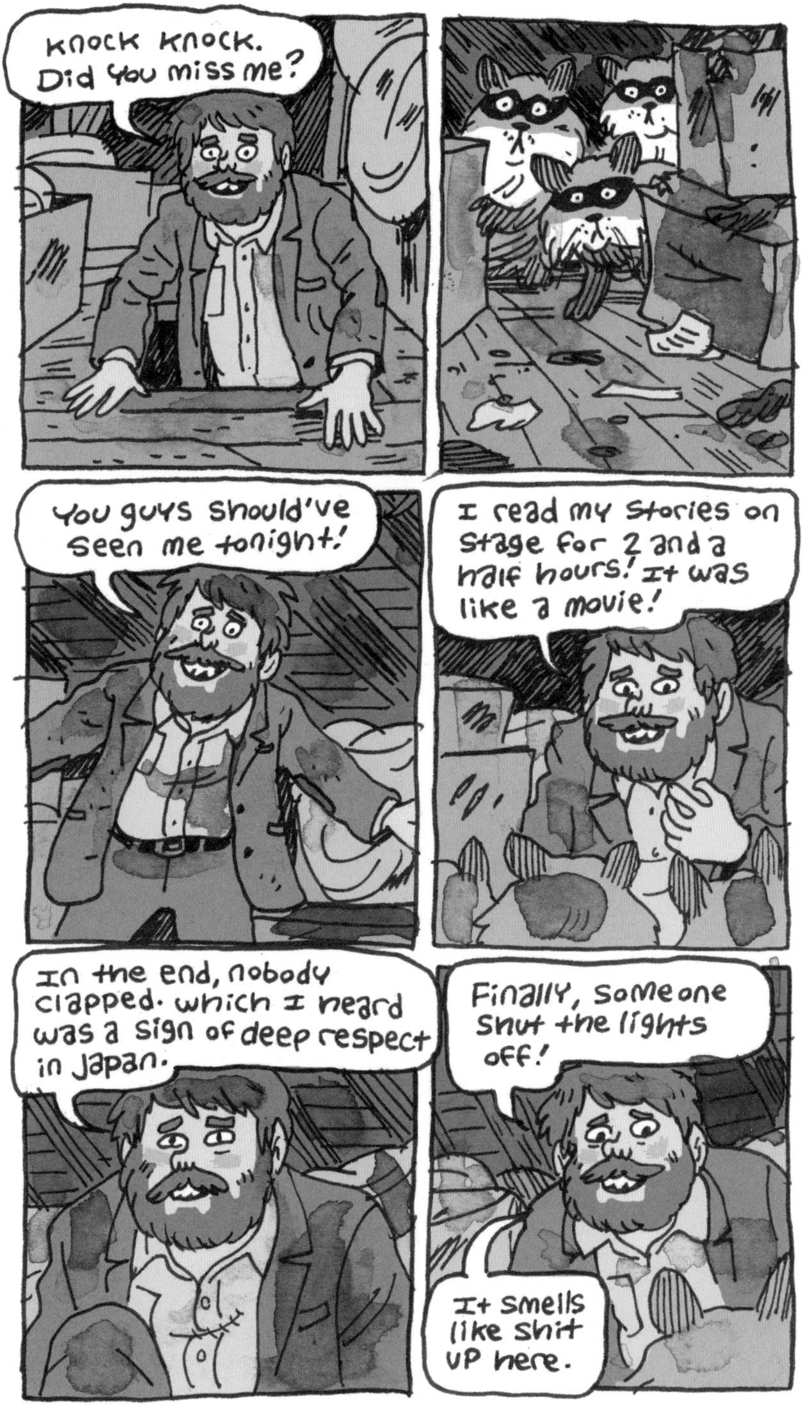
Knock Knock. Did you miss me?
You guys should've seen me tonight!
I read my stories on stage for 2 and a half hours! It was like a movie!
In the end, nobody clapped. which I heard was a sign of deep respect in Japan.
Finally, someone shut the lights off!
It smells like shit up here.

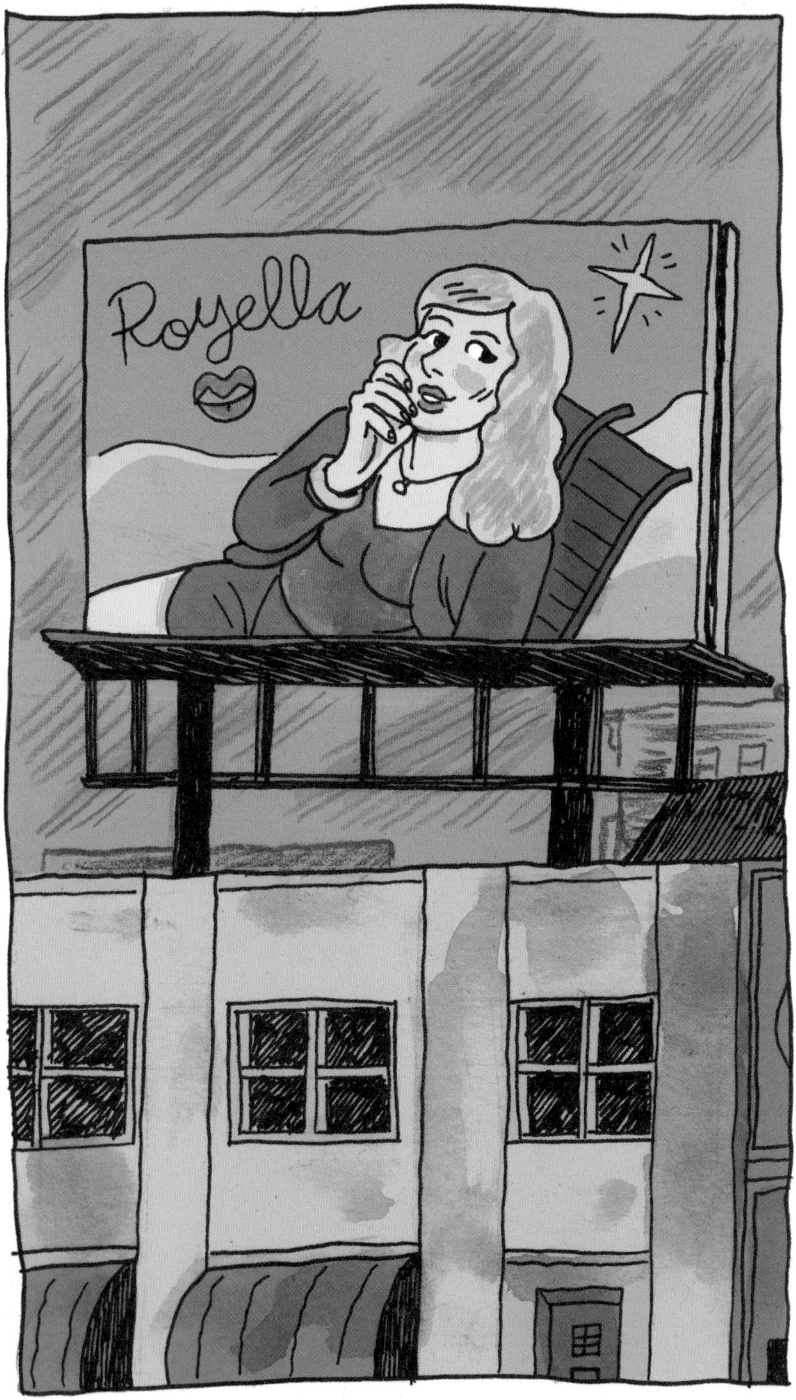
Royella

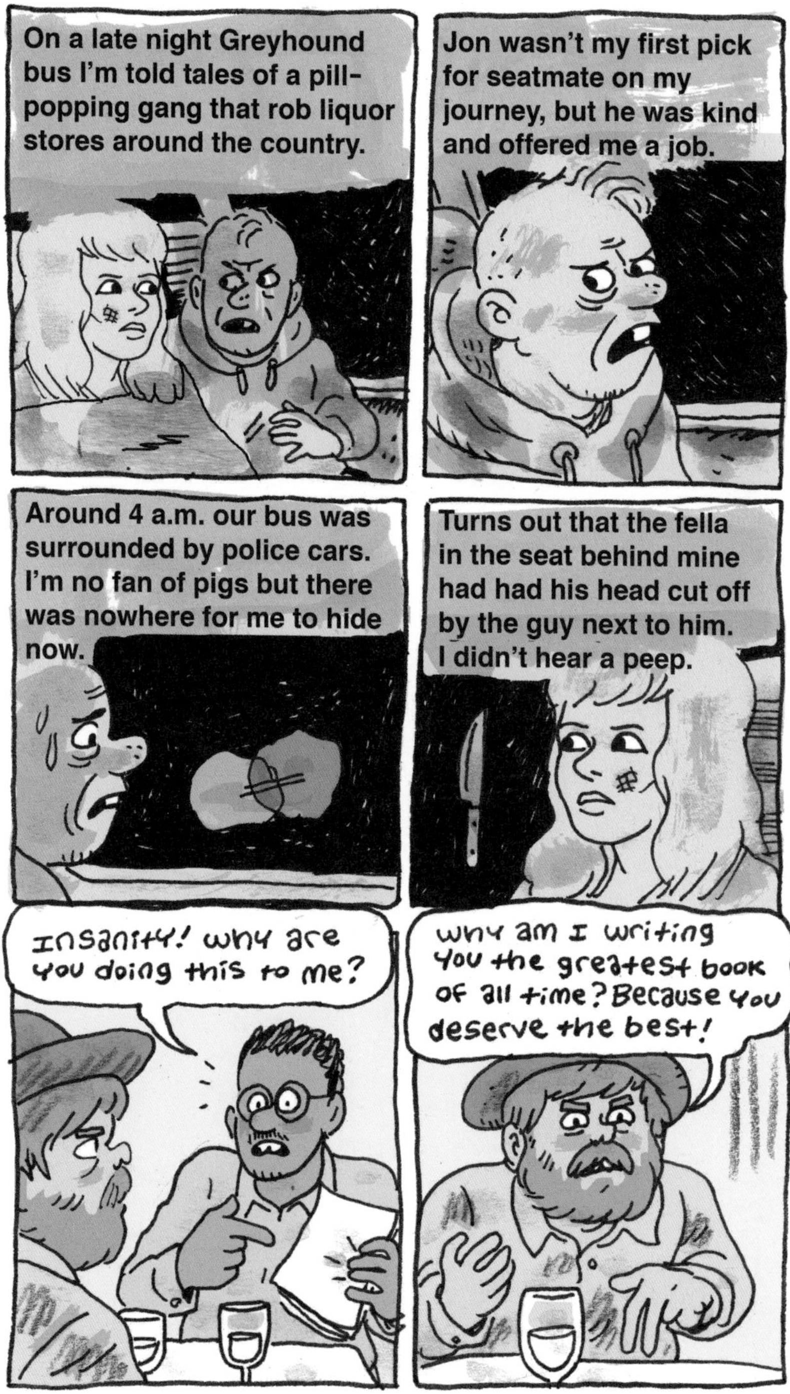
On a late night Greyhound bus I'm told tales of a pill-popping gang that rob liquor stores around the country.
Jon wasn't my first pick for seatmate on my journey, but he was kind and offered me a job.
Around 4 a.m. our bus was surrounded by police cars. I'm no fan of pigs but there was nowhere for me to hide now.
Turns out that the fella in the seat behind mine had had his head cut off by the guy next to him. I didn't hear a peep.
Insanity! Why are you doing this to me?
Why am I writing you the greatest book of all time? Because you deserve the best!

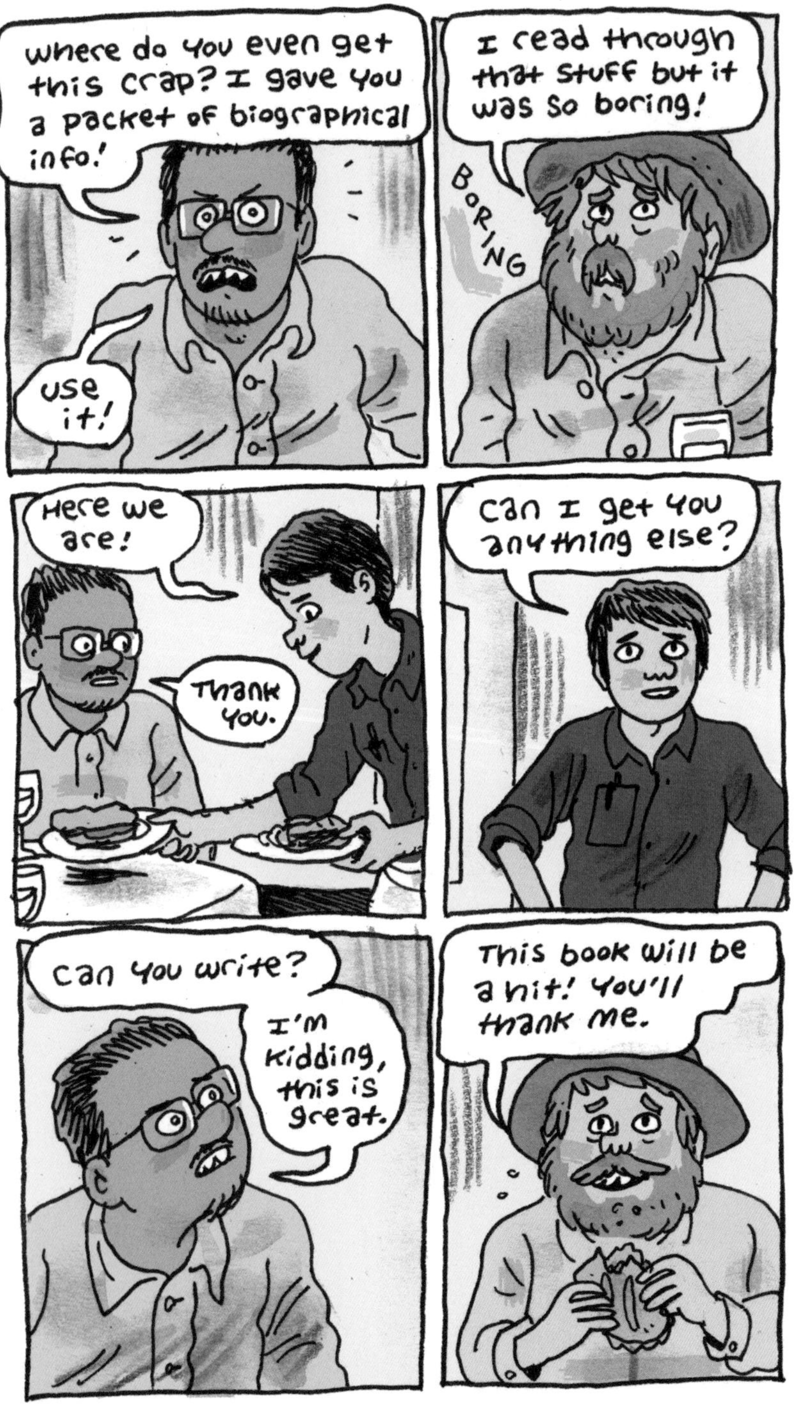
where do you even get this crap? I gave you a packet of biographical info!
use it!
I read through that stuff but it was so boring!
BORING
Here we are!
Thank you.
Can I get you anything else?
Can you write?
I'm kidding, this is great.
This book will be a hit! You'll thank me.

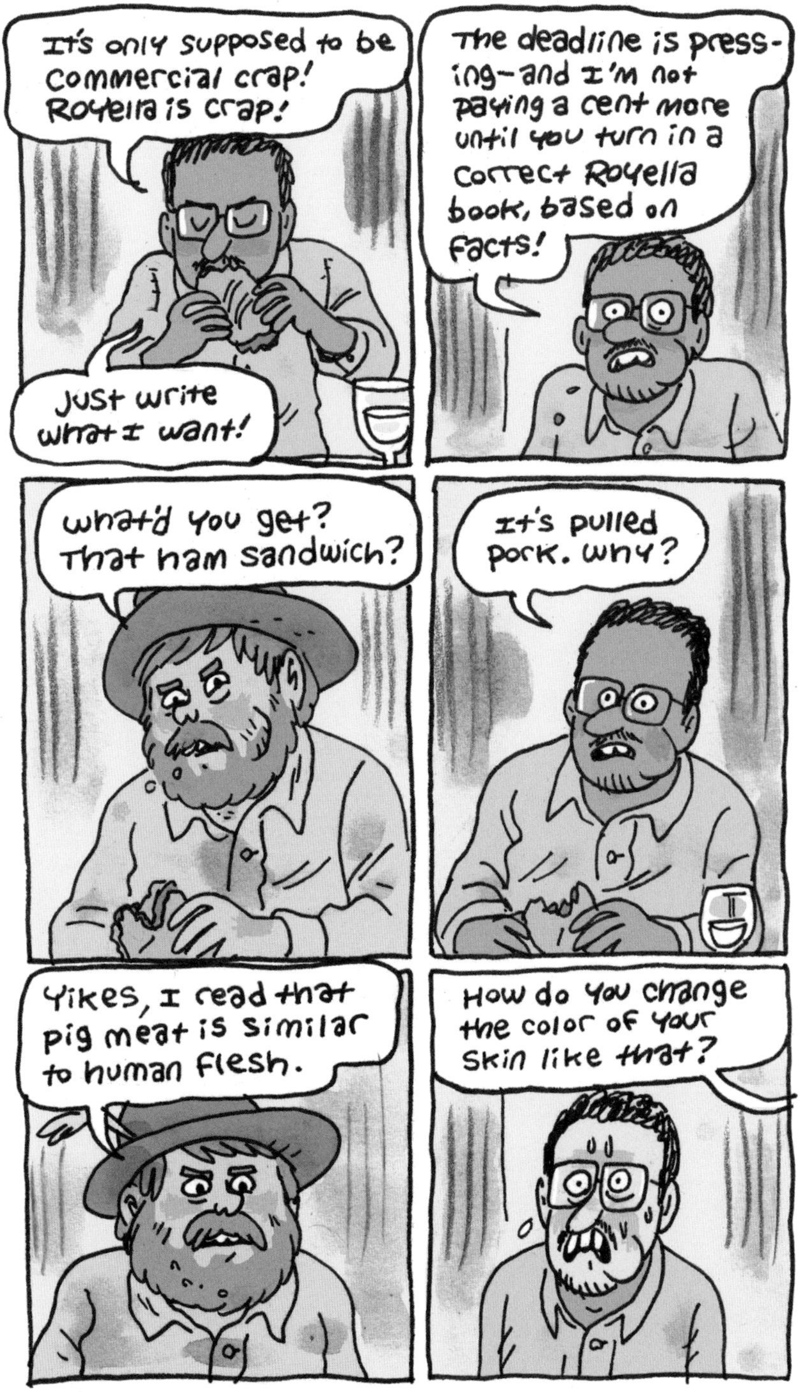
It's only supposed to be commercial crap! Royella is crap!
Just write what I want!
The deadline is pressing—and I'm not paying a cent more until you turn in a correct Royella book, based on facts!
What'd you get? That ham sandwich?
It's pulled pork. Why?
Yikes, I read that pig meat is similar to human flesh.
How do you change the color of your skin like that?

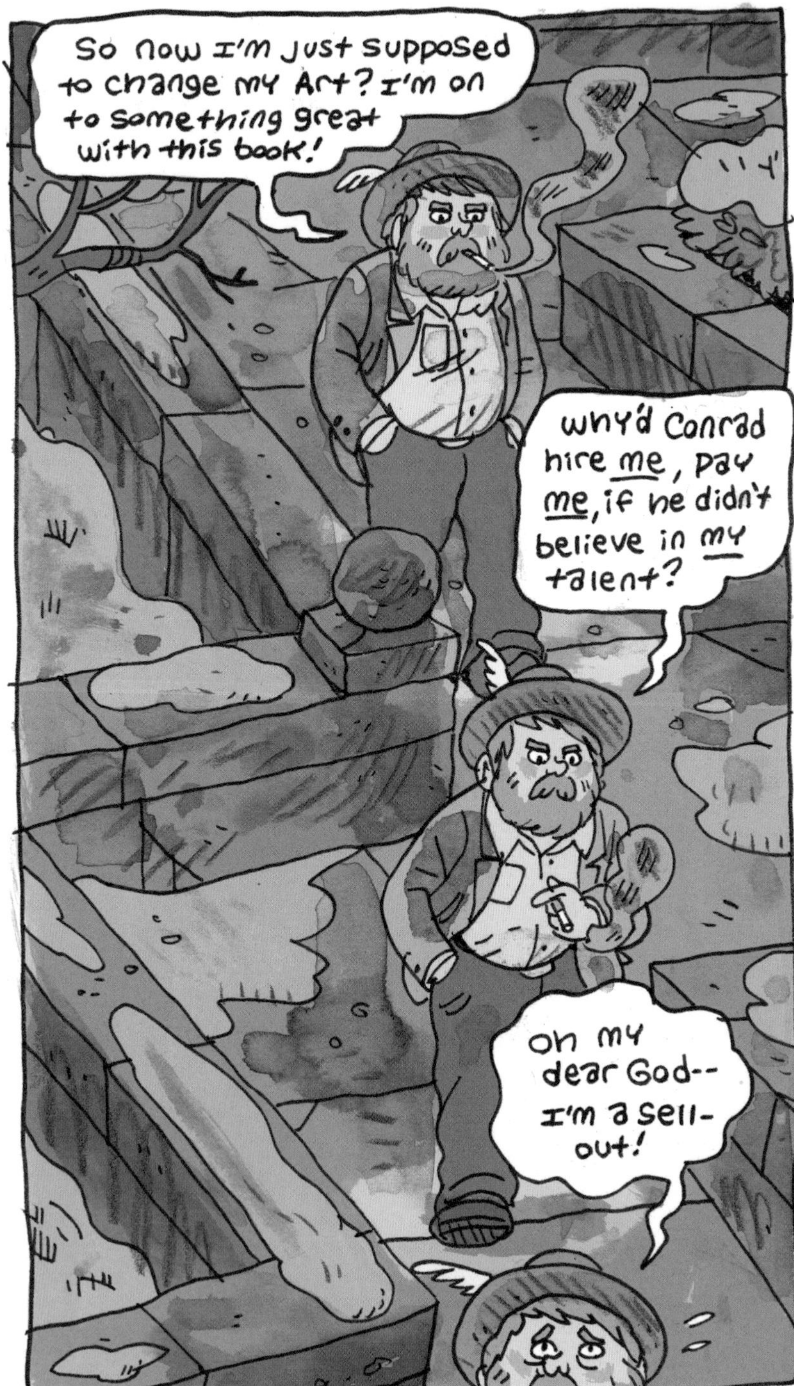
So now I'm just supposed to change my Art? I'm on to something great with this book!
Why'd Conrad hire me, pay me, if he didn't believe in my talent?
Oh my dear God-- I'm a sell-out!

Norma at work.

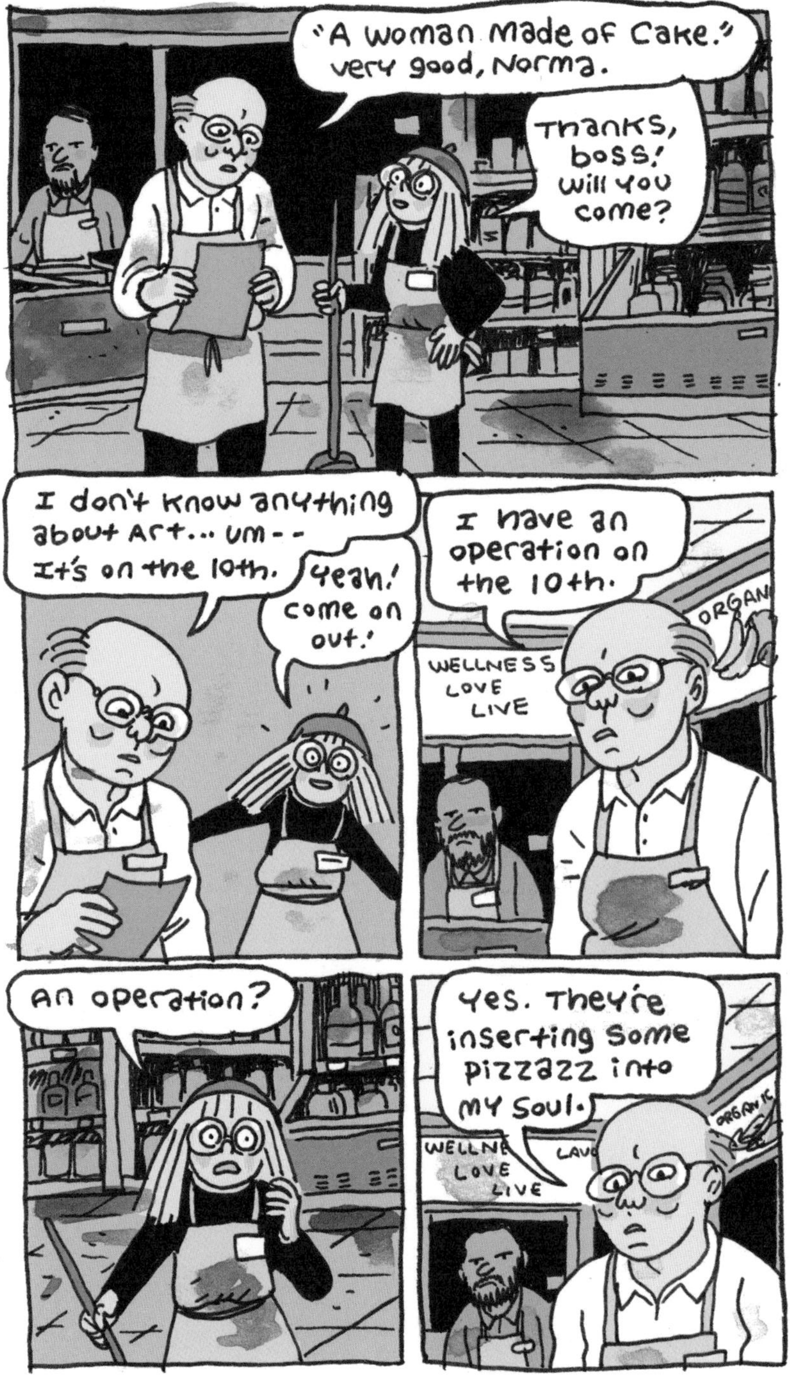

"A woman made of cake." very good, Norma.
Thanks, boss! will you come?
I don't know anything about Art... um-- It's on the 10th.
yeah! come on out!
I have an operation on the 10th.
WELLNESS LOVE LIVE
ORGAN
An operation?
yes. They're inserting some pizzazz into my soul.
WELLNE LOVE LIVE
LAV
ORGANIC

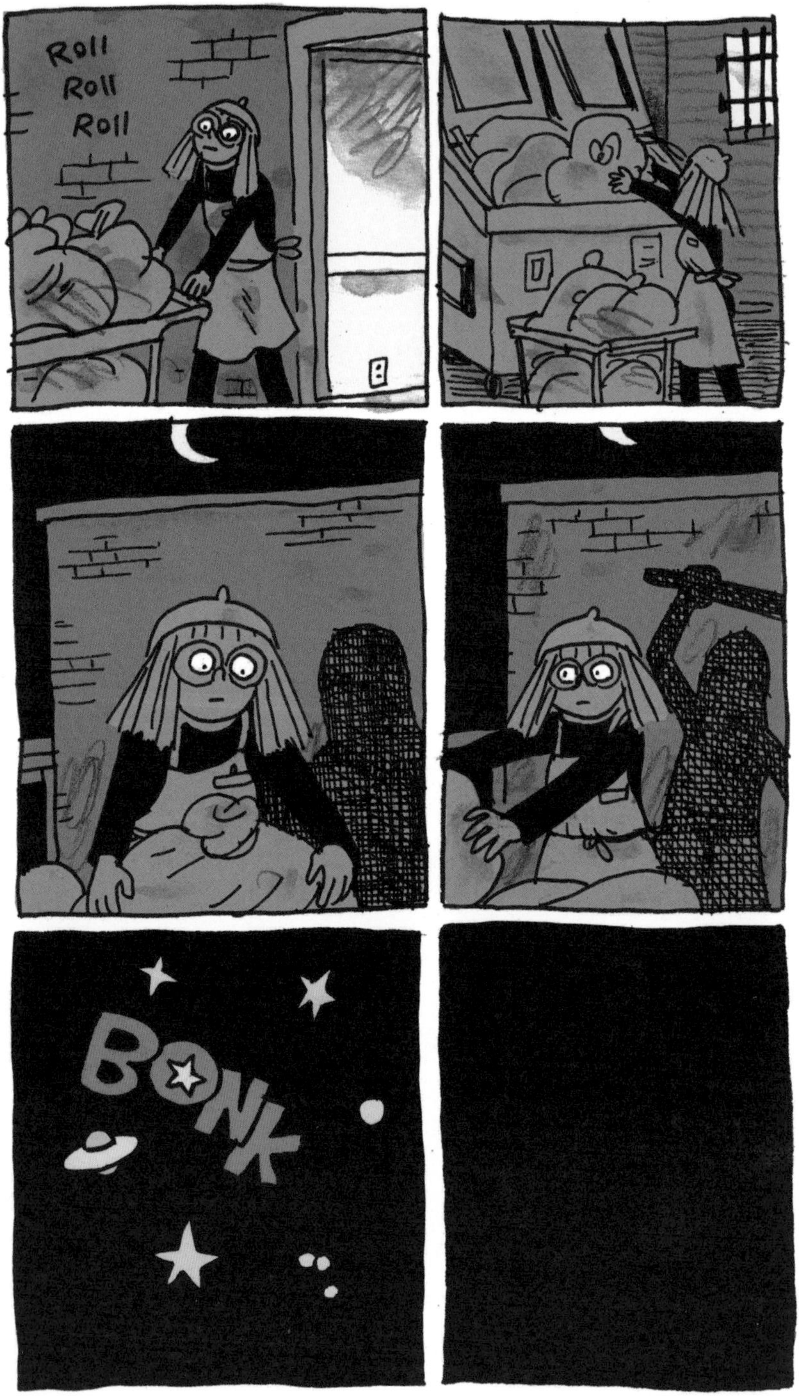
Roll
Roll
Roll
BONK

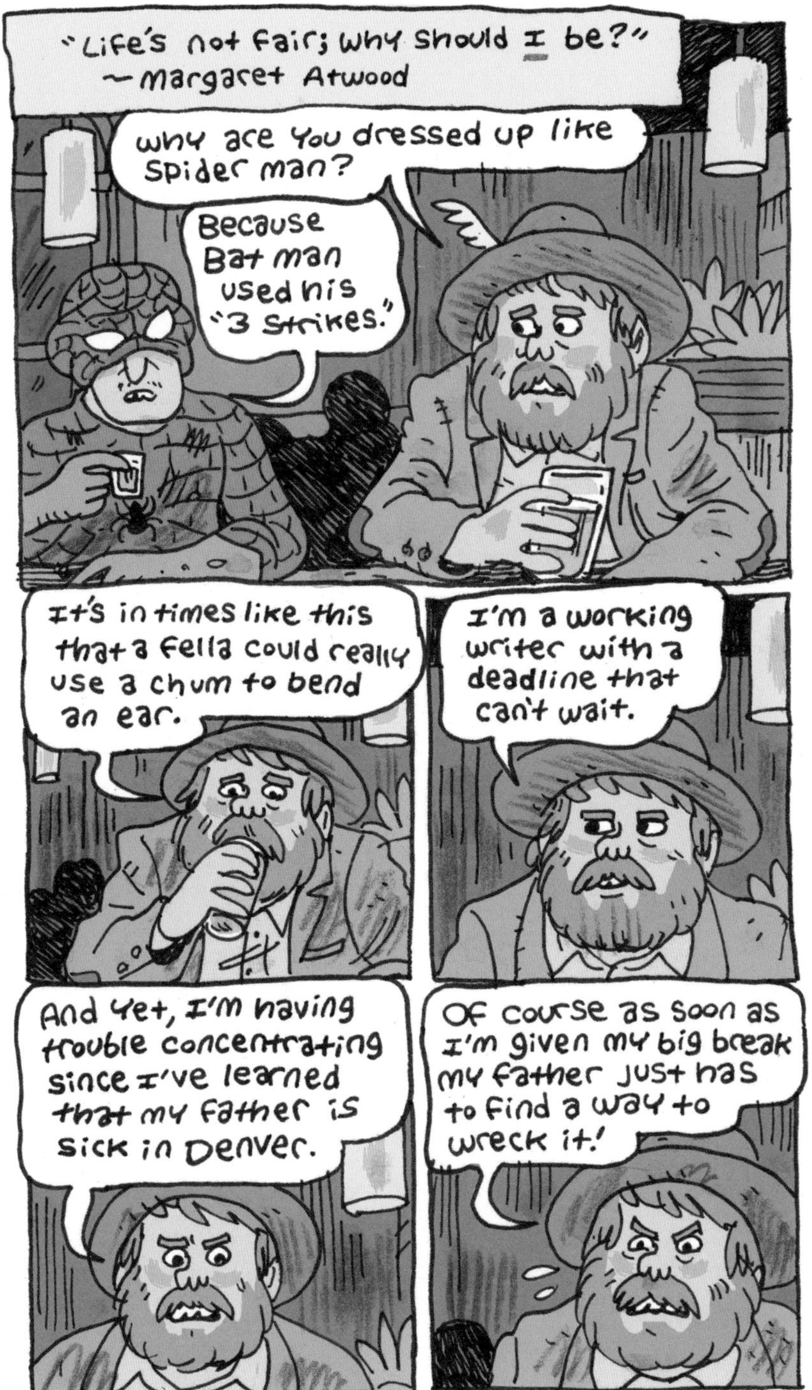

"Life's not fair; why should I be?"
~Margaret Atwood
Why are you dressed up like Spider man?
Because Bat man used his "3 Strikes."
It's in times like this that a fella could really use a chum to bend an ear.
I'm a working writer with a deadline that can't wait.
And yet, I'm having trouble concentrating since I've learned that my father is sick in Denver.
Of course as soon as I'm given my big break my father just has to find a way to wreck it!

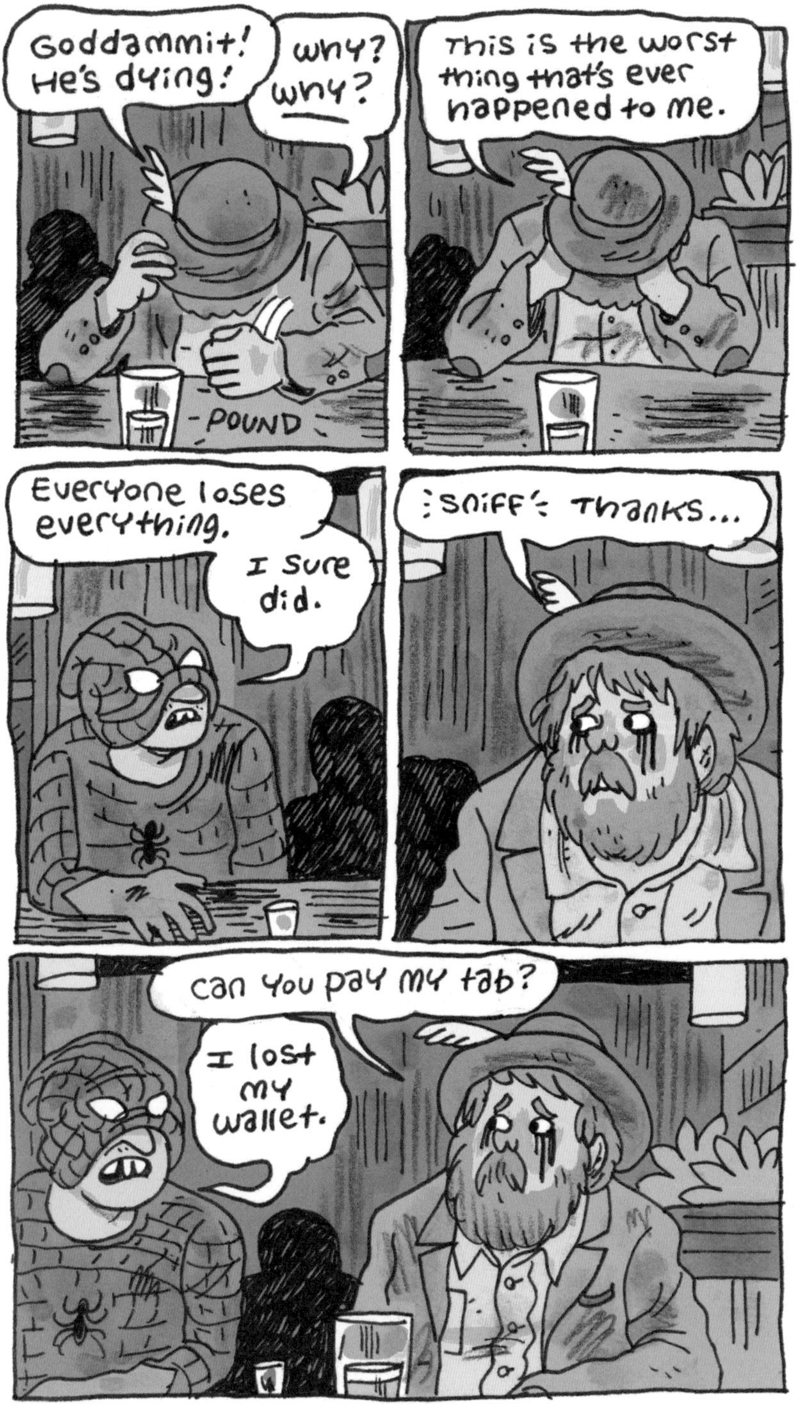
Goddammit! He's dying!
why? why?
POUND
This is the worst thing that's ever happened to me.
Everyone loses everything.
I sure did.
SNIFF Thanks...
Can you pay my tab?
I lost my wallet.

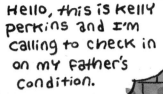

Hello, this is Kelly Perkins and I'm calling to check in on my father's condition.

Ah, yes, Kelly, good of you to call. Your father is still in a coma caused by his stroke.

I'm sorry to say.

Is my mother with him?

She's been by his side. Don't worry.

Y'know, I have a plane ticket... I'll be there soon. It's just that I wanted to pay for it myself and it was cheaper to fly at a later date.

Heaven is hiring angels, and Mr. Perkins is being interviewed for the gig.

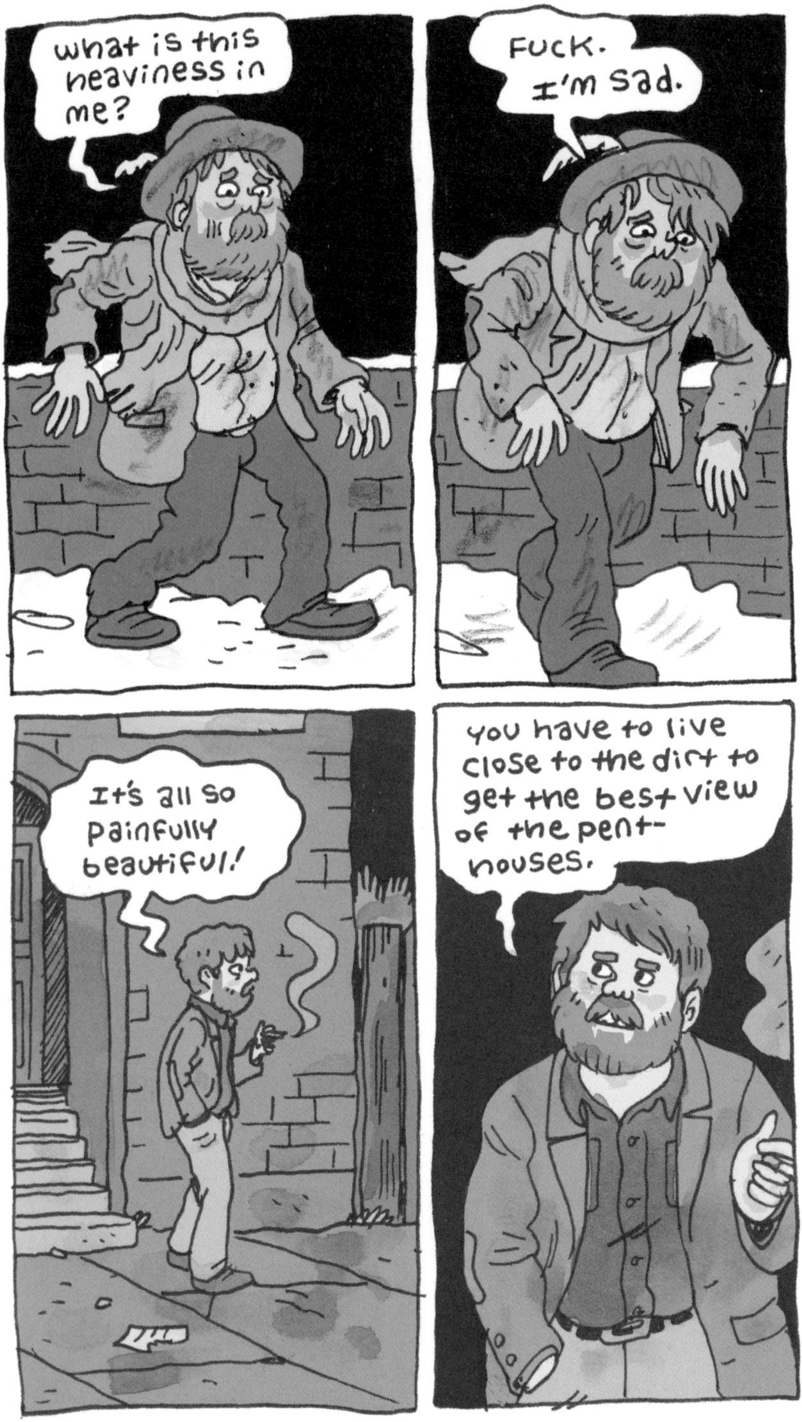
what is this heaviness in me?
Fuck. I'm sad.
It's all so painfully beautiful!
you have to live close to the dirt to get the best view of the pent-houses.

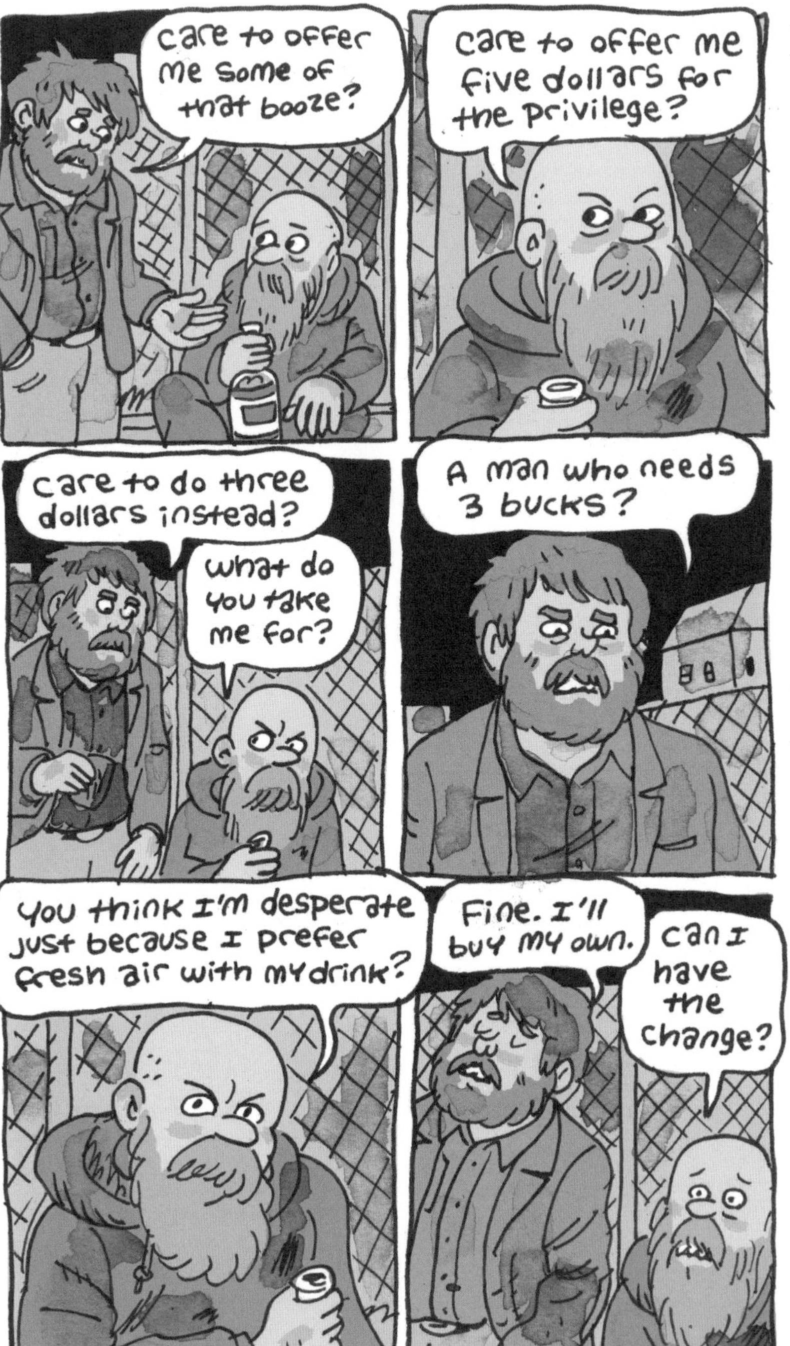
Care to offer me some of that booze?
Care to offer me five dollars for the privilege?
Care to do three dollars instead?
What do you take me for?
A man who needs 3 bucks?
You think I'm desperate just because I prefer fresh air with my drink?
Fine. I'll buy my own.
Can I have the change?

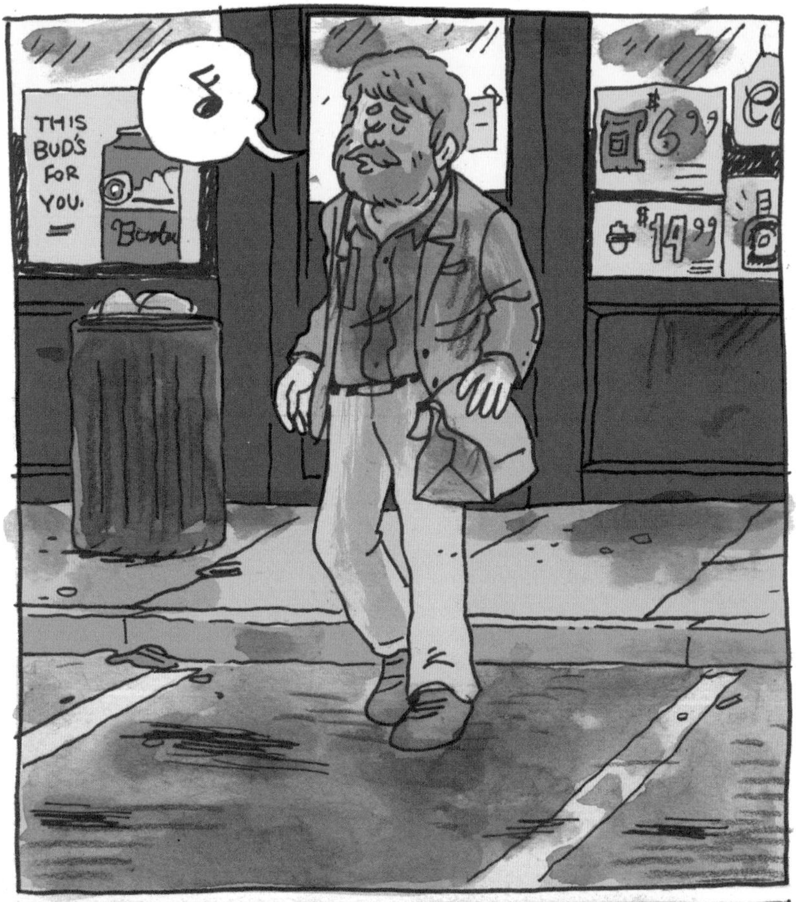
THIS BUD'S FOR YOU.
$6.99
$14.99

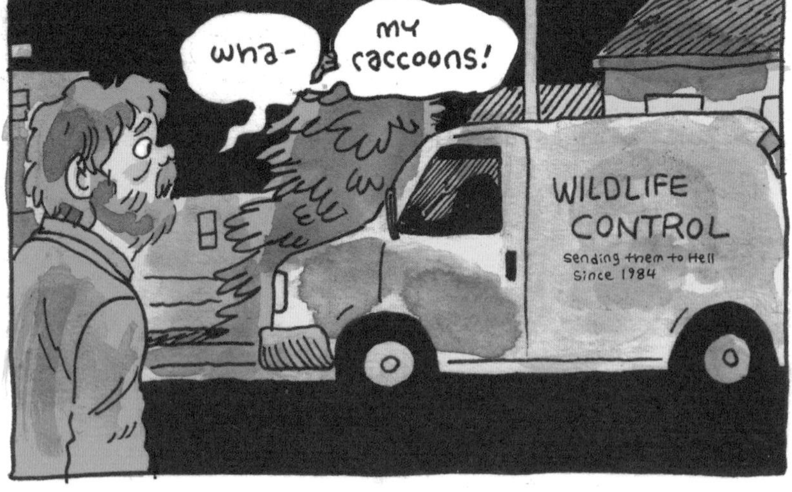
wha-
my raccoons!
WILDLIFE CONTROL
sending them to Hell Since 1984

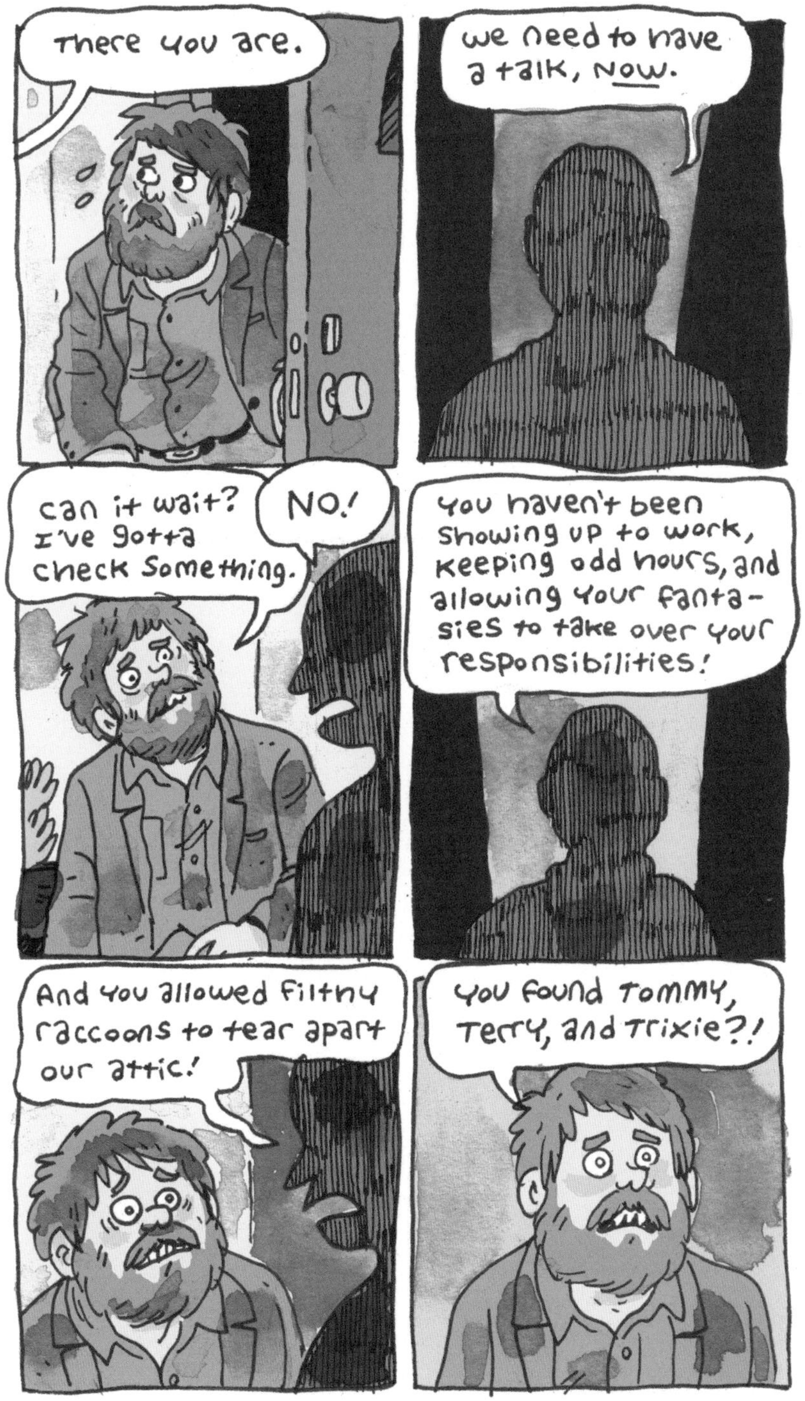
There you are.
we need to have a talk, NOW.
can it wait? I've gotta check something.
NO!
You haven't been showing up to work, keeping odd hours, and allowing your fantasies to take over your responsibilities!
And you allowed filthy raccoons to tear apart our attic!
You found Tommy, Terry, and Trixie?!

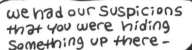
we had our suspicions that you were hiding something up there—

we prayed it wasn't a dead hitchhiker.

what have you done?

what have you done with my friends? Father, what have you done?

Friends? whatever happened to your real friends? Call Curtis once in a while.

Curtis?

Curtis is a jock!

Raccoons are not your friends and neither are dead writers!

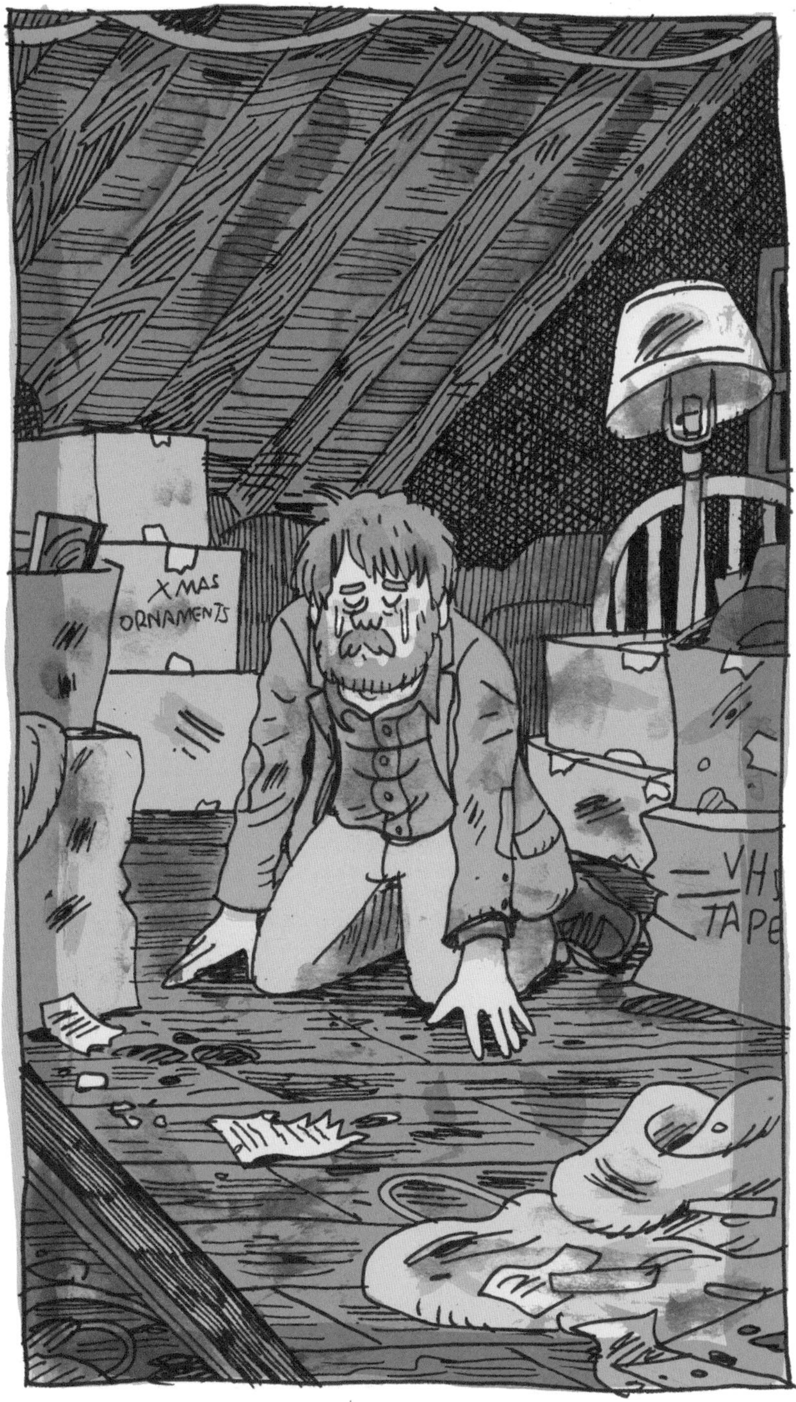
XMAS ORNAMENTS

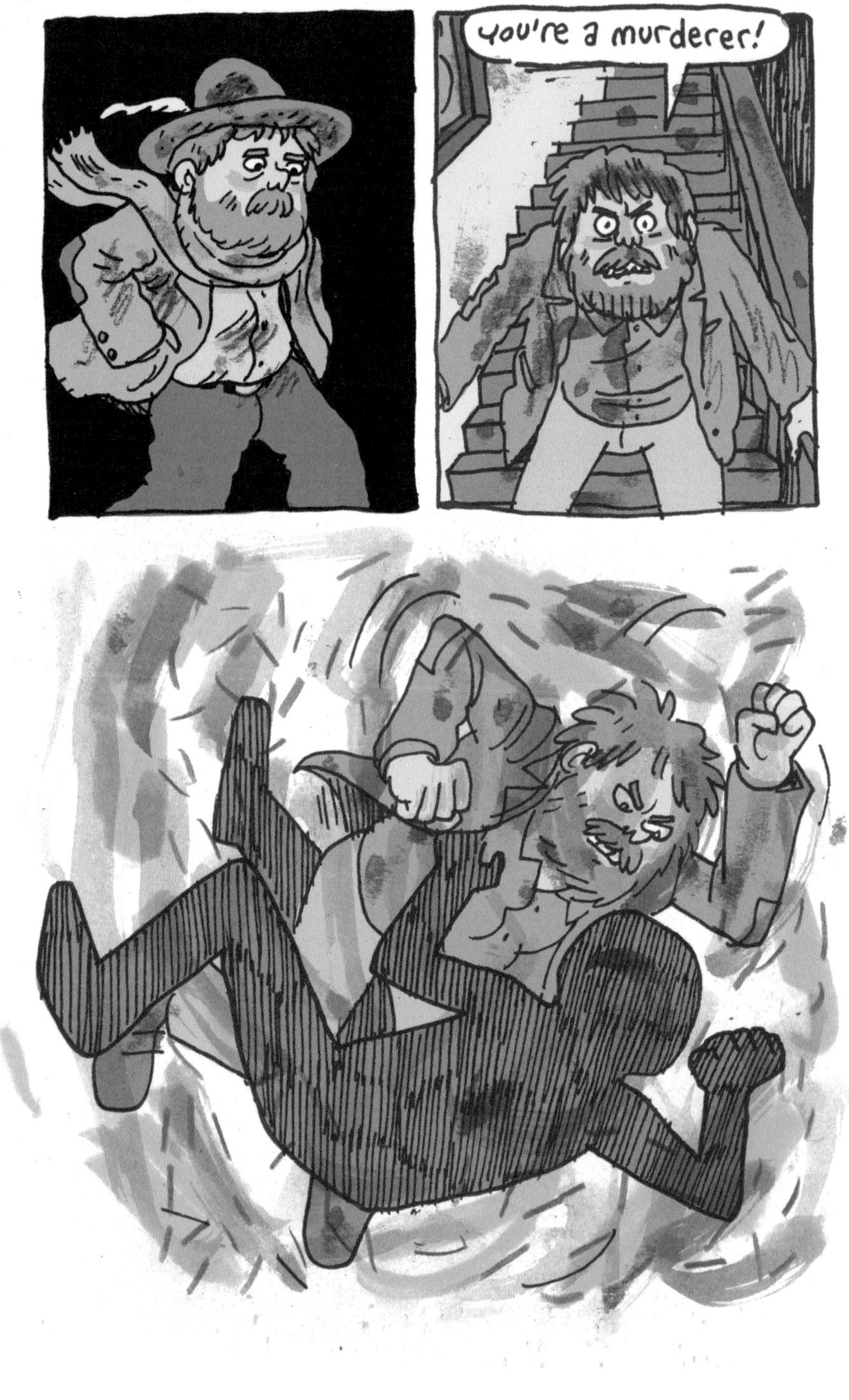
you're a murderer!

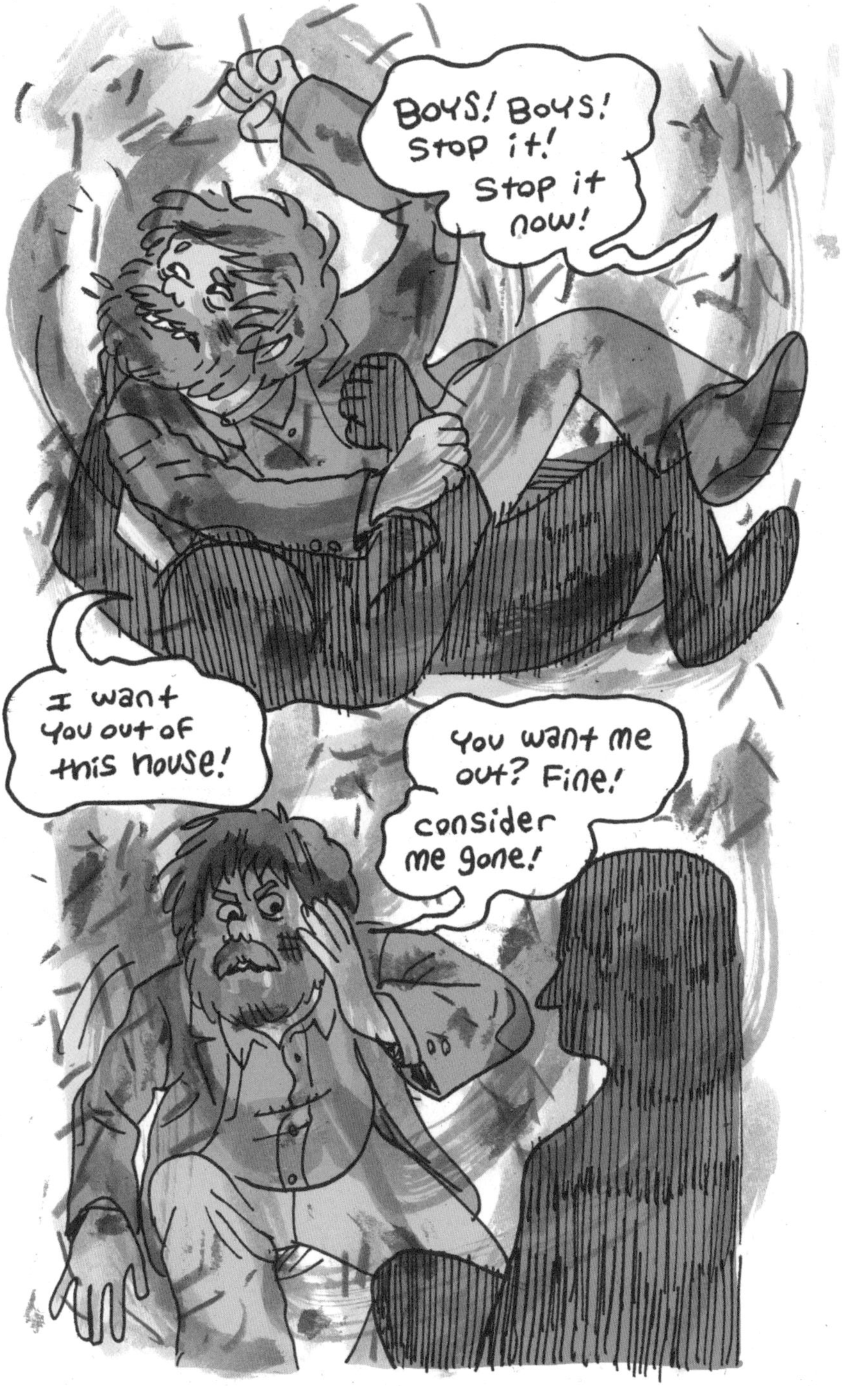
BOYS! BOYS! Stop it! Stop it now!
I want you out of this house!
You want me out? Fine! consider me gone!

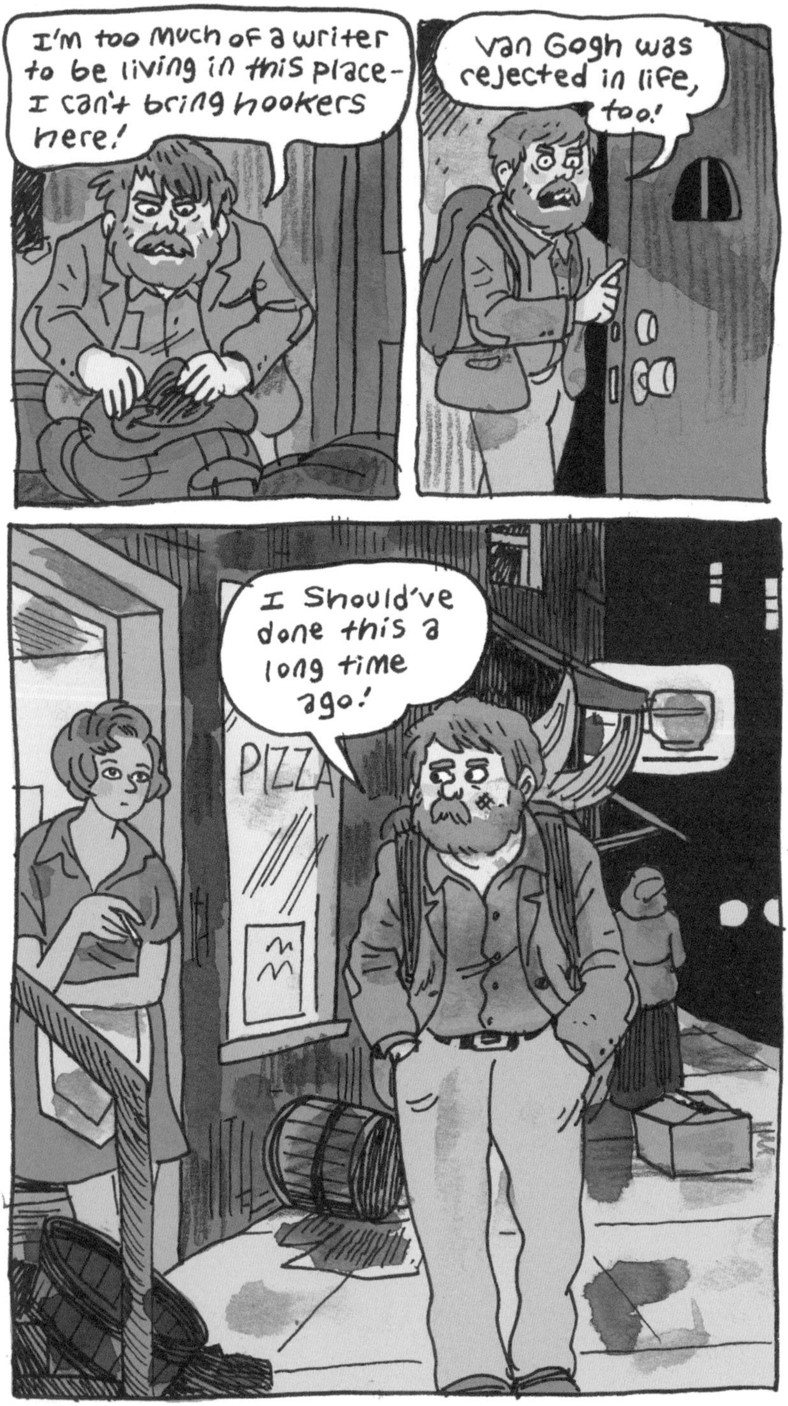
I'm too much of a writer to be living in this place- I can't bring hookers here!
Van Gogh was rejected in life, too!
I should've done this a long time ago!
PIZZA

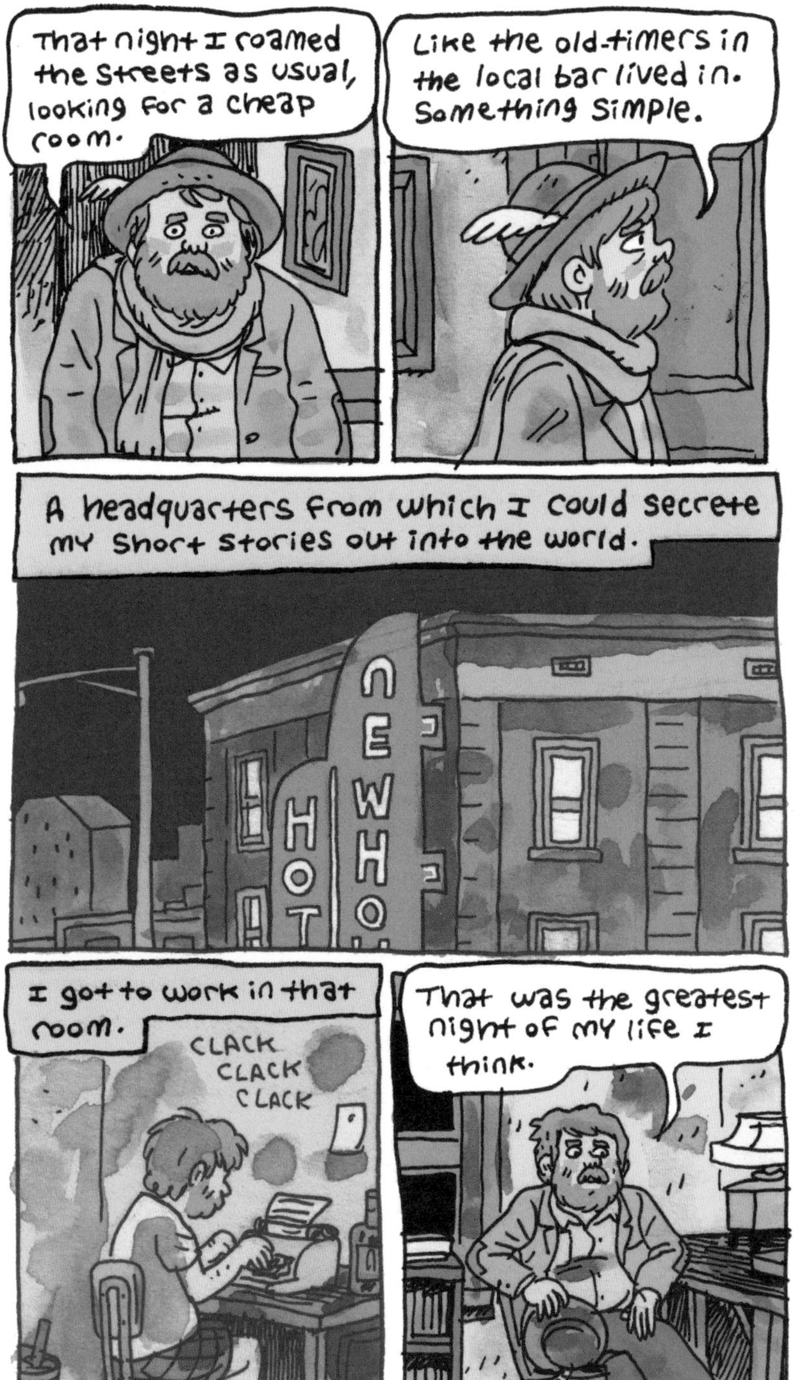
That night I roamed the streets as usual, looking for a cheap room.
Like the old-timers in the local bar lived in. Something simple.
A headquarters from which I could secrete my short stories out into the world.
NEW HO
HOT
I got to work in that room.
CLACK CLACK CLACK
That was the greatest night of my life I think.

Uh oh, Fante.

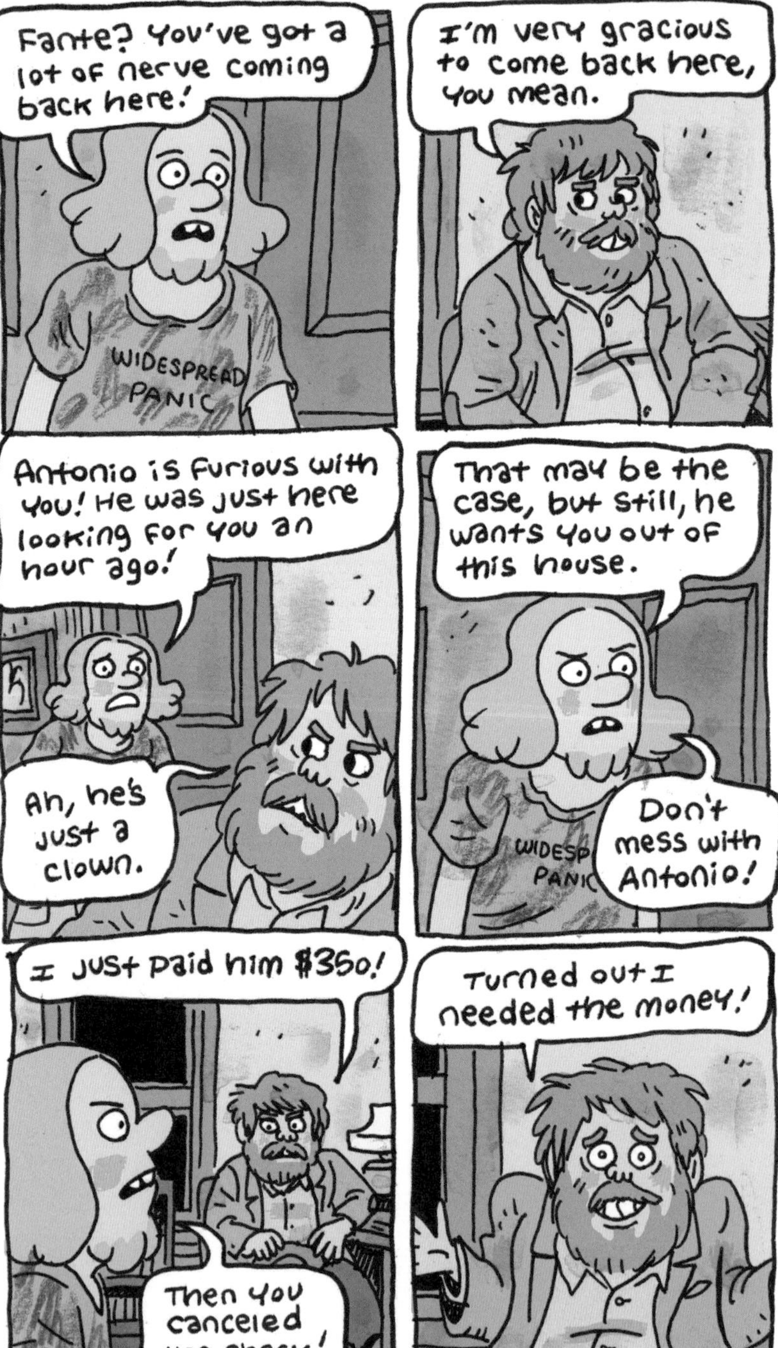
Fante? You've got a lot of nerve coming back here!
I'm very gracious to come back here, you mean.
WIDESPREAD PANIC
Antonio is furious with you! He was just here looking for you an hour ago!
Ah, he's just a clown.
That may be the case, but still, he wants you out of this house.
Don't mess with Antonio!
I just paid him $350!
Then you canceled the check!
Turned out I needed the money!

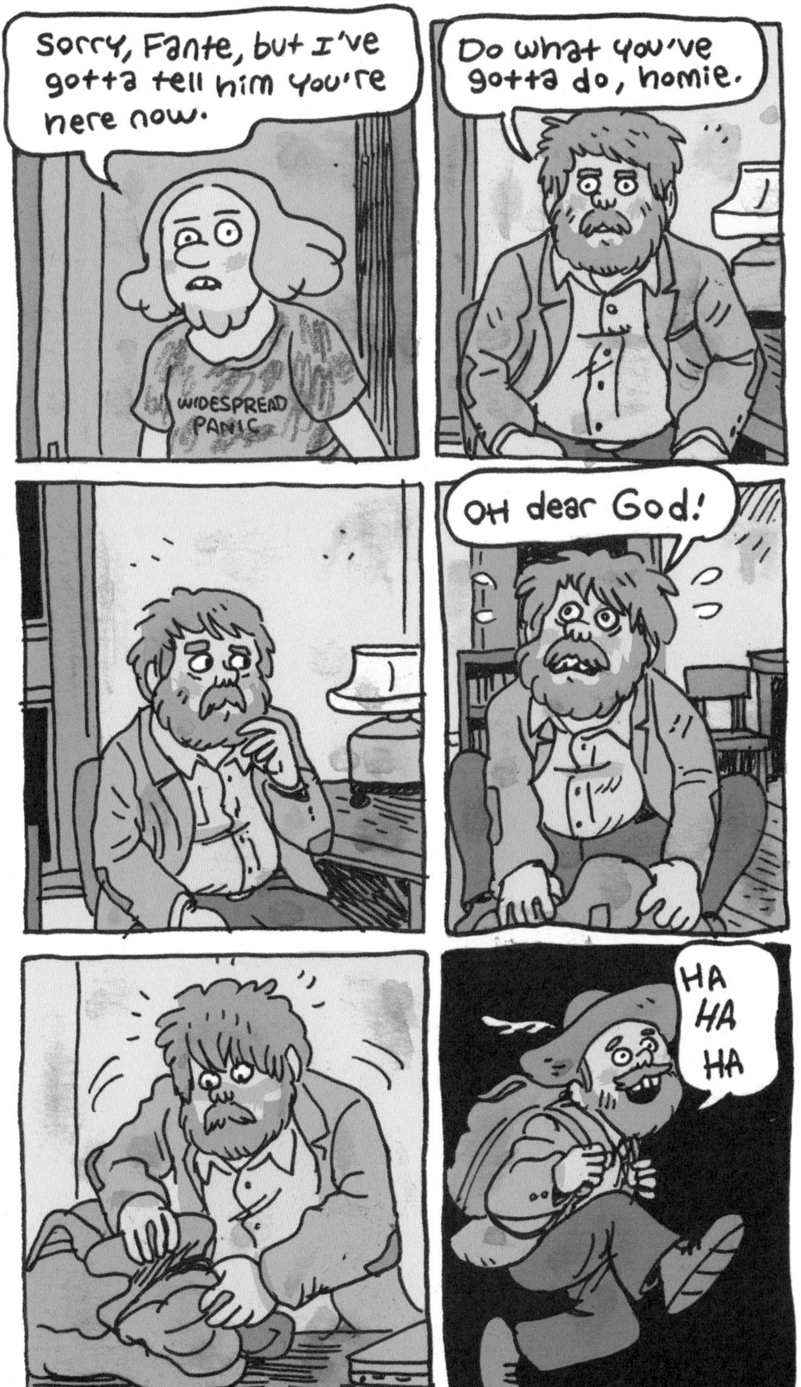
Sorry, Fante, but I've gotta tell him you're here now.
WIDESPREAD PANIC
Do what you've gotta do, homie.
OH dear God!
HA HA HA

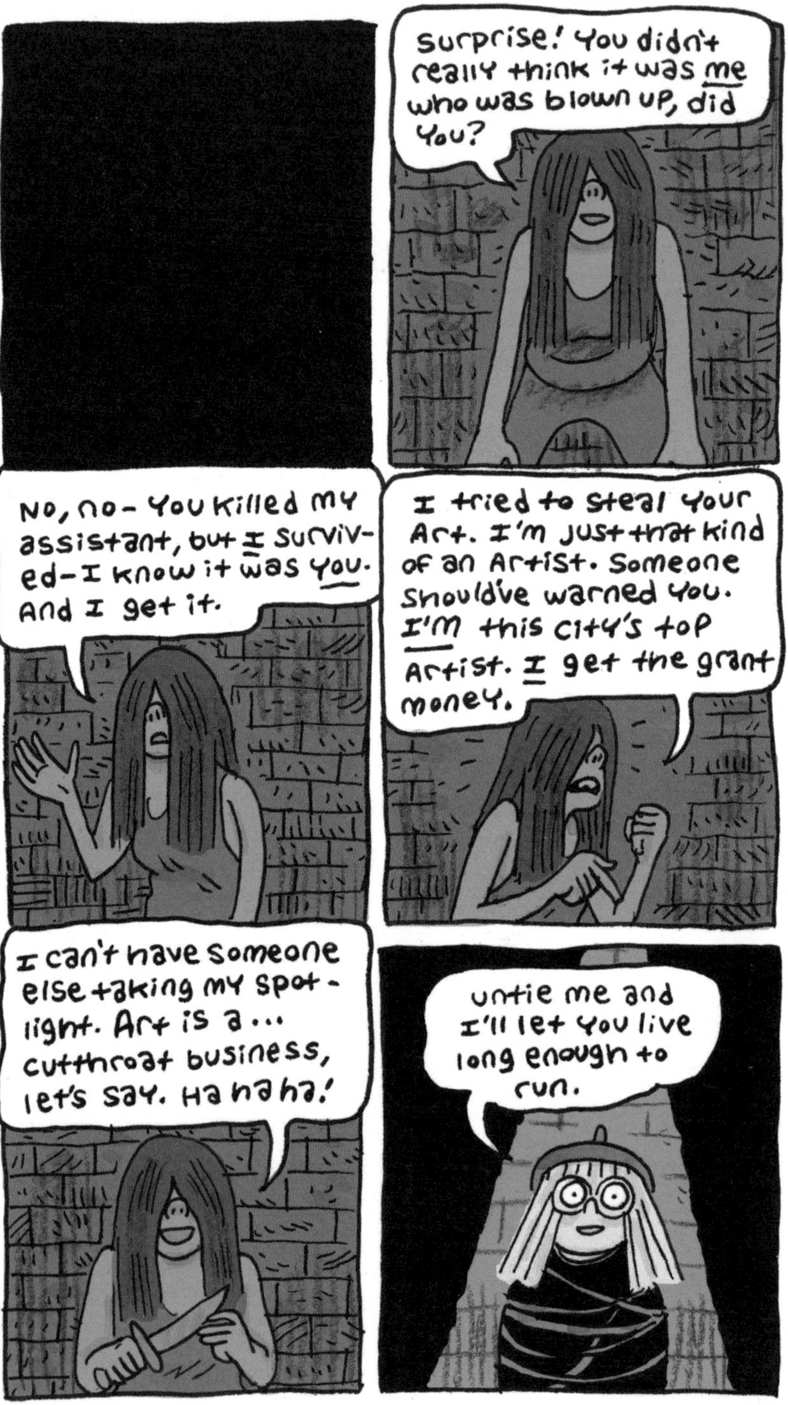
Surprise! You didn't really think it was me who was blown up, did you?
No, no- You killed my assistant, but I surviv-ed-I know it was you. And I get it.
I tried to steal your Art. I'm just that kind of an Artist. Someone should've warned you. I'M this city's top Artist. I get the grant money.
I can't have someone else taking my spot-light. Art is a... cutthroat business, let's say. Ha ha ha!
Untie me and I'll let you live long enough to run.

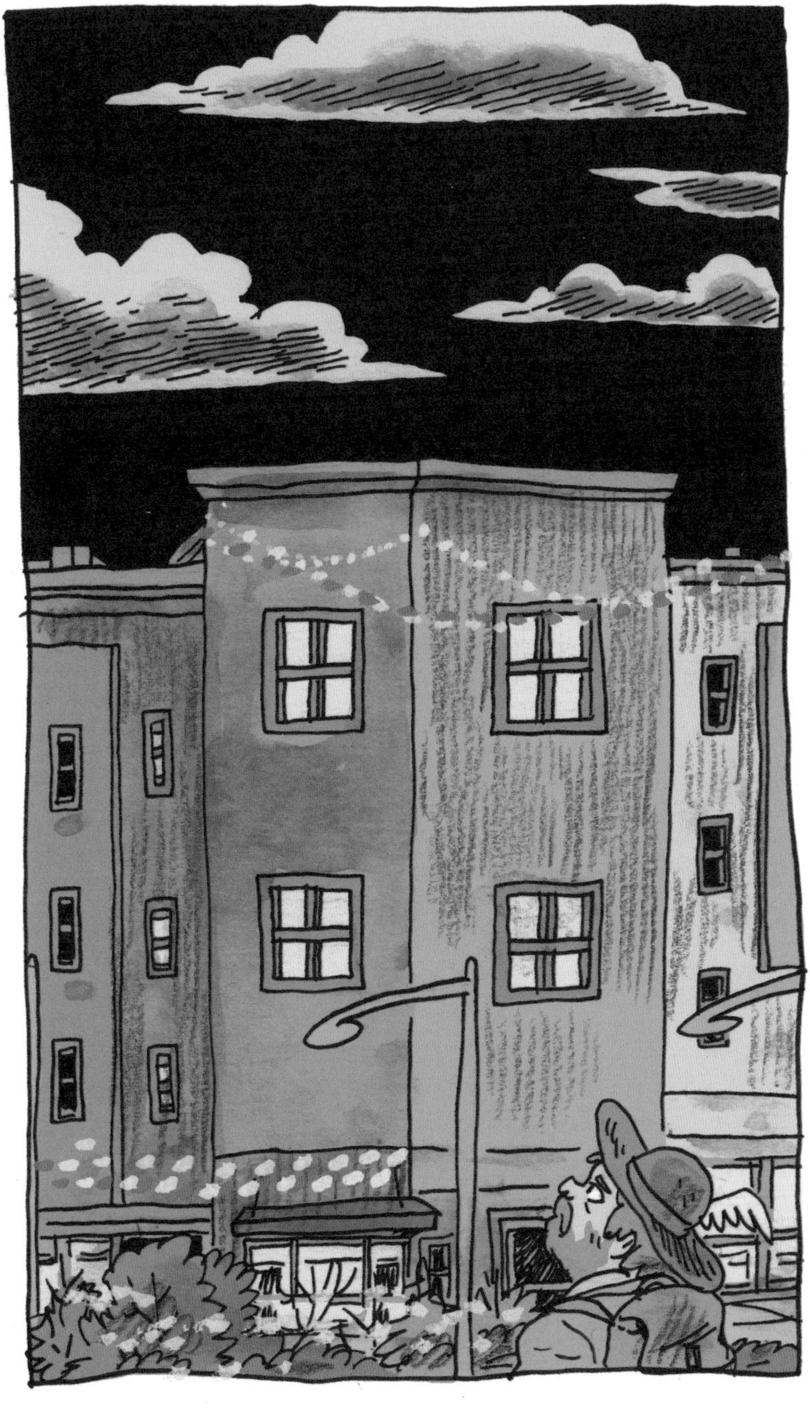

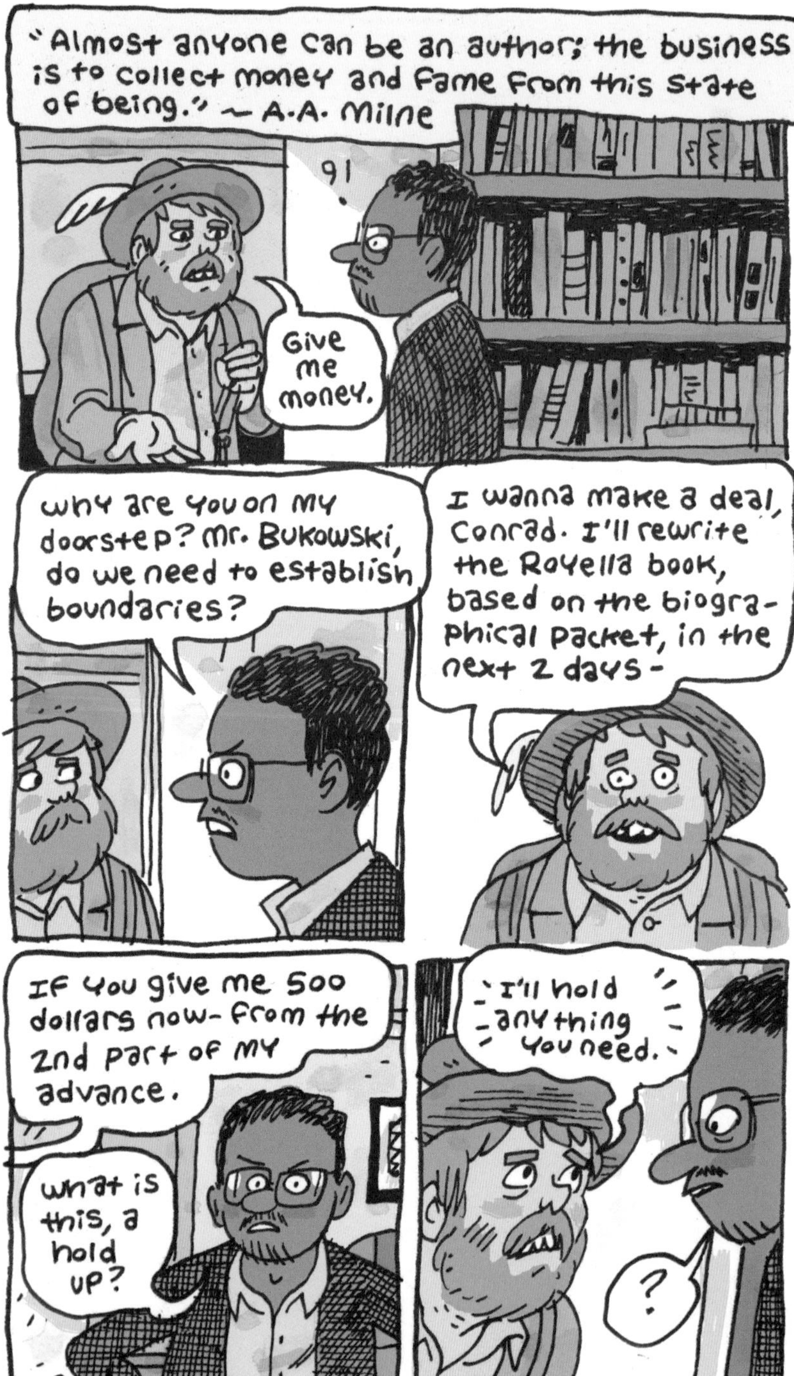
"Almost anyone can be an author; the business is to collect money and fame from this state of being." ~ A.A. Milne
?!
Give me money.
Why are you on my doorstep? Mr. Bukowski, do we need to establish boundaries?
I wanna make a deal, Conrad. I'll rewrite the Royella book, based on the biographical packet, in the next 2 days -
If you give me 500 dollars now- from the 2nd part of my advance.
What is this, a hold up?
I'll hold anything you need.
?

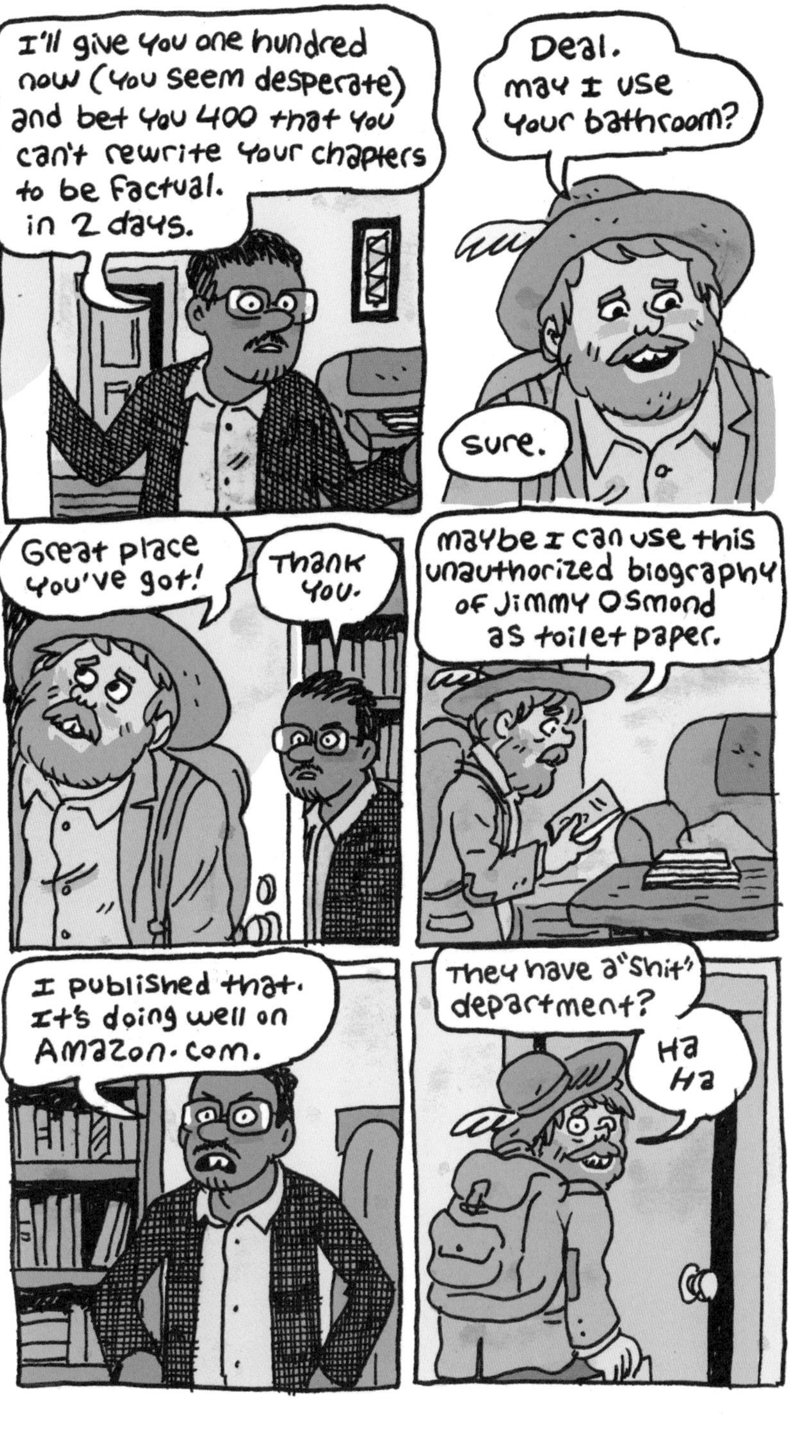
I'll give you one hundred now (you seem desperate) and bet you 400 that you can't rewrite your chapters to be factual. in 2 days.
Deal. may I use your bathroom?
sure.
Great place you've got!
Thank you.
maybe I can use this unauthorized biography of Jimmy Osmond as toilet paper.
I published that. It's doing well on Amazon.com.
They have a "shit" department?
Ha Ha

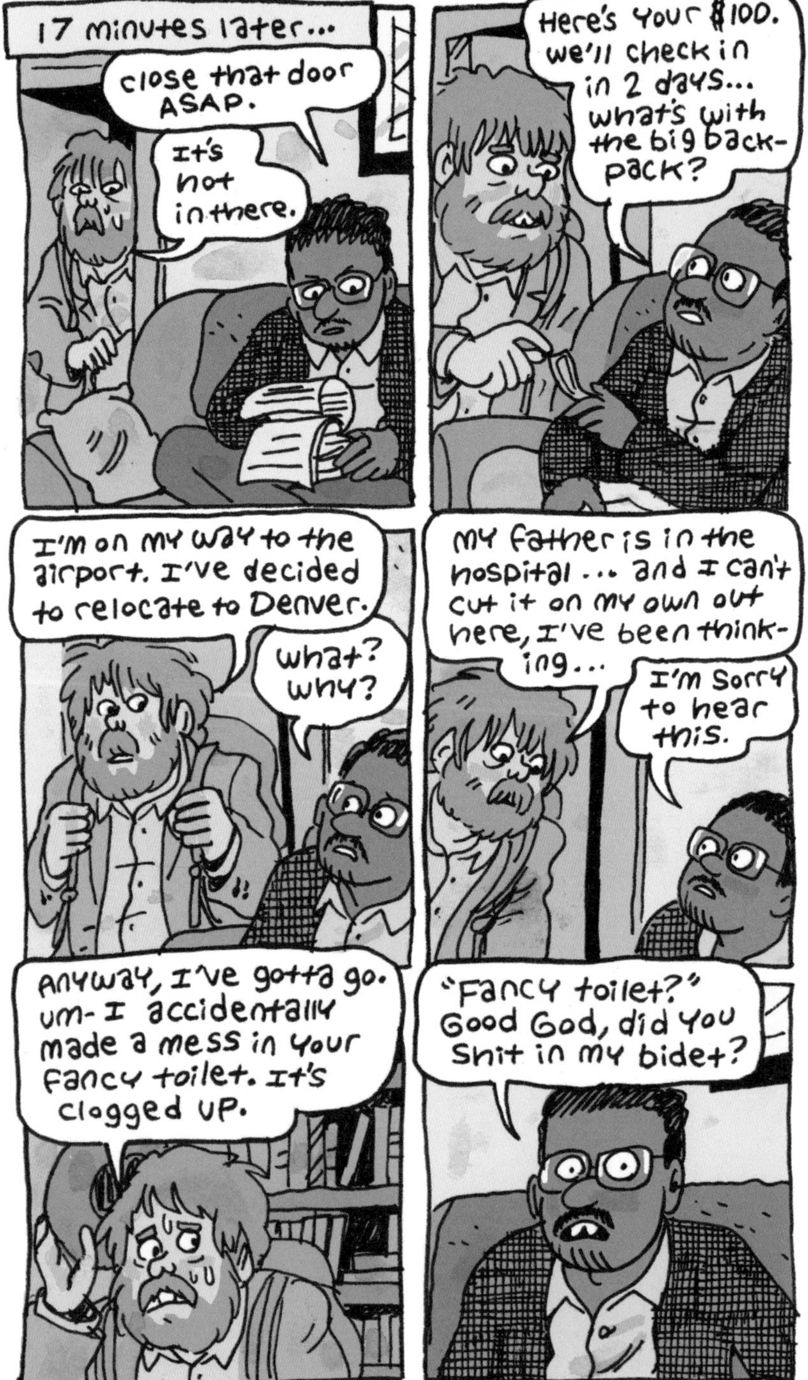
17 minutes later...
close that door ASAP.
It's not in there.
Here's your $100. we'll check in in 2 days... what's with the big back-pack?
I'm on my way to the airport. I've decided to relocate to Denver.
what? why?
My father is in the hospital ... and I can't cut it on my own out here, I've been think-ing...
I'm sorry to hear this.
Anyway, I've gotta go. um- I accidentally made a mess in your fancy toilet. It's clogged up.
"Fancy toilet?" Good God, did you shit in my bidet?

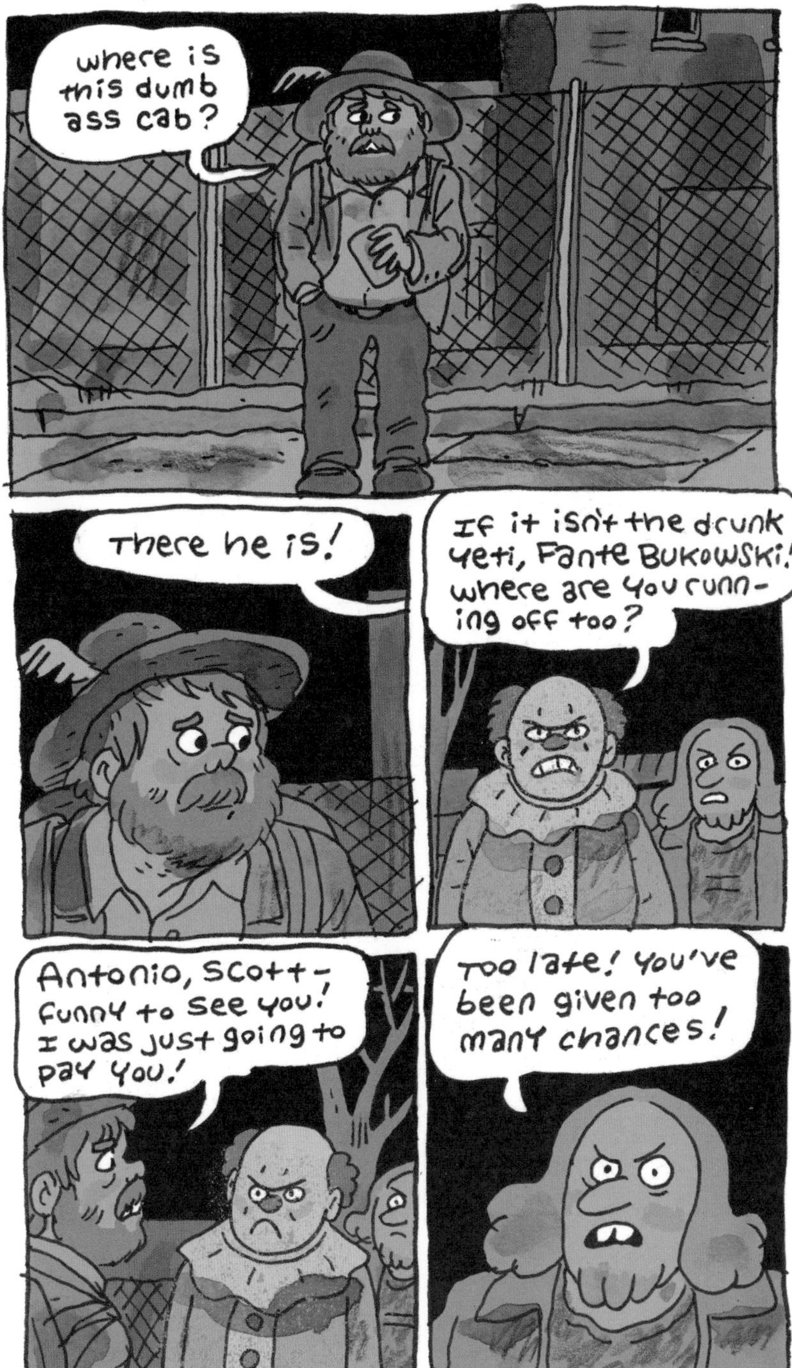
where is this dumb ass cab?
There he is!
If it isn't the drunk yeti, Fante Bukowski! where are you running off too?
Antonio, Scott- funny to see you! I was just going to pay you!
Too late! You've been given too many chances!

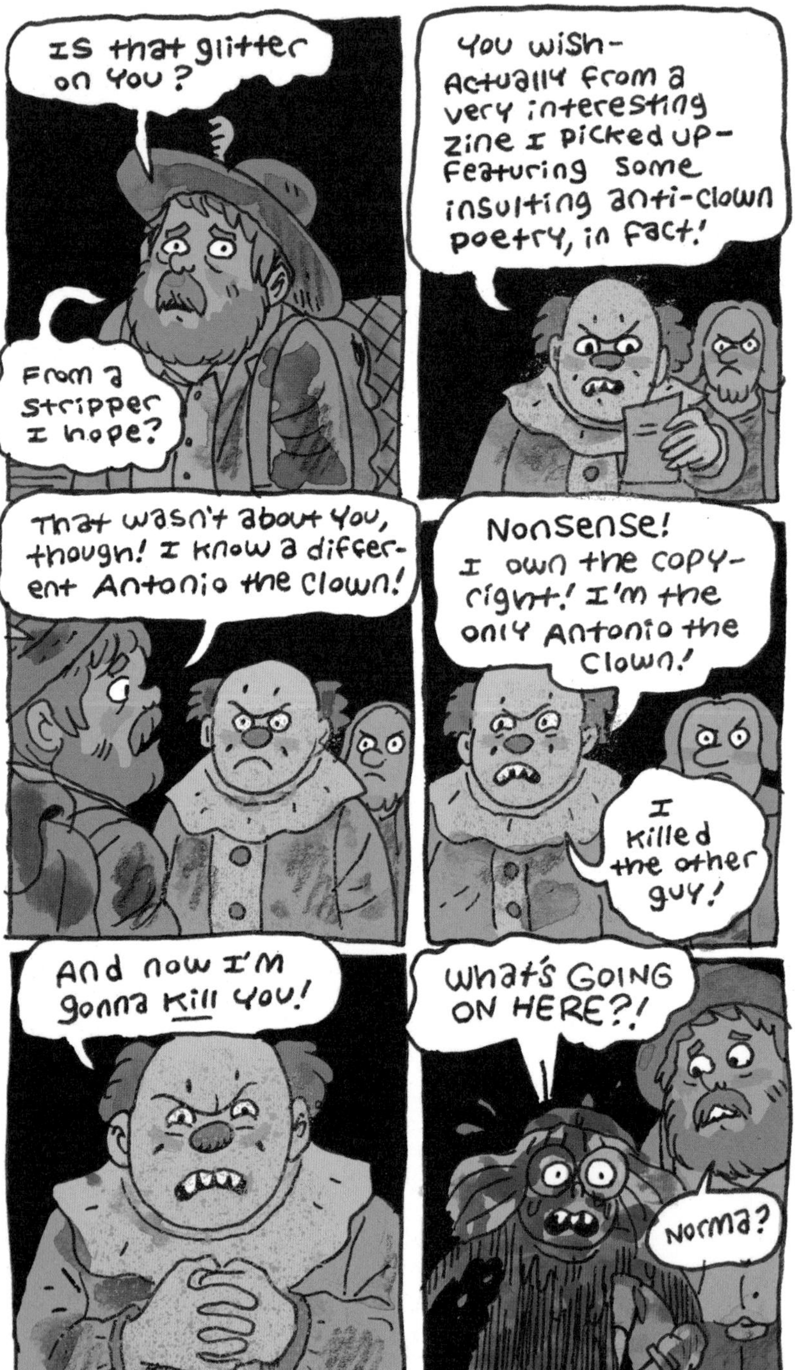

Is that glitter on you?
From a stripper I hope?
You wish- Actually from a very interesting zine I picked up- Featuring some insulting anti-clown poetry, in fact!
That wasn't about you, though! I know a different Antonio the clown!
Nonsense! I own the copyright! I'm the only Antonio the Clown!
I killed the other guy!
And now I'M gonna kill you!
What's GOING ON HERE?!
Norma?

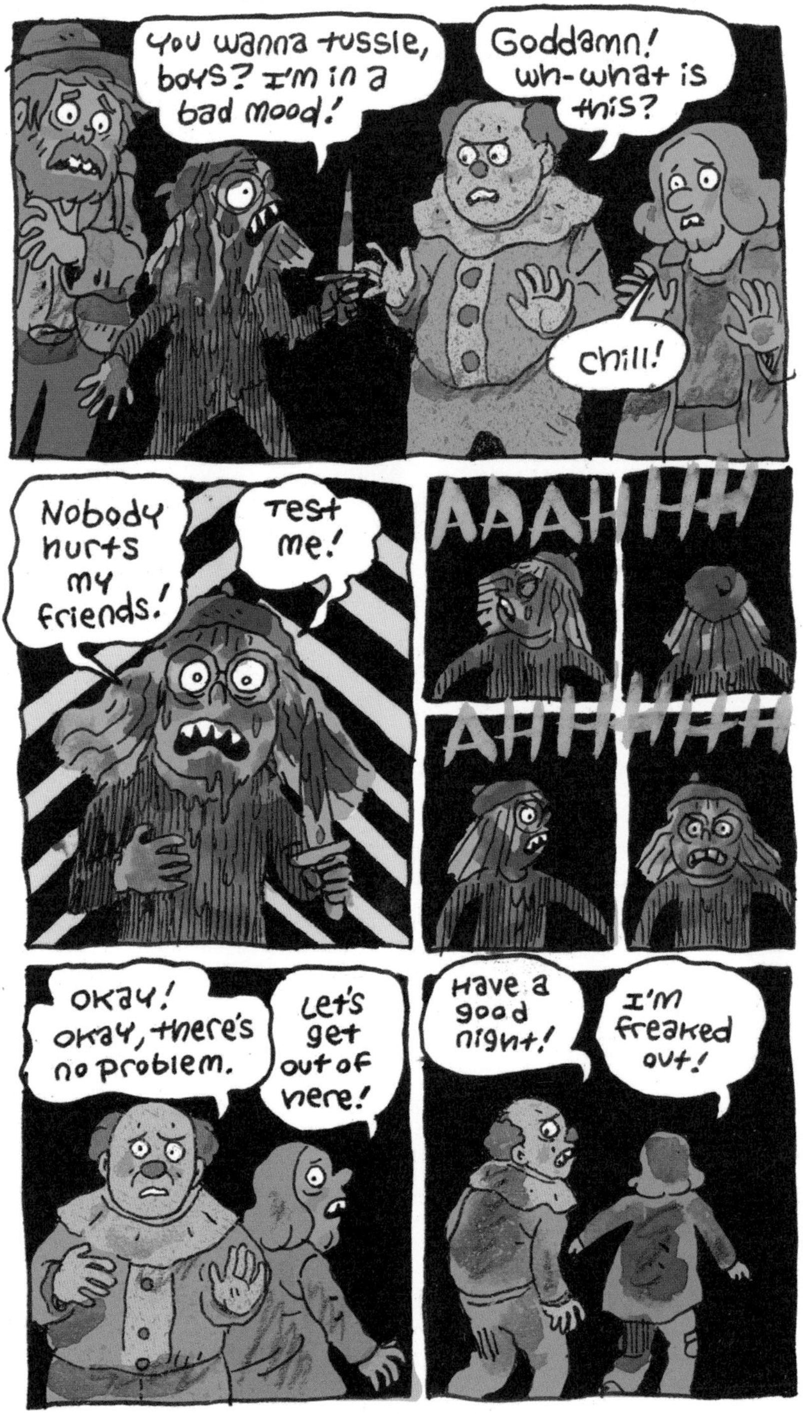
You wanna tussle, boys? I'm in a bad mood!
Goddamn! Wh-what is this?
Chill!
Nobody hurts my friends!
Test me!
AAAHHHH
AHHHHHHH
Okay! Okay, there's no problem.
Let's get out of here!
Have a good night!
I'm freaked out!

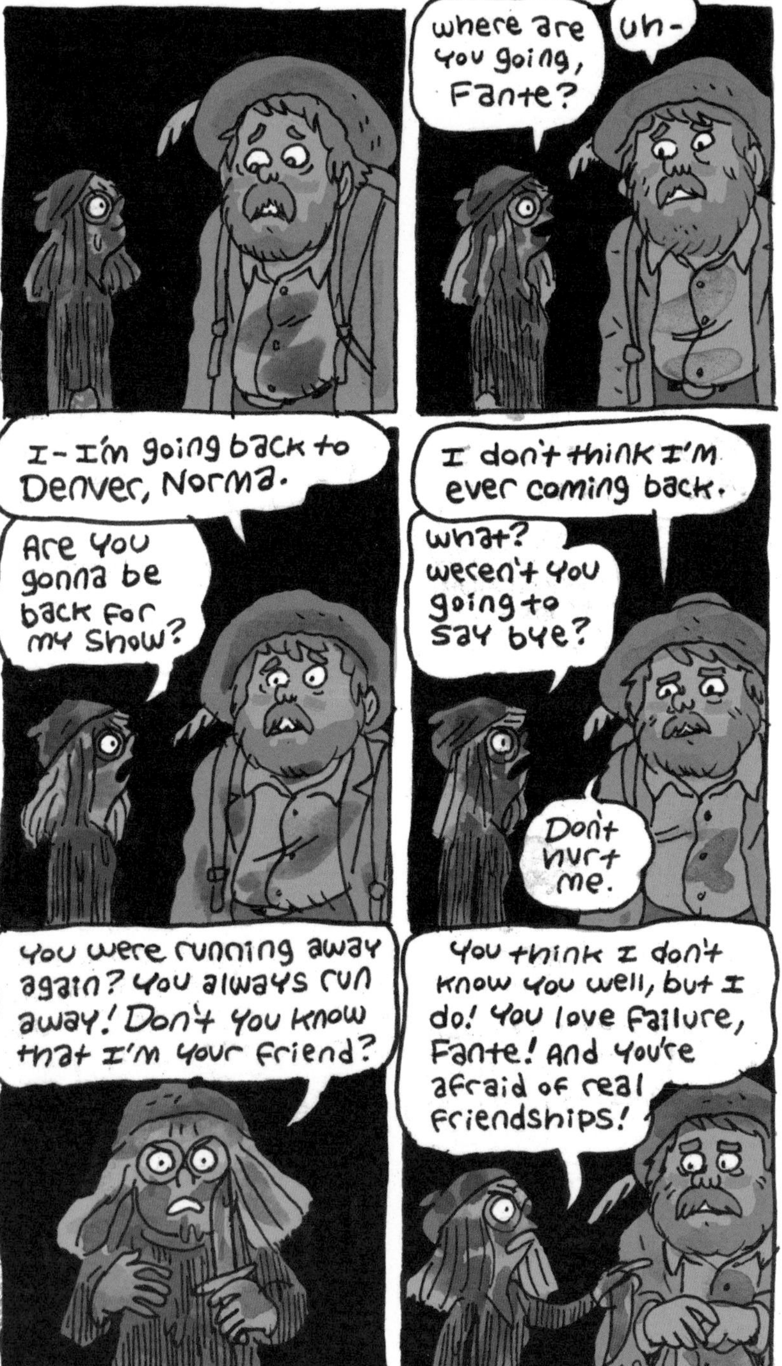
where are you going, Fante?
uh-
I- I'm going back to Denver, Norma.
Are you gonna be back for my show?
I don't think I'm ever coming back.
what? weren't you going to say bye?
Don't hurt me.
You were running away again? You always run away! Don't you know that I'm your friend?
You think I don't know you well, but I do! You love failure, Fante! And you're afraid of real friendships!

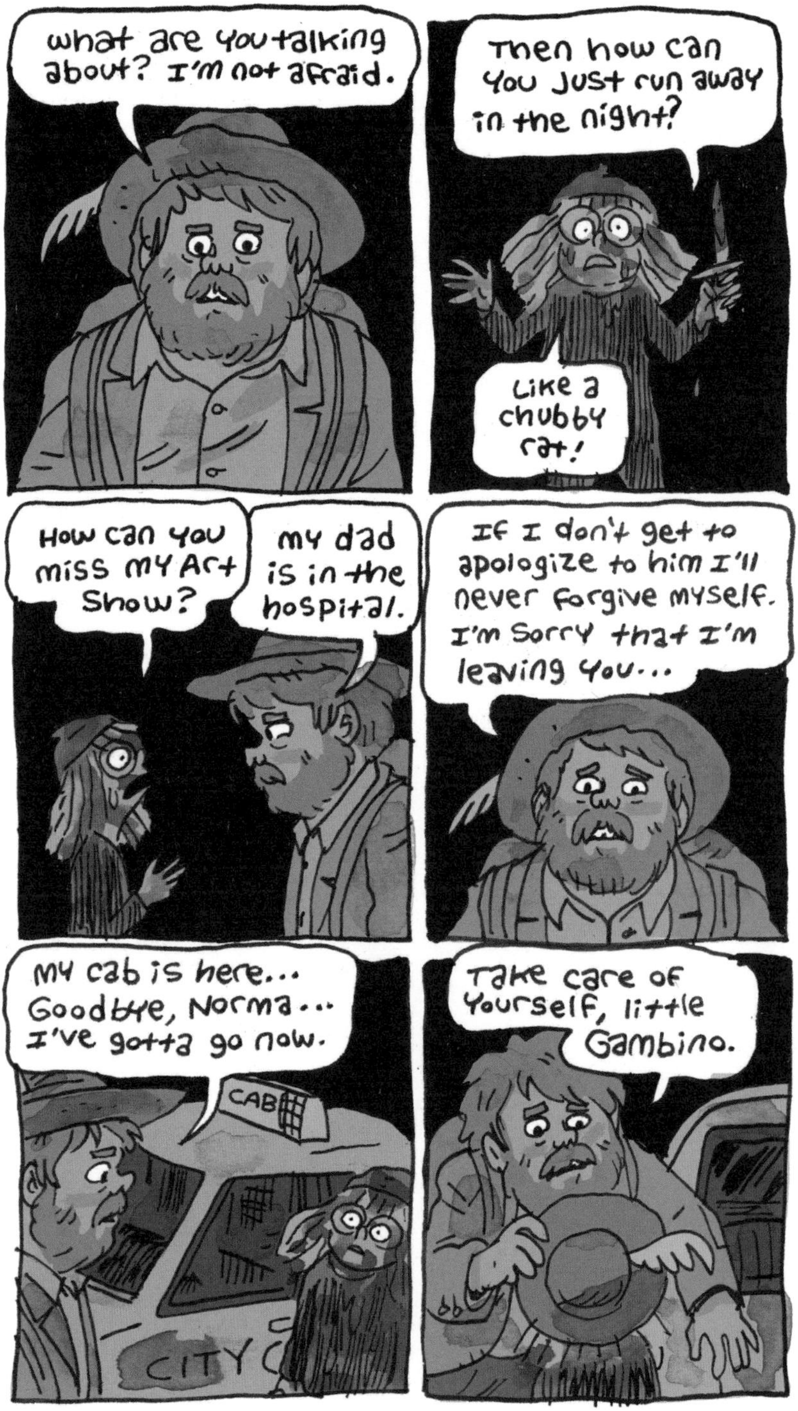

what are you talking about? I'm not afraid.
Then how can you just run away in the night?
Like a chubby cat!
How can you miss my Art Show?
my dad is in the hospital.
If I don't get to apologize to him I'll never forgive myself. I'm sorry that I'm leaving you...
my cab is here... Goodbye, Norma... I've gotta go now.
CAB
CITY
Take care of yourself, little Gambino.

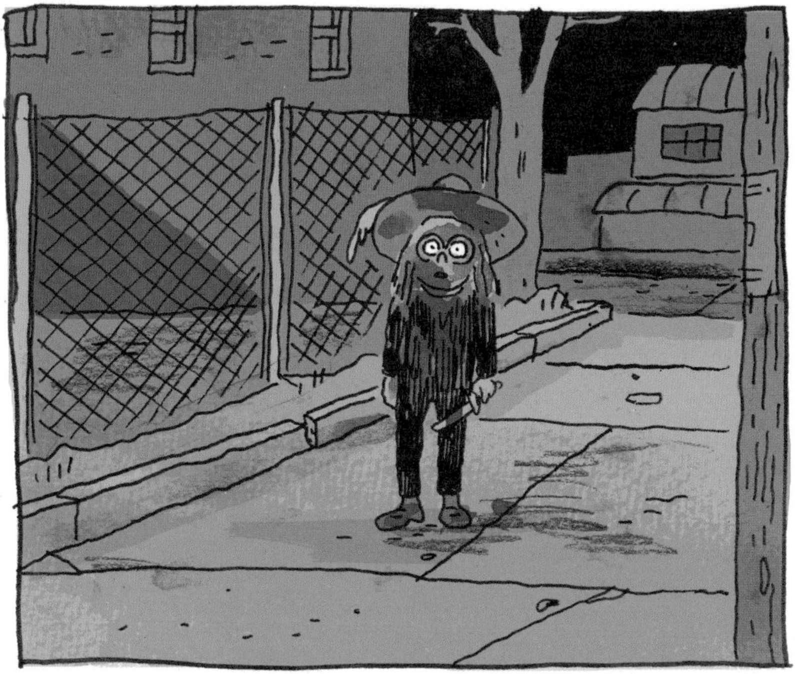

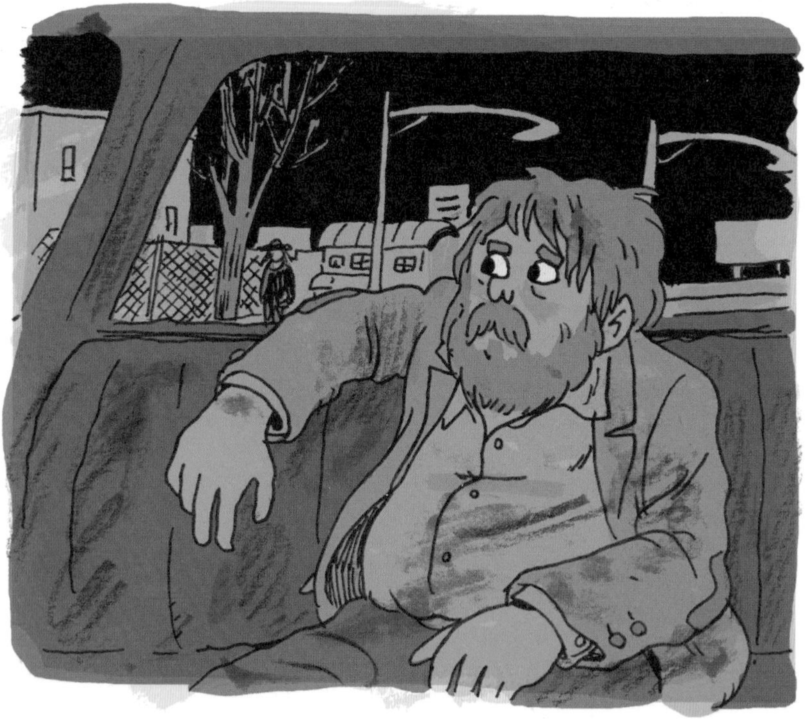

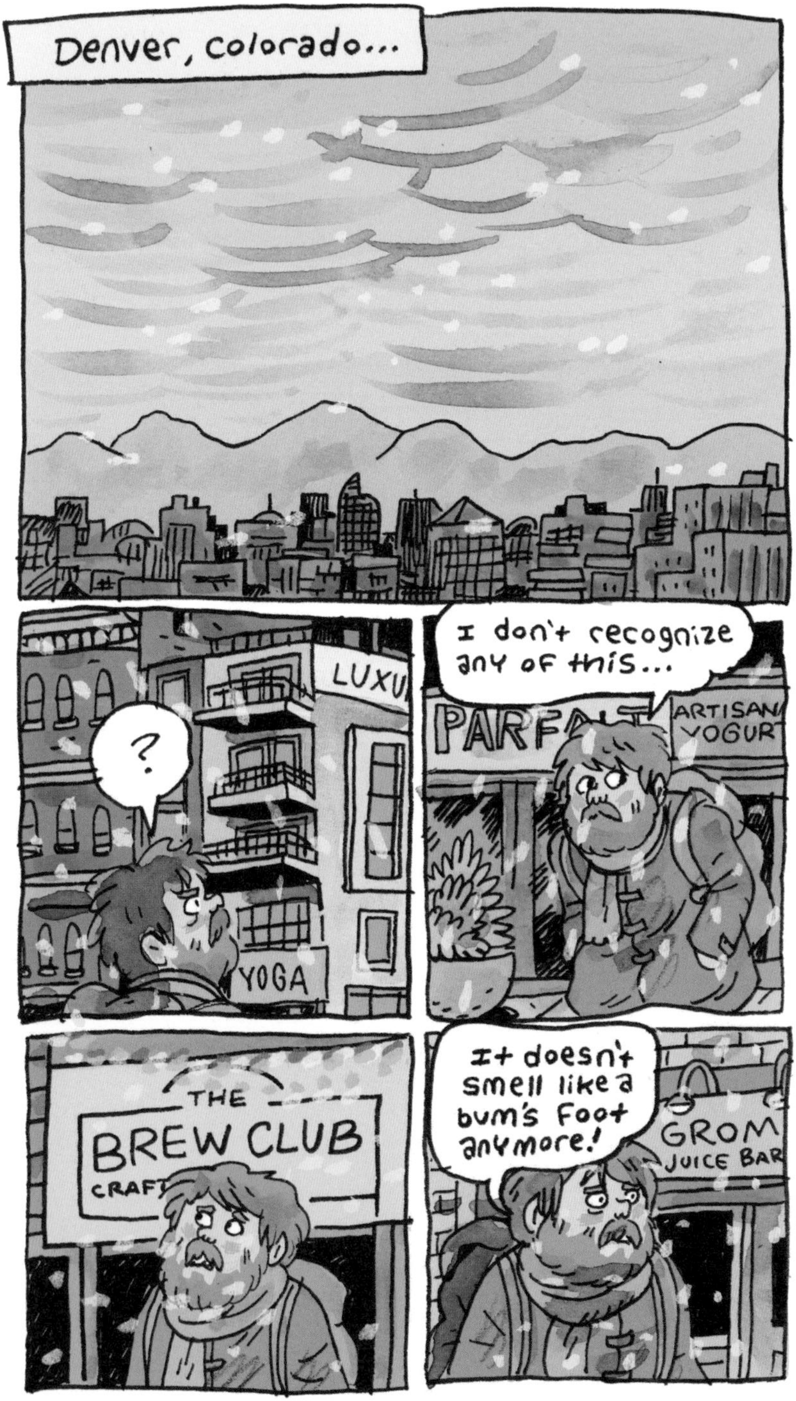

Denver, colorado...
LUXU
?
YOGA
I don't recognize any of this...
PARFAIT
ARTISAN YOGURT
THE
BREW CLUB
CRAFT
It doesn't smell like a bum's foot anymore!
GROM
JUICE BAR

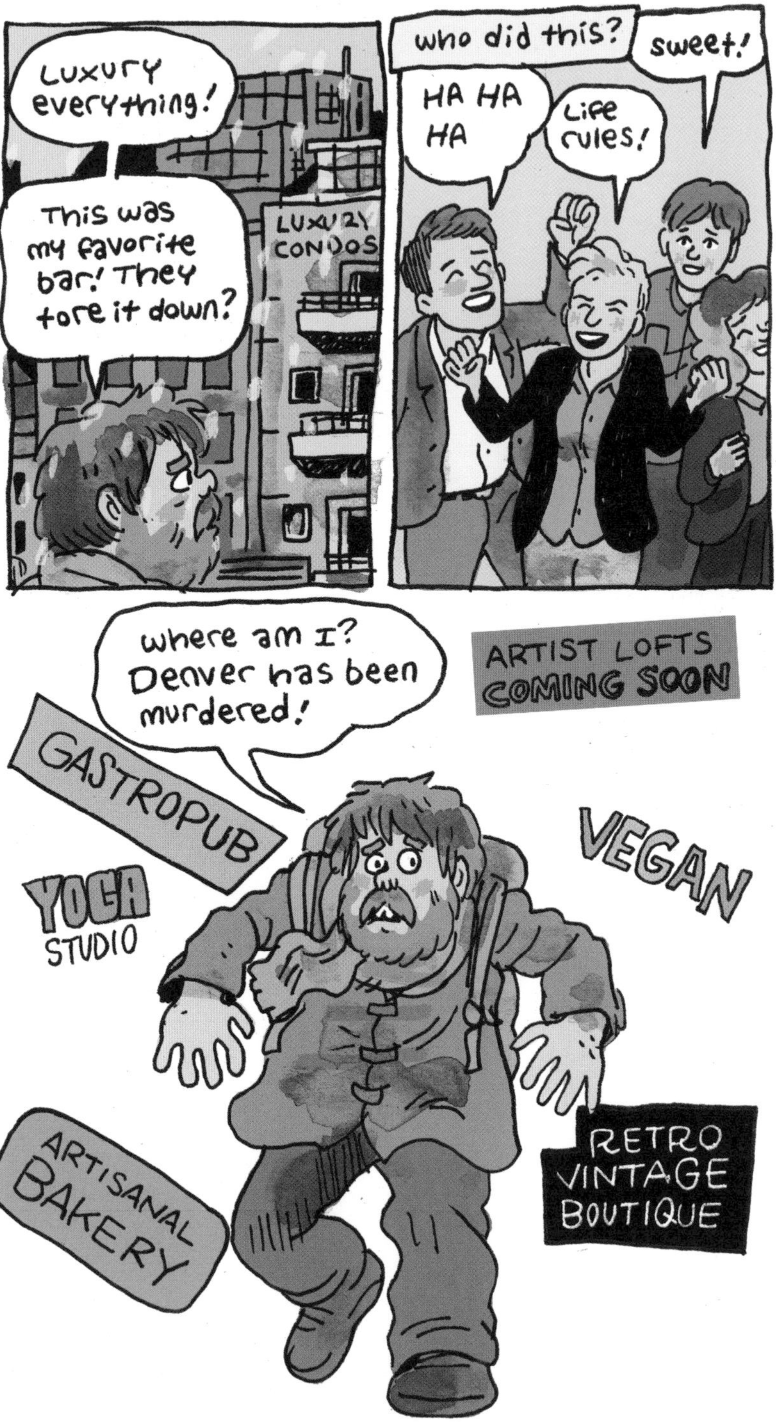
Luxury everything!
This was my favorite bar! They tore it down?
LUXURY CONDOS
LUXURY
who did this?
sweet!
HA HA HA
Life rules!
where am I? Denver has been murdered!
ARTIST LOFTS COMING SOON
GASTROPUB
VEGAN
YOGA STUDIO
ARTISANAL BAKERY
RETRO VINTAGE BOUTIQUE

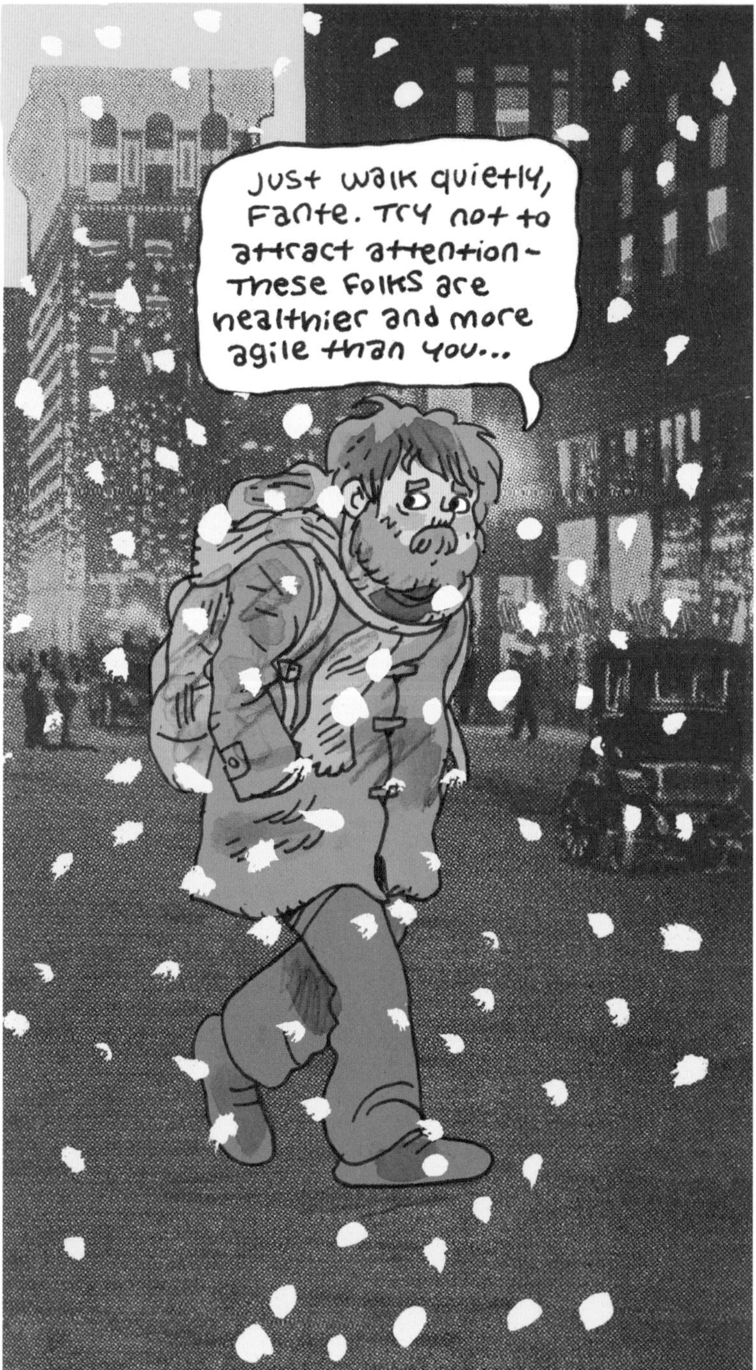
Just walk quietly, Fante. Try not to attract attention- These folks are healthier and more agile than you...

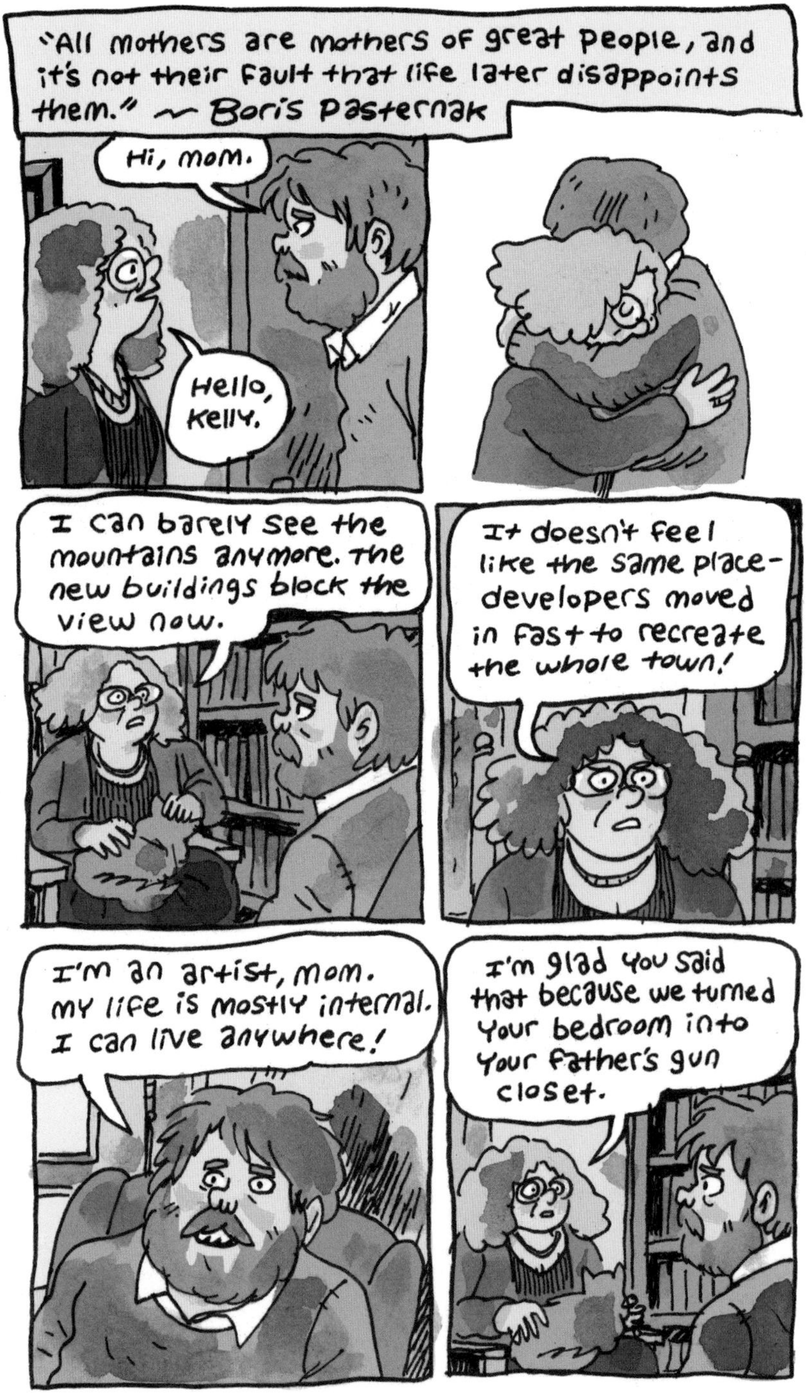
"All mothers are mothers of great people, and it's not their fault that life later disappoints them." ~ Boris Pasternak
Hi, mom.
Hello, Kelly.
I can barely see the mountains anymore. The new buildings block the view now.
It doesn't feel like the same place- developers moved in fast to recreate the whole town!
I'm an artist, mom. My life is mostly internal. I can live anywhere!
I'm glad you said that because we turned your bedroom into your father's gun closet.

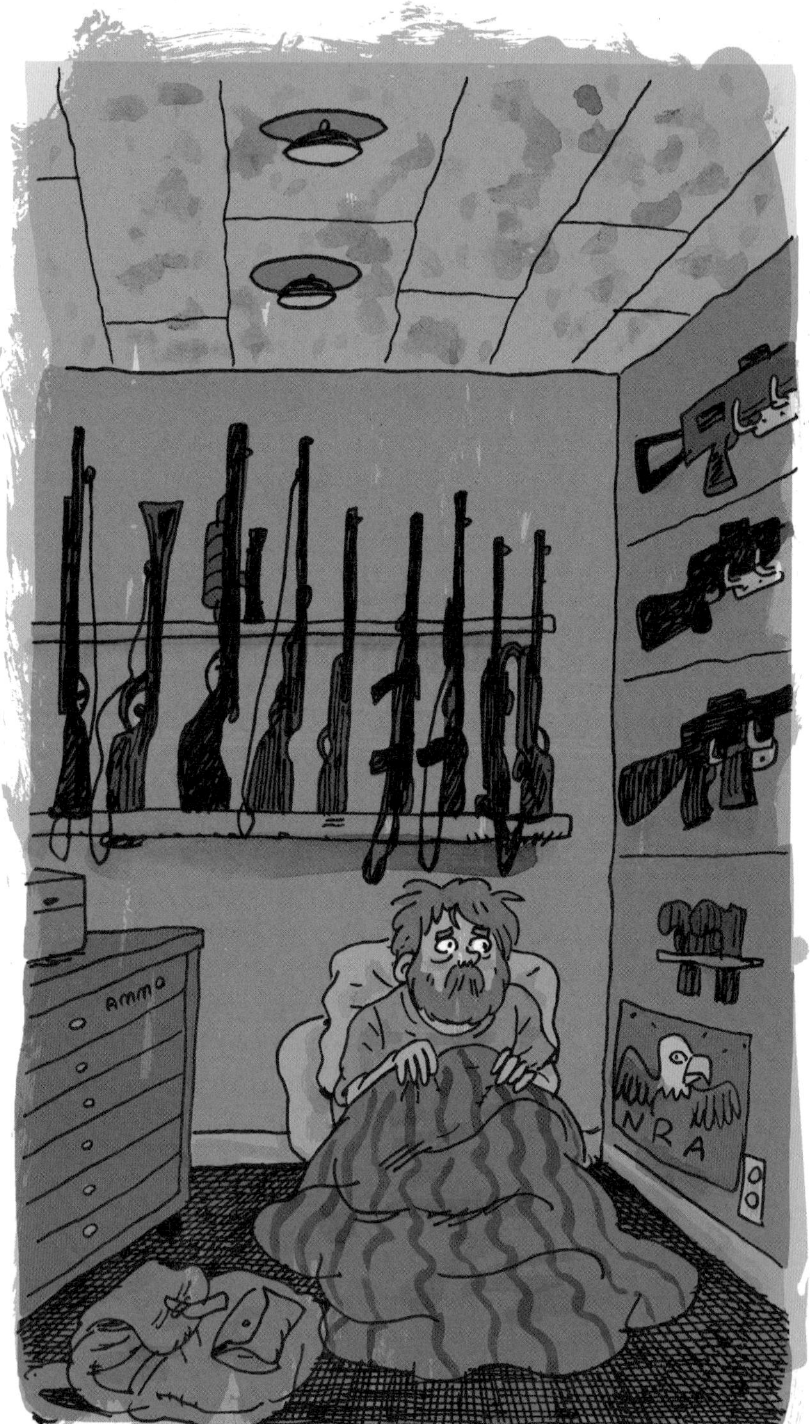
Ammo
NRA

"writing a book is like telling a joke and having to wait 2 years to know whether or not it was funny." ~Alain de Botton

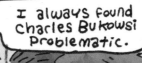

I always found Charles Bukowsi problematic.

I've gotta concentrate on this Royella book. There's a bet to win.

She won a beauty pageant at the age of 15 and was discovered by a Disney scout.

Where's the struggle?

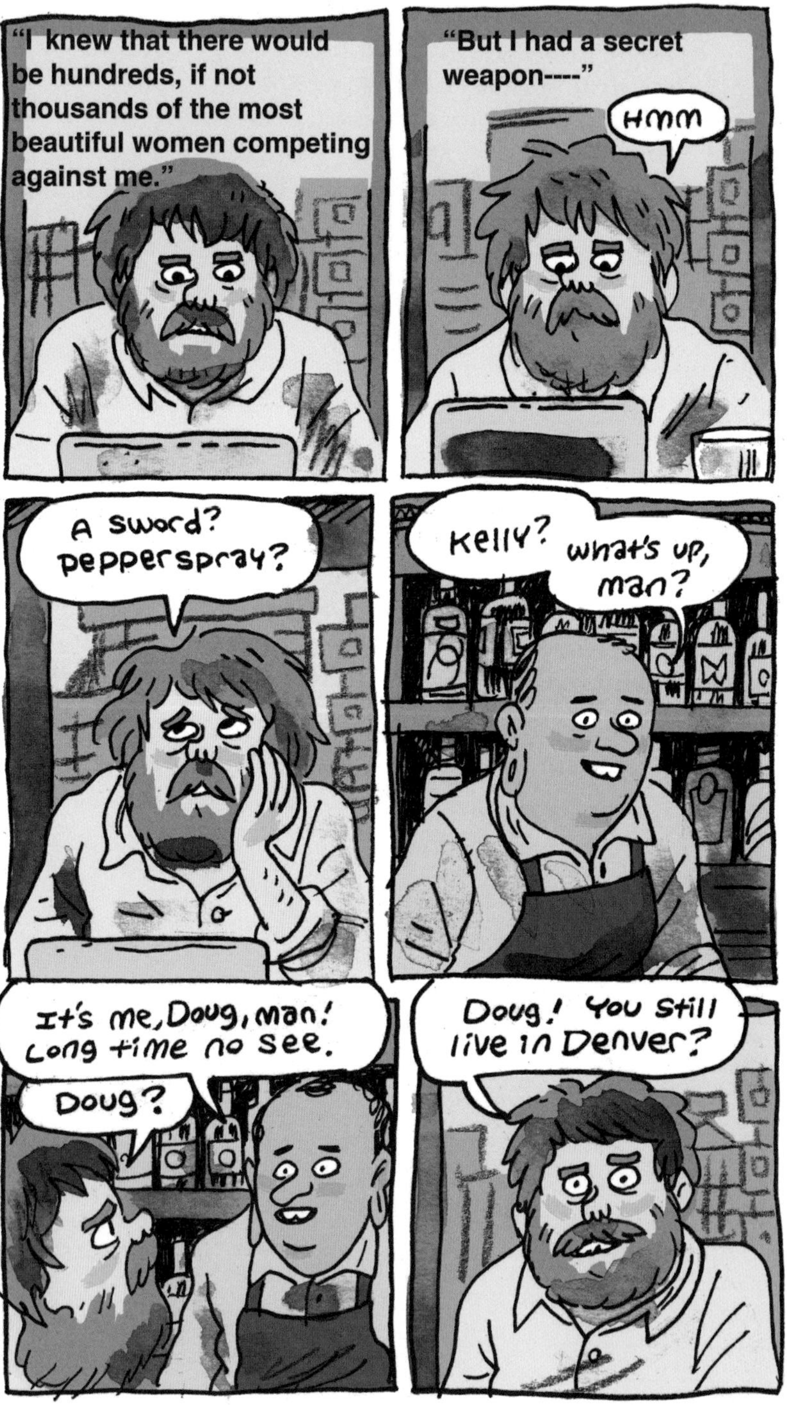
"I knew that there would be hundreds, if not thousands of the most beautiful women competing against me."
"But I had a secret weapon----"
HMM
A sword? pepperspray?
Kelly?
what's up, man?
It's me, Doug, man! Long time no see.
Doug?
Doug! You still live in Denver?

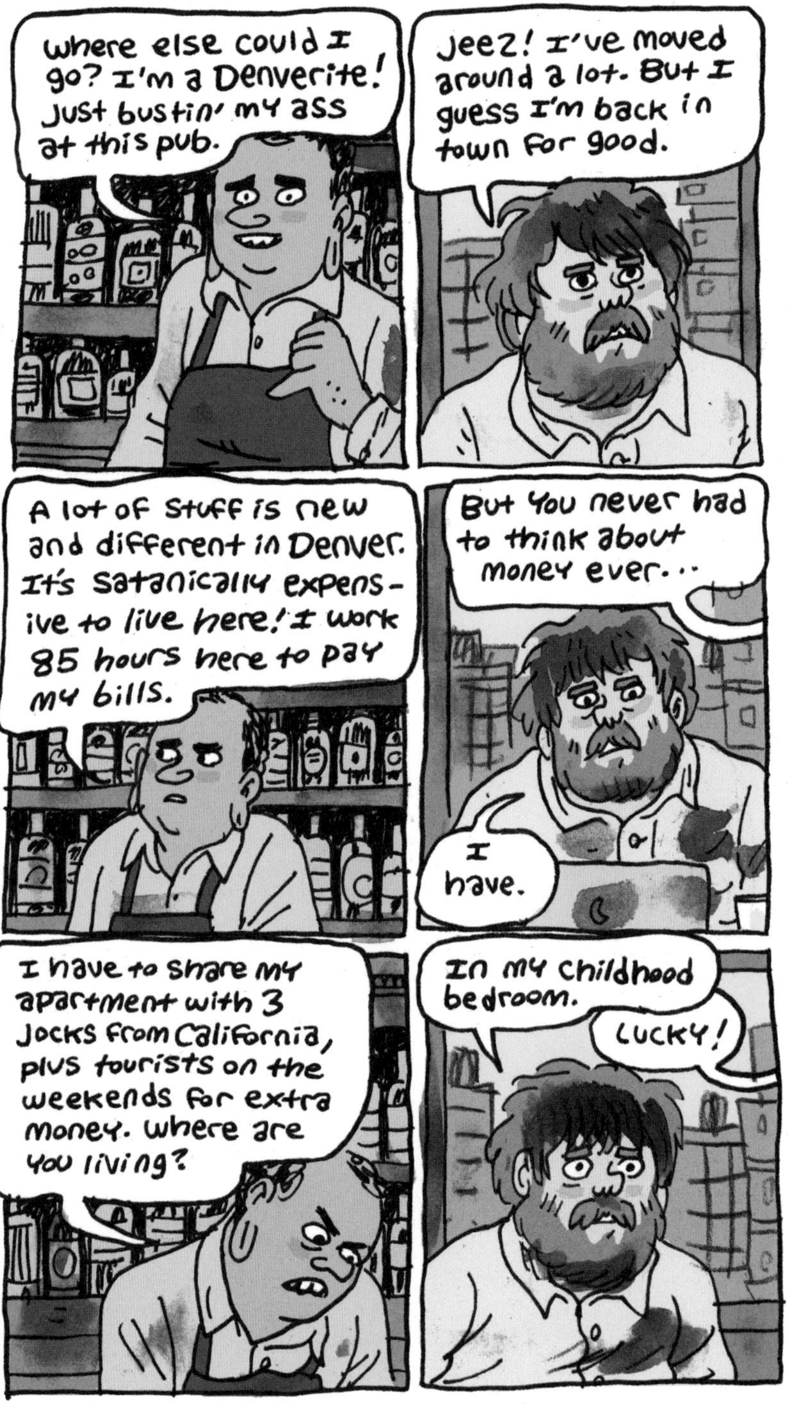
Where else could I go? I'm a Denverite! Just bustin' my ass at this pub.
Jeez! I've moved around a lot. But I guess I'm back in town for good.
A lot of stuff is new and different in Denver. It's satanically expensive to live here! I work 85 hours here to pay my bills.
But you never had to think about money ever...
I have.
I have to share my apartment with 3 jocks from California, plus tourists on the weekends for extra money. Where are you living?
In my childhood bedroom.
Lucky!

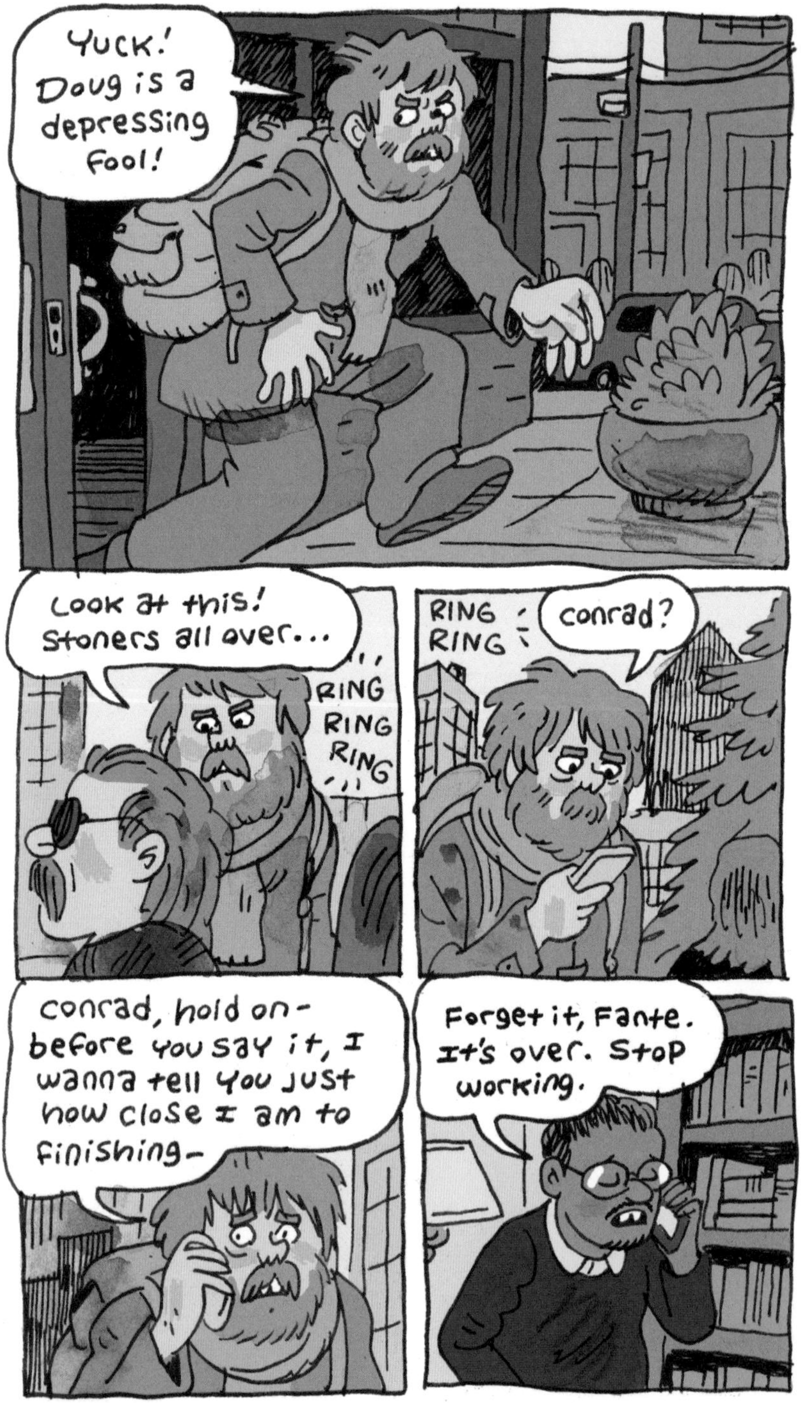
Yuck! Doug is a depressing fool!
Look at this! Stoners all over...
RING RING RING
RING RING
Conrad?
Conrad, hold on- before you say it, I wanna tell you just how close I am to finishing-
Forget it, Fante. It's over. Stop working.

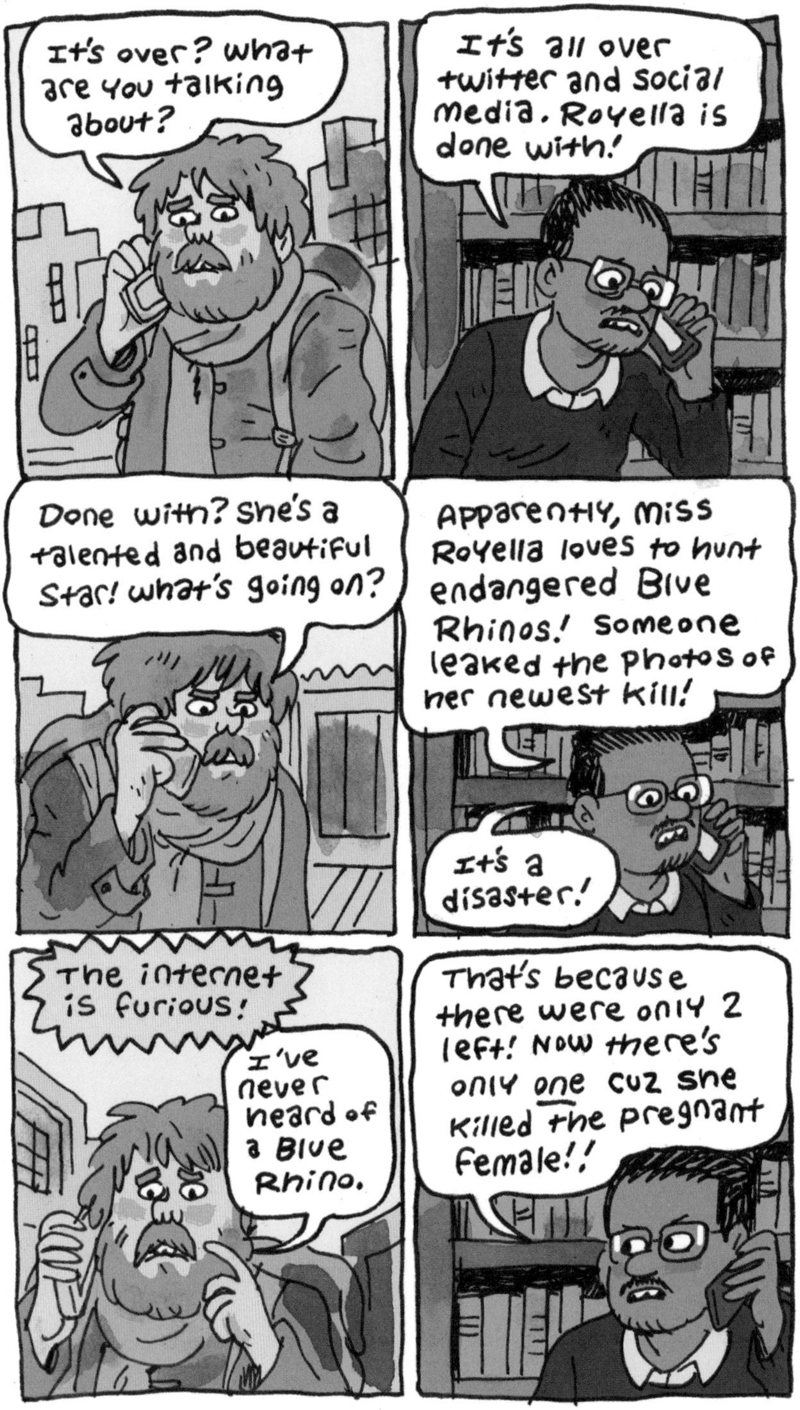
It's over? what are you talking about?
It's all over twitter and social media. Royella is done with!
Done with? she's a talented and beautiful star! what's going on?
Apparently, miss Royella loves to hunt endangered Blue Rhinos! Someone leaked the photos of her newest kill!
It's a disaster!
The internet is furious!
I've never heard of a Blue Rhino.
That's because there were only 2 left! Now there's only one cuz she killed the pregnant female!!

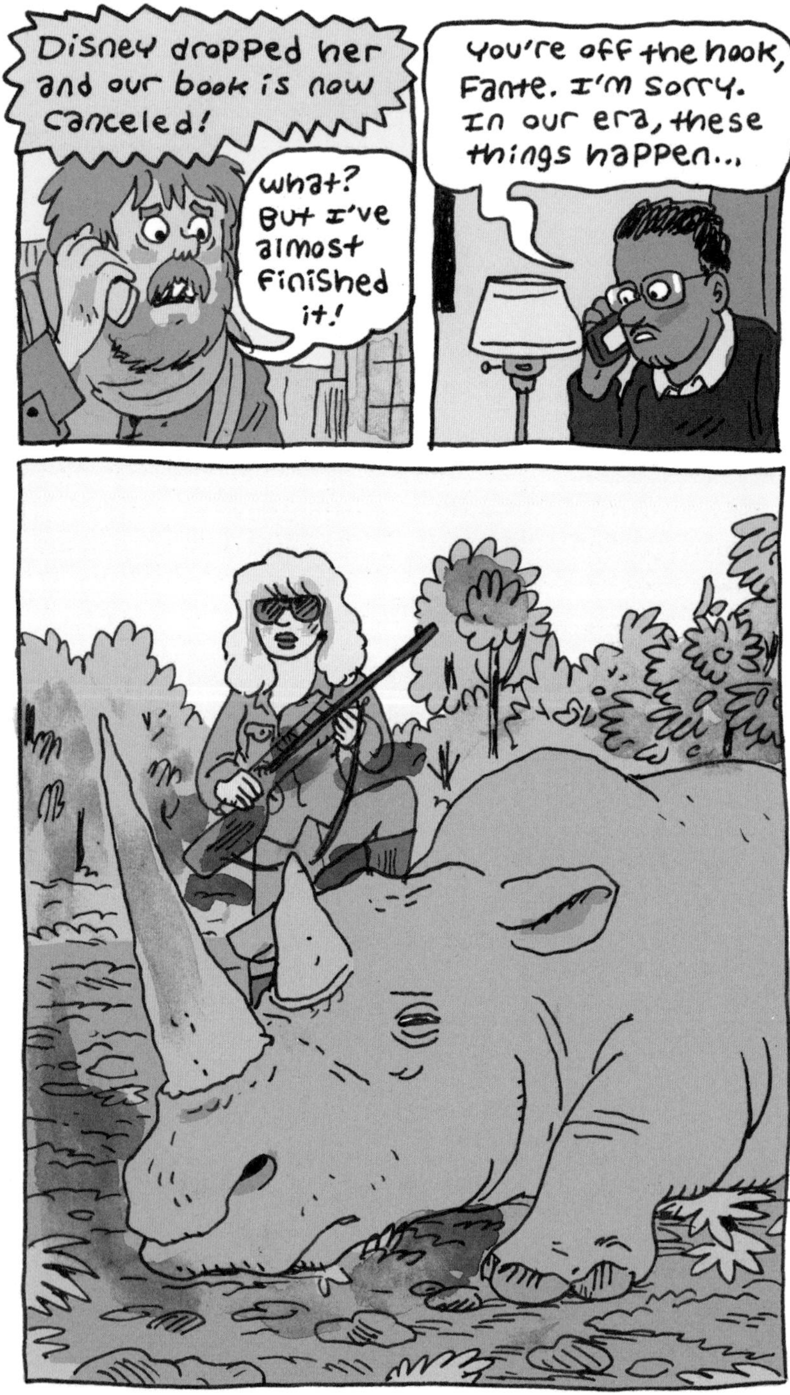
Disney dropped her and our book is now canceled!
What? But I've almost finished it!
You're off the hook, Fante. I'm sorry. In our era, these things happen...

~~Fante~~ Kelly visits his father.

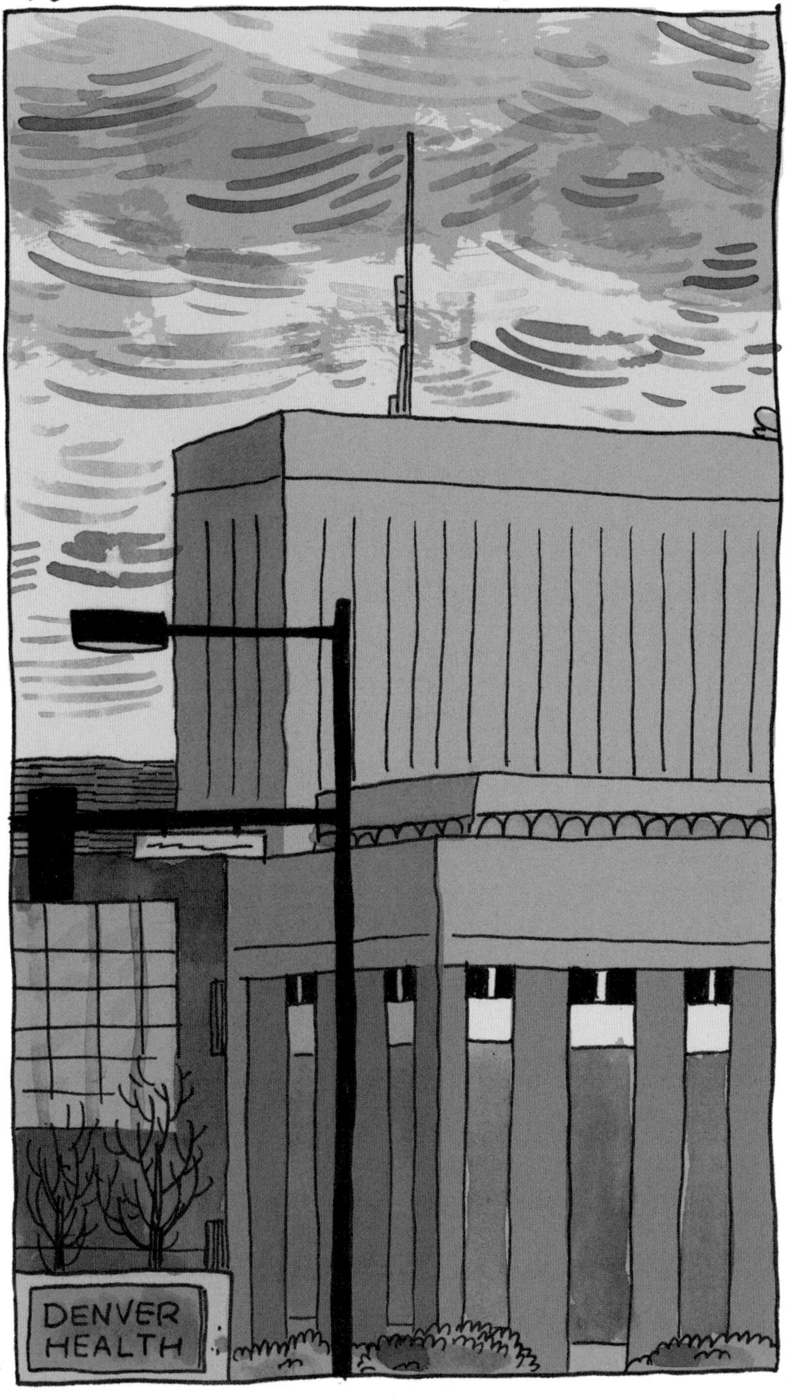
DENVER
HEALTH

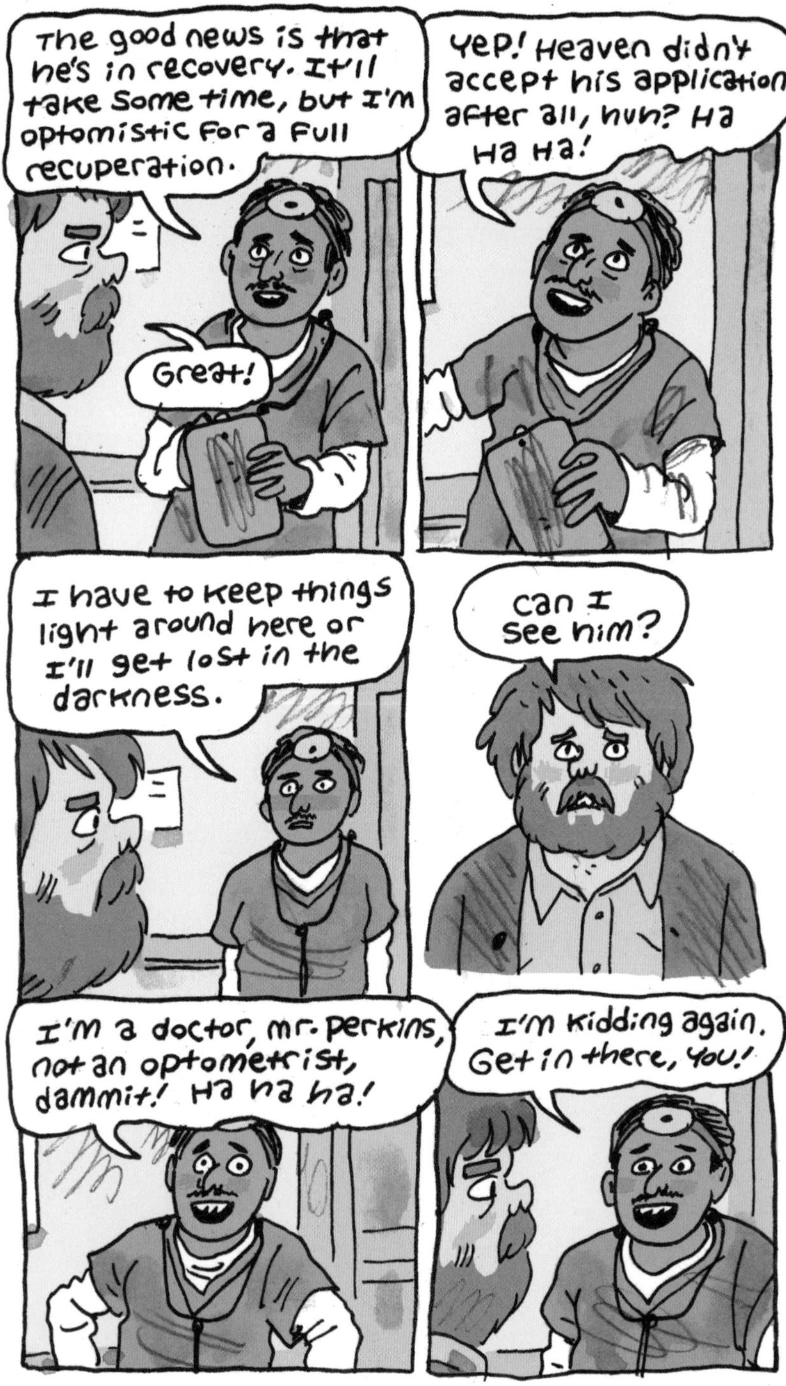
The good news is that he's in recovery. It'll take some time, but I'm optomistic for a full recuperation.
Great!
Yep! Heaven didn't accept his application after all, huh? Ha ha ha!
I have to keep things light around here or I'll get lost in the darkness.
Can I see him?
I'm a doctor, mr. Perkins, not an optometrist, dammit! Ha ha ha!
I'm kidding again. Get in there, you!

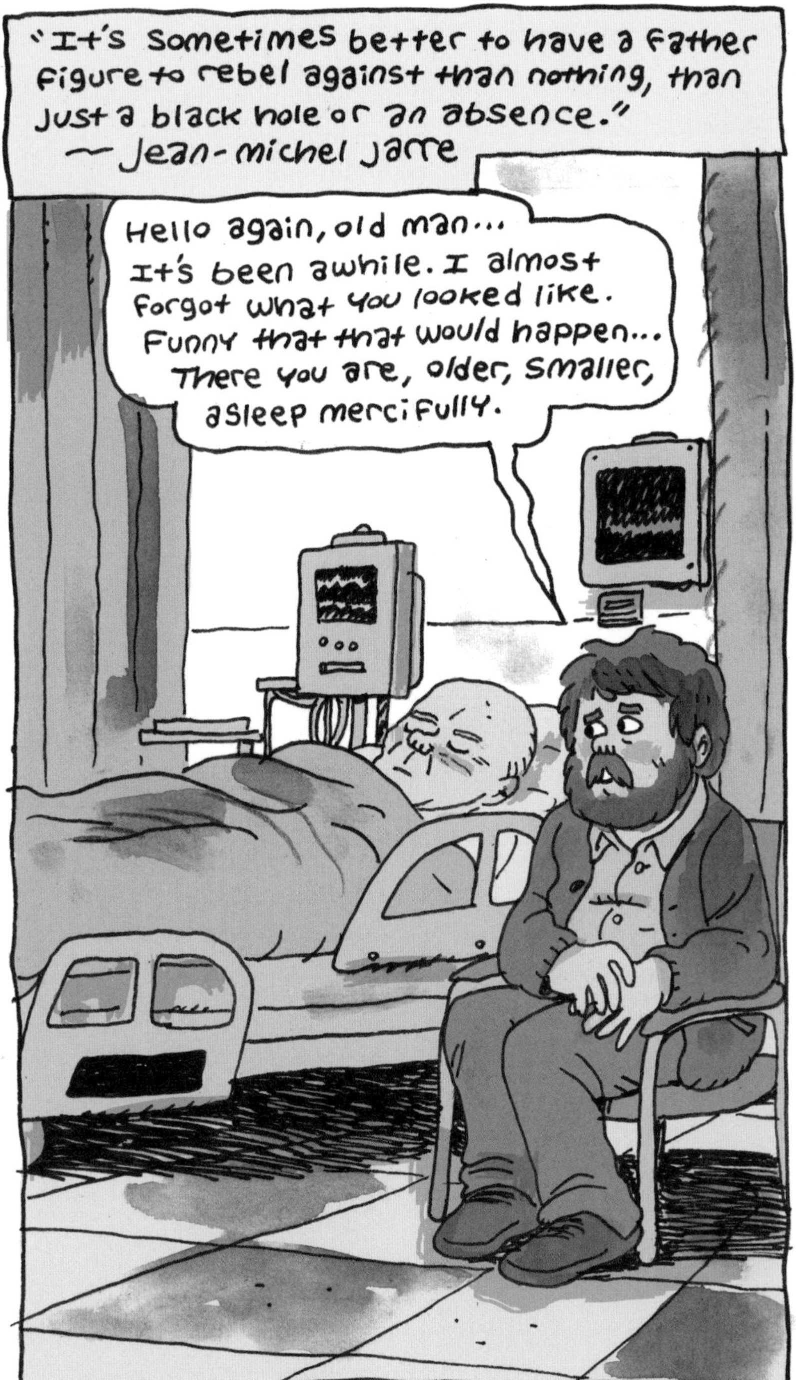
"It's sometimes better to have a father figure to rebel against than nothing, than just a black hole or an absence."
~ Jean-Michel Jarre
Hello again, old man... It's been awhile. I almost forgot what you looked like. Funny that that would happen... There you are, older, smaller, asleep mercifully.

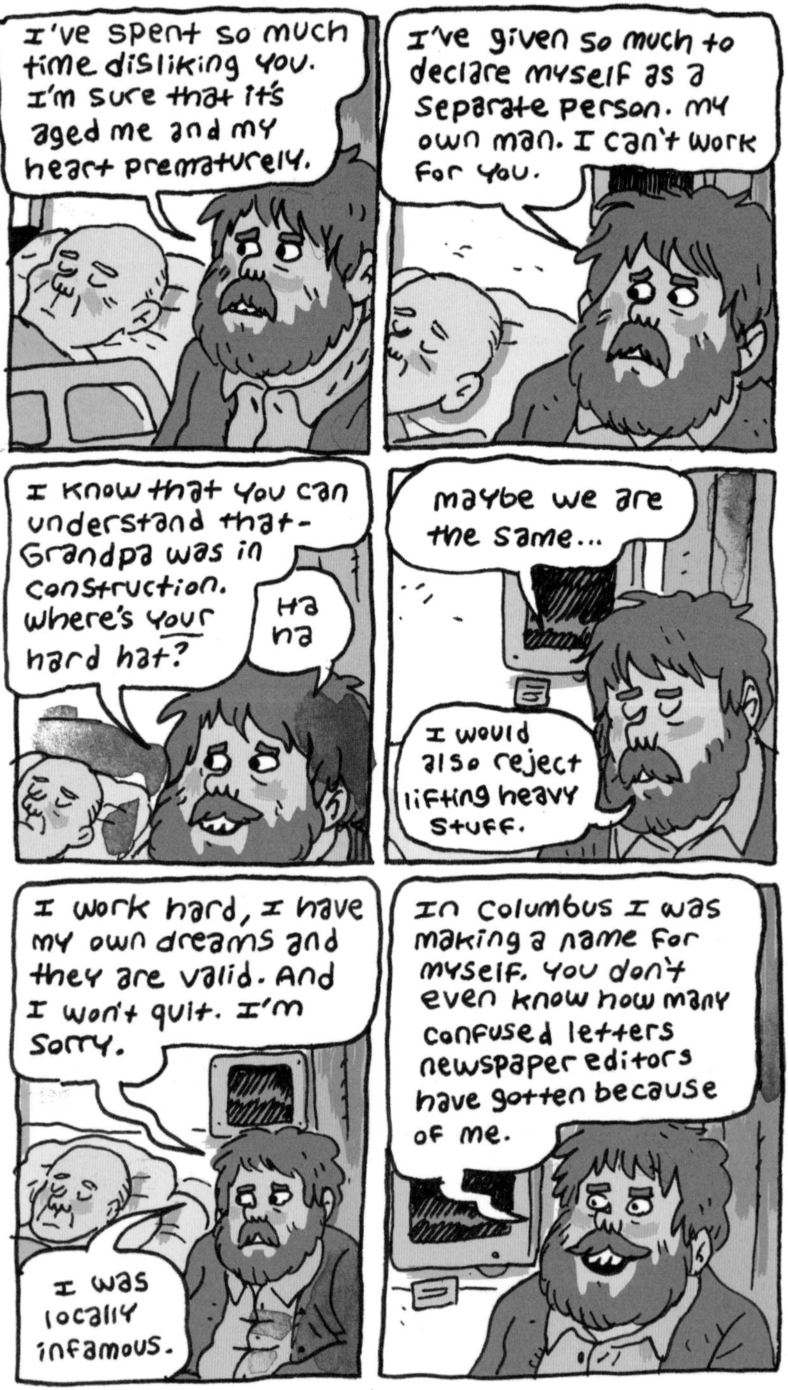
I've spent so much time disliking you. I'm sure that it's aged me and my heart prematurely.
I've given so much to declare myself as a separate person. My own man. I can't work for you.
I know that you can understand that- Grandpa was in construction. Where's your hard hat?
Ha ha
Maybe we are the same...
I would also reject lifting heavy stuff.
I work hard, I have my own dreams and they are valid. And I won't quit. I'm sorry.
I was locally infamous.
In Columbus I was making a name for myself. You don't even know how many confused letters newspaper editors have gotten because of me.

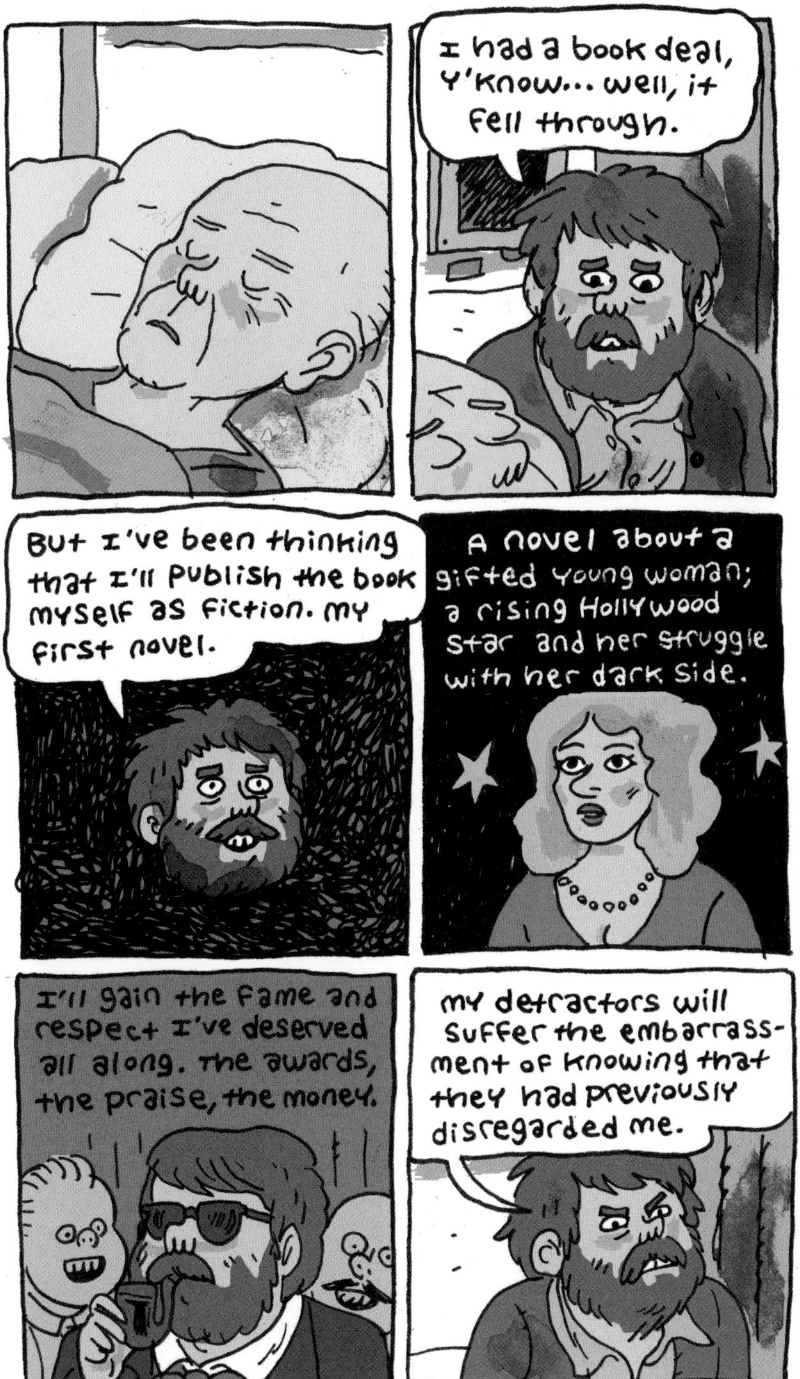
I had a book deal, Y'know... well, it fell through.
But I've been thinking that I'll publish the book myself as fiction. My first novel.
A novel about a gifted young woman; a rising Hollywood star and her struggle with her dark side.
I'll gain the fame and respect I've deserved all along. The awards, the praise, the money.
My detractors will suffer the embarrassment of knowing that they had previously disregarded me.

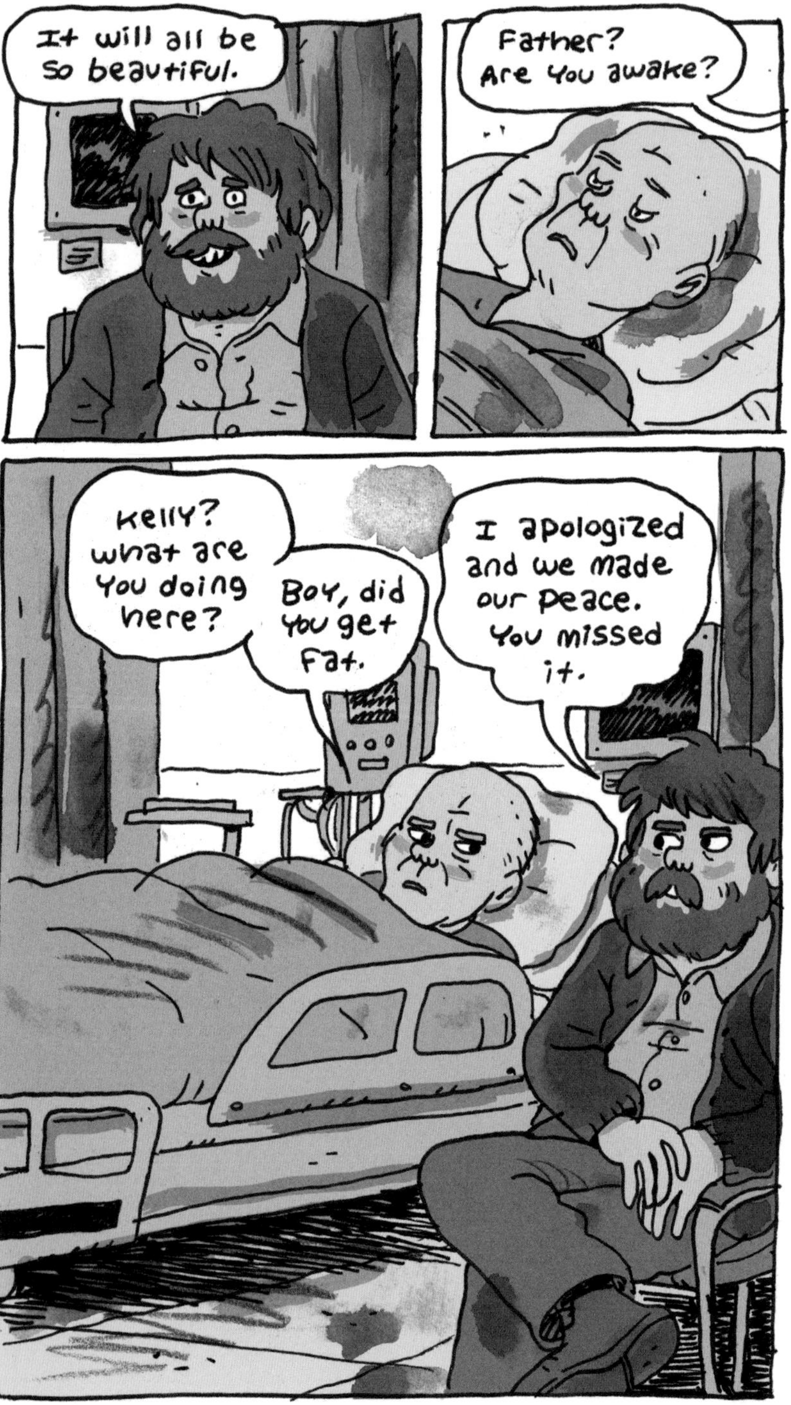
It will all be so beautiful.
Father? Are you awake?
Kelly? what are you doing here?
Boy, did you get fat.
I apologized and we made our peace. You missed it.

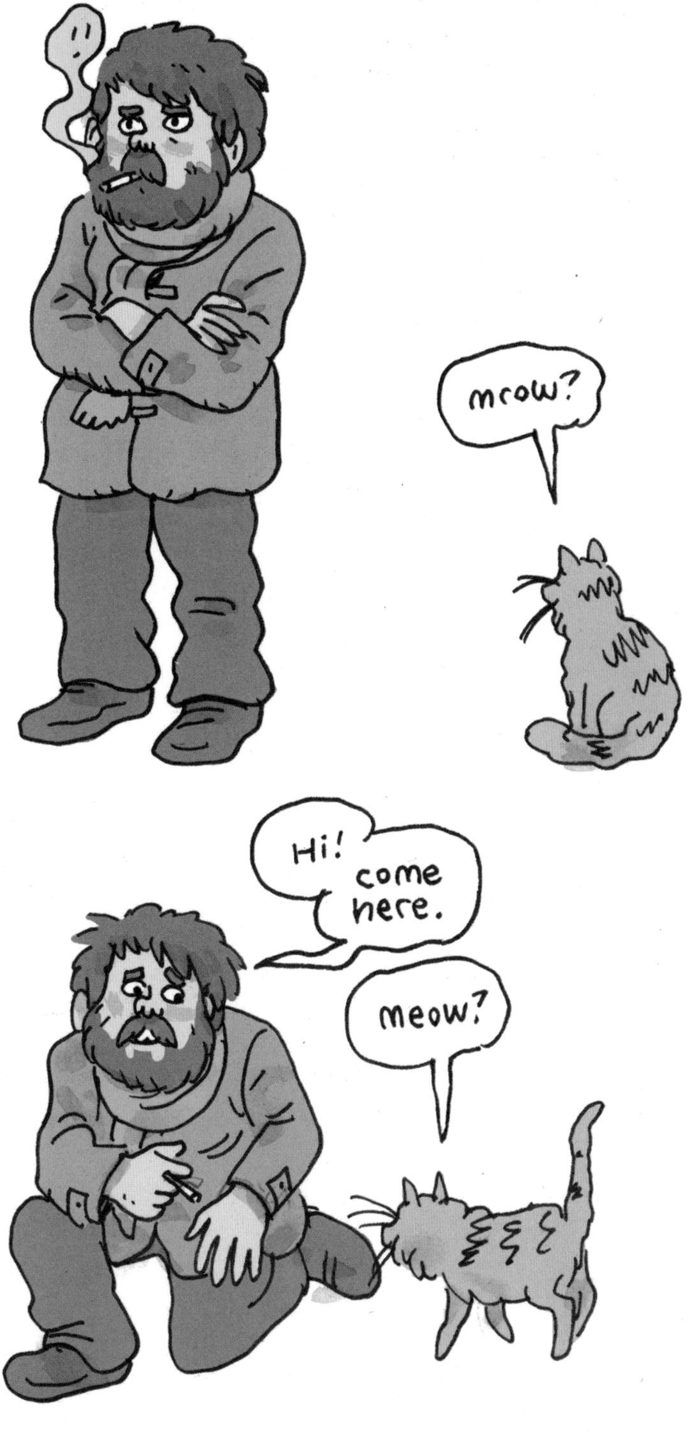
mrow?
Hi! come here.
meow?

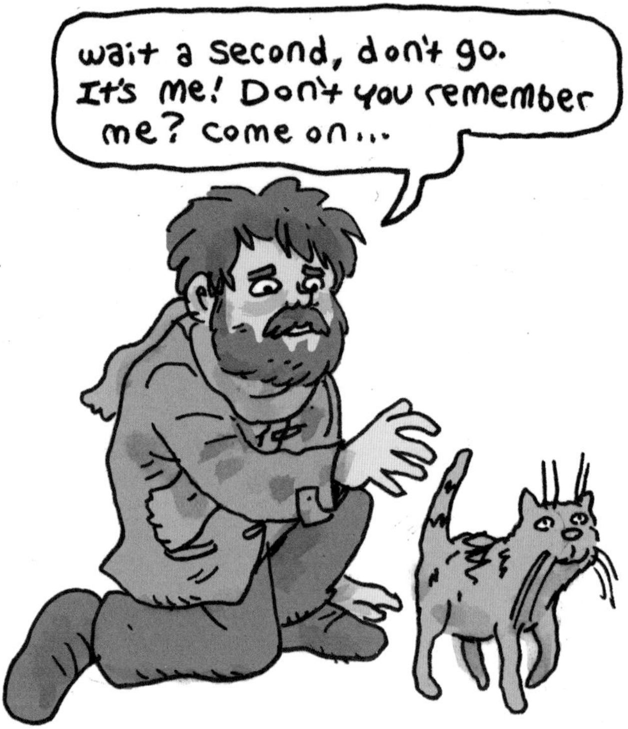
wait a second, don't go. It's me! Don't you remember me? come on...

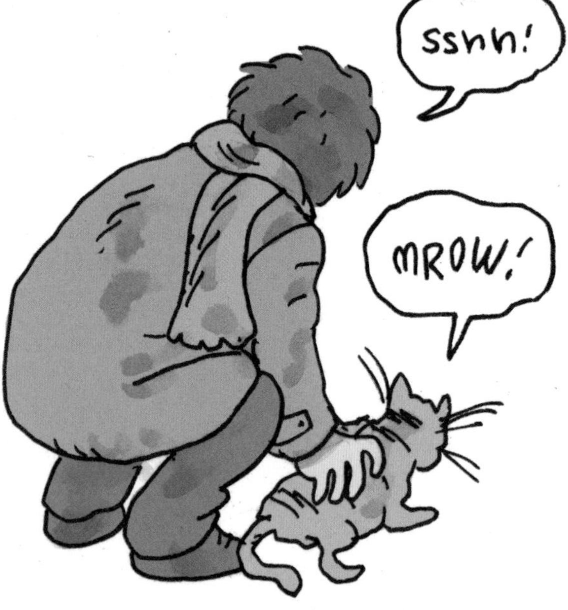
ssnn!
MROW!

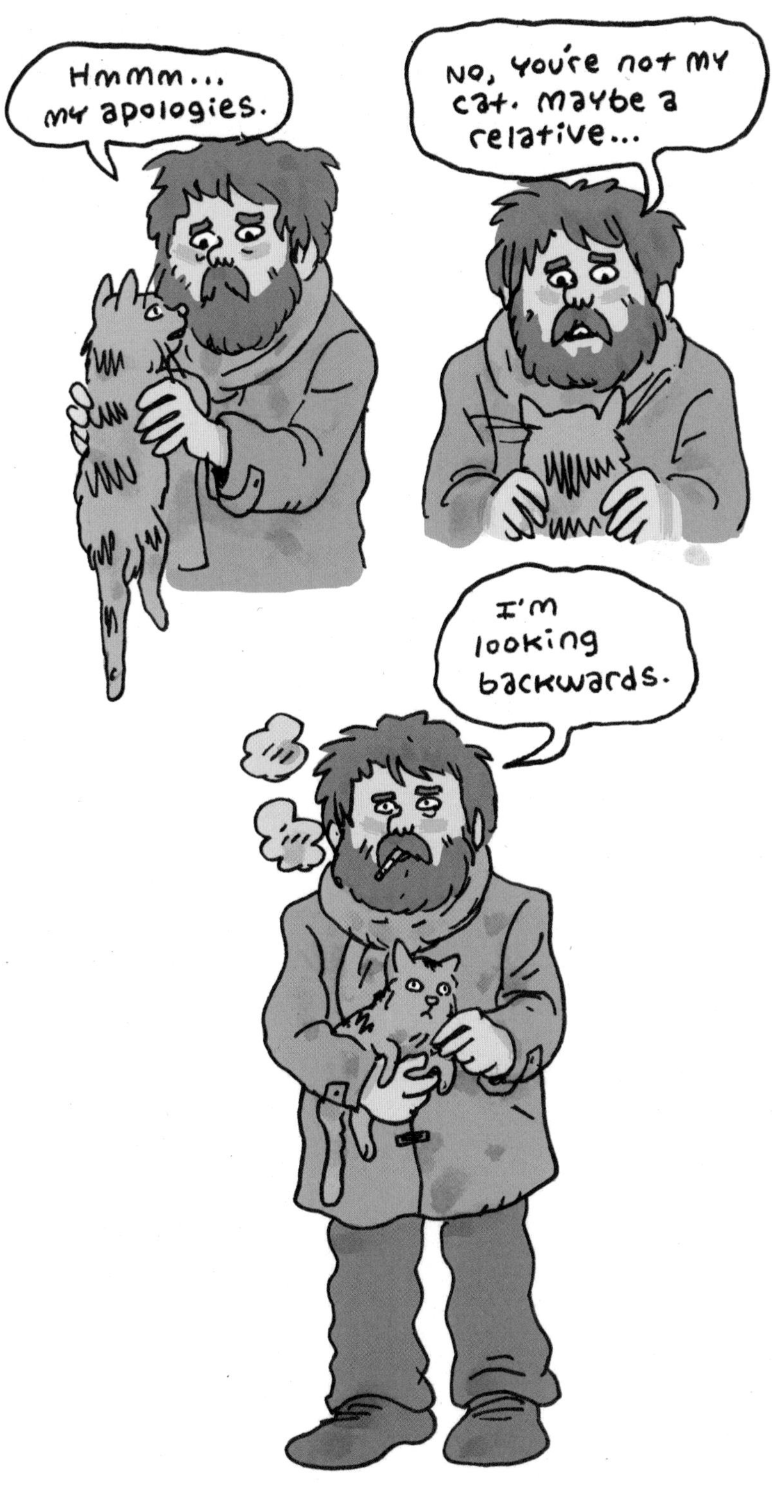
Hmmm...
my apologies.
No, you're not my cat. Maybe a relative...
I'm looking backwards.

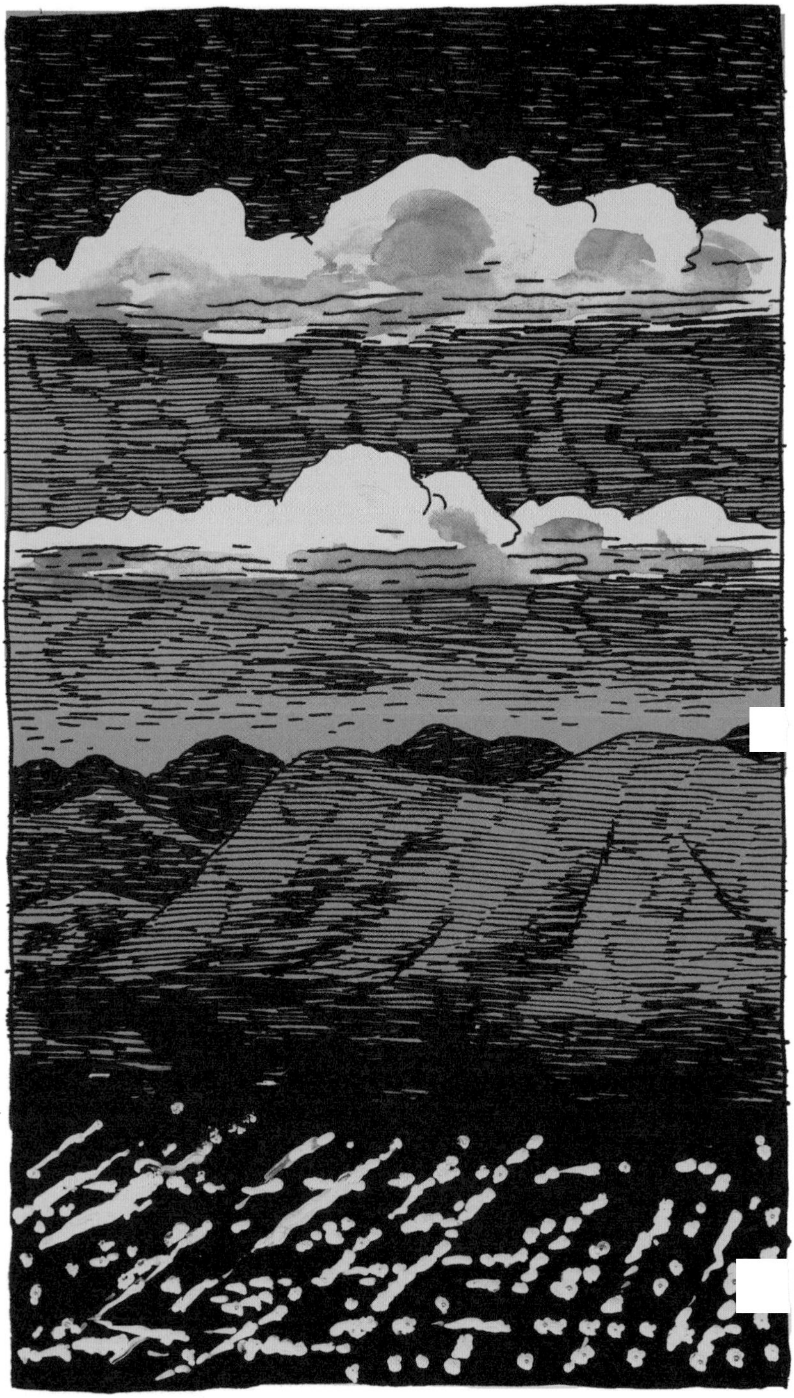

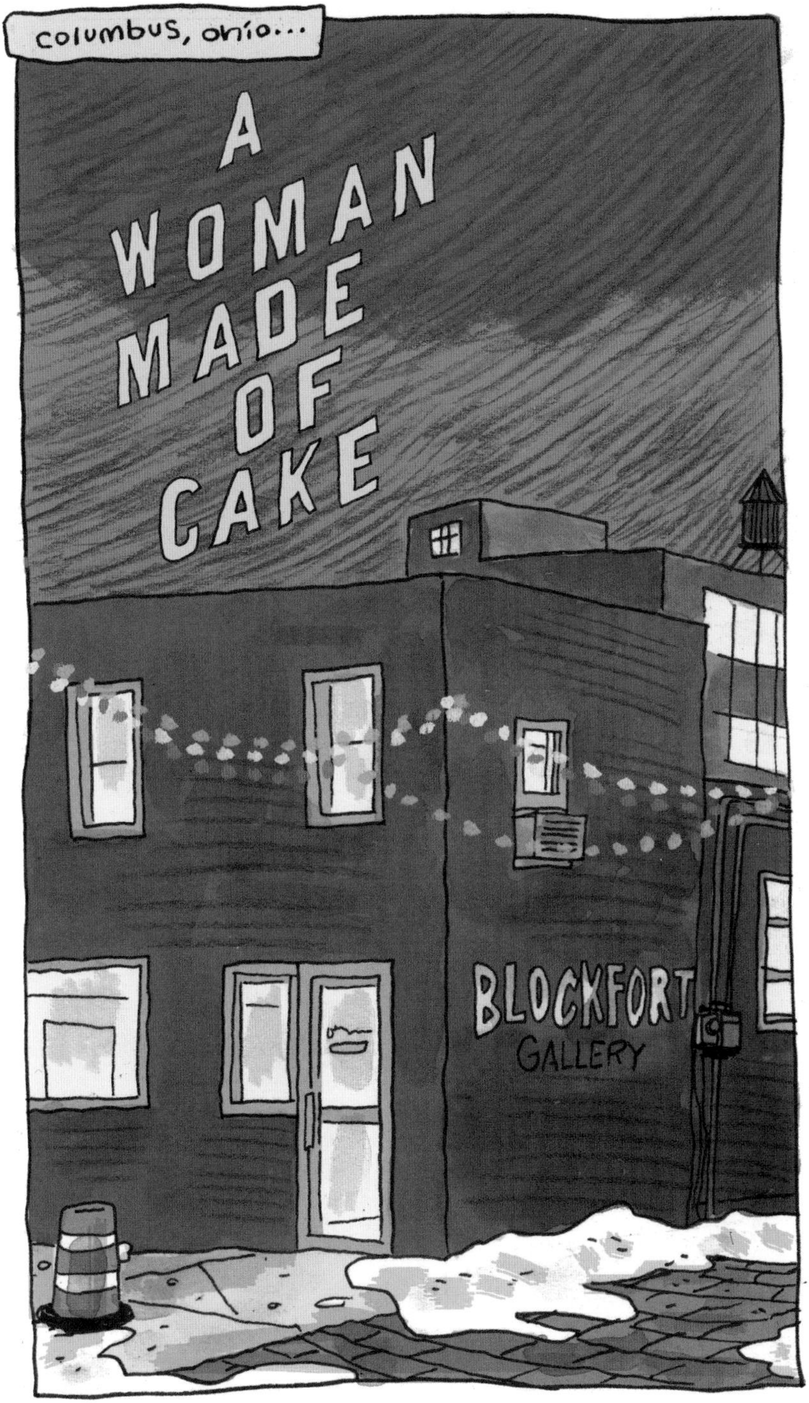
columbus, ohio...
A WOMAN MADE OF CAKE
BLOCKFORT
GALLERY

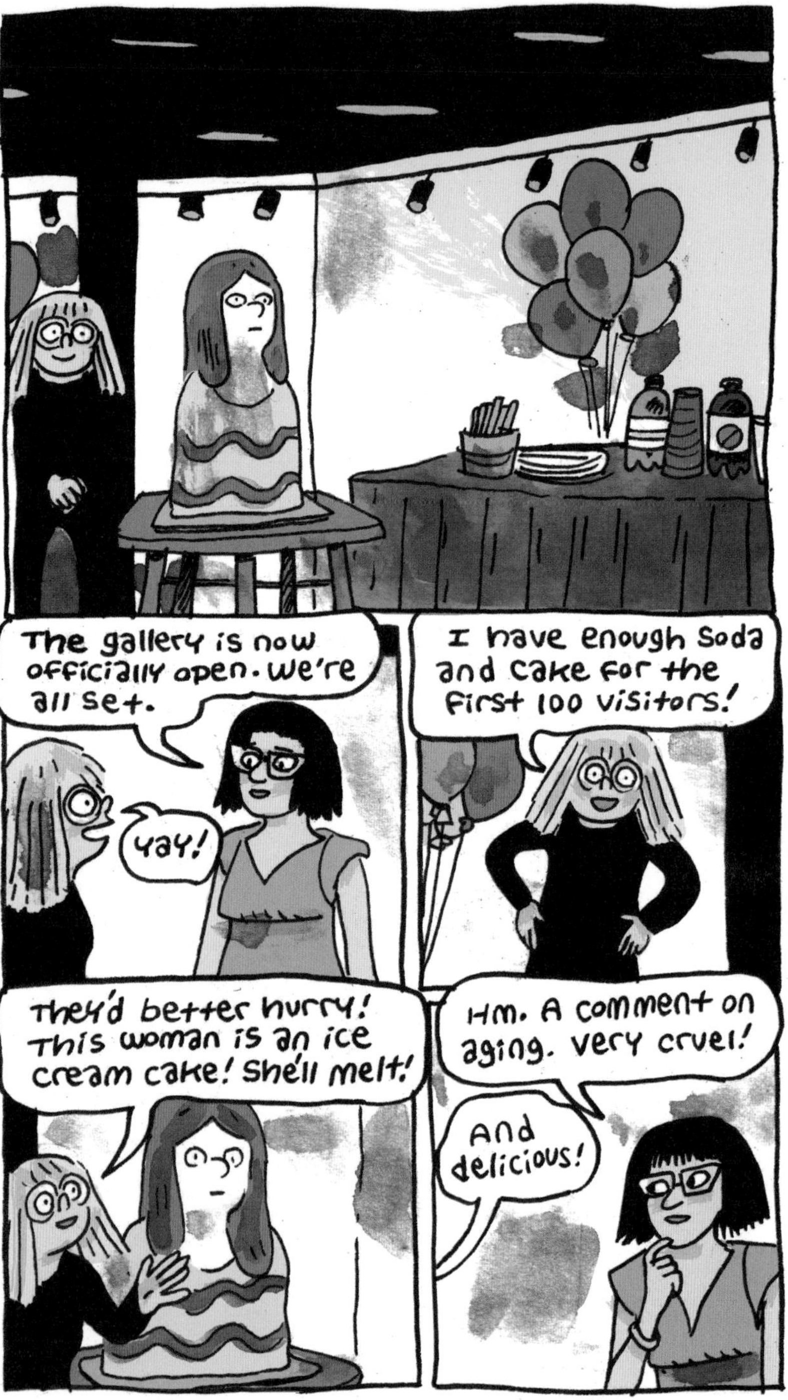
The gallery is now officially open. We're all set.
Yay!
I have enough soda and cake for the first 100 visitors!
They'd better hurry! This woman is an ice cream cake! She'll melt!
Hm. A comment on aging. Very cruel!
And delicious!

And so...

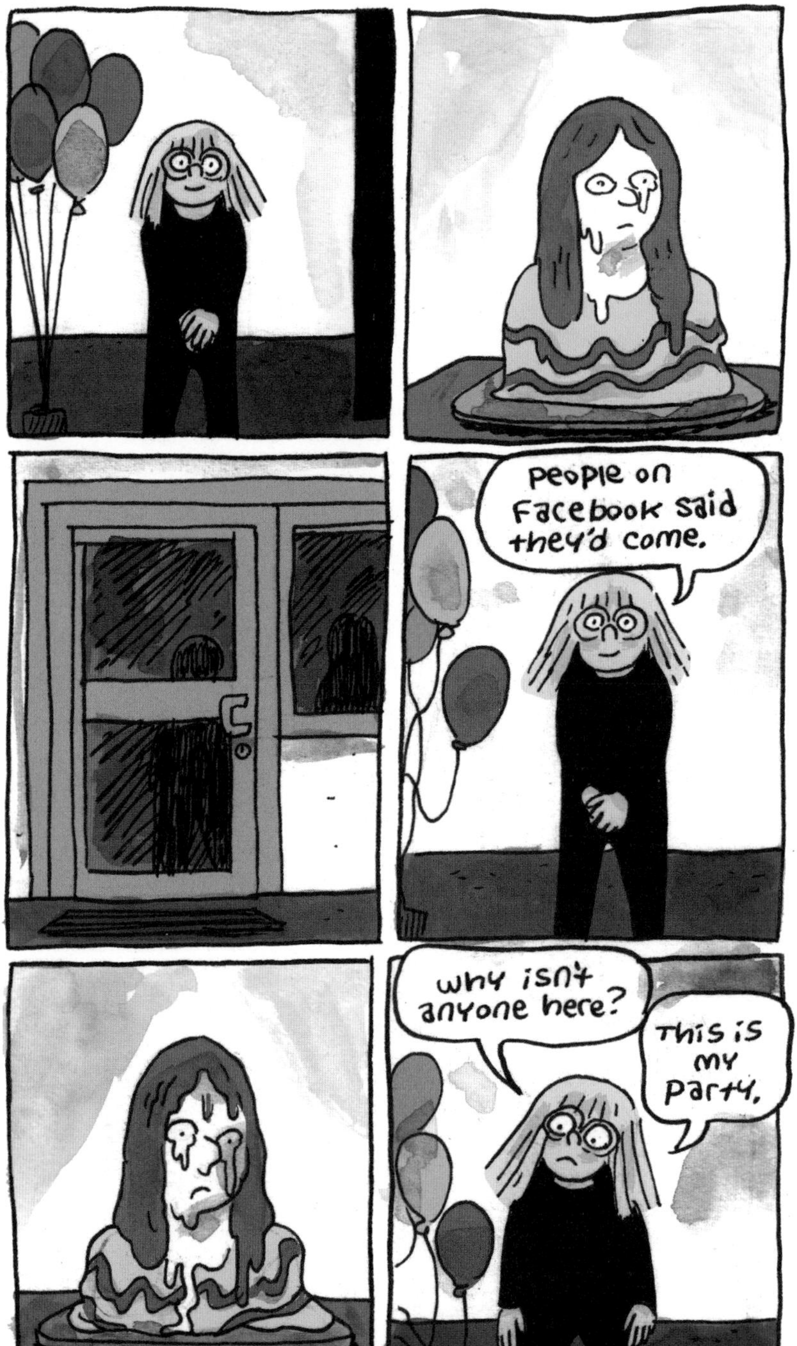
People on Facebook said they'd come.
why isn't anyone here?
This is my party.

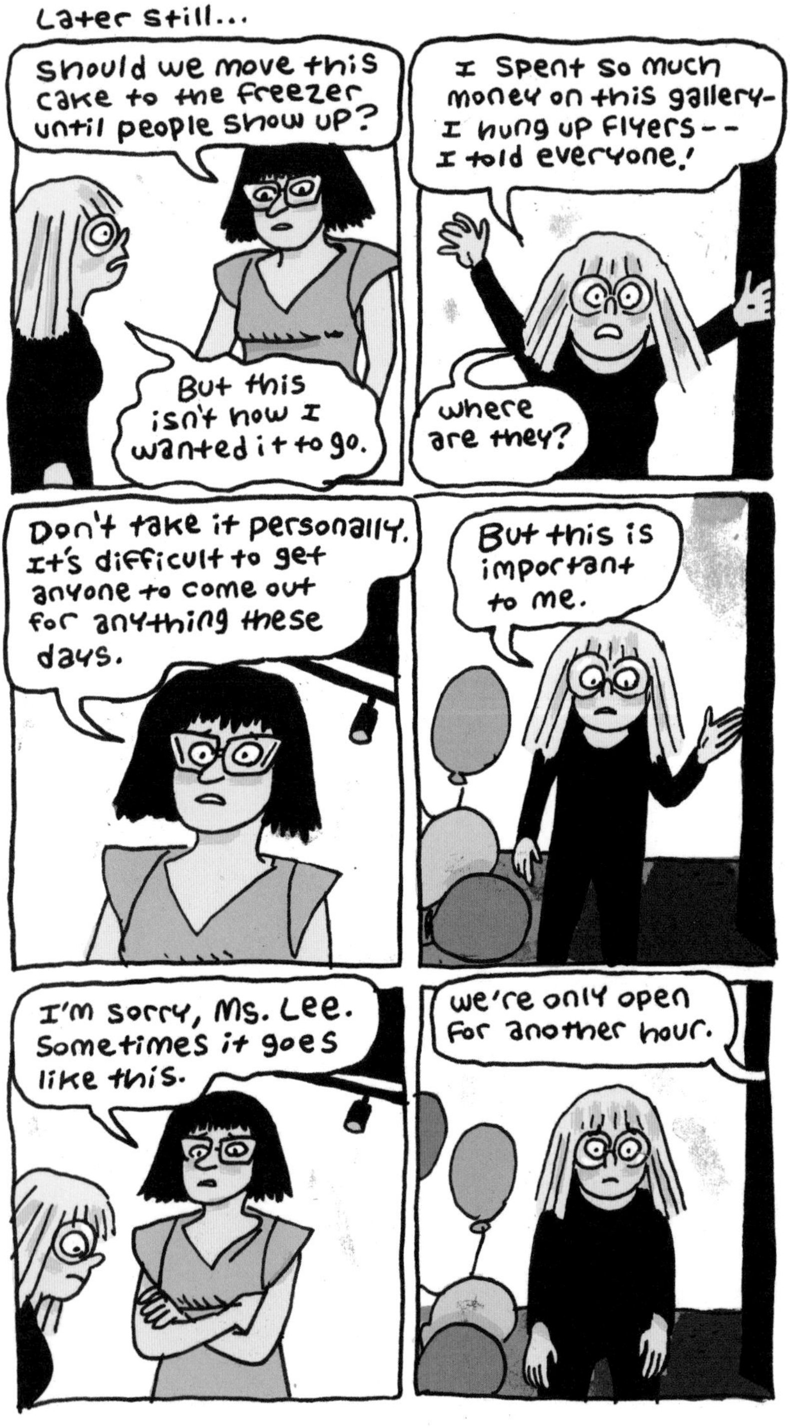
Later still...
Should we move this cake to the freezer until people show up?
But this isn't how I wanted it to go.
I spent so much money on this gallery-- I hung up flyers-- I told everyone!
Where are they?
Don't take it personally. It's difficult to get anyone to come out for anything these days.
But this is important to me.
I'm sorry, Ms. Lee. Sometimes it goes like this.
We're only open for another hour.

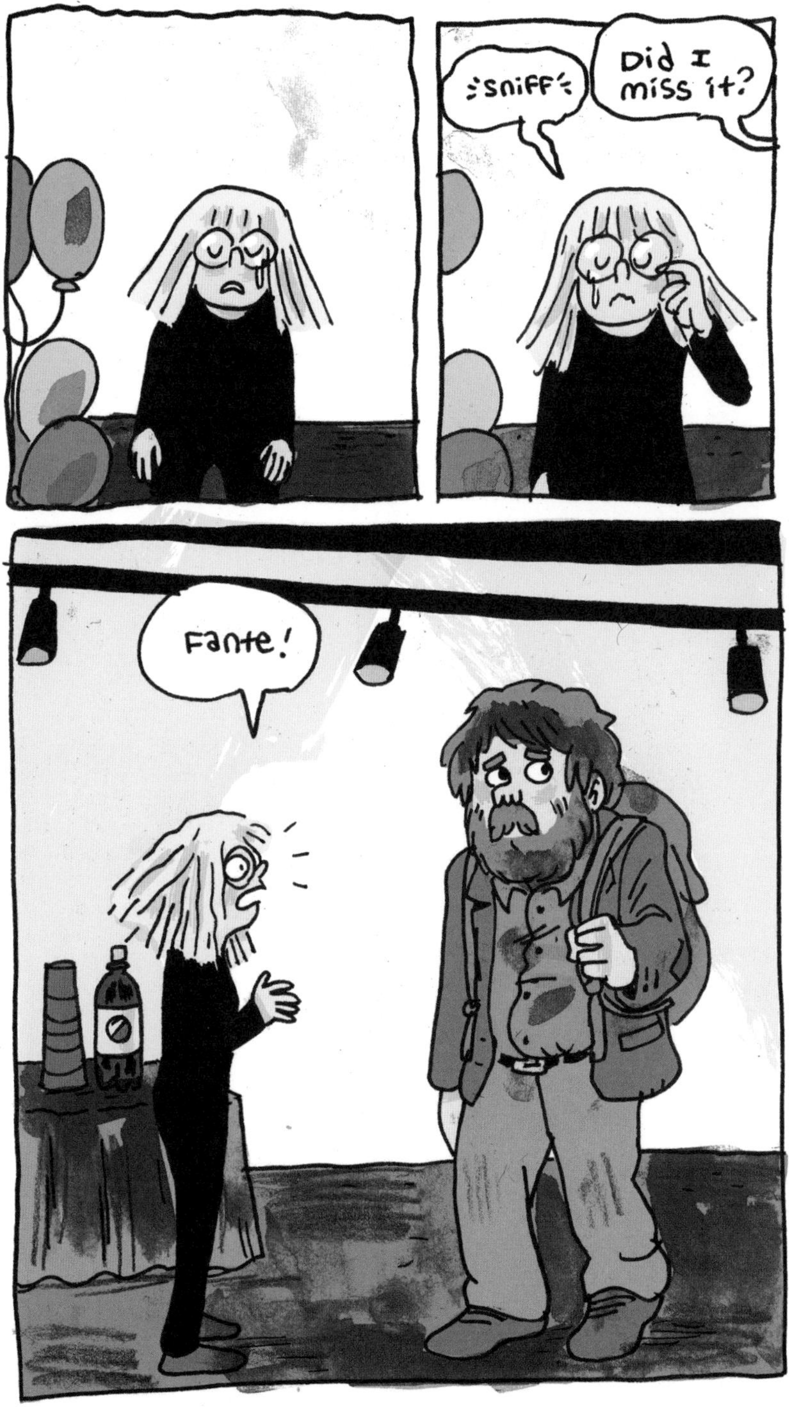

:sniff:
Did I miss it?
Fante!

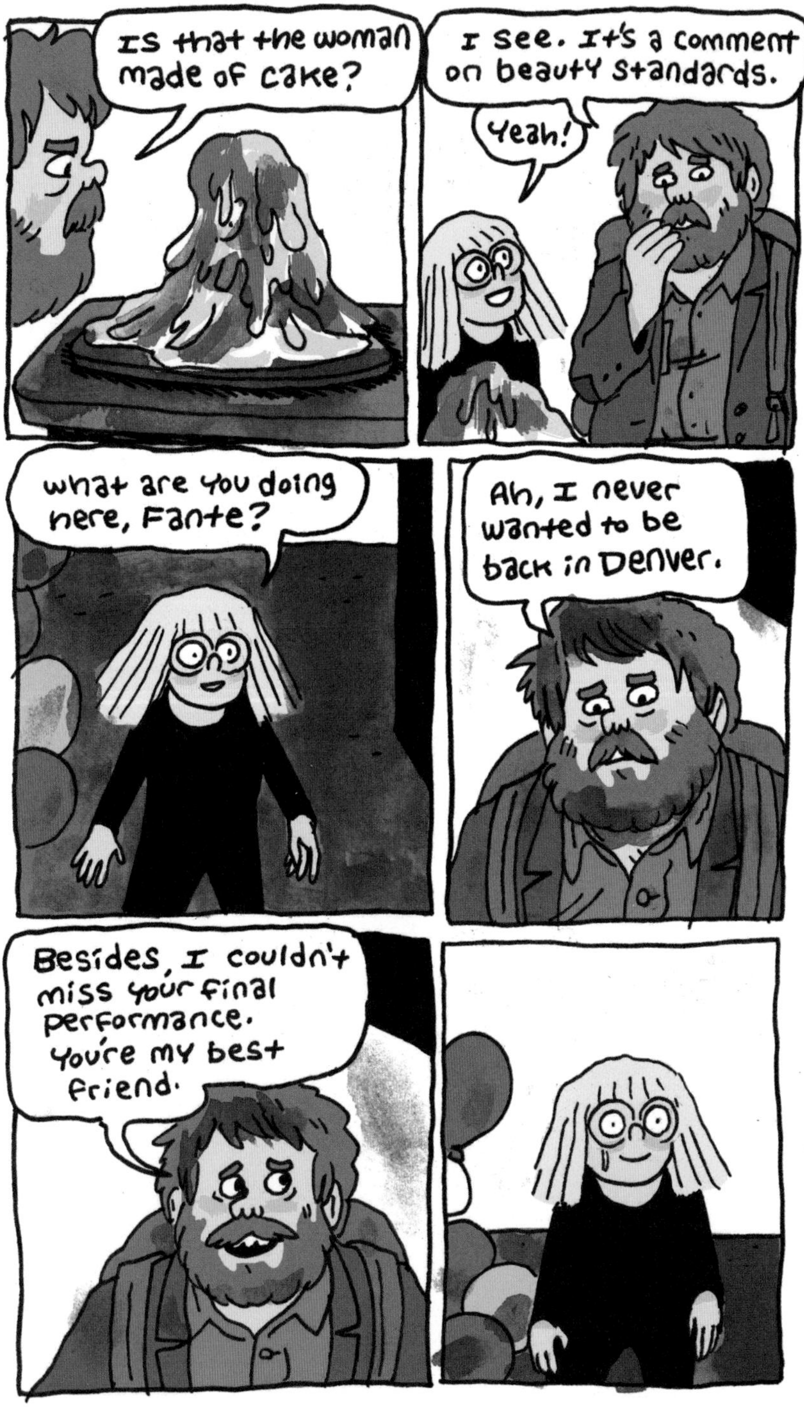
Is that the woman made of cake?
I see. It's a comment on beauty standards.
Yeah!
What are you doing here, Fante?
Ah, I never wanted to be back in Denver.
Besides, I couldn't miss your final performance. You're my best friend.

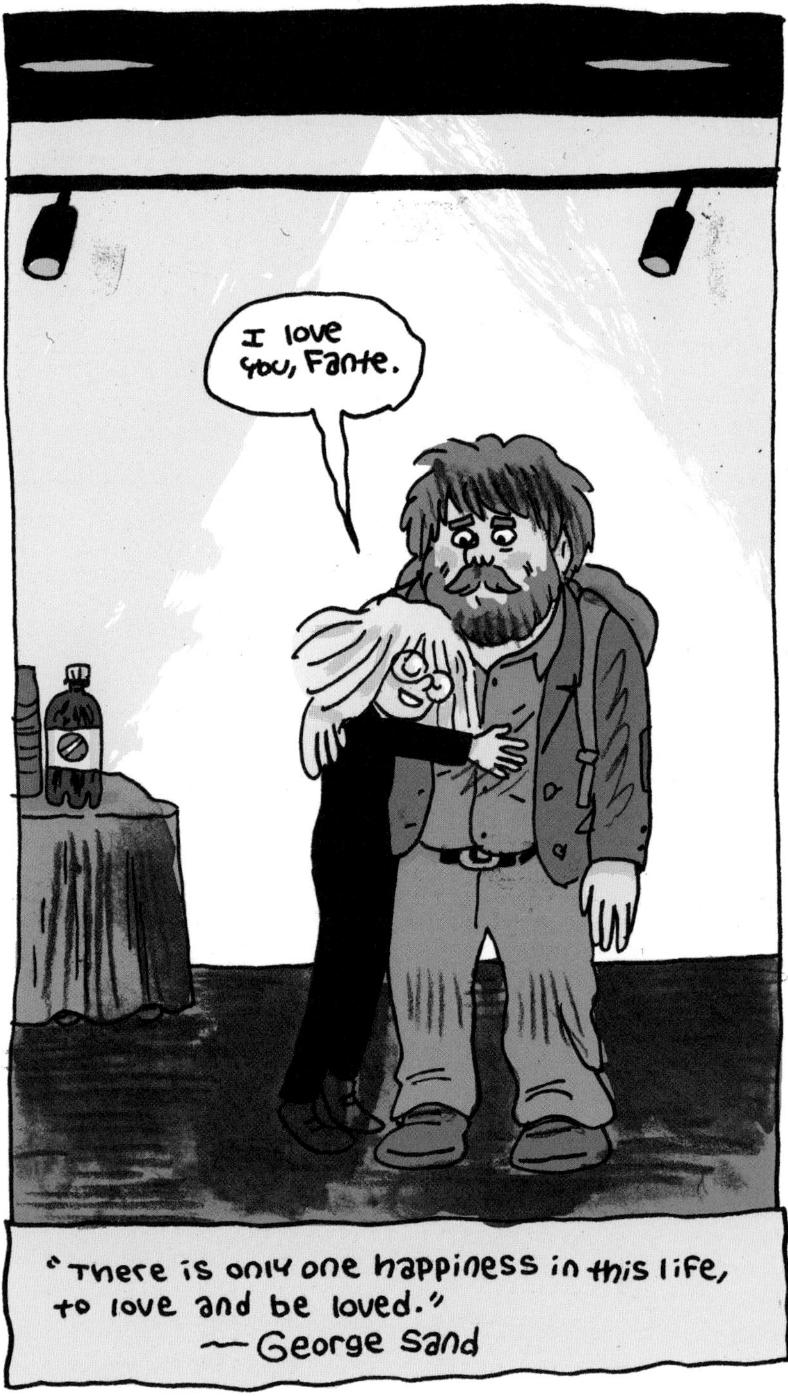
I love you, Fante.

"There is only one happiness in this life, to love and be loved."
—George Sand

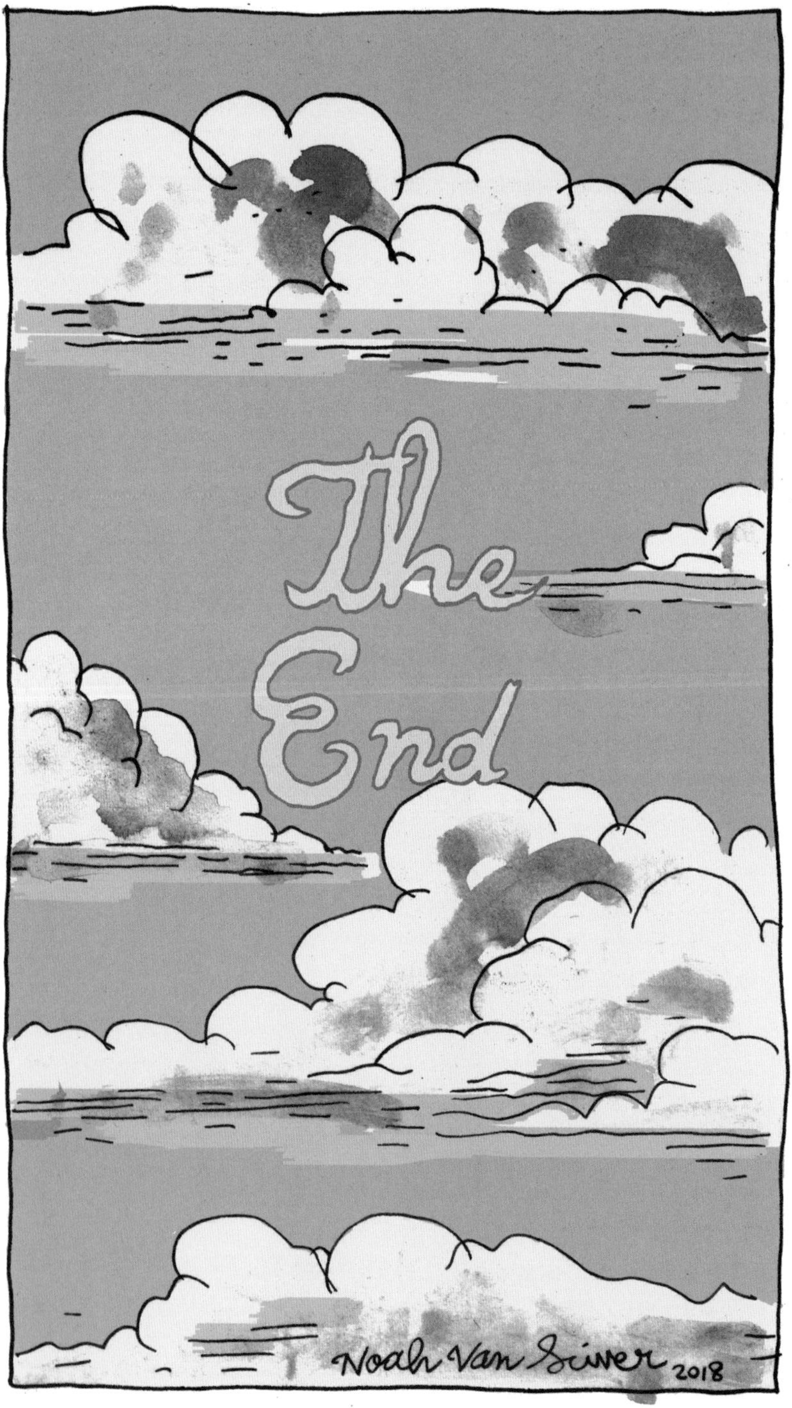
The End
Noah Van Sciver 2018

AFTERWORD

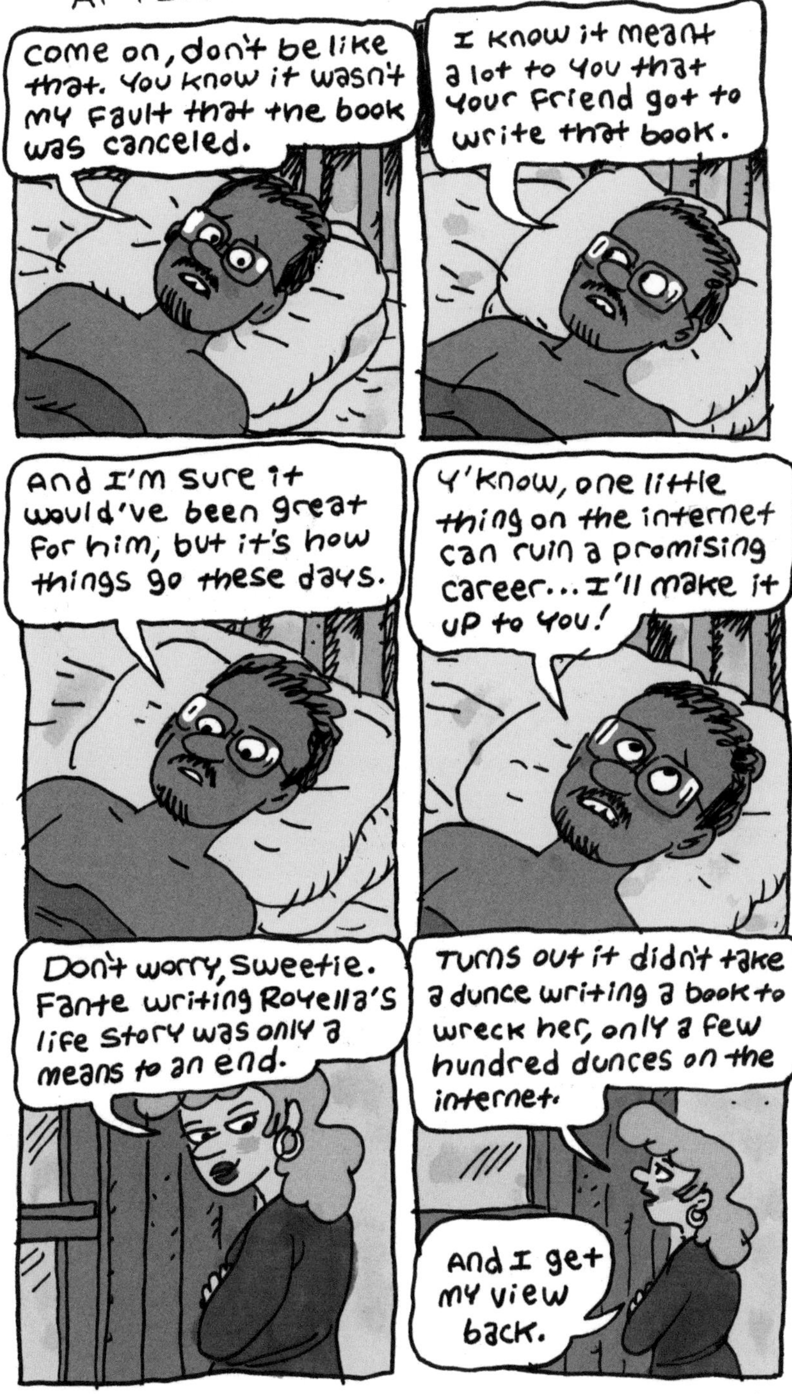
Come on, don't be like that. You know it wasn't my fault that the book was canceled.
I know it meant a lot to you that your friend got to write that book.
And I'm sure it would've been great for him, but it's how things go these days.
Y'know, one little thing on the internet can ruin a promising career... I'll make it up to you!
Don't worry, sweetie. Fante writing Royella's life story was only a means to an end.
Turns out it didn't take a dunce writing a book to wreck her, only a few hundred dunces on the internet.
And I get my view back.

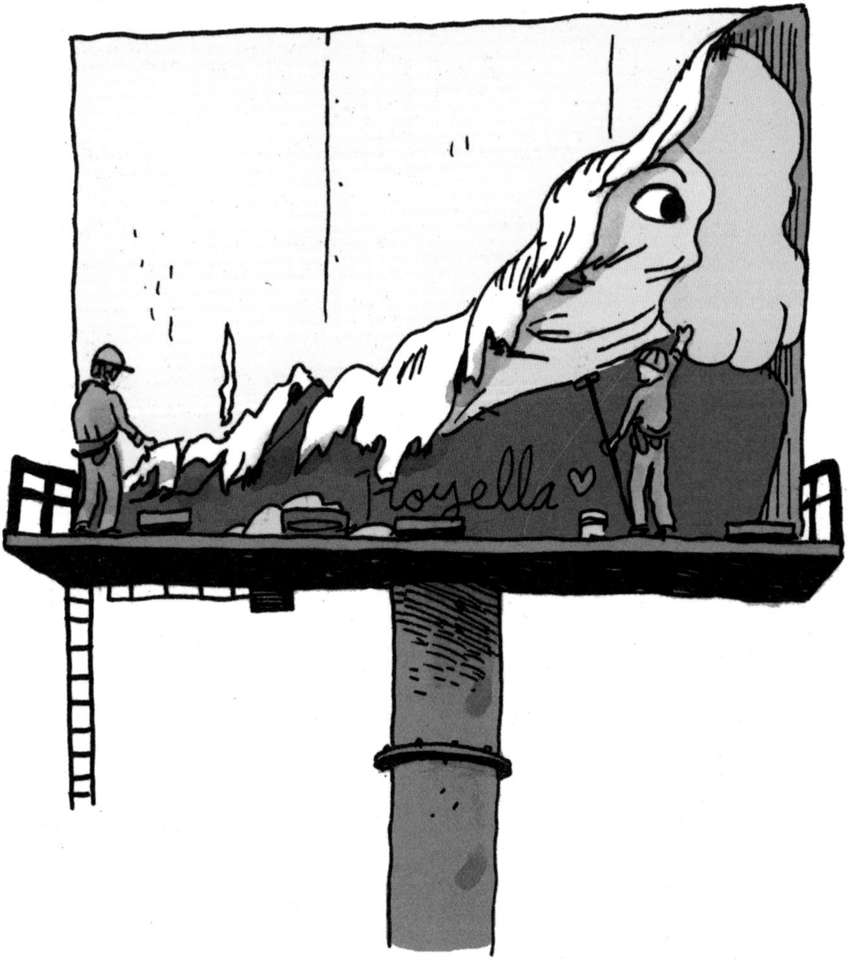
Foyella

FANTE BUKOWSKI THREE
PIN-UPS:

Alessandro Tota, Bryan Moss, Cristina Portolano,
Max de Radiguès, Giulia Sagramola, Nina Bunjavec,
Pierre Maurel, Noah Van Sciver

FANTE BUKOWSKI IN ITALY

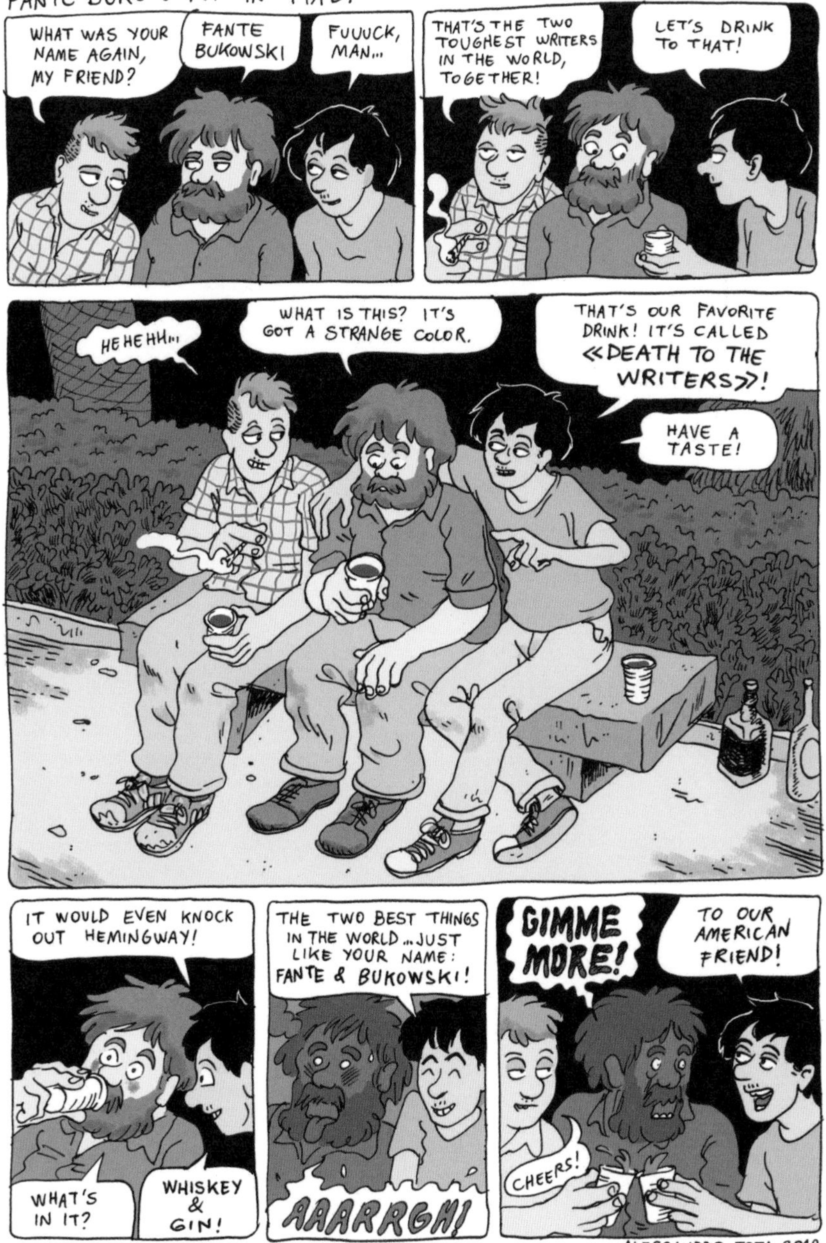
WHAT WAS YOUR NAME AGAIN, MY FRIEND?
FANTE BUKOWSKI
FUUUCK, MAN...
THAT'S THE TWO TOUGHEST WRITERS IN THE WORLD, TOGETHER!
LET'S DRINK TO THAT!
HEHEHH...
WHAT IS THIS? IT'S GOT A STRANGE COLOR.
THAT'S OUR FAVORITE DRINK! IT'S CALLED «DEATH TO THE WRITERS»!
HAVE A TASTE!
IT WOULD EVEN KNOCK OUT HEMINGWAY!
WHAT'S IN IT?
WHISKEY & GIN!
THE TWO BEST THINGS IN THE WORLD... JUST LIKE YOUR NAME: FANTE & BUKOWSKI!
AAARRGH!
GIMME MORE!
TO OUR AMERICAN FRIEND!
CHEERS!

ALESSANDRO TOTA 2018

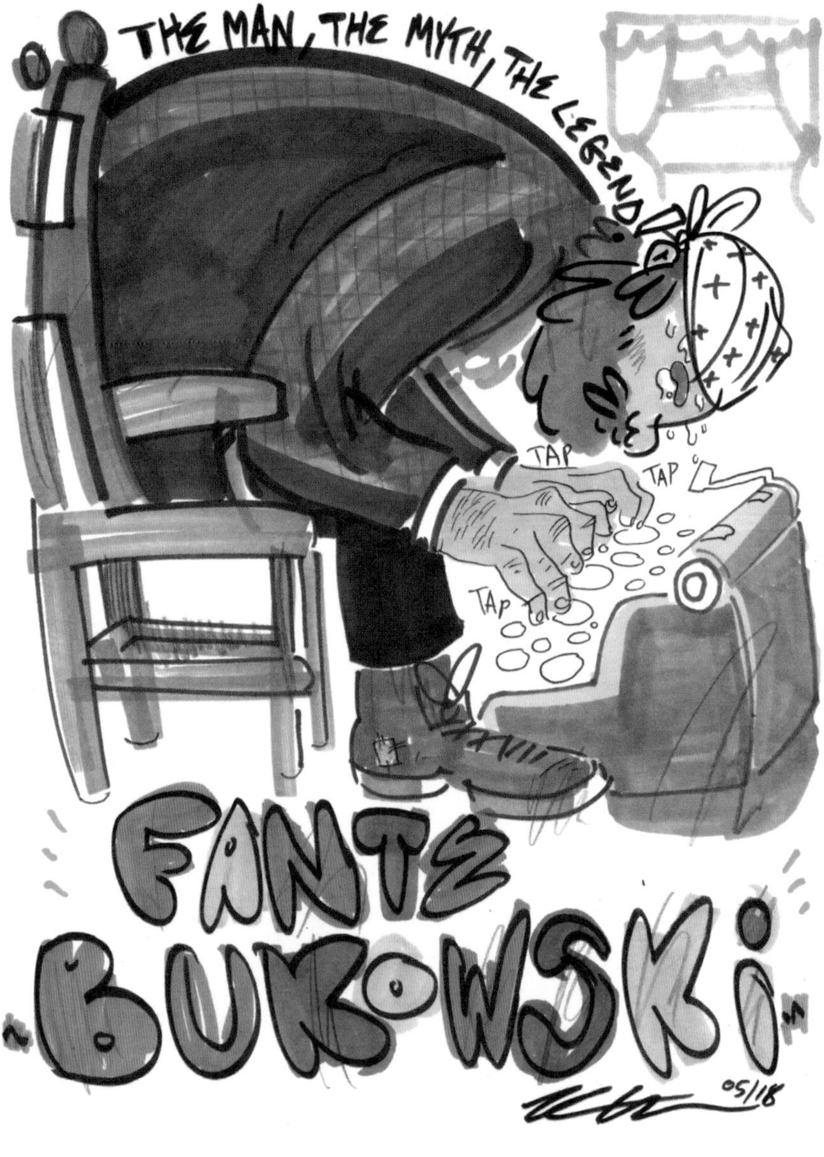
THE MAN, THE MYTH, THE LEGEND
TAP
TAP
TAP
FANTE
BUKOWSKI
05/18

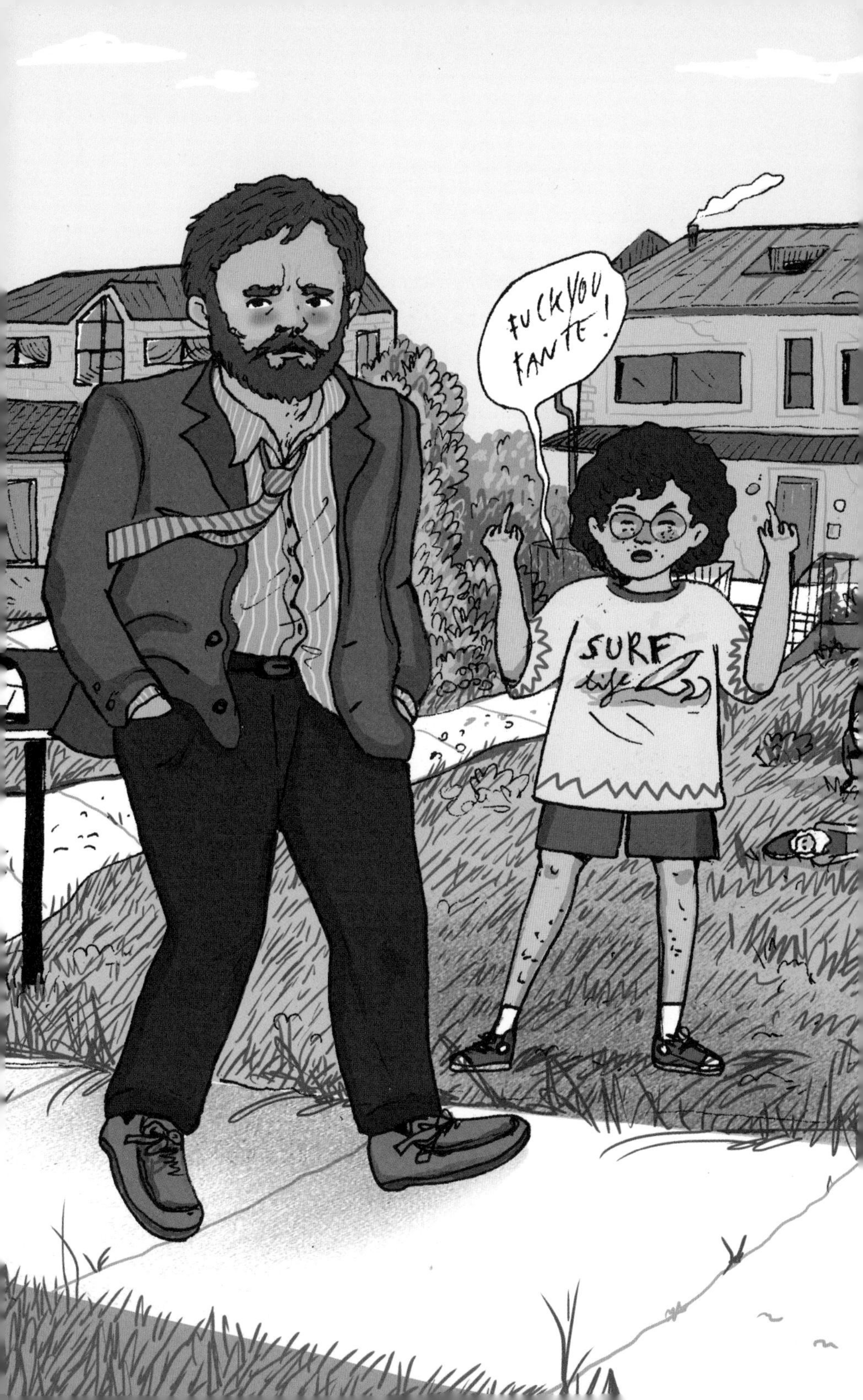
FUCK YOU FANTE!
SURF
life

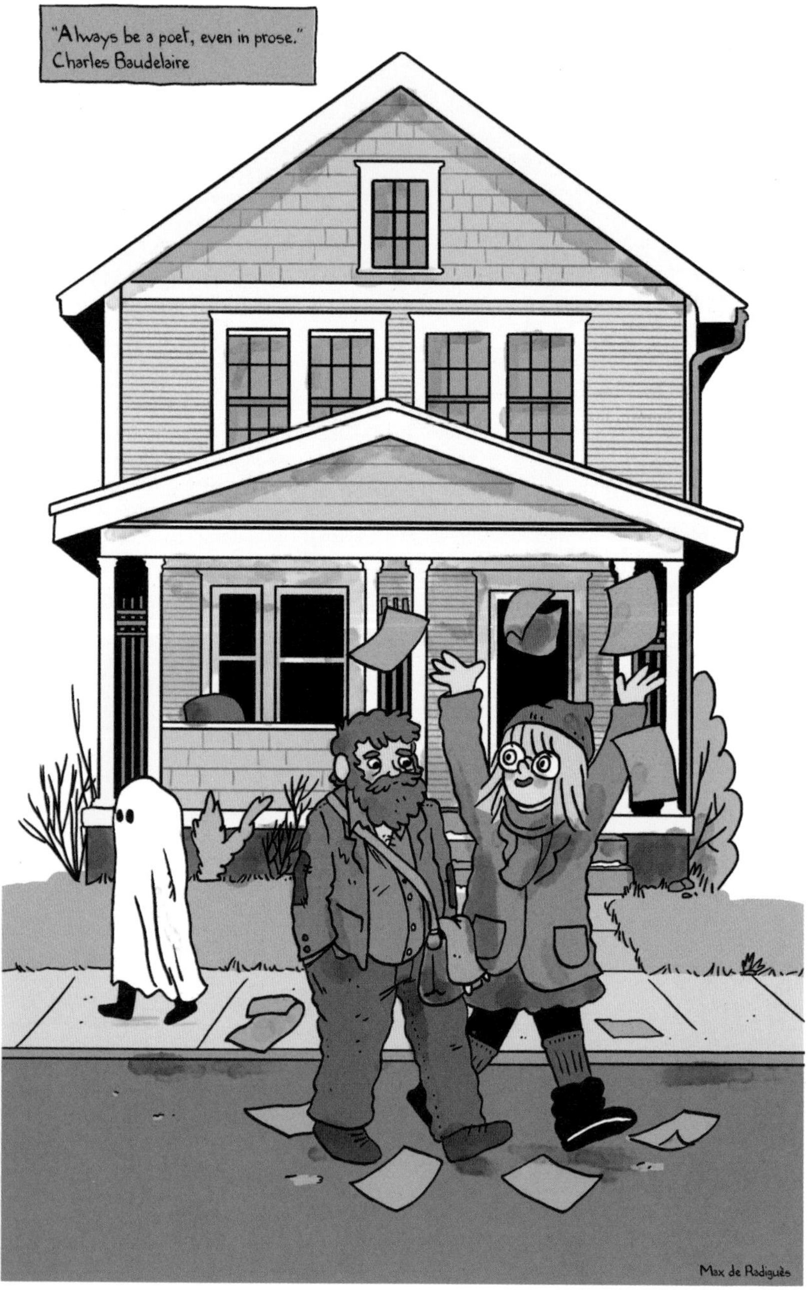
"Always be a poet, even in prose."
Charles Baudelaire
Max de Radiguès

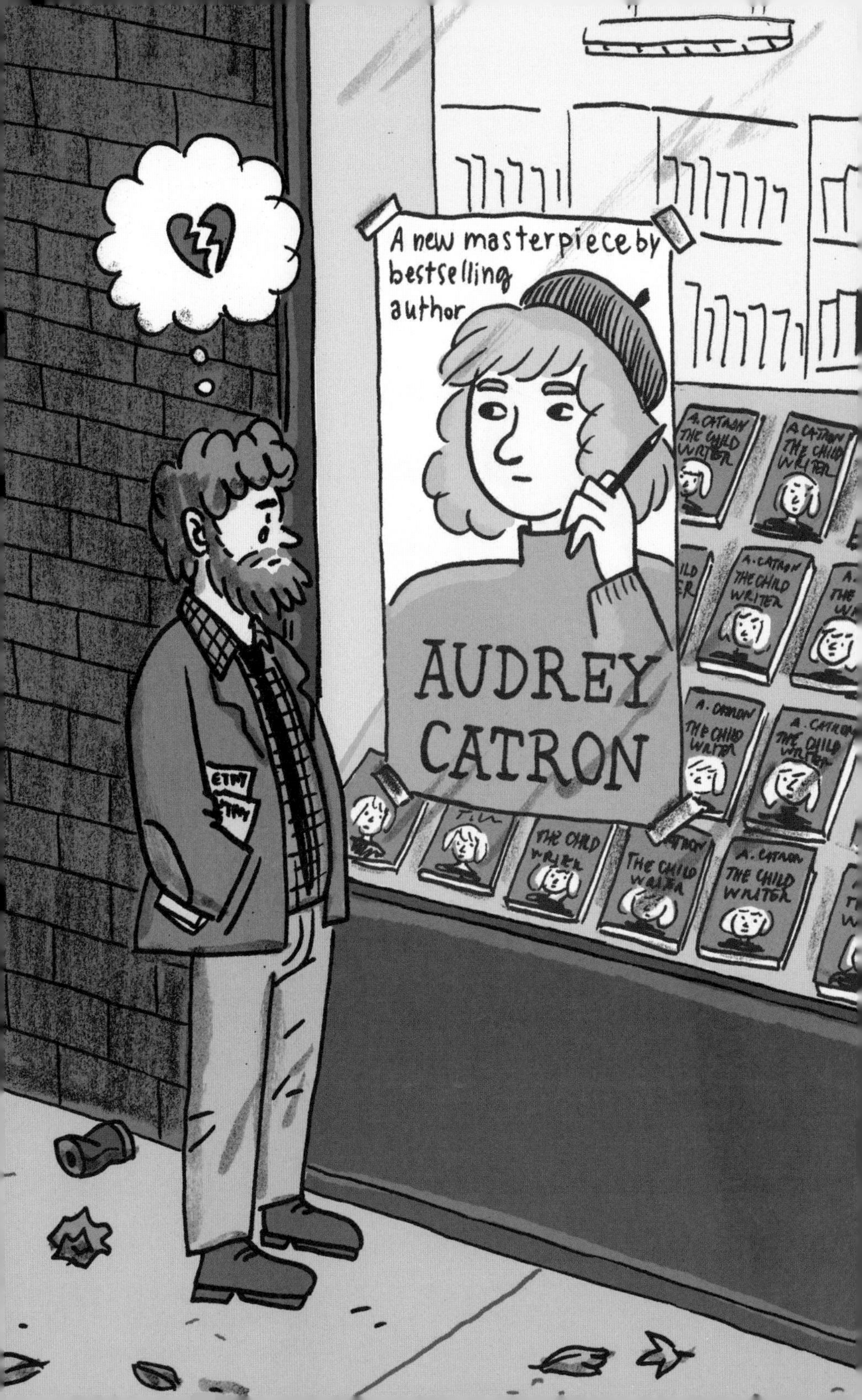
A new masterpiece by bestselling author
AUDREY CATRON
A. CATRON
THE CHILD WRITER

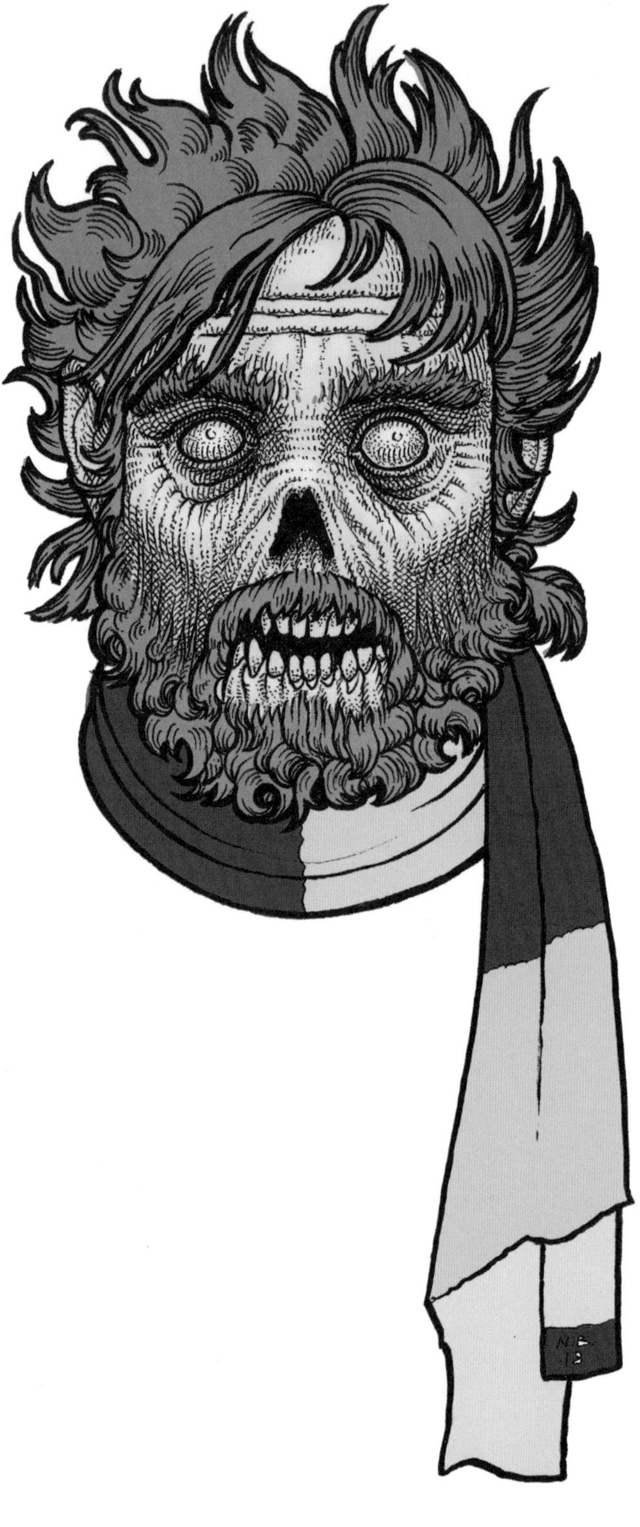

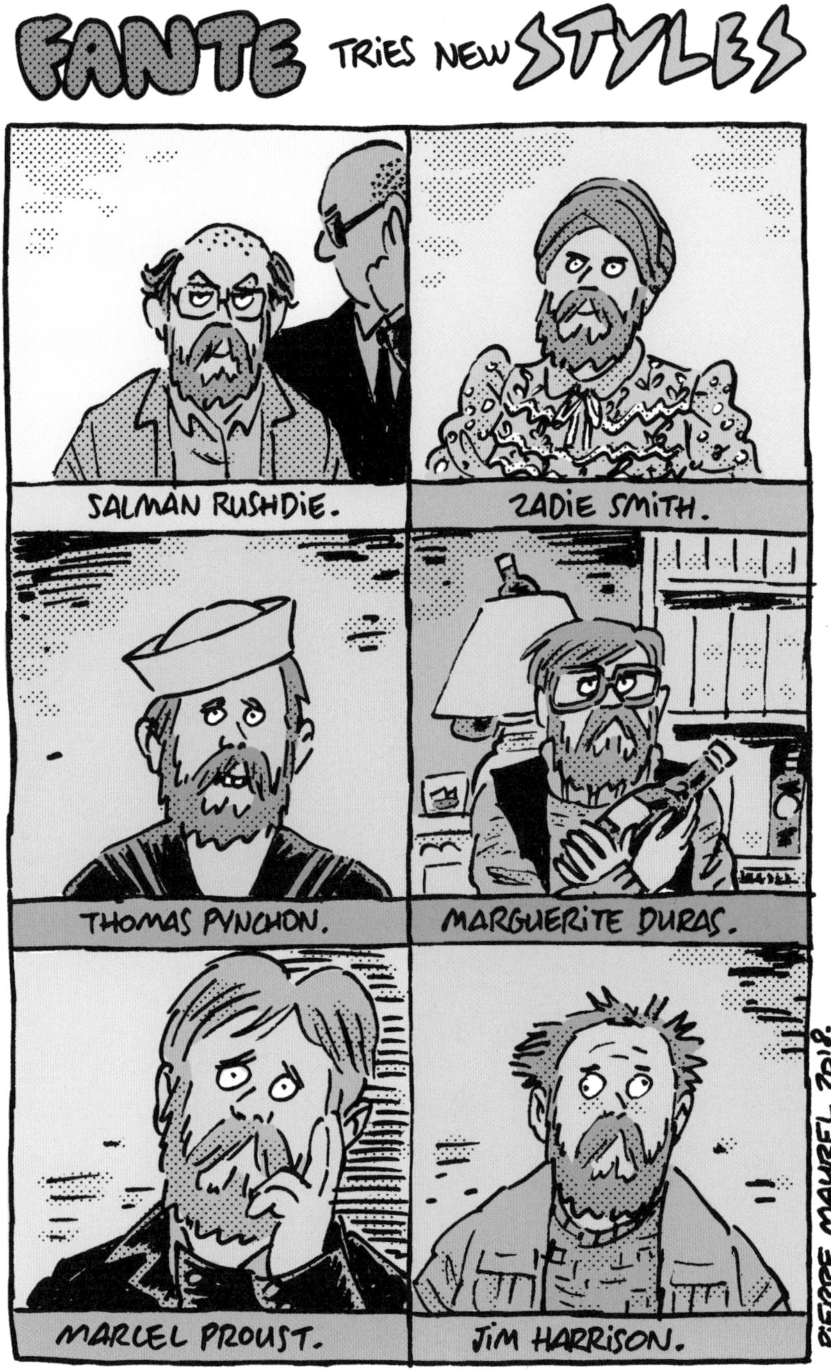
FANTE TRIES NEW STYLES
SALMAN RUSHDIE.
ZADIE SMITH.
THOMAS PYNCHON.
MARGUERITE DURAS.
MARCEL PROUST.
JIM HARRISON.
PIERRE MAUREL 2018.

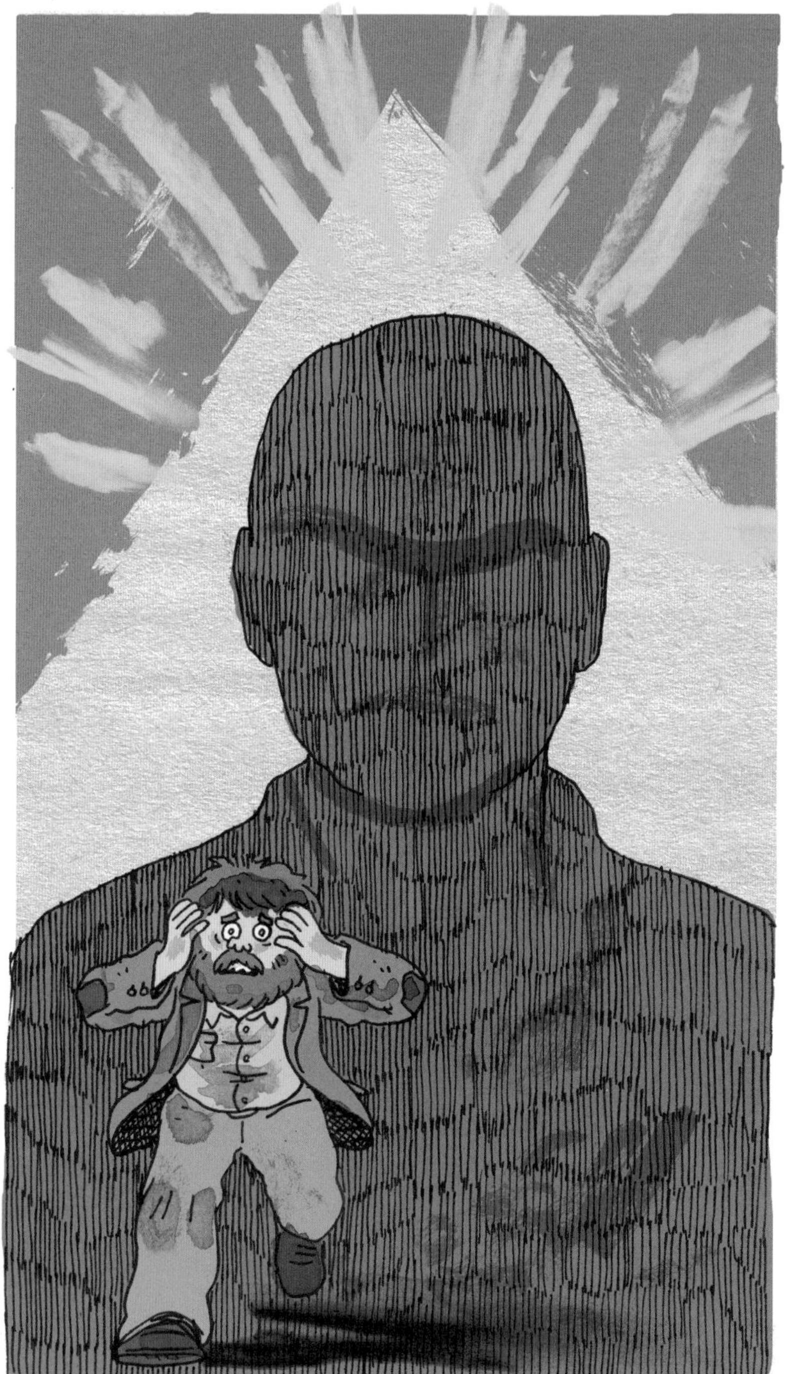

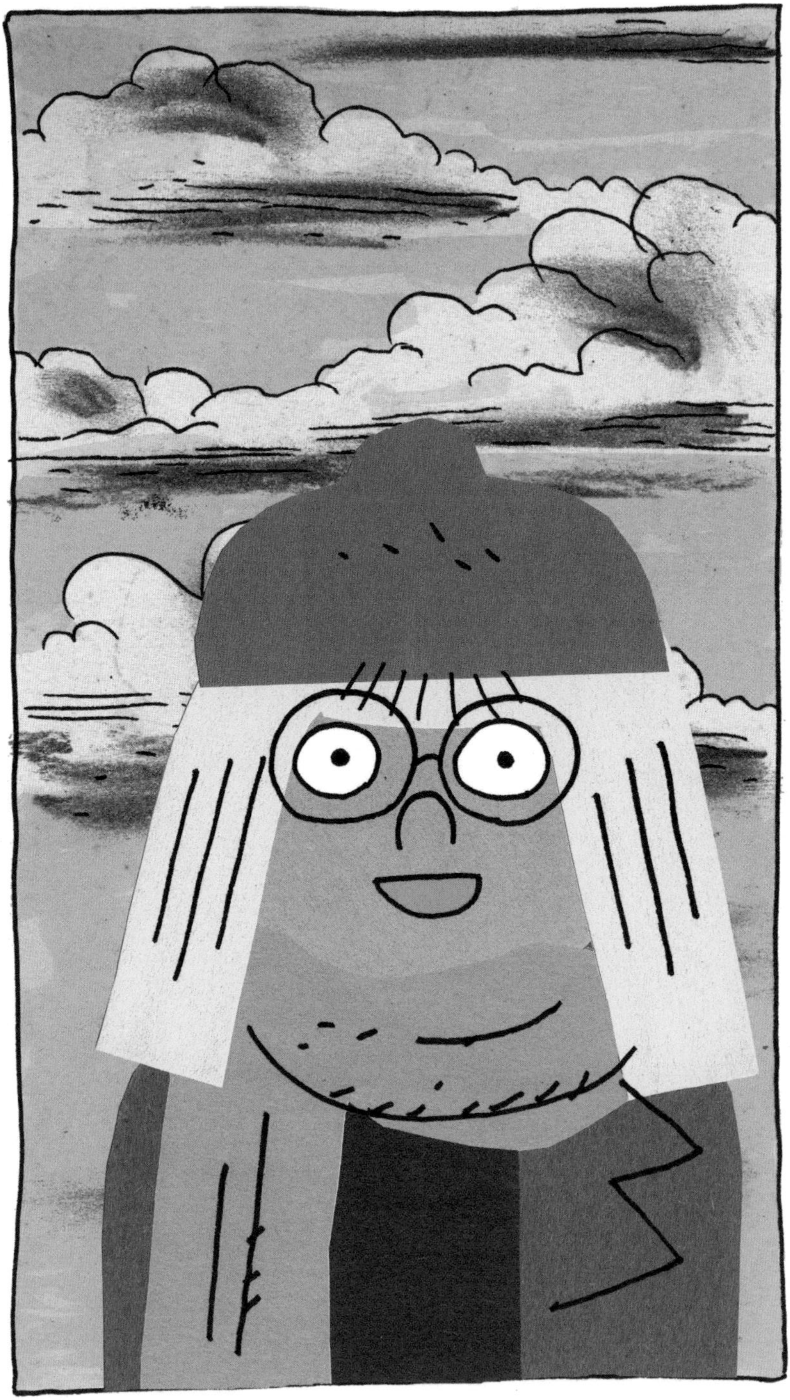

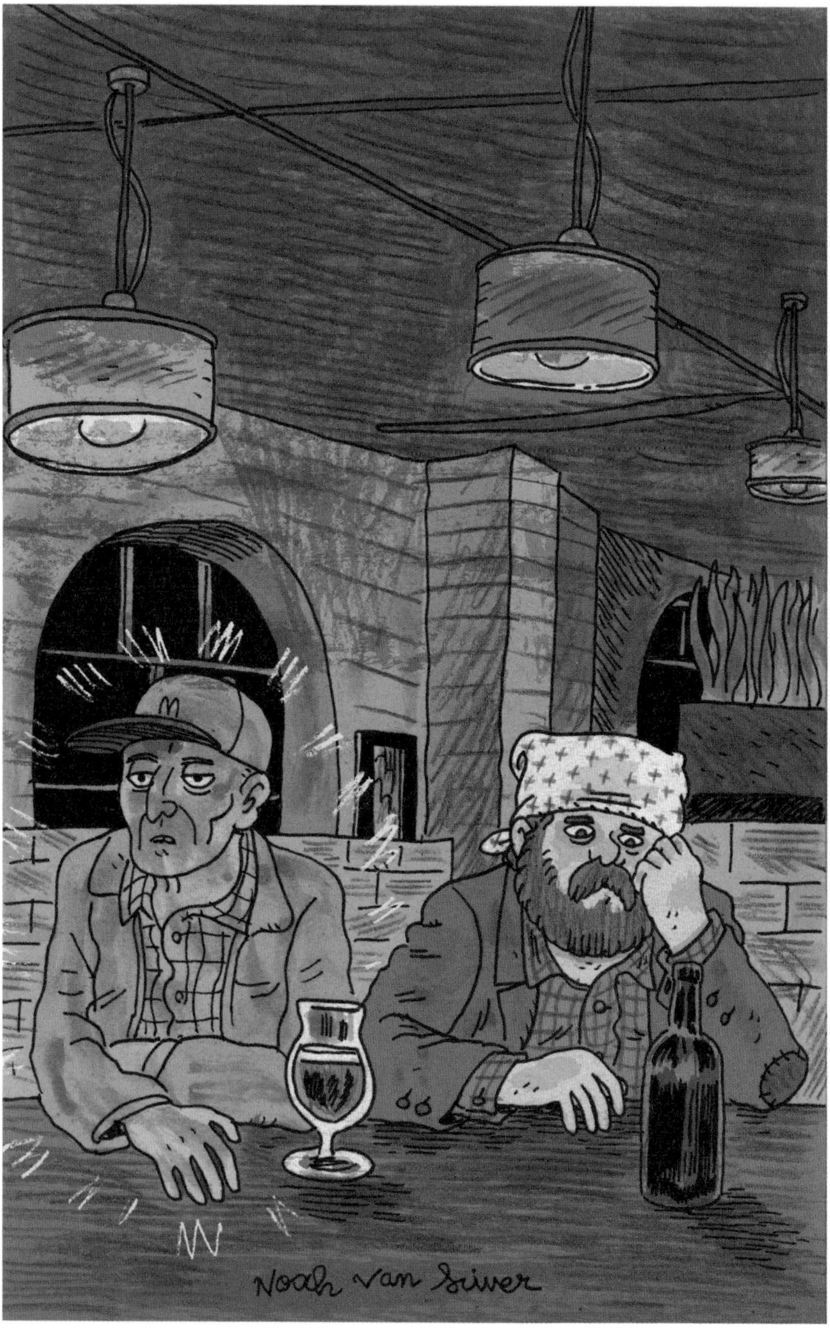
Noah van Sciver

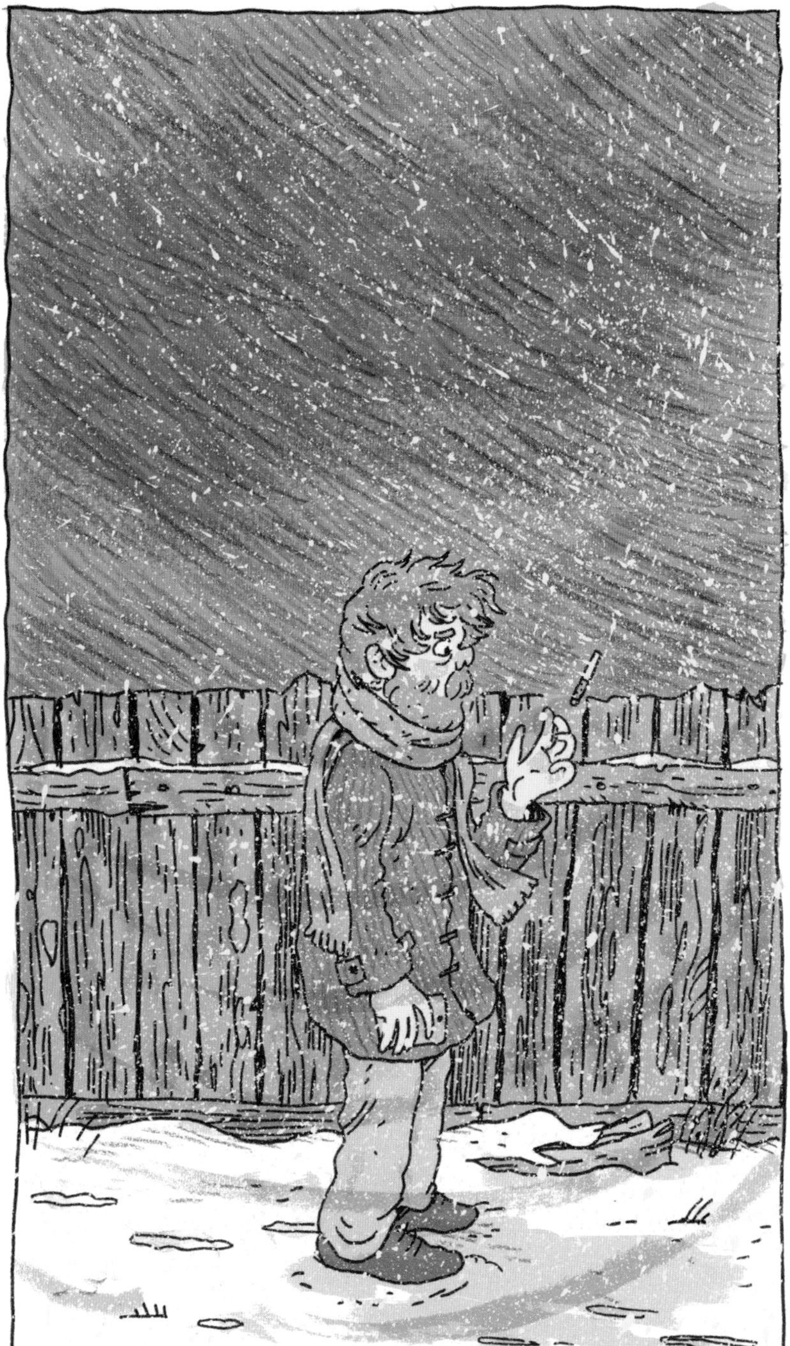

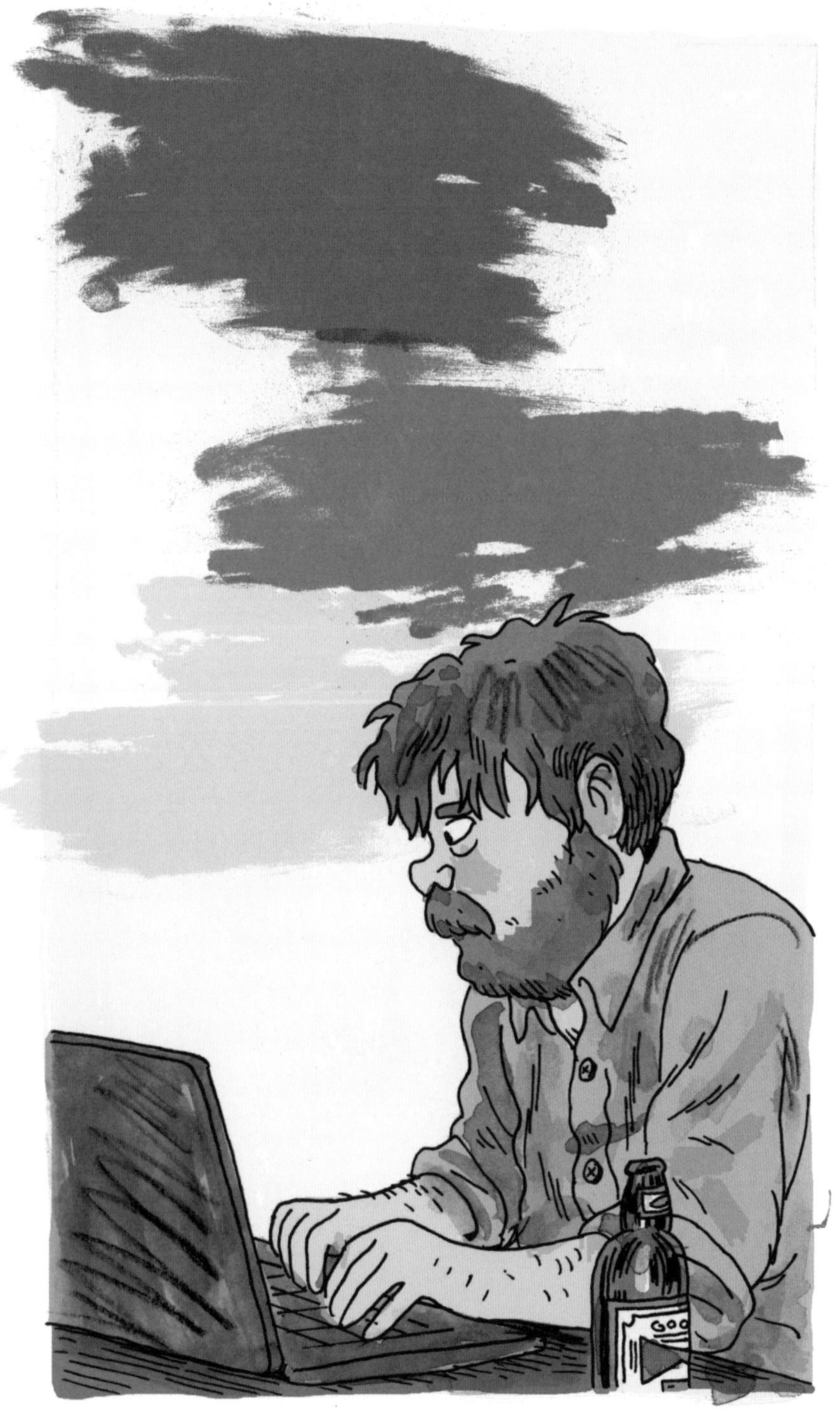

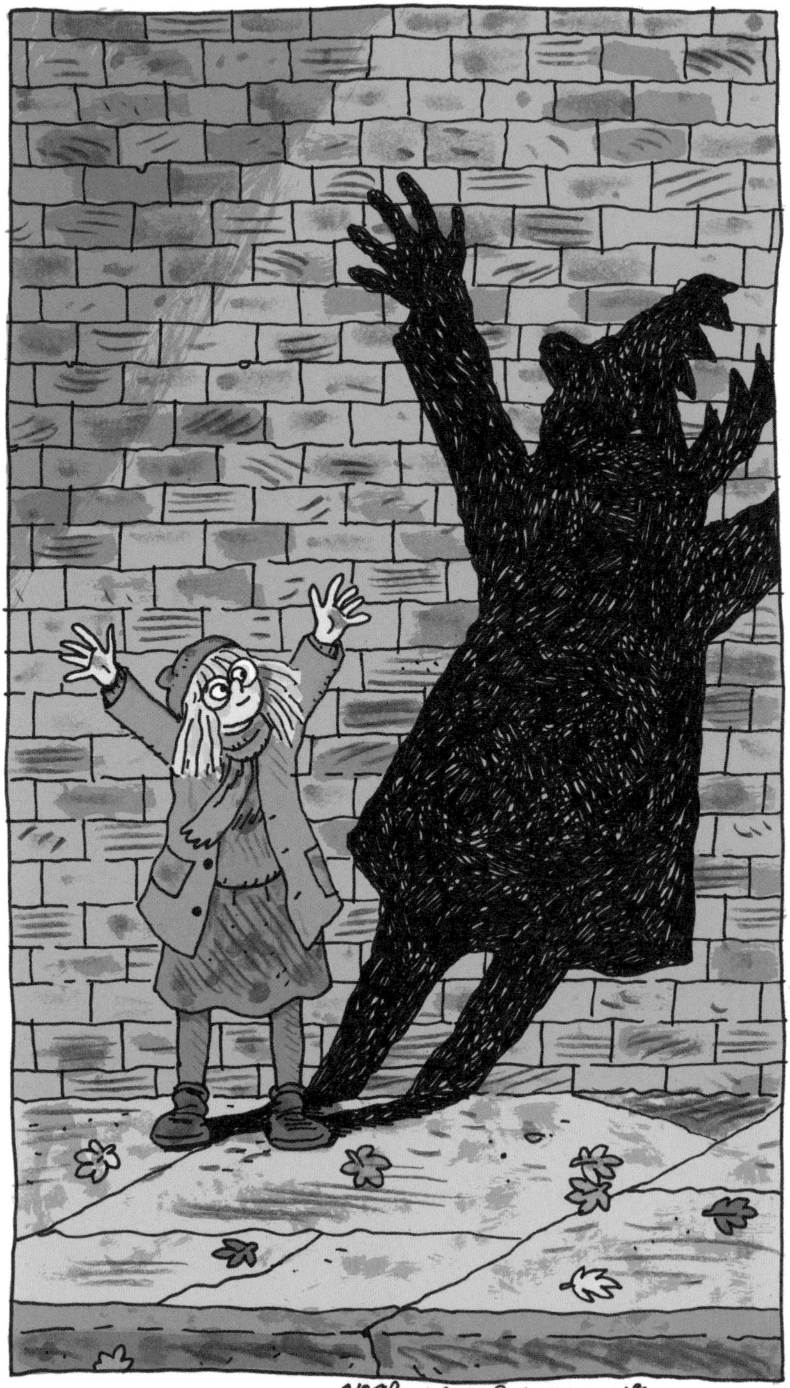
Noah Van Sciver 2018

Noah van Sciver is the award-winning cartoonist and author of many, many, many comics and graphic novels available in every corner of this god-forsaken earth...